The Mystic Chronicles

Book 1

The fate of the world lies in the echoes of eternity.

The Mystic Chronicles
Echi Eterni

BY ER HROLE NAVARRO

ECHI ETERNI.
Book One of the Mystic Chronicles Series

This book is a work of fiction. Names, characters, places, and incidents either are
the product of the author's imagination or are used fictitiously. Any resemblance
to actual persons, living or dead, events, or locales is entirely coincidental.

First Edition.
Self Published in the United States.
Kapolei, Hawaii. Visit us online at erhrole.com or www.mysticchronicles.com

Hardcover ISBN: 979-8-9905744-1-0
Paperback ISBN: 979-8-9905744-2-7
Ebook ISBN: 979-8-9905744-0-3

For every person I ever loved and ever will love in my lifetime.

~

In Loving Memory
Ethan Matthew Navarro
November 20, 2002 to October 27, 2023

ACT ONE

"Finding myself to exist in the world, I believe I shall, in some shape or other, always exist."

- Benjamin Franklin

CHAPTER
ONE

Rome, Italy, September 8, 2004 A.D.

The ancient city of Rome buzzed with secrets and whispers of history, its labyrinthine streets twisting and turning like an intricate maze. Amidst it all sat Kaira Mazza, a young woman whose dreams were as vibrant as the colors adorned the Vatican.

Her sun-kissed mane cascaded down her back like golden silk, and her piercing blue eyes reflected the endless azure skies above. Kaira stood five feet nine inches tall.

Everyone present immediately noticed her entrance into the room. As she moved, heads turned involuntarily, drawn not only by her appearance but also by the warmth that seemed to radiate from her very being. She halted to converse with a group, her voice brimming with empathy and understanding, her laughter pealing out and attracting others to her.

Her confidence was undeniable, not stemming from arrogance but from deep self-assurance that allowed her to navigate conversations effortlessly. She paid close attention, displaying genuine interest in the words of others, and her responses were insightful and knowledge-able. She was well-educated but carried her intelligence with a light touch, making her even more approachable.

As she continued to circulate, her effervescent and communicative nature kept those in her vicinity engaged, her infectious laughter making it impossible not to feel uplifted by her presence. Her compassionate spirit was evident in her actions; she provided a reassuring touch on a shoulder, her eyes connecting with those she conversed with, causing them to feel acknowledged and understood. In her essence, Kaira was a beacon of warmth and reassurance, effortlessly drawing people into her orbit.

Hailing from San Francisco, Kaira proudly embraced her cultural roots while pursuing her passion for architecture. With an early admission and scholarship to the prestigious University of California, Berkeley, she leaped at the chance to study abroad in Rome – drawn by the city's magnificent architecture and the opportunity to connect with her ancestral homeland.

But amidst the storied halls of Sapienza University and the pressure to impress her professors, Kaira grapples with internal conflicts. Balancing her dreams of becoming an architect with the demands of a long-distance relationship, she faces skeptics who question her authenticity as an Italian American in this foreign city.

"Ms. Mazza..." a man beckons to Kaira from the top of the steps leading to the library. Professor Xicato, a figure with a warmth that rivaled the Mediterranean sun, descended the steps with a slight tremor in his hands. Despite his age, there was a spark of vitality in his brown eyes as he joined Kaira.

"Good morning, Professor!" Kaira replies eagerly, her excitement palpable as she anticipates their field trip to Castel Sant'Angelo, also known as the Castle of the Holy Angel.

"It's not every day I can get my favorite student access to hidden rooms at the Tomb of Hadrian," Professor Xicato jokes with a twinkle in his eye. "I'll walk you to the car – our driver should be here any moment."

As they make their way to the waiting BMW sedan, Kaira is in awe of her mentor.

Sitting in the car, Kaira can't help but think about Emperor Hadrian – a powerful ruler who reigned over Rome a century after Jesus Christ's death. Known for his impressive architectural feats throughout

England and Europe, including the famous Hadrian's Wall, he was also a masterful architect responsible for iconic structures like the Pantheon and Temple of Venus and Roma.

"I'm going to visit the burial site of one of the most influential architects of all time," Kaira whispers to herself, closing her eyes briefly as she feels a surge of inspiration and determination.

The sleek BMW sedan glided through the bustling streets of Rome, weaving through traffic with the finesse of a seasoned charioteer. Kaira sat in the backseat, her eyes drinking in the sights that passed by in a blur of ancient and modern allusion.

As Professor Xicato sat beside her, his presence embodied an aura of knowledge and mystery. His voice filled the car with tales of emperors and gladiators, wars fought, and alliances forged, painting vivid images of Rome's storied past. She had heard all the stories time and time again, but she could never grow tired of hearing them.

Castel Sant'Angelo

As they approached Castel Sant'Angelo, the imposing structure loomed before them like a guardian from a bygone era. Its cylindrical form rose majestically against the azure sky, its weathered stone walls whispering secrets of centuries ago.

The car stopped, and Kaira stepped onto the cobblestone path leading to the castle's entrance. The air was thick with anticipation, and a sense of history hung heavy around them as if they were almost in another world.

As Kaira followed Professor Xicato through the winding corridors of Castel Sant'Angelo, her heart raced with excitement and trepidation. The ancient fortress seemed to hold secrets in its walls, whispering stories of the past that begged to be unveiled.

She had always dreamed of exploring the castle's hidden depths and uncovering the mysteries buried within its stone embrace. And now, with the professor as her guide, she finally had the chance to do just that.

But as they descended deeper into the castle's bowels, Kaira couldn't shake the feeling that there was more to this journey than a simple archaeological expedition. The air seemed to grow heavier with each step, thick with anticipation and the weight of centuries past.

Professor Xicato, too, seemed to be harboring a secret. A knowing gleam shone in his eyes as he traversed the maze-like corridors with a confidence that hinted at a more profound intention. Kaira's curiosity burned brighter with each twist and turn, her mind racing with possibilities of what lay ahead.

Finally, they came to a halt before a nondescript door, its weathered wood and rusted hinges misrepresenting the significance of what lay beyond. Professor Xicato turned to Kaira, his expression a mix of solemnity and barely contained excitement.

"This," he said, producing a large iron key, "is where our real adventure begins."

Kaira knew Hadrian's tomb was in the mausoleum. While the official tour guide would take tourists to the imperial burial room, many scholars debated whether his remains were moved when the Catholic Church took over the fortress. There were many secret rooms still waiting to be found, much like the pyramids of Egypt.

"Professor Xicato, where did you get this key?" Kaira took a deep breath, trying to steady her racing heart and calm her nerves.

The professor's gaze remained fixed ahead as he prepared to answer her question, pausing momentarily before speaking. "Archaeologists found this room a few months ago. An old colleague reached out. She has connections." He looked at Kaira with a confident smirk and smiled.

"Connections indeed," Kaira echoed, unable to deprive her voice of the doubt that had seized her. She studied the key with widened eyes, taking in its rustic charm, its age evidenced by the oxidized metal and the worn grooves that bore an uncanny resemblance to a relief map. Professor Xicato unlocked the door, pushing it open with a soft creak reverberating through the silent corridor. A wave of calm, musty air spilled out from within, carrying fine dust particles that sparkled as they caught the stray beams of sunlight. Kaira crossed the threshold into a cocoon of whispers from an ancient time.

"You can look, but don't touch," Professor Xicato said jokingly. "As you are aware, there are many secrets left to unlock in all of the ancient architecture you are here to study. You, my dear Kaira, are one of the lucky few who get to see a room very few people know exists. They believe this is the true burial location of Emperor Hadrian."

Astonishment widened Kaira's blue eyes. "The real burial location?" she echoed, her voice a mere whisper against the pressing silence of the ancient room.

Professor Xicato nodded gravely, his gaze sweeping the remnants of faded frescoes and artifacts with reverence. "Indeed. Our historians have been reevaluating the evidence for some time now. The Church records from the 14th century hint at a relocation of Hadrian's remains during a period of upheaval and change. This place," he gestured at their surroundings, "bears some telling signs that it could be the actual resting place."

As she entered the dimly lit room, Kaira's breath caught in her throat. The flickering light revealed ancient artifacts and frescoes, giving a glimpse into life in Rome during Hadrian's rule. She noticed statues of familiar gods - Mars, Venus, Fortuna, Saturn, and even Mithras - standing tall around what appeared to be Hadrian's tomb. They seemed to watch over the room like silent guardians.

Mars, the God of War, stood firm and imposing on a tall carved marble pedestal. The statue embodied the relentlessness and raw brutality of war. Kaira remembered reading about how Romans used to pray for Mars' favor before embarking on battles and disputes.

Next was Venus, the Goddess of Love and Beauty. Her features were soft and serene as if frozen in eternal tranquility. Her representation here in Hadrian's resting place starkly contrasts Mars'. Kaira wondered if Venus symbolized Hadrian's love for his wife, Sabina, or his indulgence in the arts and culture.

Fortuna, the Goddess of Fortune and Good Luck, was depicted with a cornucopia in one hand and a rudder in the other - a symbol of abundance and control over destiny. Perhaps Hadrian saw Fortuna as his ally who guided him through his reign, thought Kaira.

Saturn, the ancient God of Agriculture and Time, stood with his symbolic sickle, reminding Kaira of the transient nature of time and power. As she studied the deity's weathered features and the sickle clasped in his hand, a wave of nostalgia washed over her, transporting her back to a distant memory from her childhood.

She recalled sitting on her grandfather's lap in his cozy study, surrounded by the comforting scent of old books and pipe tobacco. He would often regale her with tales from mythology, his voice rich and enchanting as he wove stories of gods and heroes, battles won and lost, and the relentless march of time.

One story stood out in her mind—the tale of Saturn, the god who devoured his children to prevent them from usurping his power. It was a grim and cautionary tale that spoke of the fleeting nature of authority and the inevitability of change.

As a child, Kaira was fascinated and unsettled by the story, grappling with the concept of time as an all-consuming force. She remembered asking her grandfather if anyone could ever truly escape the clutches of time and if there was a way to hold onto the moments and people they loved forever.

Her grandfather had smiled then, a wistful expression on his face as he gazed out the window at the changing leaves of autumn. "Time is a gift, my dear," he had said, his voice soft and contemplative. "It is the canvas upon which we paint the stories of our lives. We may not be able to hold onto it forever, but we can make the most of every moment we are given."

Now, standing before the statue of Saturn in the heart of Castel Sant'Angelo, Kaira felt the weight of those words anew. The sickle in the god's hand seemed to take on a new meaning - not just as a symbol of the harvest and the turning of the seasons but as a reminder of the preciousness of time and the importance of living each moment to the fullest.

Last of them all was Mithras - a deity associated with soldiers and oath-keeping, his presence indicating the level of trust Hadrian had in his legions. She imagined the Emperor praying to Mithras for strength and loyalty amongst his men, especially during times of discord.

As she studied each deity in this silent congregation, her gaze finally settled on the grand sarcophagus at the center, which potentially held the remains of Emperor Hadrian. It was a simple but imposing stone structure devoid of ornate carvings or precious gems usually associated with royal tombs. Yet, its austere presence commanded respect.

"May I?" Kaira asked Professor Xicato hesitantly, gesturing towards the sarcophagus. He nodded in affirmation, and she stepped forward.

Kaira's heart raced as she gazed upon Hadrian's tomb because she was overwhelmed by the historical significance of the moment. As an architecture student with a deep passion for ancient Roman history, standing in the presence of the final resting place of one of the most influential emperors was a profound and awe-inspiring experience. The realization that she was directly connecting with a pivotal figure from the past, whose legacy had shaped the world she studied, filled her with excitement, reverence, and a sense of personal fulfillment.

The marble surface beckoned to her, cool and unyielding, as if hiding secrets within its inscriptions. She traced the ancient words with a trembling hand, feeling a strange energy emanating. Her mother's ring passed down through generations, began to vibrate on her finger, matching the rhythm of her quickening pulse. A primal force surged within her, drawing her towards the tomb with an indescribable pull, unlike anything she had ever felt.

The room seemed to yell at her, its walls vibrating with a latent energy that made her hair stand on end. Kaira took a deep breath, trying to steady her nerves.

A shiver ran down her spine as her fingers brushed over a particular inscription. The carving seemed familiar - like something in her dreams or another life entirely. Her breath caught in her throat as she read the words *Time is a river, where past and future mingle and become one.*

A deafening, bone-shattering boom of thunder reverberated through the city as a massive storm materialized above it. The sound blasted its way to the secret tomb, bouncing off the walls and causing small rocks to tumble from the ceiling. At that moment, Kaira could have sworn she saw the statues surrounding the emperor come to life, their stone eyes blazing with wrath.

"Kaira, we need to find shelter!" Professor Xicato's voice was barely audible over the deafening roar of thunder and blinding flashes of lightning emanating from each of the statues of Roman gods. Their electric bolts struck the walls and floor like furious spears of light, threatening to tear apart the structure they were standing in. Kaira's heart raced as she realized they were in grave danger and needed to escape before it was too late.

Terror gripped her as she took one last look at her surroundings, her hand seemingly glued to the ancient inscription. A sense of foreboding washed over her, as if she had just unlocked Pandora's Box. Time seemed to stop as a flash of blue light surrounded her and exploded.

Just like that, Kaira Mazza was gone.

CHAPTER
TWO

C amp Pendleton, California, August 26, 2024 A.D.

The sun blazed down on Camp Pendleton, casting a golden hue over the ranks of crisp uniforms and gleaming medals. Command Sergeant Major Elan Durant stood at attention, his posture impeccable as the solemnity of his retirement ceremony washed over him in waves of pride and nostalgia.

"Attention to orders," boomed the presiding officer's voice, snapping the assembled Marines into an even more rigid formality. The ceremony was a testament to years of discipline and dedication—a tribute to a career that had shaped the very core of Elan's being.

As the accolades were read aloud, recounting valor and steadfastness, Elan's mind wandered fleetingly to Kaira, whose memory clung to him like the shadow of a guardian angel. Her absence, a silent companion through all his years in uniform, lay upon his heart with a weight he could neither lift nor lighten.

The crisp declaration, "I am the flag of the United States of America. My name is Old Glory," initiated the flag-passing ritual, accompanied by the strains of America the Beautiful. It pierced his contemplative state, yanking him back to the present. The youngest Marine commenced a salute, her attire a stark contrast to the azure heavens behind her. Elan's heart brimmed with a poignant blend of reverence and the creeping, aching awareness of an ending.

"Long may I wave, dear God, long may I wave." Sergeant Major Durant executed the concluding salute with flawless synchronicity as the banner descended a terminal instance from his longtime comrade and compatriot across myriad deployments. Elan advanced to accept the standard, an emblem of his dutiful toil and tribulation. The pennant was creased with solemn import and proffered unto his gnarled digits, which caressed the material, charting the luminaries and bands with veneration.

The Sergeant's voice, an unfaltering grip incarnate in auditory form, conveyed his sentiment. "Your steadfast service is deeply cherished, Sergeant Major Durant."

"Semper Fidelis," Elan replied, his voice steady despite the tumult within. He pivoted, facing the crowd, and found his mother's eyes. Rose's gaze held all the support and fierce love of a lifetime. Elan crossed the space between them, the American Flag cradled like a newborn. As he passed it to her, it was not just a tribute but a shared legacy.

The applause echoed, a cascade of respect and recognition swelling around him. Yet within Elan's chest, a silent battle raged—memories of war zones mingling with personal demons. But the presence of friends and family was a bulwark against the tide of uncertainty.

Reagan Mazza's nod from the sidelines was the unspoken promise of camaraderie that transcended their different paths—military and law enforcement. It spoke of battles fought and yet to be faced, of a future uncertain yet not uncharted.

Elan's eyes swept over the assembly one final time before he stepped back, his decorated career encapsulated in a single, crystalline moment of closure. His heart beat a staccato rhythm, fueled by the adrenaline of action and the quiet dread of what lay beyond.

"Dismissed!" The command released the formation, soldiers dissipating like smoke on the wind. And as they did, Elan felt the mantle of his military persona begin to lift, revealing the raw edges of a man about to embark on his most daunting mission yet—the quest to rediscover himself in a world he had left behind two decades ago.

"Congratulations, Elan," Reagan approached him with a warm smile, offering a firm handshake that quickly turned into a warm embrace. "You've earned this."

"Thank you, Reagan." Elan's voice was steady, but his thoughts raced as he pondered the shape of his future. The structure and camaraderie of the Marines had been his haven for so long, and facing the unfamiliar landscape of civilian life filled him with trepidation.

"Have you given any thought to what you'll do now?" Reagan inquired, sensing his friend's unease.

"I'm still figuring it out," Elan admitted, trying to quell the disquiet that gnawed at him. "Maybe I'll find something in private security or law enforcement. But honestly, I'm not sure yet."

"Take your time, my friend. You don't have to decide right away." Reagan's words were meant to reassure, but they also reminded Elan of the freedom to choose that he'd been granted—a gift and a burden wrapped in one.

Elan's mind wandered through the labyrinth of memories—tours in the Middle East, postings worldwide, and the bonds forged under fire. They were the threads that had woven the tapestry of his identity, but now, that tapestry seemed fragile, frayed at the edges by the looming uncertainty.

"Promise me one thing, though," Reagan said, pulling Elan back to the present. "Don't forget about us when you're charting your new course. We'll always be here for you, no matter what path you take."

"Of course, Reagan," Elan replied, gratitude infused in his voice. It was a lifeline, a tether connecting him to the people who mattered most. She was like a sister to him. Looking at her, he saw the similarities she shared with her sister. And as he looked around at the familiar faces gathered to celebrate his retirement, he knew he had a support system—a foundation to build his new life.

San Francisco, California

Under the sun's relentless heat, a beautiful green house in San Francisco stood tall, its shadows stretching and swaying in the midday heat. This was no ordinary house; it was Elan's childhood home. After years of being away, he returned to spend time with his mother, Rose, and enjoy retirement together while also figuring out his next steps as a veteran. But for now, he just wanted to take a walk through the city and soak in the familiar sights and sounds and think.

The air was thick with an undercurrent of brine as if the city was pausing to take a deep breath before exhaling its secrets to the windswept bay. Towering above the bustling crowd, the majestic spires of St. Mary's Cathedral stood sentinel in proximity, their gargoyles seemingly scowling at the hubbub below. This was Elan's city, his home, and now, it was time to take it all in, at least for a short while.

The weight of his decision to retire from the Marines, to leave behind the only life he'd known for the past two decades, was beginning to sink in. He thought back to the ceremony earlier that week, the crisp folding of the American flag, its deep red, white, and blue hues symbolizing the country he'd sworn to protect, now draped in his arms like a shroud, marking the end of an era.

The decision hadn't come easily. Memories flooded his mind in a whirlwind of chaos—the faltering steps of a young recruit, the adrenaline-fueled firefights deep in hostile deserts, and the camaraderie of brothers-in-arms forged in the crucible of war. He'd seen more than his fair share of bloodshed and loss, but he'd also witnessed the resilience of the human spirit and the power of love and faith to transcend even the darkest times. It was a technique he watched most of his Marines and Sailors master but one he was struggling to accomplish on his own.

As Elan approached Fisherman's Wharf, the sights, sounds, and smells transported him back to a cherished childhood memory. He recalled a foggy, chilly night when he was just six years old, and his father had taken him crabbing along the San Francisco Bay.

The air was thick with the briny scent of the sea, and the fog horns echoed in the distance, adding to the mysterious atmosphere. Elan's small hand was engulfed by his father's calloused palm as they made their way down to the docks, the old wooden planks creaking beneath their feet.

His father had prepared their crab nets earlier that day, each baited with fish heads and chicken necks. Elan watched in fascination as his father tossed the traps into the dark, murky water, the splash breaking the eerie stillness of the night.

As they waited for the crabs to take the bait, Elan's father regaled him with stories of his own childhood, of the countless nights he had spent in the Philippines, learning the secrets of the sea from his grandfather.

When it was time to pull up the nets, Elan's heart raced with anticipation. He watched as his father hauled in the heavy traps, the metal cages clanging against the side of the dock. Inside, the crabs scuttled and clawed at the bars, their shells glistening in the dim light of the fishing lamps.

Elan's father showed him how to handle the crabs safely and how to measure them to ensure they were of legal size. Elan marveled at the strength and dexterity of his father's hands as he deftly sorted through the catch, tossing back the smaller crabs and placing the keepers in a large bucket filled with seawater.

As they made their way home, the bucket heavy with their prize, Elan felt a sense of pride and accomplishment that would stay with him for years. He had braved the cold, foggy night and learned valuable lessons from his father, forging a bond that only lasted his childhood.

Reaching the edge of the sea wall, Elan stopped and took in the panoramic view of the bay. The Golden Gate Bridge was a majestic sentinel in the distance, its copper-clad towers shrouded in a veil of fog. Gulls soared on the wind, their cries mingling with the low drone of the city. Beneath him, the choppy emerald waters of the bay lapped at the breakwater as if the very currents of fate were ushering him toward his destiny.

Elan closed his eyes, the chill wind biting at his cheeks. He'd come to San Francisco searching for answers but found something far more precious: a renewed sense of purpose. Slipping his hand into his jacket pocket, he felt the cold, smooth edges of the photograph he'd carried with him for so long. His family's smiling faces stared back at him, their love a tether to a life he'd thought lost.

The dark, musty basement of Elan's childhood home suffocated him as he sat alone in the stillness of the night. Exhausted from a draining discussion with his mother, his mind struggled to process everyone else's opinions about his future. The cluttered space was filled with forgotten boxes and trinkets, an eerie reflection of his conflicted thoughts.

But then his attention fell upon a box labeled "Kaira and Elan." Memories came flooding back - Kaira's laughter, her passion for architecture, her acceptance into U.C. Berkeley. A bittersweet ache settled in his chest as he opened the box and sifted through its contents.

A small, unopened parcel addressed to Elan lay tucked at the bottom of the box, its postmark dating back years to just after his enlistment and deployment with the Marines. He assumed his mother had placed it there and neglected to give it to him. As he handled the package, the sound of shifting wrapping paper inside piqued his curiosity but also stirred a sense of unease. Carefully unwrapping it, a leather-bound scroll tumbled into his grasp, containing a cryptic message alluding to the circumstances of Kaira's disappearance.

Elan's hands shook as he read the letter; his heart raced with fear and determination. The carefully scripted words spoke of a family heirloom and sinister forces that sought to exploit it. He knew he had to act as he sat in his basement, surrounded by shelves overflowing with books.

With a deep breath, Elan made up his mind. He would travel to Kaira's childhood home, find the mysterious trinket mentioned in the letter, and journey to Italy to uncover the truth about her fate. The message warned him to be discreet, for there were those who would stop at nothing to get their hands on the precious family heirloom.

As he closed his eyes and leaned back in the old recliner, memories of Kaira's grandmother flooded Elan's mind. She had always told stories of her devout Catholic upbringing in Italy, and Elan couldn't help but wonder if she held any clues to the whereabouts of the relic. With a resolute determination to uncover the truth and bring closure to

Kaira's memory, Elan made a mental note to visit Kaira and Reagan's grandmother in the morning.

Elan took a deep breath. His mind raced with thoughts of Kaira and the mysterious scroll. He couldn't shake the feeling that there was more to her disappearance than met the eye. He wondered what dark forces were at play and how he could help her if she was alive.

THREE

The early morning fog enveloped Kaira's cozy home, hiding the landscape and transforming her surroundings into an indistinct, misty haze. Shadows seemed to dance in the mist, making the familiar surroundings appear eerie and unfamiliar. Perhaps it was the anxiety Elan was feeling from the night before. Elan paused on the front porch, his heart pounding against his chest as a hundred questions swirled in his mind. What would he say to Kaira's grandmother? Would she even entertain letting him search through her family's treasured heirlooms? He didn't even know what he was looking for.

"Let's get this over with," he murmured, remembering Elan's countless times with Grandma Mazza and his best friends. Taking a deep breath, Elan knocked on the heavy oak door.

The door creaked open, revealing not Kaira's grandmother but Reagan, her eyes alight with excitement. "Elan!" she exclaimed, throwing her arms around him. "You won't believe it, I'm here for the weekend! I flew in late last night and wanted to surprise you."

"Reagan? I didn't think I would see you so soon." Elan blinked, taken aback by her sudden appearance. A part of him was relieved to see his old friend, yet he couldn't shake the feeling of urgency that gnawed at him. He forced a smile though his thoughts raced with concern.

"Hey there," Elan said, hugging her back. I'm glad you're here. I need your help." His voice grew quieter and more serious. "It's about Kaira."

"Kaira?" Reagan's expression shifted, her brow furrowing with concern. "What's going on?"

"Can we go inside?" Elan asked, glancing over his shoulder. "It's a long story, and I don't want your grandmother to overhear us."

"Of course," Reagan nodded, stepping aside to let him in. As they crossed the threshold, Elan felt an odd sense of comfort enveloping him. Despite the gravity of the situation, he knew that with Reagan by his side, they would find answers.

As the door closed behind them, Elan's determination burned brighter than ever. The search for the truth had taken an unexpected turn.

The sun cast a golden glow through the faded red curtains of Kaira's living room while Elan and Reagan settled into plush armchairs. The scent of freshly brewed coffee emanated through the air, offering a comforting familiarity amidst the uncertainty that weighed heavily upon them. Elan took a deep breath, his gaze meeting Reagan's concerned eyes.

"Reagan, I found a scroll," he began, his voice tense with urgency. "I believe it's connected to Kaira. I know it is. I think there's an heirloom here that might help us understand its meaning."

Reagan leaned forward in her chair, her expression shifting from worry to confusion. "What are you talking about? An heirloom? In this house? Where did you find a scroll?"

"I know how this must sound," Elan replied, running a hand through his messy black hair as he considered the enormity of the situation. "But I have no idea where to start looking or what it even looks like. Someone mailed me a package shortly after Kaira…disappeared. It's been sitting in my mom's basement ever since!"

"Wait," Reagan's eyes widened as if struck by a sudden realization. "I think I know which heirloom you're talking about." Her voice lowered to a whisper as if sharing a secret. "Grandma used to tell Kaira and me stories of an artifact passed down through generations of our family. Grandmothers pass them to their granddaughters when it's time."

A glimmer of hope danced in Elan's eyes as he spoke. "That artifact holds the answers we need to uncover Kaira's fate."

"Maybe," Reagan nodded, her resolve strengthening. "We'll have to find it first to know for sure."

"Where do we begin?" Elan questioned, his fingers tapping restlessly against his leg as his military instincts kicked in, strategizing and evaluating every possible course of action.

"Grandma's bedroom," Reagan replied without hesitation. "That's where she keeps all the family treasures. She's out at the fish market this morning, so we can go get it right now."

Reagan swiftly ascended the stairs, with Elan closely trailing behind her, until they reached her grandmother's room.

"Grandma keeps everything important in her armoire," Reagan whispered, pointing towards an ornate wooden wardrobe that stood majestically in the corner of the room. "If the heirloom is anywhere, it's in there."

"Let's hope we find what we're looking for," Elan murmured, his heart pounding in anticipation as Reagan eased open the armoire door.

As they rummaged through the antique trinkets and relics that lay within, the weight of their mission settled upon them, binding them together in a shared purpose. Their determination grew with each item they examined, fueled by the knowledge that the heirloom they sought could be the key to unlocking the secrets of Kaira's past – and perhaps even saving her life.

"Elan, look at this," Reagan breathed, her fingers trembling as she held up an ancient-looking object. "This has to be it."

Elan's eyes widened as he gazed upon an ornate rosary bead fitting in the palm of Reagan's hand. It resembled a pocket watch made of copper metal. It was definitely not like today's traditional and modern-day rosary. The two sides of the bead were exquisitely drawn, with one side depicting the agony of Christ's crucifixion and the other portraying the glory of his resurrection.

"It's beautiful," Elan murmured reverently as he took the rosary from Reagan's hand. Upon closer inspection, he noticed something peculiar. The bead was hinged and could be opened like a locket.

With bated breath, Elan gently pried open the heirloom. Nestled inside was an ancient scrap of parchment, upon which was scribbled a cryptic message in Latin.

"What does it say?" Reagan asked, peering over Elan's shoulder.

Elan's brow furrowed as he took his phone out to translate the ancient text automatically. "It speaks of a secret crypt beneath St. Peter's Basilica. This must be a clue to Kaira's location."

Reagan's eyes flashed with intensity. "Then we know where we need to go. Rome."

As Elan gripped the prayer bead tightly, he gave a grave nod. "Looks like I'll finally cash in all those frequent flyer miles. I'll book seats for us on the first flight out of SFO tomorrow morning."

Reagan placed a steadying hand on Elan's shoulder. "We're going to find out what happened to her," she said, her voice brimming with resolve.

Elan met her unwavering gaze, confidence surging through him.

Come what may, they would find Kaira - or die trying.

CHAPTER

FOUR

Rome, Italy, September 8, 2024 A.D.

Elan and Reagan emerged from the terminal at Leonardo da Vinci International Airport, the din of Rome enveloping them instantly. They clutched their bags tightly as they navigated the bustling crowds, keeping the precious rosary bead tucked safely in Elan's pocket.

Despite the urgency of their quest, they paused for a moment to take in the majestic sight of the Eternal City unfolding before them. As they stood amidst the commotion, memories of Elan's sole visit to Rome as a fresh-faced Marine Private surfaced in his mind. Back then, his youth and inexperience blinded him to the splendor and rich heritage the city had to offer. Ancient ruins and Renaissance palaces gleamed in the bright sunlight, infusing the modern metropolis with its storied past.

"Where do we even start?" Reagan wondered aloud, scanning the myriad streets and alleys spidering in all directions.

Elan considered for a moment. "The clue mentioned a crypt beneath the Vatican. We should start our search there."

Reagan nodded. "Right. Let's grab an Uber to St. Peter's and see if we can find a way into the crypts underground."

Securing a ride, they soon drove past the imposing facade of St.

Peter's Basilica. Elan's pulse quickened. They were close—he could feel it.

As the driver dropped them at the edge of St. Peter's Square, the basilica loomed before them, its ornate dome seeming to touch the heavens. The crypt from the rosary's clue lay beneath its hallowed halls and chapels.

Squaring their shoulders, Elan and Reagan joined the throngs filing into the ancient church. The game was afoot.

When Elan stepped into the cavernous space within St. Peter's Basilica, he sensed the burden of history descending on him. He pondered what it must be like for Kaira to reside in a metropolis filled with the very architectural wonders she had studied in her chosen field. Golden light filtered down through Michelangelo's magnificent dome, illuminating the ornate marble altars and effigies of saints that lined the nave.

"Where to now?" Reagan murmured under her breath as they slowly walked deeper into the basilica.

Elan glanced around discreetly. "The crypts are usually accessed from a side chapel or passage. We need to break away from the main part of the church. We can visit them one by one. The Vatican Grottoes, the Necropolis, the Scavi? I don't know. I'm shooting in the dark here…"

They drifted casually towards the north transept, scanning the shadowy side chapels branching off from the main space. Elan's sharp eyes caught on a small, unassuming wooden door between two Baroque altars.

"There," he whispered. Reagan followed his gaze and nodded slightly. Waiting until no one was looking, they quickly slipped through the door into a narrow stone passageway beyond.

As the door closed behind them, the din of the church was muted, replaced by an eerie silence. Dripping water echoed down the passage as Elan fished a small flashlight from his pack. Flicking it on revealed a steep staircase plunging down into darkness.

Elan met Reagan's eyes, seeing his own exhilaration and trepidation reflected back at him. Reagan, always the level-headed and analytical one, had been his rock throughout their journey. Her quick wit and sharp intellect had gotten them out of countless scrapes, and her unwavering loyalty was a constant source of comfort in an ever-changing world.

But beneath her calm exterior, Elan knew that Reagan harbored a deep well of emotion. He had seen it in how her eyes sparkled when she spoke of her dreams for the future and how her voice wavered ever so slightly when she recounted stories of their childhood adventures.

Now, as they stood on the brink of their greatest challenge yet, Elan could see that same depth of feeling shining through. Reagan's face was a mix of determination and apprehension, her jaw set and eyes blazing with a fierce intensity.

"Ready?" Elan asked, his voice barely above a whisper.

Reagan smiled tightly, her hand reaching out to squeeze his own in solidarity and support. "Let's do this."

With Elan in the lead, they began their cautious descent into the crypts beneath the Vatican. The temperature dropped as they wound deeper, their breath pluming before them. The flashlight's beam glinted off damp stone walls on either side, revealing niches containing crumbling bones and relics.

Elan and Reagan continued down the winding staircase, their footsteps echoing in the enclosed space. The air grew colder and damper as they descended deeper into the earth below the Vatican.

After hours of walking and what felt like an eternity, the stairs finally ended at an arched wooden door bound in black iron. Exchanging a tense glance, Elan gripped the ancient handle and pulled. The door creaked open reluctantly, stale air rushing out to meet them.

Stepping through, Elan's flashlight revealed a small chamber lined with stone sarcophagi and racks of scrolls and artifacts. Reagan gasped as she caught sight of a familiar symbol engraved into one sarcophagus - the Mazza family crest.

"I can't believe it. Do you know what this is? My family crest! This is it," she breathed. "If there are any clues about Kaira, they must be here."

Elan was already examining the scrolls, unrolling them with care.

Most were faded and crumbling with age, but his keen eyes caught sight of a sketch in one that was unmistakably Kaira. Heart pounding, he scanned the text, picking out references to a ritual and a hidden temple.

"Reagan, look at this," he called urgently. She quickly crossed the room to peer over his shoulder at the scroll. As she read the text, her eyes went wide.

"This is the break we've been waiting for," Reagan said, her voice trembling with excitement and desperation. Her eyes glistened with unshed tears as she clutched the ancient map, her knuckles turning white with the force of her grip.

Elan could see the pain etched into every line of her face, the weight of Kaira's loss bearing down on her like a physical force. He knew that Reagan had been carrying the burden of her sister's disappearance for years, never allowing herself to fully grieve or let go of the hope that they might one day find her.

Now, as they stood on the brink of a potential breakthrough, Elan could feel the raw emotion emanating from Reagan in waves. Her breath came in short, sharp gasps as she fought to maintain her composure, the map in her hands a lifeline to the answers she so desperately sought.

"If we can find that temple," Reagan continued, her voice barely above a whisper, "we can find out what happened to Kaira. We can bring her home, Elan. We can finally give her the peace she deserves."

Elan's heart ached at the mention of Kaira, his own loss, a constant companion in the years since her disappearance. But seeing Reagan like this, so vulnerable yet fiercely determined, reminded him of their unbreakable bond.

He reached out and pulled Reagan into a tight embrace, feeling her body shudder with the force of her emotions. They clung to each other like two survivors adrift in a storm-tossed sea, drawing strength from their shared grief and unwavering commitment to finding the truth.

"We'll find her, Reagan," Elan murmured into her hair, his voice thick with emotion. "I promise you; we won't stop until we bring Kaira home."

Elan rolled up the scroll carefully and tucked it into his pack. "What are the chances we find this right away? This seems too easy. We'd better get moving. Kaira's waiting."

Vatican Library, Vatican City

With the ancient scroll secured in Elan's pack, the pair hurriedly entered the most beautiful library he had ever seen. The magnificent architecture stretched up towards the sky, and the grand entrance adorned with statues and intricate carvings was a sight beyond wonder. The library itself boasted high ceilings and walls lined with endless shelves of books and scrolls, each carefully labeled and preserved.

The library's grand entrance revealed intricately carved wooden doors adorned with gold, leading to an expansive room with towering shelves filled with countless ancient scrolls and texts. The white marble floors reflected the warm glow of the ornate chandeliers hanging from the high ceilings. Rays of sunlight pour through arched windows, illuminating the intricate details of the space.

As Elan and Reagan walked with a purpose, the librarian raised an eyebrow as they passed, but their determined expressions left no room for questioning. Reagan and Elan paused to catch their breath, their hearts racing from the discovery.

"Where do we start?" Elan asked, his military instincts kicking into high gear as he surveyed their surroundings with a practiced eye. His posture straightened, shoulders squaring and jaw setting in a way that was all too familiar to those who knew him as a Marine.

Elan's gaze swept over the area, taking in every detail with a sharpness honed by years of training and experience. He mentally cataloged potential threats and advantageous positions, his mind already formulating strategies and contingencies.

His hand instinctively went to his hip, fingers brushing against the reassuring weight of his sidearm. It was a habit he had never quite been able to shake, even after leaving the service. The muscle memory was as ingrained as the instinct to assess and adapt to any situation.

Elan's breathing slowed, a deliberate and measured cadence that helped to clear his mind and focus his thoughts. He could feel the adrenaline beginning to course through his veins, sharpening his senses and heightening his awareness.

As he continued to scan the surroundings, Elan's eyes narrowed, his brow furrowing in concentration. He was looking for anything out of place, any sign or clue pointing them in the right direction.

His mind raced with possibilities, each one evaluated and either discarded or filed away for further consideration. He knew that every decision he made from this point forward could mean the difference between success and failure, between finding Kaira and losing her forever.

After a final sweep of the area, Elan turned back to his companions, his expression grim and determined. "We'll need to establish a perimeter," he said, his voice calm and authoritative. Work our way inward, looking for any signs of recent activity or disturbance."

He paused, his gaze locking with each of theirs in turn. "Stay sharp and stay focused. We don't know what we're walking into, but we're going to face it together."

"According to the scroll, the hidden temple is within the catacombs beneath Rome. It's a vast labyrinth, but it's our best shot at finding the truth," Reagan replied, in a steely voice.

Elan nodded, his mind already working through possible strategies. "Let me talk to the librarian. I can ask him for manuscripts or historical documents to help us navigate the catacombs."

Reagan agreed. "Great idea, Elan. I wish I had paid more attention to my grandmother when she talked about our family history. While you gather those documents, I will see if I can dig up any information on the family history. There's a section dedicated to Heraldry."

Reagan headed towards the Heraldry section while Elan approached the desk where an elderly Italian man sat reading through a thick tome.

Elan cleared his throat, praying that his app-learned Italian wouldn't betray him. "Buongiorno, signore. Mi scusi, ma potresti aiutarmi a trovare documenti sui catacombe di Roma? Siamo in un viaggio di ricerca personale." Good day, sir. Excuse me, but could you help me find documents about the catacombs of Rome? We are on a personal quest.

The librarian's eyes sharpened, but he seemed unfazed by the unusual request. He waved them to follow him along a narrow aisle lined with crumbling tomes before stopping abruptly before a section marked "Miscellanea."

Hours later, in a dimly lit area of the library, Reagan was immersed in her research on the family history. Elan delved into the ancient tomes, cross-referencing with the scroll's notes. He was rewarded with a small triumphant exclamation. "Reagan, I think I've found it!"

Joining him, Reagan skimmed the yellowed pages of the tome he held out, a frown furrowing her brow. "It talks of a hidden temple near the Catacombs of San Callisto. The entrance is supposedly marked by... wait for it... a statue of a lioness with her two cubs."

Elan raised an eyebrow. "That narrows it down."

Reagan smirked humorlessly. "Well, it's more than we had before. Let's go before sunrise tomorrow and make our move. We don't want to attract any unwanted attention."

"We'll need supplies: flashlights, maps, anything that might help us navigate the maze down there." Elan stood up with a burst of energy. Reagan agreed, and they quickly set off to gather what they needed.

As they ventured to purchase supplies, Elan couldn't help but feel the weight of responsibility on his shoulders. He knew their success depended on his ability to think quickly and adapt to the unknown. And yet, he also knew that he could rely on Reagan's unwavering loyalty and resourcefulness to see them through any roadblocks they might encounter.

Reagan's hand gently touched Elan's shoulder. "We've got this, Elan," she said, her tone filled with conviction. "You and me, just like old times."

Elan couldn't help but smile at the memory of their childhood adventures, the scrapes and close calls they had navigated together. Even then, Reagan had been the one to keep a cool head, always ready with a clever plan or a quick escape route.

Her keen gaze swept the surroundings, searching for overlooked paths or ways to traverse the crowded avenues as she advanced. Reagan had a way of seeing things others might miss, a talent that had served her well as a police officer.

"There," she said suddenly, pointing to a faint impression in the soft earth. "Let's take this street; it'll be faster."

As they pursued the path to the shop, Reagan's thoughts were already at work, assembling their subsequent actions, surpassing their immediate goal.

Elan nodded, his own tactical mind considering the possibilities. "Good thinking," he said, impressed by her strategic insight. "We'll need to be prepared for anything."

Reagan flashed him a grin, her eyes sparkling with excitement and determination. "That's why you've got me," she said, bumping his shoulder with her own, "I've always got your back, no matter what."

With those words, Elan felt a rush of gratitude and affection for the woman beside him. Reagan's loyalty and resourcefulness were more than abstract qualities; they were tangible forces that had seen them through countless challenges and would continue to do so, no matter what lay ahead.

As they pressed on, Elan knew that they could face anything with Reagan by his side. Her quick thinking and unwavering support were the pillars upon which their partnership was built, a foundation that would not crack or crumble under even the greatest of pressures.

The night was still young as Elan and Reagan hurried through the busy streets of Rome, the air teeming with life. The smell of freshly baked bread and espresso mingled with the scent of exhaust fumes, creating a heady mix that Elan found both invigorating and intoxicating. Brightly lit storefronts displayed various wares, from designer clothes to souvenirs, each vying for their attention. They ducked into an electronics store, the fluorescent lights bathing them in a harsh glow as they purchased flashlights and other necessary gear. Their steps echoed against the tiled floor as they moved quickly about. A pair of young lovers shared a kiss outside a gelato shop, their tongues dancing like elves in a snow globe while they held each other close.

As they emerged onto the cobblestone street, Elan couldn't help but be reminded of Kaira and her infectious laughter. He swallowed the lump in his throat, eyes glistening with unshed tears. Reagan nudged him with her elbow, a fleeting gesture of understanding and support.

Elan stopped on the sidewalk as Reagan paused beside him, her expression a mixture of compassion and inquisitiveness. "Elan, it's been twenty years since Kaira…. I mean, I love her too, but why haven't you stopped to settle down and…move on?"

Elan looked at Reagan. "I don't know Ray. I struggle with that every day. No one compares to Kaira. I know I was a kid, but man… I loved her. I tried. I tried to love others. I've tried to *find* love. I know it's all in my head, but I think I can't even love myself because my heart was lost the day your beautiful sister disappeared."

Reagan stared into her best friend's eyes and determinedly put her hand on his shoulder. "You're a hopeless romantic, bro. I love you for that."

The map store was their next stop, where they acquired a detailed map of the catacombs and the surrounding area, marking the location of the Catacombs of San Callisto with a silver pin. The elderly shopkeeper eyed them curiously but said nothing as they paid in cash and left briskly.

Elan and Reagan spread out their meager supplies on the bed at their hotel room, double-checking everything meticulously.

"We'll head out before dawn tomorrow," Elan said, dark eyes alight with determination. "Kaira, we're coming for you. No matter what it takes."

"Are you ready?" Reagan asked as they stood at the entrance to the catacombs, their flashlights casting eerie shadows on the ancient stone walls.

Elan took a deep breath and looked into Reagan's eyes. "Let's do this. For Kaira."

Together, they stepped into the darkness, driven by love, friendship, and the unbreakable bond that united them in their quest to find Kaira and uncover the truth.

As they ventured deeper into the catacombs, the air grew colder, and a heavy silence enveloped them. They could feel the weight of history pressing down on them as if the very walls were trying to keep their secrets hidden.

"Can you believe we're walking through centuries of history?" Reagan whispered, her voice barely audible in the oppressive gloom.

Elan glanced over at her, noting how her shoulders tensed and her eyes glistened with unshed tears. He knew that beneath her brave facade, Reagan was grappling with the same overwhelming emotions that threatened to consume him.

"I can't imagine how hard this must be for you," he said softly, his hand reaching out to give hers a gentle squeeze. "Kaira was your sister, your blood. The bond you shared..."

Reagan drew in a shaky breath, her grip tightening on Elan's hand like a lifeline. "It's like a part of me is missing," she whispered, her voice cracking with the weight of her grief. "Every day, I wake up, and for a moment, I forget that she's gone. And then it hits me all over again, like a wave crashing over me, pulling me under."

Elan felt his own throat tighten, the raw pain in Reagan's words mirroring the ache in his own heart. "I know," he murmured, blinking back the tears that threatened to fall. "But we're here now, walking in her footsteps. We're going to find her, Reagan. We're going to bring her home."

Reagan smiled, a flicker of hope sparking to life in her eyes. "More than that," Elan continued, his military training keeping him focused on their mission. "We're walking through Kaira's past, a connection to her that's been lost for generations."

Their flashlights flickered over the ancient inscriptions and faded frescoes, each a testament to the lives once lived and the stories now forgotten. It was humbling and inspiring, a reminder that they were part of something far more significant than themselves.

"Elan, look at this," Reagan said, her voice tinged with excitement as she pointed to a worn inscription on one of the walls. "Do you think it could be related to Kaira?"

Elan scrutinized the inscription, his heart racing at the possibility.

The text was difficult to decipher, but he could make out what appeared to be a name: 'Kyra.'

"Reagan, I think we might be onto something here," he said, the hope in his voice unmistakable.

The two friends pressed on, following a winding path through the seemingly endless network of tunnels. Every now and then, they would pause to examine another inscription or piece of artwork, their determination to find Kaira growing stronger with each discovery.

"Wait," Elan said suddenly, stopping in his tracks. "Do you hear that?"

Reagan strained her ears, listening intently. At first, there was only silence, but then she heard it too – a faint, distant sound, like the echo of a voice calling out in anguish.

"Do you hear that?" Elan cried, his heart pounding with a mix of fear and hope. He took off down the tunnel, Reagan close on his heels, their flashlights slicing through the darkness as they raced toward the sound.

As the voice grew louder, it became clear that it was coming from a hidden chamber deep within the catacombs. Elan and Reagan exchanged a determined glance, knowing they were drawing closer to the truth with each step they took.

Together, they pushed open the ancient door, bracing themselves for whatever awaited them. But nothing could have prepared them for the sight that met their eyes – a room filled with relics and artifacts, each one a piece of Kaira's past waiting to be rediscovered.

"Elan," Reagan called, her hand trembling as she picked up an exquisite golden locket with her family crest. Inside was a portrait of a young woman on one side and a man on the other who resembled Kaira.

"Kaira's ancestors?" Elan breathed, his heart swelling with emotion. "I mean, *your* ancestors? We're getting closer."

Their search continued, the relic guiding them like breadcrumbs along a path that led further into the depths of history. Each discovery, since the night in his mother's basement, brought them one step closer to finding the truth regarding Kaira, fueling their quest to find out what really happened to her.

"Elan, look!" Reagan's voice rang out, her flashlight illuminating an ancient parchment wedged between two crumbling stones. Written in Latin, it appeared to be a diary entry or letter; the ink faded with age but was still legible in places.

Elan carefully removed the delicate parchment and squinted at the text. He could make out a few words, enough to send shivers down his spine: "Darkness... Prophecy... Sacrifice... Kaira..."

"This is it," he said, the pieces beginning to fall into place. "It's all connected to Kaira and her disappearance."

"But how?" Reagan asked, her eyes wide with wonder.

"I've been waiting for you." A voice said from the shadows.

Reagan and Elan whirled around to see an elderly man emerge from the shadows. He was tall and thin, with a long white beard and piercing blue eyes that seemed to stare right through them.

"Who are you?" Elan asked warily, instinctively moving to shield Reagan.

The old man smiled gently. "I am a friend. I have been guarding this chamber for many years, knowing that one day you would arrive seeking answers."

Reagan peered past Elan to study the man closely. "Answers about what?"

"*You* sent that scroll to me twenty years ago," Elan added.

"Indeed, Elan Durant. Reagan Mazza, yes, about your sister Kaira," the man replied. "And about the role she is destined to play in the coming battle between good and evil. But first, let me show you something."

The old man wore simple robes, and his white hair was pulled back in a severe bun, giving him the air of a wise sage.

"Who are you?" Elan demanded.

"I am Nykronus," the man said, his voice deep and heavily accented. "I have been expecting you. And I know where Kaira went and how to bring her back."

Elan and Reagan exchanged a skeptical glance, but the old man's eyes were filled with such conviction that they could not look away.

"Tell us more," Elan said cautiously. "Please."

Nykronus took a long, slow draw from his pipe, exhaling a swirling cloud of smoke that seemed to hang eerily in the air.

"The gods did not act lightly in taking Kaira," he continued, his voice low and resonant in the cramped chamber. "Dark forces are stirring, and Kaira has a role to play that the Fates themselves decreed long ago."

Elan clenched his fists, jaw tight. "So how do we get her back? You said you knew how."

Nykronus nodded. "There are certain...doorways that can be opened. But it will take an extraordinary relic - one forged by the gods themselves."

"What kind of relic?" Reagan asked eagerly.

Nykronus' eyes glinted in the dim light. "A weapon. One that belonged to Michael, the Greatest of Archangels, Champion of the Heavenly Host. His sword - *Winterstar*- was crafted by Vulcan himself. The way can be opened with it to where Keira has been taken."

Elan frowned, skepticism etched on his face. "Michael's sword? That seems like a fairy tale."

But Reagan looked thoughtful. "I don't know, Elan. If what Nykronus says is true, then maybe *Winterstar* really exists. And if it can lead us to Kaira..."

Hope bloomed in Elan's chest, but he forced himself to remain cautious. "Even if it is real, how would we ever find a heavenly relic like that?"

"You must seek out the Order of Saint Michael," Nykronus said.

"The Order of Saint Michael?" Elan repeated in disbelief. "Is this some kind of secret society?"

Nykronus nodded, his expression grim. "Indeed, though few in number now. For centuries, they have safeguarded artifacts like *Winterstar*, keeping them hidden from those who would misuse their power."

He lowered his voice conspiratorially. "Gaining access will not be easy - the Order trusts no outsiders. You first need to travel to Castel Sant'Angelo to the last place Kaira was seen alive."

Reagan's eyes shone with excitement. "We'll convince them, no matter what it takes. If *Winterstar* can bring Kaira back, we have to try."

Elan placed a hand on her shoulder, pride swelling in his chest at her determination. They would brave any trial if it meant finding her.

Nykronus looked at the two people who cared most for Kaira in this world. "I have no doubt you will do what it takes. I knew this moment would come. I will see you soon."

CHAPTER
FIVE

Castel Sant'Angelo

The wind whispered through Castel Sant'Angelo's ancient corridors as Elan and Reagan stood before its imposing entrance, their shadows casting dark silhouettes against the stone façade. The cryptic message that had led them here seemed to pulsate with energy as elusive as its concealed secrets.

"Are you ready?" Elan's voice was low and steady, betraying only a hint of the uncertainty that gnawed at him.

Reagan, her eyes scanning the aged structure, nodded. "As ready as I'll ever be."

Together, they pushed open the castle's heavy doors, stepping into the dimly lit interior with nothing but their determination and the knowledge that their quest was far from over. The air was heavy with the weight of secrets spanning centuries, and the walls, adorned with age-old frescoes, told tales of valor and conquest.

"Remember," Reagan said, her voice echoing through the vast hallways, "we trust our instincts and rely on each other's strengths." Her eyes burned with resolve, her faith in Elan unwavering.

"Agreed," Elan responded, his Marine Corps instincts kicking in as he assessed their surroundings. Each detail, no matter how insignificant, was etched into his memory. He noted the ancient stone walls, the weathered texture, and the faint traces of old frescoes that hinted at the castle's rich history. He took in the placement of each doorway and arch, mapping out potential escape routes and choke points in case of an ambush.

Elan's ears strained to pick up any sound that might betray the presence of hidden dangers - the faint scurry of rats in the walls, the distant echo of footsteps on stone, the whisper of wind through unseen cracks. He knew that even the smallest detail could mean the difference between success and failure, between life and death.

As they moved deeper into the castle, Elan's nose caught the musty scent of centuries-old dust and decay, mingling with the damp earthiness of the underground passages. He could taste the staleness of the air on his tongue, a reminder of the secrets buried within these walls.

Elan's fingers traced the rough stone as they walked, feeling for any irregularities or hidden triggers that might activate long-forgotten traps. His sense of touch was heightened, every nerve ending alive and attuned to the slightest change in pressure or temperature.

The labyrinthine nature of the castle would not deter them; together, they were a formidable pair, unstoppable in their pursuit of truth. Elan's Marine Corps training had honed his senses to a razor's edge, allowing him to process and analyze a staggering amount of information in mere seconds.

He knew Reagan was doing the same beside him, picking up on details others might overlook. Together, their combined skills and instincts formed a powerful tool, a weapon against the unknown and the unseen.

As they pressed on, Elan's mind continued to whir, processing and cataloging every piece of information, every sensory input. He was building a mental map of the castle, a blueprint to guide them through the twists and turns ahead.

They navigated the shadowy depths of Castel Sant'Angelo, guided by the light of their conviction and the unseen hand of fate. Every twist and turn, every fork in the path held the promise of discovery – or danger – yet they pressed forward, undaunted.

"Sometimes, I wonder if we're just pawns in someone else's game,"

Reagan mused as they paused momentarily, catching their breath. "It feels like we're being manipulated like there's some grand plan we're not seeing."

"Maybe, sis," Elan conceded, his gaze fixed on the path ahead. "But we choose our roles. We may not control destiny, but we'll fight to shape it." With a reassuring nod, he added, "And I believe that there's still hope for us yet."

Reagan smiled, her faith in their mission rekindled by Elan's unyielding resolve. "You're right. Let's keep moving."

As they ventured further into the castle's heart, the air grew colder, the whispers of the past growing louder with each step. The stones beneath their feet thrummed with ancient, powerful energy.

"Whatever lies ahead," Elan thought, his hand instinctively reaching for the hilt of *Winterstar*, "we'll face it together."

Beneath the flickering glow of ancient torchlight, Elan and Reagan forged their path through the dimly lit corridors of Castel Sant'Angelo. It was wild to think this massive fortress was a museum for tourists, knowing what really lies behind the interior walls.

"Left or right?" Reagan inquired, her breath hushed, her eyes scanning the intersecting passageways for any sign of hidden danger.

"Left," Elan decided, surging forth like a guiding compass. "I sense something... familiar in that direction."

"Trust your instincts," Reagan nodded, her intuition adding weight to Elan's decision. "They've never failed us before."

As they pressed on, the air grew thick with tension, each step further into the castle's depths to fuel and challenge their resolve.

"Elan," Reagan began, her voice cautious and measured, "do you ever wonder what awaits us at the end of all this? Will we find the truth we seek?"

"The truth will set us free," Elan mused, tightening his grip on his sword's hilt. "But our journey will reveal answers, wanted or not."

"Then let's hope we're prepared for what we find," Reagan whispered, her hand resting on the dagger at her side.

"Hope is our most powerful weapon," Elan considered.

"Let's keep going," Elan declared, his voice resolute.

"Agreed," Reagan replied, her eyes shining with fierce determination.

After hours of navigating through the catacombs, Elan and Reagan found themselves standing in front of an ancient door. Elan inserted a key Nykronus gave him. The door creaked open, revealing a chamber bathed in soft blue light. Dust swirled in the air, disturbed by their presence after centuries of undisturbed slumber. Elan and Reagan exchanged glances, feeling the weight of history surrounding them as they stepped into the room.

"Look at all this," Reagan marveled, her eyes wide with wonder as she gazed upon the multitude of historical artifacts that filled the chamber.

"I know…" Elan agreed, his voice hushed with reverence. "These relics must hold secrets we could never dream of."

They moved slowly through the chamber, their footsteps echoing softly off the walls laden with remnants of the past. The air was heavy with anticipation, each artifact whispering its story to those who dared listen.

"Elan," Reagan called, her voice tinged with awe, "check this out."

He walked towards her, finding her standing before a dusty tapestry depicting an epic battle between angels and demons. The intricate details were breathtaking, and Elan couldn't help but feel humbled by the craftsmanship and history it represented.

"This is incredible," he exhaled, his fingers lightly tracing the edges of the ancient fabric.

"Can you imagine the stories these walls could tell?" Reagan mused, her gaze sweeping across the room, lingering on the artifacts. "The truths we will uncover here? How can so many places be unexplored in such an ancient city?"

"It's wild!" Elan replied, his heart swelling with pride for their shared purpose. "Together, we will unlock the mysteries of the past and forge a new future."

"But we need to be careful," Reagan cautioned. "The power these artifacts hold. They're locked away for a reason."

"Agreed," Elan affirmed. "Let's proceed with caution and respect."

As they continued to explore the chamber, their thoughts echoed one another—both keenly aware of the significance of their discovery and the immense responsibility that rested on their shoulders. In this hallowed space, where history converged with destiny, Elan and Reagan found themselves bound by a common purpose—to uncover the truth and restore balance to a world teetering on the edge of darkness.

"Let's just hope," Elan murmured, as they stood shoulder to shoulder, "that these ancient relics will take us on the right path."

"They will," Reagan whispered.

Elan's eyes scanned the chamber, his attention drawn to the assortment of relics that seemed to shimmer in the dim light. Reagan moved silently at his side, her intuition guiding her as though by some unseen force.

"Look at this," Reagan whispered, crouching to examine a small wooden box nestled among the artifacts. With a gentle touch, she opened it to reveal a rosary inside. "It's beautiful."

Elan's gaze narrowed as he noticed something peculiar about the rosary. "There's a bead missing."

Reagan's brow furrowed as she studied the strand, her fingers tracing the smooth beads. "You know what I'm thinking, right?"

"Take it out," Elan replied, his voice heavy with conviction. "It looks like it would be a perfect fit!"

Reagan reached into her bag and pulled out the rosary bead they had found at her grandmother's house just days before. She placed the bead into the empty notch on the rosary. The relic glowed as if surrounded by a blue fire. The blue hue brightened the room, revealing an immense stone statue.

Elan and Reagan stood in awe as they beheld an enormous statue of St. Michael before them. The Archangel towered over them, his wings outstretched and poised for battle. His eyes seemed to pierce their very souls, and the air around them crackled with otherworldly energy.

"Holy shit…" Reagan whispered, her voice barely a breath. "This… this is St. Michael."

"Damn," Elan marveled, his eyes tracing the lines of the celestial warrior's armor, the lifelike folds of his robes. He could feel the power emanating from the statue as if it were imbued with a divine presence.

"Look! It's the sword Nykronus was telling us about! Stellata d'Inferno. *Winterstar*." Reagan exclaimed, pointing to the sword held aloft in the Archangel's grasp. Its blade connected to the ceiling by shimmering bolts of lightning that danced and flickered above their heads.

The rosary's same blue aura pulsed gently around the empty pool beneath the statue, casting eerie reflections on the damp stone walls. Elan furrowed his brow, his mind racing with questions. "What purpose does this serve?" he wondered aloud, his voice echoing through the chamber.

"Maybe… it's a test," Reagan suggested hesitantly, her gaze locked on the ethereal glow. "A trial we must overcome in order to prove our worthiness."

"Or it's a trap," Elan countered, his Marine Corps instincts kicking in as he scanned the room for potential threats. His heart began to race, pounding against his ribcage like a war drum, sounding the alarm. The hair on the back of his neck stood up, a primal response to the unseen danger that lurked in the shadows.

Elan's muscles tensed, coiled like springs, ready to launch him into action at the slightest provocation. His palms grew slick with sweat, his body's natural response to the adrenaline that surged through his veins. He could feel the weight of his weapon pressing against his hip, a reassuring presence in the face of the unknown.

As his eyes darted from one corner of the room to the other, Elan's breathing became shallow and rapid, his lungs struggling to keep pace with the demands of his racing heart. The air seemed to grow thicker, pressing down on him like a physical weight, making each breath a conscious effort.

Every sense was heightened, every nerve ending alive and crackling with electricity. Elan could hear the faintest whisper of fabric as Reagan shifted beside him, the soft scrape of stone on stone as something moved in the distance. He could smell the musty odor of centuries-old dust, mingling with the acrid tang of his own fear.

The room seemed to close around them, the walls pressing in like the jaws of a giant beast. Elan's skin prickled with the sensation of unseen eyes watching, waiting, ready to strike at the first sign of weakness.

And yet, despite the fear that gnawed at his gut, Elan remained focused, his mind sharp and clear. He knew that their survival depended on his ability to anticipate and react to any threat, to think two steps ahead of their enemy.

"Nykronus *said* it would be heavily guarded," Reagan declared, her resolve steeling her nerves. "We've come too far to give up, and Kaira needs us. United in purpose. For love, for hope, and for the truth."

"Then let's do this!" Elan said, stepping towards the pool, the rosary clutched tightly in his hand. "May St. Michael guide us and protect us."

"I mean he is looking down on us," Reagan echoed, her heart pounding in anticipation as they moved closer to the pulsating pool.

The blue aura grew brighter as they approached, bathing them in its ethereal glow. His hand quivering faintly, Elan extended the rosary above the shimmering surface, his mind drifting to Kaira and the treacherous path that had brought them to this pivotal juncture.

"Are you ready?" he asked Reagan, his voice steady despite his trepidation.

"Always," she replied, her hand reaching for his in solidarity and support.

Elan's eyes locked on the statue of St. Michael as he prepared to face the unknown.

The dimly lit chamber seemed to breathe with anticipation, as if aware that its long-held secrets were about to be uncovered. Elan's eyes scanned the room, lingering on a small wooden table at its center. Upon closer inspection, he realized it held an ancient manuscript, its cover worn and weathered by time.

"Look," he whispered to Reagan, beckoning her with a wave. "This has to be what we've been searching for."

Reagan approached cautiously, her eyes widening in awe as she closed in on the ancient book. She reached out a trembling hand, fingertips brushing against the rough surface.

"I can feel it, Elan," she murmured. "There's power in these pages, a history of past battles, of love and sacrifice. It's all connected to St. Michael... and to us."

Elan's fingers traced the intricate symbols etched into the book's spine. He could almost hear the echoes of prayers whispered fervently by those who had sought guidance and protection from the celestial warrior throughout the ages.

"Elan, do you think this could help us find Kaira?" Reagan asked, her voice quivering with hope.

"It has to," he replied thoughtfully, lifting the heavy tome from its resting place. "But first, we need to decipher its pages and understand the purpose it serves in our quest."

"Then let's get to work," Reagan said with determination, her fear momentarily replaced by a fierce resolve to see their mission through to its end. Together, they huddled over the ancient manuscript, their minds racing to unlock the knowledge contained within.

As they delved deeper into the spell book, Elan couldn't shake the feeling that something significant was about to transpire. There was a subtle shift in the air, an unseen force tugging at the edges of his consciousness. He glanced at Reagan, who seemed to sense it too—her eyes met his, wide and full of wonder.

"Elan," she breathed, her fingers hovering above a specific passage on the page. "I think this might be it."

"Read it aloud," he urged, his heart pounding in anticipation.

Reagan's voice wavered as she began to recite the ancient words, their meaning slowly revealing itself like a puzzle coming together piece by piece. As the final syllable left her lips, a shudder ran through the chamber as if the very foundations of the castle were responding to the power invoked by the spell.

"Something's happening," Elan whispered, his gaze darting around the room for any changes. He felt an inexplicable pull, drawing him closer to the center of the chamber where the statue of St. Michael stood sentinel.

The shadows of the chamber seemed to recede as Reagan lifted the book from its resting place, unveiling a hidden slot beneath it. The shape and size of the slot matched perfectly with the blade held by St. Michael's statue, beckoning Elan to make the connection.

"Elan, look at this," Reagan beckoned, her voice trembling with excitement. She pointed at a letter tucked between the pages of the manuscript, its script composed of elegant strokes that bespoke its ancient origin. "It has instructions for our quest."

"Read them," Elan urged, his eyes darting between the sword and the slot, a sense of urgency taking hold.

Reagan unfolded the letter carefully as if she feared the parchment would crumble under her touch. Her eyes scanned the text, her brow furrowing as she pieced together its meaning. Finally, she began to read aloud:

"O seeker of truth, thou hast come far in thy journey, yet further still must thou venture. With the sword of St. Michael in hand, unlock the power of the pool, and let the tides of time guide thee towards the light."

As Reagan spoke these words, Elan's heart raced with anticipation. He glanced around the chamber, his gaze returning to the empty pool bathed in a soft, blue aura. It seemed almost alive, waiting to be awakened.

"Elan, I think we need to place the sword into the slot," Reagan said, her tone resolute. "It's the key to unlocking whatever lies beyond."

Elan nodded, his determination mirrored in Reagan's eyes. They approached the statue, the weight of their mission bearing down upon them. At that moment, they knew their lives would never be the same.

With a deep breath, Elan grasped the sword's hilt, feeling an electric hum resonating through his very being. He lifted it from the statue's grasp, the bolts of lightning that had once tethered it to the ceiling dissipating into nothingness.

"Ready?" he asked Reagan, his voice steady despite his heart pounding.

"Always," she replied, her eyes shining with an unwavering resolve.

Elan stepped toward the slot and, with a swift motion, inserted the sword. The chamber trembled as if in response to the union of blade and stone, the air humming with energy. Moments later, the pool began to fill with water, its surface shimmering and radiating ethereal blue light.

The water seemed to have a life of its own, its surface shimmering and dancing. It cast a soft glow on the surrounding area, bathing Elan and Kaira in its luminescence. The blue light pulsed gently, as if in time with the beating of an unseen heart, adding to the enchanting atmosphere.

As the pool continued to fill, the sound of the water transformed into a soothing babbling, reminiscent of a tranquil brook winding its way through a mystical forest. It was a sound that invited relaxation and contemplation, a gentle lullaby that could easily lull one into a trance-like state.

Elan and Kaira found themselves inexplicably drawn to the pool, their senses heightened and alert. They noticed a subtle yet distinct aroma wafting from its depths. It was a scent unlike anything they had ever encountered - a delicate blend of crisp, clean air, reminiscent of the moments just after a refreshing rainfall, mingled with the faintest hint of an unknown, exotic flower.

The fragrance was invigorating and calming, filling their lungs with rejuvenation and peace. It cleared their minds and sharpened their focus as if preparing them for the journey ahead.

As the pool reached its capacity, the sound of the water shifted once more, becoming a gentle lapping against the stone edges. It was a soothing, rhythmic sound, like the soft caress of waves upon a tranquil shore.

Elan and Kaira stood at the water's edge, transfixed by the ethereal beauty. The shimmering blue light, the enchanting sounds, and the mysterious, alluring scent all combined to create an atmosphere of wonder and anticipation, a sense that they were standing on the precipice of something truly extraordinary.

The transformation was mesmerizing, a testament to the ancient magic that permeated their surroundings. Elan couldn't help but wonder what lay beyond this point in their journey – what secrets awaited them in the depths of time.

"My God." Reagan murmured, her eyes locked on the transformation unfolding before them. Reagan ventured, her voice barely audible, "Elan, do you think...?"

"Think what?" he asked, tearing his attention away from the pool.

"Is it possible that this pool is a portal to another world?" she hesitated, her expression a mix of trepidation and curiosity.

"Anything's possible at this point. Less than a week ago, the world made sense to me." Elan replied as he was analyzing every possibility. The cryptic instructions from the letter resurfaced in his mind, and he contemplated the idea that the pool could serve as a portal to a different dimension – a place where the truth would be revealed and their questions answered. A small part of him clung to the hope that Kaira would thrive in this other world unharmed. He longed to discover the reasons behind her unfortunate circumstances and finally learn of her whereabouts.

"Ready?" Reagan asked, her hand reaching out for his. He grasped it firmly, their fingers intertwining as they stood on the brink of the unknown.

"Let's go," Elan said, his voice laced with resolve. They stepped closer to the pool's edge, its surface rippling with an eerie luminescence.

"Whatever we find on the other side," he thought, "we'll face it together." And with that, Elan Durant, retired Marine Sergeant Major, and Reagan, the intuitive police officer, stepped into the glowing waters, united by their shared purpose and the promise of untold adventure.

The water surged around them, its ethereal glow casting an eerie light on their faces as they waded deeper into the pool. Elan's heart pounded in his chest, his senses heightened by the prospect of what lay beyond. He could feel the weight of Reagan's hand in his, their fingers laced together in a bond forged by friendship and shared purpose.

"Elan," Reagan said suddenly, her voice wavering. "There's something I need to tell you."

"Reagan?" he asked, furrowing his brow in concern as he studied her face. The dancing light of the pool reflected in her eyes, revealing a depth of emotion that caught him off guard.

She took a deep breath, her grip on his hand tightening. "I... I can't go with you," she stammered. "This is where my journey ends."

"Wh-What are you talking about?" Elan demanded, his mind racing with confusion. "We're in this together. We have been from the start."

"Elan, listen," she implored, tears glistening in her eyes. "You need to find my sister, and I believe you will. But I... I have a feeling that I'm not meant to be a part of it. There's something else waiting for me, something I need to do here. I can't explain it, but I just know it. I'm going to go find Nykronus."

"Reagan, no," he protested, unwilling to accept her words. "We've come so far together. I can't just leave you behind."

"Elan," she whispered, her voice thick with emotion. "Maybe not by blood, but you're my brother. You know that, right? And I'll always be with you in spirit. But this is where I need to do what I can from here and let you continue without me. Something tells me this is bigger than just finding Kaira. I trust you. I know you can do this without me."

He struggled to find the words, his mind grappling with the enormity of her decision. "Reagan, I... I don't want this to be the last time I see you."

"Elan," she said firmly, "This is not the last time you're going to see me. It's just a parting of ways for now so we can maximize our efforts. I know there's more to do here. I know the Jarhead standing in front of me knows that. We *will* see each other again, I promise you that. Plus, you're bringing my sister home to me."

"Can you do one thing for me, then?" he asked, his voice barely more than a whisper.

"Anything," she replied, her gaze never leaving his.

"Promise me you won't give up your own quest," Elan implored. "Whatever it is that you feel you need to do…whatever you find out from Nykronus, face it with courage and determination. Don't let anything stand in your way."

"I promise," Reagan vowed. "Now go, Elan. Find Kaira. Fulfill your destiny."

With a nod, Elan released her hand, feeling like a piece of his soul was being torn away as he stepped deeper into the pool. As Reagan stepped out of the pool, the blue glow intensified around Elan, wrapping him in its embrace as he prepared to step into the unknown.

"See you later, Ray," he reluctantly said, his voice thick with a mix of sorrow and hope.

Elan took one last look at Reagan, their eyes met in a moment of unspoken understanding before he closed his eyes and whispered the words from the ancient manuscript:

"Per aspera ad astra."

As Elan plunged forward, the waters closed over him like a shroud, enveloping him in a world of muted sound and ethereal blue light. The moment he broke the surface, he felt the shock of the water's temperature, a cold that seemed to penetrate his very bones. It stole the breath from his lungs, causing him to gasp involuntarily as his body tried to adjust to the sudden change.

The water's embrace was comforting and unsettling, a sensation of weightlessness that made him feel disconnected from the world above. Elan could feel the pressure building in his ears as he sank deeper, a dull ache that grew more insistent with each passing second.

His heart raced, pounding against his chest as if trying to escape the confines of his body. The adrenaline coursing through his veins made his skin tingle, a prickling sensation that intensified the deeper he went.

Elan's lungs burned with the need for air, a desperate urge to breathe that he fought against with every ounce of his willpower. His chest felt tight, constricted by the weight of the water pressing in on him from all sides.

Elan's senses were overwhelmed by the strange, otherworldly environment as he sank further into the depths. The silence was deafening, broken only by the muffled sound of his heartbeat echoing in his ears. The ethereal blue light that suffused the water seemed to pulse and shimmer, casting eerie shadows that danced across his vision.

And yet, despite the physical discomfort and the eerie surroundings, Elan felt a sense of purpose and determination that drove him forward. He knew this was a journey he had to make, a path he had to follow, no matter where it might lead.

With each stroke of his arms and kick of his legs, Elan propelled himself deeper into the unknown, his body a vessel carrying him toward an uncertain future and the answers he desperately sought.

The pool's blue light reflected on Reagan's face, casting a celestial glow as she watched Elan disappear beneath the surface. She stood at the edge, her heart thrumming in her chest, knowing that this farewell was necessary—that it was for the greater good.

"Go forth and find your destiny," she whispered, her words carried away by the chamber's echoes.

Reagan's intuition had always been a guiding force in her life, a quiet whisper in the back of her mind that steered her toward her true path. It was a feeling that defied logic or explanation, a deep-seated knowing from a place beyond conscious thought.

As she watched Elan disappear beneath the pool's surface, Reagan felt that familiar tug in her heart, a bittersweet mix of love and sorrow that seemed to echo through her very soul. She knew, with a certainty that couldn't be shaken, that her journey would take her down a different road, requiring her to make sacrifices and face challenges she had never encountered.

It was a knowledge born from years of self-reflection and spiritual exploration, a connection to something greater than herself that had always been a part of her. Reagan had spent countless hours meditating, delving deep into her own psyche and the mysteries of the universe, seeking answers to questions she hadn't yet learned to ask.

Through this practice, she developed a keen sense of intuition, an ability to see beyond the veil of the physical world and glimpse the truth beneath. It was this intuition that now spoke to her, whispering of a destiny that was hers alone to fulfill.

Reagan didn't know where this path would lead her or what trials she would face. But she knew, with a bone-deep certainty, that she had to trust her heart's wisdom to follow her intuition's call wherever it might take her.

And so, as she watched Elan vanish into the pool's depths, Reagan steeled herself for the journey ahead. She knew their paths would diverge, and they would each have to face challenges and overcome obstacles.

As she turned from the pool, her eyes caught sight of the imposing statue of St. Michael. The angelic figure seemed to watch over her, its sword now bathed in the same ethereal blue light that emanated from the waters. She felt its presence momentarily, a reassuring warmth that spoke of protection and guidance.

"St. Michael," she said softly, "grant me the strength to see this through."

With those words, she pivoted and strode back towards the hidden chamber, her resolve unwavering. As she passed the myriad artifacts that littered the room, her hands brushed against the rosary, now complete with her family heirloom. Clutching it tightly, she felt a renewed sense of purpose course through her veins.

"Elan will succeed," she vowed, determination lacing her every thought. "And I... will too."

"Reagan," a voice called out, echoing through the dimly lit hallways. Startled, she looked up to see a figure emerging from the shadows, their face shrouded in darkness.

"Who are you?" she asked, her hand instinctively reaching for a weapon she no longer possessed.

"Someone who shares your cause," the figure replied. Reagan's eyes widened in surprise and recognition as the figure stepped into the blue light that spilled from the pool

"Professor Xicato?" she said, extending her hand.

The elderly man grasped her hand, their grip firm and unwavering. In that moment, a new alliance was forged, born from sacrifice and bound by a shared sense of purpose. And as Reagan took her first steps into the unknown, she knew that whatever lay ahead, she would face it with courage and conviction.

"Elan, I promise you," she whispered, her voice filled with determination. "We will set things right – for us, for our families, and for the world."

ACT TWO

"I am certain that I have been here as I am now a thousand times before, and I hope to return a thousand times."

- Goethe

CHAPTER

SIX

A sudden rush of cold air kissed Elan's cheeks as he blinked, finding himself standing in the heart of a barren field. As if waking up from a bad dream he couldn't remember, he found himself confused and disoriented. His senses were bombarded with a mishmash of unfamiliar sounds: the shrill cry of a distant bird, the rustle of dead grass underfoot, and the setting sun quickly bringing darkness over the desolate landscape. He felt the weight of the world pressing down on him like a stone slab. What would be normal sounds on an average day was overwhelming.

"Where am I?" Elan said in a barely audible whisper. They seemed drowned out by the relentless gusts whipping around him. With scrunched brows and slightly clenched fists, Elan stumbled forward, his boots dragging on the dry earth beneath him. Every step felt heavy, burdened with the uncertainty of the situation.

The constant feeling of being trapped in a never-ending nightmare was consuming him. He desperately wanted to escape, but at the same time, he couldn't help but feel like this was indeed a reality. It was a tug-of-war between wanting to run away and facing the terrifying truth that this might be the new norm. Suddenly, patrols in Afghanistan felt much more manageable.

"Get it together, Elan," he muttered, drawing upon the resourcefulness that had served him well during his time in the Marines. "What's the last thing you remember?"

As Elan fought to clear his foggy mind, a sudden noise snapped him to alertness—a low growl from behind. Turning, he saw a pack of feral dogs emerging from the shadows, their eyes hungry and fixed upon him. Instinctively, Elan changed the pace of his walk to a double time. "Move, Elan, move!" he commanded himself, his feet picking up a faster pace as the dogs began their chase.

The chase was frantic. Elan's heart pounded in his chest as he navigated through the rough terrain, the dogs' snarls a constant threat at his heels. His thoughts briefly flashed to Kaira—the reason for his determination to survive—and a promise to find her again. "I've got to make it through this," he panted, pushing his body to its limits.

Finally, seeing an outcrop of rocks ahead, Elan made a desperate dash towards it and clambered up with all his remaining strength. The dogs circled below, their barks echoing in the chilly air, but they couldn't reach him. He was safe, for the moment. Panting heavily, Elan scanned the horizon as the last rays of the sun painted the sky with strokes of crimson and gold.

"Elan Durant does not give up! I will find Kaira. I will find answers, and I *will* make it back home," he reassured himself, his voice firm with conviction despite his exhaustion. After what seemed to be hours, he watched the dogs slowly retreat into the fading light, their figures becoming more part of the landscape.

Darkness settled, and the chill of the night began to creep in; Elan's resolve hardened. He couldn't stay here forever. With cautious movements, he descended from his temporary refuge and continued his journey, his muscles aching but his spirit undeterred.

And then, just as he was about to give in to the weariness that threatened to overwhelm him, a faint glimmer of light appeared in the distance. It shimmered like a beacon through the darkness. "Please, let it be real," he prayed, his weary legs carrying him toward the hopeful light.

As he approached, the light grew steadier and brighter, revealing that it was no illusion—there were indeed others in this desolate place.

Filled with relief and anticipation, Elan quickened his pace, eager to connect with anything other than a pack of wild dogs.

"Maybe I can find some clues to figure out where I'm at," he thought, his heart swelling with hope. The wind continued to howl through the field, a stark reminder of his isolation, but the promise of human contact gave him new energy.

As the distance closed, Elan prepared himself for whatever lay ahead. Would the first people he met be friend or foe? His former Commanding Officer's words echoed in his mind: "Trust is earned, not given freely." He knew he had to be cautious but open-minded. He needed help, but he couldn't afford to compromise his own safety.

"Keep moving," he commanded himself, ignoring the ache in his muscles and the emotional turmoil swirling within. He had faced worse than this.

Finally, as he stepped into the radiant embrace of the light, he saw a silhouette standing before him—his back turned only to put Elan on alert.

Amid the light's radiant glow, Elan knew anything was possible in this dangerous land, where shadows loomed large, and dangers lurked at every turn. He wondered if this was a friend or foe, and there was only one way to find out.

CHAPTER

SEVEN

Elan's boots sank into the forest floor, almost at attention - a force of habit showcasing his Marine Corps discipline. The campfire's glow beckoned him forward, slicing through the veil of darkness that draped the woods. He advanced with measured steps, every sense attuned to the environment. A shudder ran through the night air, a palpable charge that seemed to resonate with the very beat of his heart.

The shadows danced around the fire's edge as if there was a mutual understanding to cloak the figure that stood there—a mysterious silhouette against the flickering light. Elan felt the weight of unseen eyes upon him, assessing his approach with intensity. There was power here, old and mysterious, coiled within the quietude of the scene like a sleeping serpent.

As Elan approached cautiously, the figure stirred. The firelight caught the edges of a spacious cloak, revealing the glint of an ornate clasp at the shoulder—a sigil. Its intricate design shined with the promise of ancient power. A symbol of great importance, it seemed to pulse with energy, emanating from the center towards the edges. It was a radiant design of golden wings enveloping a green cross.

The air crackled anew, this time with the echo of a voice that seemed woven from the threads of history itself and hauntingly familiar.

"Elan Durant," the voice intoned, rich with the timbre of authority. "You were always meant to be here at this moment."

As the voice declared Elan's destiny, skepticism and curiosity waged war within him. His military mindset resisted the unfounded assertion, yet a spark of intrigue ignited and challenged him to consider a greater narrative. Conflicting emotions brewed—a resonant validation pulled him to accept this long-awaited truth while self-doubt shadowed his worthiness to fulfill such a role. Despite the doubts, the statement propelled Elan into deep reflection, confronting his past, present, and future far from the certainties of military life. This moment became a crucible for transformation, nudging him towards a destiny intertwining martial prowess and the mystical and setting him on a path of profound growth and discovery.

Nykronus stepped forth from the embrace of the shadows, his presence commanding even as it exuded serene wisdom.

His eyes showed the marks of time, yet he appeared younger - perhaps even younger than Elan himself. The hot flames shimmered in his pupils as he held Elan's gaze with a stock-still concentration.

"Destiny is not a path trodden by chance, but one shaped by the will of those called to its service," Nykronus continued. His hands, emerging from the folds of his cloak, moved with a grace that belied their appearance. "I am Nykronus, once of Rome, now servant to the Order of St. Michael. It is my charge to guide you towards what awaits."

Elan's stance remained guarded, the Marine within him bristling at the supernatural relevance. Yet, as he stood before the enigmatic guardian, he could not deny the resonance of truth in the man's words. The emblem on Nykronus's cloak seemed to pulse with an inner light, a beacon calling to Elan's own unacknowledged yearning for purpose.

He was standing in front of a younger version of a man he had just seen yesterday. He remembered the time travel movies he had watched throughout his lifetime and wondered if there were consequences or a possibility of altering the future. His mind became chaotic, and his anxiety kicked into overdrive. Elan was also relieved knowing he was still on Earth and gazed up to the sky, noticing the familiar constellations from his past - or, in this case, his future.

"Prophesied meeting. Nykronus, we've met. I'm from the future." Elan's voice was a low rumble, skepticism, and intrigue warring beneath the surface. "Why me?"

"Because within you lies the confluence of courage and compassion, strength forged through battles waged in both light and shadow," Nykronus replied. "The Order has watched, and now the time comes when your role in the grand tapestry shall be revealed."

Elan glimpsed fragments of another existence in the dance of the flames, one where duty extended beyond the corporeal realm. Nykronus's presence was a beacon amidst the uncertainty, promising answers to questions Elan had yet to voice.

"Guide me then," Elan said, the decision resonating within him like a call to arms. "Show me this so-called destiny."

"Follow and learn," Nykronus said, turning to face the abyss beyond the campfire's reach. "For what lies ahead is both a burden and a gift, and you must be ready to bear its weight."

Together, they stepped into the night, the fire's glow at their backs, Venus shining brightly in front of the constellation Leo high above them, and the whispers of an ancient order filling the air with promises of revelations yet to come.

Elan trailed behind Nykronus, his combat boots sinking slightly into the soft earth with each step. The campfire's light waned behind them, casting long, quivering shadows across the forest floor that seemed to reach out like grasping fingers, desperate to pull him back into the safety of the known. Elan was relieved they were walking away from the barren field he traveled through.

"To you, your path is linear, but I am telling you, that path," Nykronus began, his voice a blend of command and solace, reverberating in the space between the ancient trees, "is inscribed with the ink of fates not yet realized."

Elan's anxiety intensified under the weight of Nykronus's words. He had faced terrorists and navigated the myriad of war zones. Still, this incomprehensible talk of destiny was a different battlefield altogether—one he wasn't sure he believed in or was ready for.

"Trials await that will test your heart beyond the physical fray you know so well," Nykronus continued, his eyes reflecting the silver of moonlight. "Tenacity is but one virtue you'll need to harness; wisdom, restraint, and sacrifice will be your silent weapons."

Elan listened, the flames of skepticism burning in the back of his mind. Yet, something in the pit of his stomach—a raw, primal instinct —resonated with the truth buried in the riddles. The tales Nykronus spun were not merely stories; they hinted at a reality far grander and more perilous than any Elan had encountered.

"Give it to me straight," Elan demanded, his voice a mixture of frustration and curiosity. "What battles? What sacrifices?"

"Every choice casts a stone upon the waters of destiny, Sergeant Major Durant," Nykronus answered, pausing to study Elan's face as though reading an ancient script engraved upon his soul. "The ripples you create will either uphold the balance or send us teetering into darkness. Your actions, unwittingly, have already begun to shape this future—your future, my future, humanity's future."

Nykronus' words "balance" and "darkness" felt foreign to Elan as his thoughts churned, grappling with the significance of his prophecy. The phrase "Same shit. Different day" echoed his life of service and sacrifice, a cycle reminiscent of his years in uniform. One poignant memory stood out: a mission gone awry in Afghanistan, a young Marine's life slipping away, a stark reminder of war's cost. These moments of loss tangibly expressed the abstract ideal he lived by—the belief that their struggles served a higher cause.

Standing before Nykronus, the words took on new meaning, bridging the gap between his past battles and the mystic struggles that awaited. Though the battleground had shifted, the essence of the conflict remained: a fight against darkness, a testament to human resilience. This realization strengthened Elan's resolve, and he was ready to face the cosmic battle between light and darkness with the same commitment that had always guided him.

"Listen, Nykronus," Elan said, his voice threaded with resolve. "I have to be honest with you—I'm here for one thing and one thing only.

I need to find out what happened to Kaira. She's the reason I stepped through that portal in the first place."

Nykronus, eyes reflecting a depth of centuries, nodded slowly. "I understand, Elan. Your heart drives you as it should. But remember, our paths are intertwined. The quest to uncover the truth about Kaira's disappearance is part of a larger tapestry."

"But it's Kaira who matters to me," Elan pressed, his gaze intense. "She vanished from our time, left without a trace or reason. Finding her, bringing her back, or learning what happened... that's my goal, Nykronus. That's why I'm here."

"I respect your dedication," Nykronus replied, the ancient wisdom in his voice softening. "And I assure you, aiding you in your quest for Kaira is part of our shared journey. We are allies in this, Elan. Your purpose is not forgotten."

"Then let's not lose sight of that," Elan concluded, a firm determination settling over his features. "Finding Kaira is my main priority. Everything else comes second. I just want to be clear on what it is you want with *me*."

"Elan Durant, you've been brought to this era for a purpose," Nykronus asserted. "Your quest and the truths I've shared are intertwined more closely than you know. There's a grander design at play here, one that extends beyond your current understanding. We must delve into the shadows, unravel the schemes of darkness, and tilt the scales back towards the light. The Order of St. Michael depends on it— and on you."

"Tell me what I have to do," Elan finally said confidently as he squared his shoulders against the unknown challenges Nykronus alluded to. "If what you're saying is true, then I'm ready. I have what it takes. I know that. You know that. I've done this before. Insert bad guy here. But I want you to know. I don't march into battle blindly."

Nykronus nodded, a ghost of a smile gracing his lips as if he'd expected no less from the warrior before him. "In time, all will be revealed," he promised. "For now, walk side by side with me, Elan. Walk the path of those who guard the flickering light of humanity from the encroaching shadows."

And so, beneath the cathedral of stars and whispers of ancient spirits, Elan stepped forward, his skepticism slowly yielding to a blossoming alliance with the serendipity Nykronus wove—a tapestry of love and war, of sacrifice and hope, interlaced with the eternal struggle between light and darkness.

"Centuries have passed since the Order of St. Michael first took its silent oath," Nykronus began, his voice carrying the weight of history and the unseen burden of countless battles. "In the shadows of the world, away from mortal eyes, we have waged a relentless war to maintain the fragile equilibrium between light and darkness."

The star-filled sky illuminated Elan's face, casting shifting shadows across his face as he listened with an expression of profound reflection. The ancient and clandestine chronicle of the Order resonated deep within him, intertwining with his lifelong commitment to obligation and the price he had paid. However, even as the tale of this veiled conflict struck a chord with his personal journey, a singular question nagged at the edges of his concentration, tugging at the tapestry of his thoughts: What part did Kaira have in the grand scheme of things? The allusion to struggles waged beyond the sight of the world conjured her visage in his mind's eye, weaving her recollection into this newly discovered calling.

"Hidden wars?" Elan's words were measured, grappling with this revelation. "Wars fought in secret—how is it that the world is still this ignorant in the future? Ancient conspiracies…"

"Because, as you are already aware, Elan, the most dangerous battles are often those fought in silence, where the clash of swords never reaches the ears of the innocent." Nykronus's eyes gleamed with an intensity that held Elan captive. "The Order has been the bastion against the forces that seek to tip the scales towards eternal night."

Nykronus reached into his satchel, retrieving an object wrapped in cloth. He unraveled the fabric, revealing a tome bound in leather so old it seemed a part of the earth itself. He carefully opened the volume to a page marked by a green ribbon with words indelibly marked in metallic gold. Words inscribed in a language older than any Elan had encountered flowed across the parchment.

"Ut infra, sic supra," Nykronus intoned. Though the language was foreign, Elan recognized and understood the Latin words striking a chord within Elan—an echo of something primal and known.

"As below, so above," Elan realized Nykronus was speaking to him in English the entire time.

Nykronus locked eyes with Elan. "Our actions in the shadows reflect upon the world in ways unseen but deeply felt. Understand the secrets of the past, and you will learn to navigate the labyrinth of the present."

With each syllable spoken, Elan could feel the weight of centuries unfold before him, a mosaic of hidden knowledge slowly coming into focus. The mystic's words were not just a history lesson; they were a key to understanding the very fabric of reality.

"Secrets of the past," Elan repeated, allowing himself a moment to absorb the magnitude of what he was learning. "You speak as if time itself bends to your will."

"Time is but a river, Elan, and we, the Order of St. Michael, have learned to swim against its currents," Nykronus said, closing the tome with a sound that echoed like a distant bell. "To be one with the Order is to see beyond the veil of the temporal—to protect, to serve, and to sacrifice in the name of the greater good."

Nykronus's words left Elan pondering the Order's mastery over time and the commitment required to join their ranks. As he considered the expanse of duty before him, he focused on how this journey through history might lead him to Kaira. The promise of serving a greater cause resonated within him, yet his quest to reunite with his lost love remained intertwined with every fiber of his being. Elan silently wondered how his pursuit intersected with the path to find Kaira and how the Order's timeless war connected to the heart of his own quest.

Elan felt the last remnants of his skepticism dissolve in the silence that followed. The dance of twinkling stars, the ancient text, and the solemn wisdom in Nykronus's eyes—all spoke of a truth far greater than he could ever dream. And somewhere deep within, a spark of resolve kindled, ready to ignite into the blaze of a warrior's spirit.

Elan scrutinized the shifting shadows cast by the bright stars. The air crackled with an energy that seemed to resonate with the very beat of his heart—an echo of a distant drum, trumpeting a call to arms from ages long past. It was like hearing the trumpet before playing the National Anthem every morning - a patriotic reminder. A battle cry. As Nykronus began to speak again, his voice was both a balm and a blade, cutting through Elan's doubts and pulling them toward the gravity of his own purpose.

"Your role, Elan Durant, is not one of mere chance or coincidence," Nykronus intoned, his words weaving toward the star-pricked sky. "You stand at the convergence of fate and free will, where every choice carves the future out of the monolith of destiny."

Elan felt the weight of those words settle upon his shoulders like an ancient mantle, heavy with the dust of fallen empires and the whispers of lost souls. It was as if he was stepping onto a battlefield that spanned beyond time, where every step was laden with the responsibility of countless lives yet to be touched by the darkness. It was as if he had been part of this war his entire life.

"Tell me about these heroes," Elan demanded, his voice steady despite the tumult. "What sacrifices have they made? What are their greatest triumphs?"

"Ah, the annals of the Order are overflowing with valor and sacrifice," Nykronus replied, gesturing to the fire that seemed to flare with his every word. "There was Lucius, who stood alone against the hordes of hell, his faith a shield against their desecration. His flesh was torn, but his spirit never broke."

The story unfurled, and with it, images danced in Elan's mind—a mosaic of defeat and victories. He saw faces engrained with determination, eyes alight with fervor, and hands clasped in prayer before clashing with unspeakable evil.

"And then there was Seraphina, whose love for her soulmate knew no bounds. She fought with the ferocity of a lioness, even as her heart bled from the ultimate betrayal," Nykronus continued, his gaze locked with Elan's. "In their darkest hour, when all seemed lost, it was their love that rekindled hope—a beacon that pierced the veil of despair."

"Love as a weapon?" Elan mused aloud. The concept resonated with him, striking a chord deep within his soul where the memory of Kaira lingered—an ember of passion that refused to be extinguished.

Elan contemplated love as a weapon, recalling the strength drawn from his profound love for Kaira. Their love was a formidable force, capable of driving back the darkest shadows. It was his shield and sword, the light guiding him through the darkness, the beacon leading him home. This realization spurred his determination. In battles faced, whether external or internal, the unwavering love for Kaira fortified his resolve, transforming it into an unbreakable weapon. With this love, he was invincible—not undefeatable, but with reason to fight, no matter the odds.

"Indeed," Nykronus affirmed. "But remember, where there is love, there is also the potential for profound loss. Each guardian of the Order has grappled with this duality, their sacrifices engrained into the very essence of our legacy. You have felt this. You have lived this. Don't you see it?"

Elan felt a solemn purpose stir within him, a resonance with the tales of yore that spoke of a path strewn with glory and grief. In the tales of the Order's champions, he recognized the echoes of his own life —a Marine's life—where each victory came at a cost, and each act of bravery was a step closer to redemption or ruin. He thought of spending his last moments with the love of his life and being robbed of the opportunity to say goodbye or see her one last time.

"You know I'm in. I'm here. I know my role in this legacy with honor," Elan declared, the boldness in his voice matching the steely kindle of his eyes. "For Kaira, for those we've lost along the way, and for the ones we can't see who seek only the light."

Nykronus nodded, approval evident in the slight upturn of his lips. "So shall it be," he said. "As it was with the heroes of old, so it now falls to you to wield the torch of hope against the encroaching shadows."

As Elan watched the starlight fade, as dawn approached, he was reminded of a similar moment of clarity and purpose he felt long ago —on the eve of his first deployment with the Marines. Back then, surrounded by his brothers-in-arms, the weight of duty and the antici-pation of the unknown had forged in him a sense of invincibility and a deep commitment to something greater than himself. But upon retir-ing, that sense of direction and passion had slowly dissipated, leaving him adrift in a sea of uncertainty, struggling to find a purpose that matched the intensity of his days in service. As the stars disappeared and Nykronus's words echoed in his heart, Elan rediscovered that fervor. It was as if the pieces of his soul, scattered and lost in the transition to civilian life, were finally coalescing once again, reignited by the promise of a new battle and cause. This rediscovery was not just a return to his roots as a warrior but an evolution, transforming his martial prowess into a beacon of hope against the encroaching shadows.

"You've brought the old me out in a way that feels new, and I can't explain it," Elan confessed, his voice a low thrum. "I've been a Marine for all of my adult life, a defender of my country without ever second-guessing that decision. And here I am now, ready to be a guardian of this world's hidden truths. I will continue to serve Nykronus."

"Indeed, you must," Nykronus replied. From the folds of his robe, he produced yet another object. With a reverence reserved for sacred rituals, he unveiled a talisman wrought in metal that shone with an otherworldly luster. Its surface was carved with symbols that seemed to dance in the flickering light and images of a goat and a ram.

"Behold," intoned Nykronus, "the Sigil of David, which belonged to St. Gabriel. Its purpose is eternal—to guide the chosen through the darkness, to unlock doors veiled by mystic forces."

Elan reached out, his hand hovering over the relic, feeling the thrum of power coursing through it. The moment his fingers brushed against the cold metal, a surge of energy spiraled up his arm, setting every nerve ablaze with a sense of destiny. It was as though the very essence of the Order now ran in his veins, bonding him to the lineage of warriors who had shouldered the weight of the world unseen.

"Where will my path take me?" Elan asked, the talisman now resting in his palm. Its celestial symbols were a map to a future yet to come.

"Through the annals of history, across the chasms of time," Nykronus answered, his voice a solemn echo. "You must seek out the fractures where darkness seeps into our realm. This sigil will be your compass, guiding you to confrontations most dire, to victories that hinge upon the strength of your soul."

"I won't let them down. I won't let you down. We're moving. We're moving forward, and I swear I'll honor the courage of those who've gone before me," Elan vowed. The weight of the artifact in his grasp was a measurable expression of his commitment—a sentinel's badge, marking him as a Temporal Knight of St. Michael's Order.

"Let the light of the sigil illuminate your journey," Nykronus said. "Remember, the balance of all things rests upon the edge of your blade and the fortitude of your heart."

"Kaira, wherever you are, this fight is for you too," he whispered with thoughts reaching out to his soulmate, his reason for sacrifice. The legacy of the Order of St. Michael was now his to uphold, a sacred duty that transcended life itself. With the sigil as his guide and his love as his anchor, Elan Durant stepped forward into the maw of adventure, where history awaited the imprint of his footsteps.

Elan's fingers closed around the sigil, its ancient metal cool against his skin. The intricate etchings seemed to pulse with a life of their own, a silent heartbeat that resonated with his own. He lifted it before his eyes, and the gem at its center, casting a radiance of light upon his aging face.

"Embrace this calling, Elan," Nykronus intoned, shouting from the forest. "Your soul is now entwined with the eternal mission of the Order."

Elan nodded, the weight of the artifact anchoring him to this new reality. "If there's one thing I've been good at, it's upholding legacy. It's my honor. I *will* uphold *this* legacy," he vowed, feeling an unbreakable chain of purpose link him to the warriors of old. His past life as a Marine had been a mere prelude and training to this grander battle—a war for the very essence of light against darkness.

"Yet know this," Nykronus said, stepping closer, his eyes aglow with a fire not reflected by any mundane flame. "The path you tread is strewn with peril, more treacherous than any battlefield you have known."

"Noted." Elan's voice was a steady drumbeat in the still night. "This is *not* my first rodeo."

"Indeed, but rely not only on your martial prowess." The guardian's hand rose, pointing to Elan's chest. "Within you resides a power yet untapped, a force born from the confluence of your spirit and the lineage of St. Michael. Trust in it as much as your blade."

A shiver ran down Elan's spine, a premonition or perhaps the awakening of something dormant within his being. He sensed the truth in Nykronus's words, the potential of strength beyond physical limits. His entire life, he struggled to trust his heart. He cringed at the idea he thought he grew up in a happy childhood home. Only recently, he realized his abandonment issues predated Kaira and stemmed from his father not being present. Even when he was present, he wasn't really there. His ability to love was stunted before he fell in love with Kaira. And when he did give his heart to the only person he ever loved, through no fault of her own, she took pieces of it with him. He wrestled with the idea of sharing and finding love in anyone else. Most importantly, he struggled to truly love himself.

"Instincts... they've brought me this far," Elan responded, reflecting on close calls and the intuitiveness that had guided him through dark alleys and war-torn streets.

"Sharpen them as you would your sword," Nykronus instructed. "For instinct is the whisper of God, guiding you when the darkness seeks to blind your eyes."

"God's whisper..." Elan echoed, the concept weaving seamlessly into his soul. His love for Kaira, the driving force behind every step, now mingled with this divine imperative. It was a transcendent love, fueling his resolve to fight for a world where such pure bonds could flourish without the taint of evil.

"Go forth, Elan Durant," Nykronus proclaimed, a note of finality in his voice. "Bear the sigil and your conviction as shields against the encroaching void."

With a last nod, Elan pocketed the sigil, its presence a constant reminder of the destiny he had embraced. His gaze was firm, his stance resolute; he was ready to delve into the secrets of his own soul, to uncover the latent power that would shape his journey ahead. For him, he knew this was barely scratching the surface.

"Remember, Elan Durant," Nykronus's ethereal and omnipresent voice resonated. "My guidance is ever at your side, a specter in the gloom to remind you of the brotherhood that stands with you."

Elan nodded, feeling the weight of centuries converge upon his shoulders—ghosts of warriors past lending him their silent strength. He was a solitary figure against the vast canvas of the world, yet not alone. The legacy of St. Michael's Order coursed through him.

"Your path is forged by your hand alone, but it traces the steps of many," Nykronus continued. "Take solace in our shared endeavor. Triumph and sacrifice are siblings in this ancient struggle."

"Thanks, Nykronus," Elan said, unsure if his words reached the invisible mentor. Gratitude filled him; for the first time since his discharge, he sensed true camaraderie—a fellowship not bound by time nor death.

With a heart beating to the rhythm of a cause larger than life itself, Elan and Nykronus strode into the embrace of the wilderness. Each step was a battle drum's beat, a proclamation of his commitment to the war that raged beyond mortal sight. Crisp morning fog wrapped around him, whispering secrets of the journey ahead, tales of valor and darkness that would test the very fabric of his being.

His breath mingled with the mist, a visible testament to the life force within him. Elan's eyes shined with resoluteness, mimicking the ancient sigil in his pocket. It pulsed against his skin as if alive with the same passion and willingness to live.

"So it begins..." he looked up to the sky, his voice steady despite the adrenaline surge that surged like a torrent in his veins. He was no longer just a man or a former Marine. He was a protector, a beacon of hope in a world besieged by nefarious forces.

A chill breeze tugged at his jacket, but within, a fire was kindling— burning hotter than the one he felt mere hours before. He could sense the malevolent forces gathering strength, a sinister tide that sought to engulf the world he vowed to protect.

As he walked, Elan's mind replayed the tales of valor Nykronus had woven into the fabric of the night. Each story was a thread in the grand tapestry of the Order's legacy—a narrative steeped in sacrifice and redemption. And now, he was to become a part of that legend.

Elan began to wonder if the Nykronus from 2024 already knew what was to come or if he was just reciting and acting from a story that had already been written. Then he remembered his path was marked with the ink of fates that had not yet been realized.

"Saint Michael, guide my blade, *your* blade..." he intoned, the words a prayer, invoking the patron of the Order that now claimed his allegiance. The sentiment carried more than religious reverence; it was an acknowledgment of the divine struggle that mirrored their own mortal combat.

And so began the burgeoning saga of Elan Durant, Temporal Knight of the Order of St. Michael.

CHAPTER
EIGHT

Papal State Territory, Rome, 842 A.D.

The moon hung low, a ghostly galleon adrift on a sea of ink, when Nykronus appeared to Elan, materializing from the shadows like a specter of ancient lore. Elan, who had been sitting on a jagged boulder with his back to the ruins of what once might have been a temple, jolted upright, every muscle in his body tensing with the instinctual readiness of a soldier.

"We must speak," Nykronus urged, haste threading his words as he approached. His eyes gleamed with a knowledge that seemed to transcend time itself.

Elan rose to his feet, his eyes narrowing as he tried to read the perplexing figure before him. "What's happened?"

"A discovery," Nykronus replied, his gaze never wavering. "I received word from the Order. There's an old farmstead nestled between the forgotten folds of this land. Its soil holds more than the sweat of toil—it cradles relics essential to our journey."

Elan's pulse quickened. "Relics? What kind of relics?"

Nykronus glanced at the sky, ensuring the stars were their only witnesses. "The kind that may give us clues as to where the location of St. Michael's feather is. But we must hasten. The forces against us grow restless with each passing hour."

"Nykronus, how do we find this old farm? And what kind of forces are against us?" Elan's questions tumbled out in a rush.

Nykronus placed a hand on Elan's shoulder, his touch strangely comforting despite the haste in his tone. "The farmstead lies on the abandoned outskirts of southern Rome, sometimes patrolled by the Byzantines trying to gain control of that territory. Our path could be dangerous, and we will have no choice."

Elan squared his shoulders, "Then let's go. I didn't come all this way to be afraid of a little skirmish or two."

Nykronus smiled. "Your spirit is commendable, Elan Durant. We shall depart at first light. Until then, rest and gather your strength."

With those words, Nykronus melted back into the shadows, leaving Elan alone with his thoughts. He settled onto the cold ground, his mind whirling with the gravity of their quest. The fate of Kaira rested in their hands, and failure was not an option.

As dawn bathed the land in golden hues, Elan and Nykronus set out toward the elusive farmstead.

The farmstead lay nestled in a secluded valley, its buildings weathered by time and neglect. Nature had begun to reclaim what man had once built, and an eerie silence blanketed the surroundings.

Nykronus led Elan through overgrown paths until they reached a small, rugged barn at the edge of the farmstead. As they cautiously stepped inside, a gust of wind stirred up dust clouds, revealing a primitive chest hidden beneath a pile of hay.

"This is it," Nykronus proudly said, his voice reverent as he unlocked the chest with a key retrieved from beneath his cloak.

The chest creaked open to reveal an assortment of relics: weathered parchment scrolls, tarnished medallions, and a palm-sized vial containing what appeared to be a single feather with a slightly golden shimmering glow.

Nykronus carefully lifted the vial from its resting place and held it to the light. "A feather from St. Michael's wings," he solemnly declared. "This will aid us in our journey."

"Unbelievable." It was the only word Elan could recite as he marveled at the idea that angels were real. After all, he had seen since he retired from the military, he began to think of the parables and Bible passages he grew up listening to at Sunday Church. It was all real.

As they prepared to depart, a foreboding sensation prickled at the back of Elan's neck. Before he could voice his concern, a supernatural howl echoed through the valley, causing him to reach for his weapon instinctively.

Nykronus placed a hand on Elan's arm. "The guardians of this place have been awakened," he said grimly. "We must make haste."

Their departure was swift but fraught with danger. Shadowy figures materialized from the mist-shrouded woods, their eyes glowing with malevolence. These were not mere bandits fighting for territory but the dark forces working behind the shadows and against everything The Order of St. Michael stood for.

With Nykronus at his side, Elan fought with unyielding determination as they escaped from the farmstead. Elan raised *Winterstar* into the air and swashed against what seemed to be wolves possessed by dark energy. At that moment, it seemed too easy.

Elan hoisted *Winterstar* skyward; its blade radiated an otherworldly luminescence, casting light upon the encroaching forms of beasts that had once been wolves but were now warped by some sinister power. These were not the majestic creatures of the untamed lands but hideous mockeries, their eyes blazing with an infernal glow, pelts tangled with shades that appeared to undulate and churn around their silhouettes. Their growls formed a dissonant chorus of fury and anguish, a bone-chilling testament to their heresy.

The wolves advanced with unearthly nimbleness, their frames elongated and misshapen, sinews swelling beneath their mottled hides in a manner that implied immense might. As they sprang toward Elan, their maws gaped wide, exposing rows of jagged fangs that pulsed with the same tenebrous vitality coursing through their arteries. It was as though the gloom had bestowed upon them a new, horrifying visage, transforming them into sentinels of the eventide, resolute in their intent to annihilate.

Winterstar sliced through the atmosphere with exactitude and poise, its blade reverberating with an ancient potency as it clashed with the wolves. Each slash unleashed crescents of scintillating energy, hurling stark illumination against the obscurity. When the blade struck the creatures, it did not merely lacerate but seemed to purify, leaving trails of dissipating murk in its aftermath. The conflict was a ballet of radiance against shadow, of virtue grappling with shame, as Elan remained steadfast against the assault, a solitary champion bathed in the blade's spectral incandescence.

As they caught their breath amid the cool embrace of nature, Elan turned to Nykronus. "What the hell were those?"

Nykronus fixed Elan with a steely gaze and did not answer Elan's inquiry, as the idea of mystical wolves was a regular walk in a park. "We have what we came for," he said firmly. "Now, we must return and begin crafting the elixir that will guide us to Kaira."

The chill of the night seemed to seep deeper into Elan's bones, but it was not just the cold that unsettled him; it was the weight of responsibility that now rested on his shoulders—a weight that Nykronus seemed all too comfortable with carrying.

"Lead on then, boss," Elan said, masking any trace of hesitation in his voice.

Together, they traversed the landscape, guided by the moon's heavenly glow and Nykronus' unerring sense of direction. They passed through groves where the trees whispered secrets older than Rome and across fields that lay fallow under the blanket of night. Elan wondered if these same trees still stood in 2024 or if gas stations and houses in an overpopulated world replaced them.

Minutes felt like hours, and the hours began to feel like days. However, there were times that could just as easily have been moments in this timeless place. They arrived at the outskirts of another old and empty farmstead. The buildings slouched like weary sentinels, their wooden frames groaning under years of neglect.

"This is it," Nykronus whispered as if the wind could betray them.

Elan surveyed the area, his marine-trained eyes missing nothing despite the darkness. "Looks abandoned."

"It is... now." Nykronus moved toward an outbuilding that looked like it might collapse. "But once, it was home to a keeper of relics—a guardian of sacred trusts."

As they approached the building, Elan's senses went into overdrive. He felt rather than heard movement within—something or someone lurking in the shadows.

"Stay alert," he cautioned Nykronus under his breath.

Nykronus merely nodded, focusing on a rotting door hanging off its hinges. With a gesture more deft than forceful, he nudged it open and stepped inside.

Elan followed closely behind into what appeared to be an antiquated storeroom filled with relics that whispered tales of old battles and forgotten pacts. Cobwebs clung to corners like remnants of veils left behind by fleeing spirits.

Nykronus moved toward an old wooden bookshelf against one wall. Its surface was scarred by time and burned with symbols that danced in Elan's vision like living things.

"This," Nykronus said softly as he knelt before it, "is where our path becomes clear."

Elan watched as Nykronus' hands hovered above an intricate lockbox—with a lock that seemed less about keeping intruders out and more about ensuring something within was ready to be released.

Nykronus closed his eyes briefly before whispering words in a language that seemed to resonate with an energy beyond mere sound. The lock clicked open without touch or key—an audible surrender to Nykronus' command.

As Nykronus lifted the lid, light spilled forth from within—not from any flame or earthly source but from something otherworldly. It bathed them both in its radiance and seemed to hum with power.

Within the lockbox lay an array of objects—small artifacts, each bearing an aura of mystery and might. Atop them all rested a parchment, its edges frayed but its contents inscribed with meticulous care.

"This," Nykronus said as he picked up the parchment and handed it to Elan, "is our map—the guide through labyrinths unseen and challenges unmet."

Elan unfolded it carefully, tracing the lines and symbols scored upon it. They depicted routes, locations, incantations, and warnings—a codex for those who dared walk this path.

"We need to study this," Elan said with determination.

Nykronus nodded solemnly. "Indeed we do—and swiftly. For each symbol, here is both shield and key against forces that will stop at nothing to prevent us from putting an end to their plans."

As they poured over the map together, Elan felt something shift within him—a sense of clarity piercing through doubt like sunlight through storm clouds. This was no longer just about finding Kaira or uncovering lost relics but about standing against darkness with a light he had yet to understand or wield fully.

And so they studied under cover of night—the Marine and the mystic—united by fate and driven by forces greater than themselves.

Nykronus moved with an ease that belied his ancient origins, his gaze sweeping across the land with a knowing that stretched beyond centuries. They had come for a tome hidden within these timeworn grounds, a key to unlocking the resources needed to find Kaira.

"Feels like stepping into a painting," Elan slightly whispered, his voice betraying none of the unease that coiled in his gut.

"Nykronus nodded solemnly. 'These fields bear the scars of ancient conflicts, from the fierce clashes between the Roman legions and the invading Gauls to the legendary stand of the Spartans at Thermopylae and the tumultuous wars against the Carthaginians led by Hannibal. Each blade of grass, each patch of earth here, has witnessed the ebb and flow of empires. The soil doesn't just remember; it's a silent guardian of history.'"

Elan remained alert as they crossed the property threshold. Vines clung to crumbling stone walls, and wildflowers reclaimed what once must have been manicured gardens. Nature had waged its war here, victorious against human abandonment.

A larger structure loomed ahead, its wooden frame stooped from years of neglect. Elan could almost hear the echoes of laughter and life that once filled it, now replaced by silence and secrets.

"We must be careful," Nykronus instructed without looking back. "The tome is protected."

Protected by what, Elan wanted to ask but held his tongue. They approached the house, each step deliberate, every sense strained for signs of danger or deceit.

Nykronus led them around to what once would have been the back of the house. There, an ancient oak spread its massive limbs like a guardian. At its base, hidden by underbrush and shadow, lay an entrance to what appeared to be a cellar.

"This is where we find our answers," Nykronus said as he pulled away the overgrowth to reveal a stone archway.

Elan followed him down worn steps into the cool darkness. His eyes adjusted slowly, revealing rows upon rows of shelves laden with scrolls and books, artifacts of times long past. A musty scent clung to the air – paper, leather, and a trace of something metallic.

As Nykronus' fingertips brushed against the weathered bindings of the archaic volumes, he murmured, "Countless enigmas lie within the Order's purview." He continued, "Certain mysteries they have vowed to safeguard, while others are woven into the fabric of their extensive chronicle. The Order of St. Michael bears a multitude of responsibilities. Its members are devoted to thwarting sinister powers, maintaining the fragile equilibrium between benevolence and wickedness, securing hallowed relics, and ushering fated souls in their crusade against iniquity. The Order's ranks include erudite scholars, fearless warriors, and enlightened mystics. They are resolved to shape momentous occasions throughout history and guarantee the ascendancy of illumination overshadowed through valor, self-sacrifice, and unwavering conviction."

They moved deeper into the cellar, where a faint light glowed from within an alcove. On a pedestal bathed in light that seemed to emanate from nowhere rested a tome bound in leather so dark that it absorbed all light around it.

"That's it," Elan breathed out.

Nykronus approached, his hand hovering above the book before gently lifting it from its resting place. "With this," he said solemnly, "we will forge our path forward."

Elan watched as Nykronus opened the tome. Pages fluttered as if stirred by an unseen wind, stopping on a page marked by an intricate drawing of a feather – St. Michael's feather.

Nykronus chanted in Latin, his voice rising and falling with a magic rhythm that seemed to vibrate through Elan's very soul.

The room shifted subtly around them, and a spectrum of lights danced along walls that had stood still for centuries. Elan felt power surge through the space—raw and ancient—and he knew they had unlocked something profound.

Nykronus closed the book with care and turned to Elan. "We must prepare."

Dawn greeted them as they stepped out from the cellar. Elan squinted, his eyes adjusting to the brightness after the dimness below.

Elan glanced back at the structure, its decrepit appearance at odds with the life-affirming light of day. His thoughts shifted to Kaira—her laughter and her passions for history and architecture—and he felt a surge of emotion.

Elan's love for Kaira guided him, but he feared she might have moved on and found happiness without him. The thought pained him, yet he wanted her joy, even if it excluded him. As he journeyed through time, fighting the unknown, he dreaded returning to find her gone. Had she waited or moved forward? Despite the hurt, he wished for her wellbeing, hoping their paths would cross again, in this life or beyond.

"Let's get started," he said with fresh resolve.

Nykronus led Elan toward a clearing edged by tall grasses whipping against rustling leaves.

They faced an old stone circle reminiscent of ancient rituals and forgotten magic. The ground within was barren.

"We plant our feet here," Nykronus instructed as he stepped into the center of the circle.

Elan followed suit but couldn't shake off an unnerving feeling creeping up his spine like cold fingers tracing his vertebrae one by one.

"Feel your connection to this place," Nykronus intoned while reaching out towards Elan with one hand.

Elan closed his eyes and tried to ground himself in sensation: the ground hardened beneath his boots, Nykronus' firm grip on his arm, the distant cry of birds above, the subtle shift in air pressure as if something unseen moved among them.

Nykronus' voice guided him through breathing exercises until Elan's heartbeat slowed to match the cadence of nature itself.

"Now the secret pages of this book are unlocked," Nykronus said more firmly than before. "We begin."

Elan studied the pages, the arcane symbols and Latin text blurring before his eyes. Nykronus leaned in, his finger tracing the lines as he translated.

"The tome speaks of an elixir that grants a clairvoyance of sorts. It will tell us what we need to find Kaira."

"Clairvoyance?" Despite Elan's recent journey through time and realms beyond imagination, the term still caught him off guard. Yet, as he reflected on his experiences—stepping through portals and navigating ancient mysteries—a flicker of hope ignited. The concept, once beyond belief, now seemed another plausible thread in the fabric of his extraordinary quest.

Nykronus nodded. "This elixir will attune your senses to hers-across realms and veils unseen. Divine intervention will put you on a path to her whereabouts."

The recipe called for ingredients that read like a medieval herbalist's dream – or nightmare, depending on one's perspective. Each component held properties that defied reason, yet Elan found himself nodding along as Nykronus listed them.

"We need the feather of an angel, which we already have; the essence of starlight captured at the moment of a comet's passing; and the heart of an oak struck by lightning yet still living."

Elan let out a low whistle. "I left these in my Amazon shopping cart. Would you like me to place an order?"

Nykronus smiled faintly. "The Order has protected these secrets for centuries. The farm has been our sanctuary, our garden for such rarities. This was once our home base."

They began their search at dusk when shadows grew long, and the wind intensified. The farm seemed alive around them, as if nature knew of their quest and stood ready to assist or hinder them.

The essence of Starlight would be tricky. Elan and Nykronus waited for hours under the open sky until a streak of silver finally cut across the heavens – a comet gracing Earth with its celestial dance.

As Nykronus held out a crystal vial, there was a moment of perfect alignment with the celestial event above them. While the essence of starlight captured within the vial remained invisible to the naked eye, its presence was undeniable—a tangible force that filled the air with a charged energy. This was no mere trick of the light or sleight of hand but a profound interaction between the material and the mystical. The comet, a fleeting visitor from the depths of space, left behind a trail not just of light but of cosmic power. As this essence entered the vial, it seemed to hum with potential, a vibration that resonated on a frequency felt in the bones—a clear signal that something extraordinary and palpable had been sealed within the glass.

"Starlight," he said with reverence. "Not just light but also time – fleeting and precious."

The heart of an oak struck by lightning was found on the edge of the property, where a mighty tree stood sentinel over its domain. Its trunk bore the scars of nature's fury—blackened and split—yet thrived.

Nykronus approached it respectfully, placing both hands upon its rough bark and whispering entreaties known only to those who speak with trees.

Elan watched as Nykronus drew forth a small piece of wood from where lightning had kissed oak—a chunk that seemed to pulse with life despite being severed from its source.

With all three ingredients secured under Nykronus' watchful guidance, they returned to what remained of an old stone altar situated in what once might have been used for gatherings or rituals long abandoned by the Order - and time.

There, they laid out their bounty: an angel feather, starlight, and lightning-charred oak – each emanating their unique energy that mingled in the air.

"Now we brew," Nykronus announced while retrieving an iron cauldron from within his cloak—how it had remained hidden there, Elan couldn't fathom—and set it upon the altar.

Nykronus carefully added water from a nearby spring—crystal clear and cold—to the cauldron before carefully placing each ingredient inside.

As Nykronus worked, he chanted in low tones that wove around them like threads binding intention to action. The water began to simmer without fire or heat—stirring itself into a gentle boil as if alive with purpose.

He watched, captivated, as natural forces and ancient magic intertwined before him. With each passing moment, his commitment deepened, his belief in their mission unwavering. He marveled at the mystical blend of elements, recognizing the significance of their impending achievement.

Finally, Nykronus ceased chanting and stepped back from the cauldron, which now contained a liquid that shimmered like dawn's first light—a potion of gold glowing against iron blackness.

"This is our elixir," Nykronus declared while reaching for another vial—one empty and waiting for this very moment—and carefully poured the concoction within it.

When Elan took the vial, its warmth flooded his palms, reminiscent of sunlight thawing cold skin. He hesitated momentarily to observe its contents; the liquid inside was alive with motion, swirling around an unseen focal point. As he brought the vial closer, a fragrance emerged, a blend of the earth after rain and the crispness of fresh pine, with a hint of something ancient and indefinable, like the memory of places long forgotten. The sight and scent of it stirred something within him, a mix of awe and an inexplicable familiarity, as if in this concoction lay the essence of the very adventures he'd embarked upon—each eddy and swirl a whisper of the paths crossed and destinies yet to unfold.

"Now," Nykronus replied with gravitas heavy on every syllable, "we drink and see through eyes unclouded by distance or darkness."

With one last look at Nykronus—who gave him an encouraging nod—Elan drank down the elixir in one long draught, feeling its warmth spread through him like wildfire, burning away doubt and leaving only clarity in its wake. Elan's senses surged with the elixir's potency as he swallowed, its essence cascading through his veins like liquid Starfire. His vision blurred, the world went completely dark, and everything around him pulsed with a spectrum of colors he had never experienced, flooding his senses. Colors brightened, sounds sharpened, and a sense of knowing settled upon him—a tether stretching out into the unseen, linking him to Kaira.

The connection was initially weak, like a distant flame in darkness flickering. But as moments passed, it grew more robust, more insistent. Elan's gaze drifted skyward, past the branches reaching toward heaven, to the canvas of twinkling stars. The starlight, captured within the elixir, served as an olive branch. A solitary star twinkled as if winking in acknowledgment of the bond now formed.

Nykronus watched with anticipation. "Do you feel it?" he asked.

Elan nodded slowly, his focus inward. "It's like a compass in my chest—a pull in her direction."

"Then we must follow," Nykronus said, gesturing for Elan to lead.

Elan stepped forward purposefully, each stride resonating with the call that beckoned him. They moved through fields shrouded in mist; the air was alive with whispers of nature and echoes of the past.

Time lost meaning as they traveled. The landscape shifted—from open fields to dense woodlands where leaves rustled with secrets and shadows danced at the edge of Elan's enhanced vision. His heart beat in sync with the rhythm of their journey—a drum announcing their passage through the night's domain.

Eventually, they came upon a river that flowed like liquid obsidian under the moonlight. Nykronus produced a length of rope from within his cloak and secured it to an overhanging branch. "We have to cross," he said as he tested the knot.

As Elan stood at the water's edge, his eyes followed the river's serpentine course through the landscape. A profound pull resonated within him, gentle and insistent force beckoning him toward the unseen, to the other side where answers—or perhaps Kaira—awaited. For a moment, he allowed himself to reflect on the significance of this pull. Twenty years of longing, of dreams, whispered into the void of night, now seemed to coalesce into this tangible force guiding him forward. This connection, this enchanted bond that had persisted through the fabric of time, now felt as real as the earth beneath his feet. It was a beacon in the tempest of his quest, a reminder of the love that had propelled him across time. The realization that he was now closer than ever to finding Kaira, to unraveling the mystery of her disappearance, filled him with a potent mix of hope and trepidation. Would she be the same Kaira he remembered, or had time reshaped her as it had him? At this moment, on the brink of discovery, the weight of his yearning mingled with the fear of what he might find, yet this connection steadied his resolve. With a deep breath, Elan stepped into the water, the remarkable current swirling around him as he committed himself to the crossing, to the culmination of his two-decade search for the woman who had never ceased to inhabit his heart.

Elan grabbed hold of the rope and stepped into the water. Treading carefully, with Nykronus right behind him, he forged ahead—each movement guided by an invisible force that drew him onward.

They emerged on the opposite bank, drenched but unphased. Elan shook off the excess water, reminiscent of a dog after a swim. They then continued their trek under a sky dotted with stars, which seemed to applaud their perseverance.

Forests gave way to hills rolling gently under a blanket of fog that clung to Earth. Elan climbed with strength and determination.

Elan stopped atop a hill crowned by ancient stones arranged in purposeful patterns. The connection thrummed within him—a beacon blazing bright enough to chase away the shadows of doubt. Elan sat down and crossed his legs, in meditation, closing his eyes. The stones around began to hum gently, in harmony, as if communicating with Elan directly. Mere minutes passed, and the stones stopped abruptly. Elan opened his eyes in revelation.

"Castel Sant'Angelo," Elan whispered, and immediately after that, he fell into a slumber, exhausted from the ritual.

"Rest, Elan Durant. The elixir has served its purpose. We leave at dawn."

As Elan awoke to the dawn's early light, its golden hues casting a serene glow over the landscape, he contemplated the future he had left behind. The beauty of this moment, so starkly contrasted with the world he knew, stirred within him a blend of nostalgia and acceptance. Deep down, he harbored the hope of returning, of stepping back through time's doorway once his quest was complete. Yet, with each passing day, each encounter that wove him further into the tapestry of this era, he began to reckon with the possibility that he might not return. This realization did not come with despair but rather a solemn resolve. If fulfilling his mission meant remaining in the past, so be it. The weight of his purpose—to find Kaira, to unravel the mysteries that had brought him here—anchored him to the present. In the quiet of dawn, Elan acknowledged this potential sacrifice, ready to face whatever the journey demanded, with the hope of reunion as his guiding star. Yet, the thought lingered: what version of himself would he bring back even if he could return? Time, love, and battles fought in the shadow of history changed a man.

He stretched, feeling the residue of the elixir's potency lingering in his bones like an afterglow. Nykronus stood nearby, eyes closed, facing the sun as it crested the hilltops, bathing him in its first light.

"We must move," Nykronus noted without opening his eyes. "Time bends to no man's will."

Elan acknowledged and rose to his feet, his muscles protesting mildly from the night spent on the hard ground. Together, they descended the hillside, their shadows long and dark against the dew-kissed grass.

As they approached Castel Sant'Angelo, a shift in the air made Elan pause. It was as if a wave of anticipation rolled off the ancient walls, stirring the atmosphere with an energy that buzzed against his skin. The castle loomed ahead—a monolith of stone and history in the making; its cylindrical shape clashed with a sky streaked with morning light.

Nykronus glanced at Elan, an unspoken understanding passing between them. "This place," he began softly, "is where past and present converge. The energy here is thick with revelation."

As they approached the castle, anticipation surged through Elan. He envisioned uncovering secrets within its walls that could lead him to Kaira, his thoughts oscillating between hope and fear. The prospect of finding clues about her disappearance fueled his determination despite the uncertainty. "I can't believe how different this place looks in my present, but it also seems so familiar," he said. "It's so surreal."

The structure that exists in the present was not identical to the one he left behind in his future. Although the grand design of Emperor Hadrian's mausoleum remained, it lacked the additional fortifications that would have made it a formidable stronghold. The castle's towers were absent, but Elan could vividly picture where they would have stood as if he had just seen them yesterday.

They approached Castel Sant'Angelo with reverence, befitting a shrine rather than a stronghold. The entrance revealed itself as an imposing gateway with statues, presumably of Hadrian and his family, watching from the top of the dome, weathered by time but no less majestic for their age. The heavy wooden doors were carved with scenes of battles and triumphs—silent protectors to centuries of conflict and resolution—and many more to come in the millennia ahead.

As Elan stepped closer, he shivered. It was as though the stones recognized their approach and were speaking to him in a language felt rather than heard—the language of emperors and popes, artists and warriors who had once walked the hallowed halls.

Nykronus raised his hand, pausing before the entrance. "Within these walls lies knowledge safeguarded through turmoil and tranquility alike."

Elan studied paintings framing the doorway—angels wielding swords with faces set in eternal vigilance. Their eyes seemed to follow him as he moved—a silent judgment from guardians of a bygone era.

"Feels like stepping through time," Elan sighed.

Nykronus nodded, his expression somber and reflective. The faint light cast deep shadows across his ageless features. "And time is what we seek to unravel."

With no visible guards or barriers to entry other than history's weighty gaze, they crossed the threshold into Castel Sant'Angelo's embrace. The heavy door groaned open at Nykronus' touch—a sound that echoed through corridors like a herald announcing their arrival.

"Where's everyone at?" Elan pondered. He thought of the tourists that swarmed these same halls in his time.

"Pope Sergius is meeting with Louis the Pioius' son, Lothair, and the entire city was invited to a celebration." Nykronus marched forward with fierce conviction.

The interior of Castel Sant'Angelo unfolded before them as pages from an illuminated manuscript brought to life. Arched hallways led to chambers adorned with frescoes that seemed to pulse with stories longing to be told.

They traversed hallways that twisted and turned—a labyrinthine journey through chambers where echoes danced upon air rich with musk and myrrh. Each step brought them deeper into Castel Sant'Angelo's heart—each footfall a note in a symphony composed across millennia.

The castle was eerily quiet except for their footsteps and the occasional drip of moisture from stones weeping with condensation—a testament to its age and resilience against Rome's changing faces.

"This fortress," Nykronus said as they moved through dimly lit passageways lit by shafts of light spilling through narrow windows, "has stood witness to humanity's best and worst."

His boots trod upon the intricate mosaic, every tile a testament to ages past, and with each footfall, Elan's mind wandered inevitably to Kaira. The bond between them seemed to intensify with every stride, her presence a scintillating beacon that pulled at him, summoning him nearer to her core. Amid the castle's sprawling tapestry of yesteryears, this swelling force within served as a wordless affirmation—a luminary in the annals of time, assuring him of his true course.

As they continued onward, each new chamber revealed treasures veiled by shadows—tapestries depicting celestial battles hung beside armor sets standing sentinel in alcoves; reliquaries holding sacred fragments lay next to manuscripts whose ink had faded but whose words still held power.

Finally, they arrived at a chamber more significant than all previous ones—an expanse whose ceiling arched high above as the heavens. In its center stood an altar backed by a towering statue of St. Michael himself—sword raised high as if caught mid-battle cry against unseen foes.

"Deja vu," Elan said as he gazed at the statue he always visited, with the same sword strapped to his back that he had carried for years. *Winterstar*.

Elan approached slowly, eyes wide, as he took in every detail—the intricacy of St. Michael's armor carved into marble, the feathers on his wings so lifelike he half-expected them to flutter, and even the serpent beneath St. Michael's heel seemed poised to strike despite being forever stilled in stone.

Nykronus stood beside Elan now, their quest converging upon this singular point within Castel Sant'Angelo, where past met present and possibility.

"Here," Nykronus whispered reverently as he stepped toward the altar, where countless souls seeking guidance or grace had laid centuries of offerings.

Elan watched as Nykronus placed both hands upon the beautiful marble surface, his expression of concentration indicating preparation for communion with something far more significant than himself or anyone else who had ever knelt before this effigy.

Then silence reigned supreme—a profound hush filled Elan's ears like music heard not outside but within one's soul—an aria awaiting only its cue to swell into a crescendo...

Elan's gaze never wavered from the statue of St. Michael as Nykronus's hands hovered over the altar.

Winterstar called as if talking to its stone counterpart, synchronizing the adventures it has seen since it left the future with Elan. Or perhaps they were discussing the dangers and perils they were about to face.

Nykronus's eyes opened slowly, his gaze settling on a scroll at the center of the altar that appeared, undoubtedly connected to the same vibrations he was feeling from his sword. It lay there as if it had always been part of the stone, its parchment aged but its presence commanding.

"This," Nykronus droned, "is what we have been seeking."

Elan seemed frustrated as if he had expected to see Kaira appear. "Let me guess. This is another clue to more questions than we find answers to."

Elan stepped closer as Nykronus carefully unrolled the scroll, revealing lines of text in a script that danced before Elan's eyes—ancient, fluid, yet completely familiar. As he translated, the symbols seemed to shift and settle under Nykronus's touch.

"It is a letter—a mission from the elders of the Order of St. Michael.

The text speaks of a ritual—a forbidden ritual. It's vague. It states that dark forces are aware of this ritual and seek out the ingredients."

Elan leaned in, absorbing every word. "What do we need for this ritual?"

Nykronus pointed to a list inscribed upon the scroll. "Elements owned by St. Michael himself. Five elements are required: A shield forged by Vulcan's Fire captured from the forge between Mount Etna; a gem containing Jupiter's Bolt struck from a storm at its zenith; scales touched by the Breath of Juno; a dragon's tooth filled with dust from Saturn's Ring, collected from the cradle of creation; and armor blessed with Neptune's Tears collected from the deepest oceans."

Elan let out a low whistle. "That's quite a list. No sweat."

Nykronus spoke with a seriousness that stilled Elan's levity. "Each element represents an aspect of the gods' power—forces that bind this realm to others."

"But how are we supposed to find these? They sound like myths."

Nykronus refolded the scroll with care before meeting Elan's eyes. "They are authentic, but beyond a single person's ability to gather alone."

"So we need a squad. Don't suppose you have any friends in mind?" Elan asked.

Nykronus nodded. "Yes, we must convene with those who have pledged their lives to guard these secrets—the remaining members of the Order."

The monumental task weighed heavily on Elan, the knowledge of traversing time to stand with Nykronus in the sacred chamber akin to wearing heavy armor. As they began a quest spanning earthly and divine realms, unease flickered at the edges of his resolve. Despite the tangible goal, Elan questioned how the ancient artifacts would lead to Kaira, the uncertainty gnawing at him amidst the mission's grandiosity. He wondered how gathering old relics tied into finding the woman whose absence hollowed out his world. The mysterious, shadowed quest offered no clear path to Kaira, yet he was compelled to follow it, driven by faith and desperation.

"What's our next step?" Elan asked.

"We must leave Rome," Nykronus said. "To Cassino."

Elan nodded. He felt as if he were standing at the edge of an abyss —with only faith in Nykronus and his determination as ropes to cling to.

The two men exited Castel Sant'Angelo under a sky transitioning from dawn to day—a canvas upon which light painted clouds into fleeting and wondrous shapes.

CHAPTER
NINE

Cassino, Duchy of Benevento, 842 A. D.

Elan Durant's boots had carved a tenacious path into the medieval Italian soil during the six weeks since he'd traversed the portal, abandoning Reagan and his former existence. As he hiked beside Nykronus, his dependable guide, through the primeval, undulating landscape that laid out before them like an emerald and amber quilt, Elan soaked in every susurration of the breeze through the foliage and each faraway bird trill. To him, Earth felt simultaneously foreign and hauntingly recognizable, invigoratingly picturesque yet imbued with the gravity of his objective. Every footfall served as a reminder of the gap from his previous reality and an attestation to the pressing mission to locate Kaira and aid Nykronus on his quest. Nykronus, always the riddle, advanced with an elegance that masked his vast comprehension of the meandering trail ahead. He conversed minimally but with a quietude that spoke volumes—a summons to vigilance that Elan sensed to his core.

As they ascended a steep incline, Elan paused to wipe the sweat from the back of his neck. "These hills," he began, catching his breath as he surveyed the expanse below them.

"They have seen empires rise and fall," Nykronus replied without turning, his gaze fixed on the horizon.

Elan replied. "Trust me. They'll witness much more."

The journey was arduous but enlightening; with each step, Elan felt the weight of his former life sloughing off him like dead skin. Regrets and conflicts shed into the crisp air—guilt over Kaira, tensions with Reagan, haunting memories of fallen comrades—leaving a man focused on the present journey and future's hope. He had been a warrior once—a title he bore with pride—and now he walked toward a battle of another kind entirely.

The sun reached its peak as they approached the Abbey of Montecassino. It stood resolute atop its hill, walls bathed in golden light as if heaven itself cast a protective glow around it. The sight stole Elan's breath; it was both serene and imposing—a fortress of spirituality that promised solace and secrets. He felt a surge of anticipation as he prepared to meet the members of this holy order.

Elan felt profoundly out of place as he stepped onto the Abbey's sacred grounds. The monks' tranquil prayers and soft footsteps contrasted sharply with his driven purpose. Their serene dedication and contemplative faces highlighted the discord between their world of quiet faith and his of urgent action.

"Peace often harbors strength," Nykronus whispered with his hands on Elan's shoulder as if he could read his mind. "Do not mistake tranquility for weakness."

They made their way through courtyards where pilgrims knelt in prayer, their voices rising like incense to the heavens. The Abbey's stones spoke of ages past when faith was both a shield and spear against the darkness.

Elan noted the curious glances cast by some of the monks; they were outsiders here—warriors among men of cloth. Yet there was no hostility in those glances, only questions that hung like unspoken prayers.

Nykronus led them to an ornate door, where they were greeted by an elderly priest whose eyes sparkled with an intelligence that reminded Elan of Nykronus himself.

"Brothers," the priest addressed them with a nod. "What brings you to our sanctuary?"

"We seek knowledge," Nykronus replied, "and allies for a quest that reaches beyond these hallowed walls."

The priest studied them for a moment before stepping aside to grant them entry. "Then may you find what you seek within."

Inside the Abbey's library was a sweltering atmosphere with the scent of parchment and candle wax. Shelves lined with ancient texts climbed toward the high ceiling like stairways to enlightenment. Here was the collective wisdom of centuries—stories and secrets waiting to be discovered.

Nykronus seemed at home among these relics of knowledge; he perused titles with reverence before selecting several volumes that held promise for their journey ahead.

Elan watched him work, feeling a mix of admiration and impatience stir within him.

"The right knowledge is worth any wait," Nykronus said without looking up from a tome emblazoned with celestial symbols.

"I'm not really the patient type," Elan grinned.

Nykronus closed the book and met Elan's gaze squarely. "But you are one for doing what is necessary."

That simple statement settled over Elan like a perfectly tailored suit; he knew then that this journey would forge him anew—into something more than he had been before.

The Abbey served as more than just a waypoint—a reminder that their quest was part of something larger than themselves. Here, amidst religious figureheads and manuscripts, lay threads woven into history's grand painting—a history they were now part of shaping.

Elan left the library with Nykronus at his side, feeling fortified not just by potential allies but by newfound purpose pulsing through him like blood through veins—steady, sure, and strong enough to face whatever lay ahead.

The Beautiful Bard

Shafts of light, filtered through the Abbey's stained glass, splashed muted hues across the weathered flagstones underfoot as the sun reached its zenith in the sky above. Elan and Nykronus made their way to the bell tower, where they had been told a bard of tremendous acclaim often entertained the monks with tales from distant lands.

As they entered the courtyard, a melodious voice rose above the mutterings of conversation—a voice that seemed to weave stories into the air. In the center of an enraptured circle of monks stood Isolde. Her black hair cascaded in braids over her shoulders, glinting like threads of obsidian in the sunlight. Her mesmerizing green eyes danced with mischief as she strutted her matching green and black lute, and her song told of a knight so handsome that even his horse fell in love with him.

Elan couldn't suppress a laugh at the story's ridiculousness and the notion that even contemporary music had its fair share of silly yet addicting tunes. Nykronus's lips twitched in amusement—a rare break in his stoic demeanor. They waited for her to finish, not wanting to interrupt the performance that had even the birds holding their breath. She was like a real-life Snow White.

As Isolde's song tapered off to laughter and applause, Elan and Nykronus approached. She sized them up with a playful glint in her eye as if already crafting their stories in her mind.

"And what brings a battle-worn soldier and a man cloaked in mystery to my humble performance, Magelight Nykronus?" Isolde asked, cocking her head to one side.

"We seek knowledge," Elan began, echoing Nykronus's earlier words at the Abbey door. "And perhaps a touch of mirth for a journey that weighs heavy on our shoulders. Hi, I'm Elan."

Isolde eyed Elan with her eyebrow raised, her interest piqued. "A journey? Tell me more. I'm all ears—except for my fingers; they're all lute."

Nykronus stepped forward. "Elan, this is the beautiful bard Isolde. Isolde, we are on a quest to find ingredients to a spell for a mission coming from the Order's elders."

"And answers to my girlfriend's disappearance." Elan interrupted.

Nykronus placed his hand on Elan's shoulder to calm him down and continued to look into Isolde's piercing green eyes. "We believe you could aid us with your knowledge of lore. We need your services."

Isolde plucked at her lute strings thoughtfully. She circled Elan in a cocky and playful manner and abruptly stopped with excitement, "Is that *Winterstar*? The sword that legends say can cleave through shadow and time?"

"The very same," Elan confirmed.

A mischievous smile played on Isolde's lips. "And here I was thinking my day would be filled with nothing more exciting than rhyming 'dragon' with 'wagon.'"

Nykronus regarded her solemnly. "Your wit is as sharp as that blade."

"Sharp enough to cut through the gloom of your grave faces, I hope," Isolde quipped.

Elan found himself grinning despite the seriousness of their quest. There was something about Isolde's levity that lightened his spirit—a reminder that even in dire times, joy could be found.

"Will you help us, Isolde?" he asked, hopeful.

Isolde strummed a final chord before setting her lute aside. "For a chance to be part of a story that will be told for ages? How could I refuse?"

As they left the cloister together, Isolde's presence infused their group with an energy lacking before—a spark that turned their grim determination into something more akin to an adventure.

They made their way through the Abbey grounds towards the library, where Nykronus had arranged for the private use of a study chamber. The monks cast curious glances at Isolde, who responded with theatrical bows and exaggerated gestures of gratitude for their silent praise.

In the study chamber, surrounded by ancient texts and scrolls, Nykronus laid out their findings so far. At the same time, Isolde listened intently, occasionally asking questions or offering insights from legends she knew by heart.

"And what makes you think these ingredients can be found?" she asked after Nykronus finished speaking.

"The scroll we discovered," Elan replied, pointing to an aged parchment on the table. "It speaks not only of the ingredients themselves but also hints at their resting places and where or how they were forged."

Isolde leaned over the manuscript, her finger tracing along lines written in languages long forgotten by most. "Clues. I've heard songs about trials like these—each designed to test strength, heart, and mind. I definitely know about this one. The gem and Jupiter's bolt. I'll ask around."

"And all the others, this is why we need you," Elan said firmly.

"Of course," Isolde smiled slyly. "But who will face the trial of enduring my company on such a perilous road?"

"I suspect it will be less enduring and more enjoying," Nykronus replied dryly.

The afternoon waned as they planned and prepared; Isolde's humor never faltered—even when discussing potential dangers—and it was infectious. Laughter found its way into even their most serious strategizing, proving itself a balm against anxiety.

As evening approached, they decided to dine together. The Abbey's refectory was alive with conversation and clinking cutlery as they took their seats at a long wooden table among monks who seemed pleased by their guest's addition.

"So," Isolde began as she broke bread with a flourish fit for theater, "I've been thinking about our quest..."

Elan raised an eyebrow in anticipation.

"...and I've concluded it needs an official anthem!" she declared.

The monks around them chuckled while Elan exchanged an amused look with Nykronus.

"I suppose it does," he conceded.

Isolde tapped her chin thoughtfully before breaking into an impromptu ballad about three brave souls venturing forth to find a gem that could pierce fate itself with lightning. The lyrics were whim-sical yet heroic; each verse brought smiles and nods from the audience.

"Three brave souls, a warrior, mage, and bard,
Set forth on a quest, their path unmarred.
Through dangers untold, they'll face their fate,
To find the gem that lightning creates.
Oh, gem of power, gem of might,

Guide these heroes through the night.
With fate unfolding, step by step,
They'll find the stone that secrets kept.
In caverns deep and mountains high
The trio searches, never shy.
United by purpose, bound by heart,
They'll claim the gem, their quest to start."

Elan found Isolde's humor reminiscent of friends from his service days, whose laughter shielded them from grief. Her wit stirred bittersweet memories of lost comrades, their absence a stinging reminder of the stakes. Yet the gathering also rekindled his flickering hope through shared purpose and connection.

As they retired for the night, Elan reflected on how one person's presence could change so much—their quest was still grave, but now it seemed less like an ominous march towards uncertainty and more like epic song lyrics waiting to unfold. And he couldn't wait for tomorrow's verse.

The Old Knight

The following day, the ancient walls of Montecassino Abbey bore silent witness to the gathering of an unlikely fellowship. Elan's mind whirled with tactical plans, a feeling familiar to him from his days in the Marine Corps Forces Special Operations Command. As Elan studied the map, his mind flashed back to a tense night operation in Iraq. He recalled navigating enemy territory with his team, their steps synchronized in the silence. It had been a race to rescue a captured ally before dawn. Every decision, from routes to surveillance pauses, was critical. His team had moved as one, a testament to their training and trust. Now, planning to retrieve ancient relics, Elan's approach remained rooted in precision, adaptability, and an unspoken bond with his companions. But this time, the battlefield and stakes were vastly different.

The rest he got last night and Isolde's contagious energy gave him an extra boost. He stood beside Nykronus, whose calm was as deep as the roots of the surrounding mountains. They awaited their final companion—a man whose reputation alone could bolster an army.

Wulfstan the Steadfast stood at the edge of the courtyard, his towering form a testament to battles fought and won— to courage. The former Templar Knight's red hair flared like a banner in the morning light, his golden armor glinting with promises of protection. His chest rose and fell with deep contemplation, eyes closed as if in prayer or perhaps a recollection of a distant, more tumultuous past. A sigil of a wolf protruded from his chest.

Nykronus approached first, his steps measured, respectful of the sacred silence that Wulfstan commanded.

"Wulfstan," Nykronus greeted him with a slight bow.

The giant opened his eyes, fixating on Nykronus with a clarity that spoke volumes of his inner strength. "Magelight," he acknowledged in return.

Elan stepped forward, extending his hand not just to greet but also to symbolize partnership. "I'm Elan Durant."

Wulfstan's gaze shifted to Elan, taking in the Marine's posture and bearing with a soldier's eye. His hand enveloped Elan's in a firm grip that spoke more than words ever could—here was an ally worth having by one's side.

"Your name has been whispered by these stones," Wulfstan rumbled. "You wield *Winterstar*?"

Elan nodded, holding Wulfstan's gaze. "I do."

The knight released Elan's hand and crossed his arms over his broad chest, regarding them both with scrutiny from years of command. "And why should I leave this sanctuary to join your quest?"

Nykronus's reply carried the forbearance only eternity could grant. "Our battle extends beyond mere self-interest—we strive for a realm unconquered by shadow. As you're aware, our ranks grow thin, and a haunting adversary skulks within the gloom, their identity yet to be unmasked."

Wulfstan snorted softly, his expression unreadable. "Pretty words for an ugly world."

Isolde emerged from behind them, her steps light but her presence undeniable. She carried her lute with ease, her green eyes alight with mischief.

"Because without you," she chimed in playfully, "who will inspire my songs? Who will be the steadfast rock against which our enemies break?"

A hint of a smile tugged at Wulfstan's lips—a rare sight on such a seasoned warrior—and then it was gone as quickly as it had appeared.

"I have seen many battles," Wulfstan said slowly. "What makes this one different?"

Elan met his question head-on. "This one might just change everything."

Wulfstan's eyes narrowed at that—analyzing Elan's resolve like a blade's edge.

"Show me this *Winterstar*," he demanded.

Elan didn't hesitate; he unsheathed the legendary sword from its scabbard at his side and held it heavenwards. The metal sang in the early light—a clear tone that resonated with power beyond mere steel.

Wulfstan watched the sword intently as if searching its gleaming surface for truths hidden from the rest of the world.

"This is Vulcan's work," he muttered under his breath before looking back at Elan. "And you believe you are worthy to wield it?"

Elan lowered *Winterstar* respectfully but did not sheathe it again just yet. He understood that proving one's worth went beyond mere words or titles; it was found in action and intent.

"I've carried burdens before—fought for those who couldn't fight for themselves," Elan said with quiet intensity. I'm no stranger to sacrifice or *service*."

Wulfstan regarded him for several heartbeats longer before returning his attention to Nykronus.

"And what role do you play in all this?" Wulfstan asked.

"There is magic we have not seen since in centuries. Without a full-fledged mage in our ranks, I am ready to put my wisdom to the test. I am guide and guardian," Nykronus replied simply yet firmly. "And I believe that together we are stronger than apart."

Nykronus's tone was wisdom—a depth that seemed to echo ancient times and resonate within Wulfstan's own experiences.

The knight let out a long breath as if releasing years of solitary contemplation along with it. He glanced once more at *Winterstar* before locking eyes with Elan again.

"If we are to do this," Wulfstan said gravely, "we do it right—no half measures."

"No half-assing, aye," Elan agreed wholeheartedly.

Isolde clapped her hands together once sharply, breaking the tension woven around them like threads of fate being drawn tight.

"Then it's settled!" she declared brightly. "We have our steadfast and courageous rock!"

Nykronus nodded his head once—approval and acknowledgment contained within that simple gesture—and Elan felt something shift within him; an assurance he hadn't known he needed until now solidified into conviction beneath Wulfstan's watchful eye.

They were complete—a fusion of skills and souls brought together by chance or perhaps destiny itself—and they were ready for whatever lay ahead on their perilous journey through time and darkness toward hope's fragile light.

Wulfstan finally stepped forward to join them fully—an act akin to an oath spoken aloud—and at that moment, they were no longer strangers bound by circumstance but comrades-in-arms preparing to face whatever trials awaited them as one united force against shadows yet unseen.

The Rogue

In the Abbey's library, where the hush of whispered reverence for knowledge was almost tangible, Elan stood amidst his newfound comrades, his gaze fixed on a map unfurled across a heavy oak table. They huddled close, their heads bowed in concentration, tracing routes, and talking strategies. Isolde hummed a tune under her breath, her fingers absentmindedly drumming on the tabletop as if to conjure the melody of their impending journey. Nykronus's finger paused over a particularly troubling section of the map, his features tightened in concentration. Wulfstan loomed over them like an ancient sentinel, his red hair a fiery crown in the dim light.

It was at that moment that Ivar Ghostcloak chose to make his entrance.

The door creaked open boldly, defying the library's sanctity. Elan's attention snapped toward the sound, his hand instinctively moving toward *Winterstar*'s hilt. The young man who stepped through the threshold moved with a swagger that seemed out of place amidst the dust-laden shelves and somber tones of monastic robes.

Blond hair cascaded in untamed waves, framing his piercing blue eyes that swept through the room with incisive scrutiny. A pronounced scar, a pale streak of rebellion, cut across his right cheek, marking a young face shaped by confrontation and resilience. He wore this mark as a symbol of honor, a testament to the skirmishes and challenges he had weathered. His attire, a mix of rugged leather and cloth, hugged his frame, practical yet worn with a nonchalant grace. Layers of fabric, chosen for mobility and durability, hinted at a life accustomed to spontaneous adventure and the need for readiness at a moment's notice. Around his waist, a belt adorned with various pouches and tools essential for a wanderer or rogue's unpredictable path.

"I hope I'm not interrupting," Ivar began, his voice carrying the lilting accent of distant Scandinavia. His eyes locked onto Elan's with an intensity that belied his years. "But word travels fast—even to ears not meant to hear."

Nykronus straightened, regarding the newcomer with a mixture of curiosity and caution. "And what words might those be?"

Ivar sauntered closer, his hands casually tucked into his breech pockets. "Words of a quest—a mission to thwart dark forces."

Elan studied Ivar carefully, weighing the confidence of his stride against the potential threat he posed. "Who are you, kid?"

The corner of Ivar's mouth quirked up in an almost smile. "Ivar Ghostcloak at your service." He paused for effect before continuing. "My brother was Leif Ghostcloak—may he feast in Valhalla now."

Isolde's strumming ceased abruptly as she caught Wulfstan's subtle nod—a sign they were familiar with Leif's name.

"Your brother was known to us," Wulfstan rumbled, "a brave soul."

Ivar's demeanor softened at the mention of Leif, but only briefly before hardening into resolve. "A member of your secret society. He fell fighting shadows not unlike those you face now," he said. "I seek revenge—to honor him. I want to take his place and do my part."

Elan exchanged glances with Nykronus and Wulfstan; each look shared spoke volumes about trust and risk—about necessity and fate intertwining.

"And what makes you think we're involved in such matters?" Elan probed.

Ivar chuckled dryly. "Let's just say I have my ways—ways that could prove useful to you."

Nykronus leaned forward, resting his palms flat on the table as he addressed Ivar directly. "This path we walk is fraught with danger— more than you've likely known."

The young rogue met Nykronus's stare without flinching, a spark igniting in his blue eyes as he spoke with conviction beyond his years. "Danger has been my cradle song since birth—I fear no shadow or beast."

Isolde observed Ivar from beneath lowered lashes; her bard's intuition told her there was more depth to this young man than what appeared on the surface—a tale yearning for its place in song.

Wulfstan folded his arms across his chest plate; he questioned not strength or courage but experience—yet something about Ivar's presence commanded attention.

"You're cocky kid. You've got some spunk," Elan said slowly, still undecided about this brazen youth standing before them. "Actions speak louder than words."

A smirk danced across Ivar's lips as he drew closer to the table. He lowered his voice conspiratorially despite no one else being near enough to overhear.

"Give me a chance," he said. "Let me show you what I can do—let me fight alongside you."

Elan pondered this proposition; he knew well enough that skill often came from unexpected quarters—and so did betrayal.

"What skills do you bring?" Elan asked sharply.

"I know things—paths unseen by most," Ivar boasted lightly but confidently. "I can move silently, strike swiftly... And I have connections in places high and low. Connections could mean information—and information could mean survival."

"And your loyalty?" Nykronus asked further.

"For my brother—for vengeance," Ivar replied without hesitation.

Elan saw something familiar in Ivar's eyes then—the same burning desire for retribution that had once consumed him after losing battle buddies in the field—the same drive that had led him here now.

"You'll need to prove yourself," Elan stated firmly, testing not just Ivar's resolve but also whether fate had indeed brought them together for this moment. Trust was not easily given—it had to be earned, like every scar on his body.

Ivar nodded once—a motion filled with determination and eagerness alike. "Give me your trial then—and watch as I pass it with flying colors."

Isolde couldn't help but smile at this exchange; here was a character fit for any epic—a rogue whose mettle would soon be tested by fire and fate.

"We'll see if your bite is as fierce as your bark," Wulfstan said, finally breaking into a rare grin himself at this new addition to their ranks—an addition that might just turn the tide in their favor against whatever darkness lay ahead waiting for them in shadowy corners or across time itself.

Nykronus studied Ivar intently before nodding once. They would give this Ghostcloak his chance—to fight for revenge—to become part of their story—to join their cause if he proved himself worthy enough through trials yet unknown but surely coming soon upon them all like storm clouds gathering on horizons unseen...

In the dimly lit chamber of the Abbey's library, a circle of five convened around the map that sprawled like a web of ink across the old oak table. The weight of their quest pressed down on them, yet there was an undercurrent of excitement—a sense that each was precisely where they were meant to be.

"Things happen for a reason," Elan thought bitterly, recalling his mother's words that always seemed hollow when he needed them most. He was tired of trying to find meaning in every setback and disappointment. But deep down, he couldn't shake the belief that there had to be some purpose behind his struggles.

Elan's eyes traced the lines on the map, his mind strategizing, planning each move like a chess player anticipating his opponent's tactics. His years as a Marine had honed his ability to lead and analyze. His tenure as a Marine had ingrained in him the fundamentals of leadership and the critical analysis skill. Serving as a squad leader, he navigated complex combat scenarios, where swift decision-making under pressure was paramount. This role sharpened his tactical acumen, teaching him to quickly assess situations, anticipate adversary moves, and devise effective strategies. The rigorous training and real-world operations honed his ability to lead and inspire confidence and trust among his team, ensuring their cohesive action in the face of uncertainty. Now, it was time to wield those skills in a game far older and more dangerous than any he'd known.

"We need to split up," Elan began, his voice low and steady. "Each relic we seek is guarded by its own trials. It'll be faster if we tackle them separately."

Isolde nodded approvingly in agreement, her fingers drumming a silent rhythm on her lute. "It makes sense," she said, "And it plays to our strengths."

Wulfstan leaned forward, his massive form casting a shadow over the parchment. "We're stronger together," he rumbled, the skepticism evident in his voice.

"Yes," Elan replied, meeting Wulfstan's gaze. "But we also need to be swift. Each moment we delay could tip the scales further into darkness."

Ivar watched the exchange with keen interest, his blue eyes flickering with unspoken thoughts. He was still an enigma to them—youthful yet scarred by loss, eager yet untested.

"And what would you have us do?" Ivar asked.

Elan pointed to a spot on the map where symbols danced in cryptic patterns. "Here lies Neptune's Tears—the armor blessed with resilience. I'll retrieve it. As for the shield forged by the same Vulcan fire as *Winterstar*, I must take that one myself so I'll get that one too."

Wulfstan grunted his approval; it was fitting for Elan to seek such items—tools of defense for one who'd dedicated his life to protecting others.

Isolde leaned over the map, her braid falling over her shoulder like a dark rope. Her finger hovered over another symbol—a gemstone cut in fine lines that seemed almost ethereal.

"The gem containing Jupiter's Bolt," she mused aloud. "As I've said, I've heard tales of its brilliance—that it can cut through deception as easily as light through shadow. Those tales were confirmed by some pilgrims I met outside the city."

Elan looked at her with newfound respect; her knowledge of lore and legend would be invaluable in deciphering clues that might confound others.

Wulfstan shifted his attention toward a mountain range drawn with jagged precision on the map's edge. "And there," he said firmly, pointing to a peak that seemed to pierce the heavens themselves, "rests Saturn's creation—the dragon's tooth filled with dust from its ring."

His choice was apt; only someone with Wulfstan's might could brave such heights and emerge victorious.

Finally, Ivar spoke up again, this time with confidence that matched his earlier bravado. "Then I'll take on Juno's Breath—the scales touched by her divine influence."

Nykronus remained silent throughout their discussion. His role was different from theirs—more ephemeral yet no less crucial. He would guide them from afar, using magic and wisdom gleaned from ages past to keep them connected across distances and unknown dangers.

"Let's go over each task," Elan suggested. "Detail what we know about these relics and their resting places."

One by one, they shared their knowledge.

Isolde described the gem's last known location—a temple hidden within an oasis that mirrored the sky itself—its waters as clear as the truths it protected.

Wulfstan recounted legends of dragons who'd once soared above mountains but are now forsaken by time—a tooth lost amidst peaks where winds whisper secrets meant only for those brave enough to listen.

Ivar revealed whispers he'd caught on windswept docks and shadowed alleyways—of scales held within an ancient merchant's vault sealed not by locks but by puzzles woven into its very walls.

Elan shared tales of armor crafted in the depths where fire and water collided. A powerful anvil was said to have been wielded by Vulcan himself, forging destiny for those brave enough to wear it. Word had it that a shield was also buried with the armor.

As they spoke, their voices wove together into a tapestry rich with anticipation and resolve—each thread unique yet part of a greater whole that would shield them against whatever trials awaited beyond Abbey walls.

"Remember," Nykronus interjected when they'd finished laying out their plans. "The relics are not just objects; they are imbued with power —and with purpose."

His words were a reminder—an anchor amidst currents that threatened to pull them into realms where mortal flesh and blood were tested against arcane and divine elements.

"We leave at twilight tomorrow," Elan said once Nykronus had finished speaking. "Get yourselves mentally and physically ready tonight; rest while you can. Gather any last-minute supplies you may need in the morning."

The Abbey had long since surrendered to the night, its ancient stones holding the day's warmth like a secret. In the charterhouse's garden, Elan sat alone on a weathered bench, his fingers tracing the intricate patterns of *Winterstar*'s hilt. The air was still, with the faint scent of jasmine and a chill that spoke of the coming dawn.

Elan remembered his drill instructor yelling, "I'll sleep when I'm dead," and he couldn't help but say it out loud in a semi-joking manner. He should have been sleeping, resting for the journey ahead, but sleep remained a stranger to him these days. Even at the end of his military career, anxiety medication and therapy couldn't cure his sleep disorder. Instead, he let his mind wander through the events that had led him here—his unexpected allies forming an eclectic tapestry of strength and skill and wondering how his family and friends were doing back home.

Amidst these reflections, his thoughts invariably drifted to Kaira, whose absence felt like a void no amount of time or distance could fill. Memories of her, vibrant and full of life, served as both a beacon and a torment, fueling his determination to uncover the truth behind her disappearance and rekindle the hope that somehow, against all odds, he would find her again.

Elan took a deep breath, trying to push away the thoughts of his family and friends. He couldn't let himself get distracted now; his mission was too critical. The sound of approaching footsteps interrupted his solitude. He turned to see Wulfstan, the moonlight casting long shadows behind the towering figure.

"Mind if I join you, Elan?" Wulfstan looked intently at Elan.

Elan nodded, gesturing to the bench beside him. Wulfstan sat, his armor clinking softly. "It's strange. In this place of peace, I find myself wrestling with ghosts."

Wulfstan sighed and stared at the brightly lit stars, "Ghosts of the past are the fiercest foes. They know our weakest spots."

Elan looked at Wulfstan, surprised by the knight's insight. "I've been... struggling with the loss of someone very close to me. Kaira. Her disappearance is why I'm on this quest. I keep thinking if I'd been there, maybe..."

Wulfstan turned to Elan, his face solemn. "The burdens of 'what ifs' are heavy chains. I, too, have known loss. Battles where not all comrades returned. It's the weight we bear but it is also what forges us."

A wave of helplessness flooded Elan as he realized he had heard this before and knew the truth but could never listen."How do *you* manage? How do you move forward?"

"By remembering that we fight not just for the past but for the hope of a future. Your quest for Kaira is more than a search. It's a testament to your strength and your commitment to those you love," Wulfstan said in a deeper and quieter whisper.

Elan considered Wulfstan's words, feeling a shift within him. "Maybe you're right. Maybe this quest... it's not just about finding Kaira. It's about confronting those ghosts and maybe... finding a bit of peace."

Wulfstan looked at Elan with excitement, "Aye, and in facing them, you honor her memory and the love you bear. Let that be your shield, Elan."

They sat in silence for a moment, the night air filled with the sounds of the Abbey. Elan felt a weight lifted, understanding that his grief and guilt, while part of him, do not define his journey.

Elan stared at the sky and looked at his new battle buddy, "Thank you, Wulfstan. I really needed to hear that."

"We're all here for a reason, Elan. Together, we'll face whatever comes. For Kaira, for ourselves, and for the future we are fighting to protect."

Wulfstan stood, clasping Elan's shoulder firmly before departing, leaving Elan to his thoughts. Elan felt a sense of clarity and purpose for the first time in a long while. He reminded her of his best friend, now separated by time.

The image of Reagan kept creeping into his mind. They had been inseparable since childhood, always getting into mischief together. But as they grew older, their paths diverged. While Elan joined the military, Reagan dove into her career in law enforcement.

He wondered how she was doing now if she was safe and having a similar quest with the Nykronus of the future. And what about Austin, another childhood friend who had always been like a brother to him? Was he still running operations in Ukraine? Elan hoped that they were all doing well without him.

But he couldn't let himself dwell on these thoughts any longer. He needed to focus on the task at hand. The fate of their world rested on his shoulders, along with those of his fellow knights of the Order.

Elan stood up from the bench and stretched, feeling the tension in his muscles ease slightly. He walked around the garden, taking in its serene beauty under the moonlight. The flowers seemed to dance in the gentle breeze, their colors muted in shades of purple and blue.

As he reached the edge of the garden, he paused and looked at *Winterstar*'s hilt glinting in the moonlight. It was more than just a sword; it represented hope for their people and held within it powerful magic that could defeat their enemies.

The thought gave Elan strength as he returned to his room in the Abbey. Tomorrow would be a long day filled with battles and uncertainty, but he promised himself he wouldn't let anyone down.

He lay down on his bed and closed his eyes, trying to relax and drift into sleep, but once again, his mind went into overdrive. He thought of Wulfstan, steadfast as the mountains he'd soon climb; Isolde, whose songs seemed to hold power beyond their melodies; Ivar, young and fierce with a heart hungry for vengeance; and Nykronus, mysterious as time itself, a well of wisdom they'd all come to drink from.

They were ready—or as ready as one could be when facing the unknown. And yet, amidst this readiness, Elan felt something else within himself—something he'd been avoiding with every strategic plan and map consulted.

Grief. In these moments, he would schedule an appointment with his therapist or call Austin or Reagan to vent. While he knew it wasn't true, he felt alone. Lonely as he has felt his entire adult life.

It crept up on him now in the quiet, away from prying eyes and ears. Kaira's absence was like a wound that refused to heal—a constant ache that no amount of time or distance could soothe. The grief pursued him relentlessly, an inescapable specter that haunted his every waking moment. Countless therapy sessions and his mother's unconditional love and support in the wake of Kaira's disappearance had done little to ease the pain. On the other hand, his father had coldly advised him to just get over it and move forward with his life. He'd thrown himself into this quest with fervor to find her and escape the guilt that gnawed at him.

Therapists, friends, and family had all given him the same advice over and over again, but he couldn't shake thoughts of Kaira from his mind. If he had been there—would she still have vanished?

Elan stood up, pacing, and picked up *Winterstar*. The sword felt heavy in his hands—a weight made not of metal but of responsibility and unspoken promises. He closed his eyes against the memories that threatened to overwhelm him—the laughter they shared, her smile that seemed to brighten even the darkest corners of his world.

Elan knew that to move forward, he had to confront these demons —not just for Kaira but for himself. His team needed him whole, not fractured by what-ifs and regrets. The path ahead required all of him— mind and soul—and he couldn't give that if part of him remained lost in the past.

With a deep breath, Elan opened his eyes and stood still. The night air felt crisper now like it, too, had come to terms with what must be done.

As dawn approached with its first tentative rays peeking over the horizon, Elan returned to gather his companions. They found each other in the Abbey's main hall—a space that seemed too vast for their small number yet somehow fitting for the gravity of their pledge.

"We stand on the edge of something greater than ourselves," Elan began, his voice echoing slightly off stone walls worn smooth by centuries of whispered prayers. "This journey will test us—our courage, our resolve."

He looked at each face in turn: Wulfstan's grim determination, Isolde's calm readiness, Ivar's restless energy, Nykronus's serene confidence.

"We might not all make it back," Elan continued solemnly. "But we commit here and now—to each other and to our cause—that we will see this through. We will face whatever comes together."

They stepped forward one by one, each placing a hand atop *Winterstar's* blade where it lay upon an altar at the center of the room.

"I vow my strength," Wulfstan declared.

"My song," Isolde added softly.

"My cunning," Ivar chimed in with a fierce nod.

"My guidance," Nykronus intoned lastly.

Elan covered their hands with his own—a final seal on their pact. "And my heart."

For a moment, they remained still—connected by touch and promise—before slowly withdrawing their hands. The bond they formed was invisible yet concrete—a chain forged not just by necessity but by shared purpose and newfound kinship.

As they prepared for departure, tension wove itself through their movements—a tapestry threaded with anticipation and uncertainty about what lay ahead.

It was Isolde who broke it first.

"You know," she said with an impish grin as she adjusted her lute strap over her shoulder, "I've composed a song for our quest."

Ivar snorted skeptically while Wulfstan merely raised an eyebrow in silent question. Nykronus smiled knowingly—as if he'd expected nothing less from their bard.

"A song?" Elan asked with curiosity, coloring his tone despite himself. He couldn't help but smile at the thought of her with a futuristic Stratocaster in her hand. He envisioned her playing at music festivals, inspiring and influencing future generations as a social media influencer or famous musician.

"Yes!" Isolde exclaimed with mock seriousness before breaking into an upbeat tune that seemed at odds with everything they faced:

"Five brave souls set forth at dawn,

To claim what's lost but not yet gone.

With sword and shield and lute in hand,

They'll face down foes across the land!"

Her voice lifted into laughter as she finished her verse—the melody lightening hearts burdened by duty's weight.

The others couldn't help but join in her mirth—even Elan found himself laughing out loud despite the heaviness he'd felt only hours before. The laughter was a balm—a reminder that even on paths fraught with danger, there could be moments of joy shared among friends beneath banners, not of blood but of bond chosen willingly amidst shadows' dance...

And so they set forth from Abbey's embrace—not just as warriors, mages, rogues, or bards—but as comrades whose laughter echoed behind them like silver bells calling out hope's promise even as they stepped into uncertainty's fold...

CHAPTER

TEN

The outskirts of Cassino, Duchy of Benevento, 842 A.D.

Behind them, stood the Abbey of Montecassino, as the party stopped at a point where they would continue their journeys on separate paths. His gaze fixed upon the distant Abbey, Elan's composure remained steady. Isolde held onto her lute like a shield, her eyes shining with the promise of songs yet to be sung. Wulfstan's hand gripped the hilt of his sword, his stance exuding unwavering strength. Ivar fidgeted anxiously, barely able to contain his restless and youthful energy.

"We each carry a thread of this tapestry in our hands," Nykronus began, his voice a deep thrum that seemed to resonate with the very earth beneath them. "May we weave a story worthy of legend."

Elan stepped forward, clasping Wulfstan's shoulder. "Your steel has been tried and tested through countless battles. May it strike true once more."

Wulfstan nodded, his grizzled face breaking into a rare smile. "And may your courage never falter, Elan."

Turning to Isolde, Elan offered a respectful nod. "Your melodies have the power to soothe savage beasts and lift weary spirits. Let them be our beacon in darkness."

Isolde curtsied gracefully, her voice soft but sure. "Every note shall be a step closer to Kaira."

Lastly, Elan faced Ivar, whose eyes sparkled with mischief and unspoken tales. "The shadows you walk in hold secrets and dangers alike. Tread carefully, kid."

Ivar's grin was quick and sly. "Shadows are just places where the light's about to shine."

They embraced briefly—a circle of warriors bound by purpose—and then turned away from one another without another word, their silent goodbyes echoing louder than any farewell could.

Antium (Present-Day Anzio), Duchy of Benevento, Italy, 842 A.D.

Elan had never ridden a horse before this five-day journey, and the experience left him feeling somewhat exhausted and sore. The constant motion of the horse, the need to maintain balance, and the long hours spent in the saddle had taken a toll on his body, leaving him with aching muscles and a new respect for the challenging nature of horseback riding. However, the idea of obtaining his objective and being one step closer to finding Kaira kept his will strong.

Elan descended into the catacombs beneath Antium, the weight of solitude settling on his shoulders like his favorite flannel shirt. The musky scent of damp earth permeated the atmosphere, while a faint glimmer of torchlight reflected on the lake's dark surface. He found himself at the edge of an underground lake, its surface dark and still as obsidian glass.

Here lay the threshold of his journey—beneath these waters rested the armor he sought.

Drawing in a deep breath, Elan shed his earthly garments for those suited to traverse Neptune's domain. He affixed an amulet around his neck—a gift from Nykronus, from the treasures of the Order—that would allow him to breathe underwater as if he were born of the sea itself. The amulet is a small, intricately carved trident suspended on a thick silver chain. Its surface is smooth, almost like glass, with an opalescent sheen that dances in the torchlight. His fingers grazed the amulet tucked securely against his skin; it hummed with energy that thrummed through his veins—a mingling of Marine prowess and arcane power.

Elan stepped into the water with zero hesitation. Cool tendrils embraced him as he fully submerged himself. He dove deeper into the abyss below with powerful strokes honed by years of service.

The light waned until darkness engulfed him—a void where only faith could guide him forward. The amulet pulsed at his chest, casting a faint glow that illuminated strange runes permanently fixed upon rocks and ancient relics lost to time.

A shadow loomed ahead—massive and unmoving—an underwater colossus carved from stone and coral that guarded the relic Elan sought: a chest plate impressed with runes that shimmered with otherworldly light and adorned with a sigil that pulsed like a living heart.

Elan approached with caution, knowing such treasures would not be left unguarded. His instincts proved true as the colossus stirred—a sentinel awakened from its eternal vigil. As Elan reached out to touch the sigil, he felt a tingling sensation in his fingertips, as if the energy of the symbol was flowing through the metal of the armor.

It rose before him—a colossal giant armored in barnacles and draped in kelp—its single eye blazing like a beacon in the deep sea gloom. As the guardian emerged from the depths, its massive form caused the water to churn and swirl violently, creating powerful currents that threatened to sweep Elan away. He fought against the surging water, struggling to maintain his position as the giant loomed over him, its presence an overwhelming force that seemed to command the very ocean itself. Elan's heart raced as he faced this immense adversary, knowing that even the slightest mistake could spell his doom in the face of such raw power and ancient might.

"You who trespass in Neptune's realm," it boomed, its voice reverberating through water and bone alike, "state your purpose or prepare to be buried below the sand at the bottom closest to the borders of Hell."

Elan felt no fear—his years had taught him respect for adversaries both seen and unseen. "I mean no disrespect. I seek only to reclaim what's needed to rescue one unjustly taken," he replied, voice steady even as currents swirled around them.

The guardian's eye narrowed, appraising Elan with a scrutiny that bore into his soul—a test of strength and conviction.

"You carry scars of battles past," it observed—a statement laced with truths both known and hidden.

Elan responded unflinchingly. "What doesn't kill us makes us stronger."

The guardian remained silent for what felt like an eternity before finally speaking again. "Your words bear weight but it is your will that must be measured."

With those words came action—the colossus moved with surprising speed for its size, thrusting forward with arms that sought to crush or cast Elan into darkness everlasting.

But Elan was no stranger to combat—his reflexes honed on distant battlefields sprang into motion instinctively. He danced around its grasp like driftwood caught in a storm—evasive yet directed towards his goal.

As they engaged in their deadly ballet beneath the waves, Elan's focus narrowed to the immediate challenge at hand. The guardian's relentless attacks demanded every ounce of his skill and strength, leaving no room for philosophical musings. Each twist and turn, each parry and strike, was an instinctive response honed by years of training and tempered in the fires of countless battles. At that moment, there was only the primal struggle for survival, the clash of two powerful forces locked in a battle of wills beneath the cold, unforgiving sea.

Each dodge was more than mere avoidance—it was affirmation; each advance was more than aggression—it was resolve crystallized in motion.

He did not simply fight—he wove his tale through every move; each feint and thrust a word inscribed upon this chapter of his journey —a narrative bound by willpower and woven through with threads of magic yet untamed.

The guardian's assault was a maelstrom of churning water and grasping limbs. Its massive arms slammed into the sea, sending shockwaves rippling through the depths that battered Elan from all sides. He twisted and turned, his muscles straining as he fought against the powerful currents, seeking to evade the guardian's crushing grip. With a fierce cry that was swallowed by the roaring water, Elan unsheathed *Winterstar*, the blade gleaming in the dim light as he gripped it tightly with both hands, ready to meet the guardian's onslaught head-on.

Finally sensing its opponent's true mettle, the guardian ceased its attack; recognition flashed within its ancient eye—a nod to courage, both martial and mystical.

"You have proven your worth," it conceded with grudging respect while motioning towards the armor resting undisturbed within their watery shrine.

Elan exhaled slowly. Victory was not triumph over another but mastery over oneself, an understanding reached not at the journey's end but at its very beginning.

Elan's heart hammered in his chest as the guardian of Neptune's realm granted him passage to a secret garden on Antium's surface. Sunlight brought warmth to Elan as a ray of light was centered specifically on the armor. He approached the armor with reverence, its surface catching the dim light, casting ethereal reflections on the water around him. The chestplate's runes glowed a soft green, pulsating gently as if breathing with the tide. The craftsmanship was exquisite, beyond anything fashioned by mortal hands—clearly a divine artifact. An artifact fit for St. Michael.

He fastened the chest plate around his torso, feeling an immediate rush of power coursing through his veins. It was as if the sea itself buoyed him, its depths and mysteries lending him their strength. The armor clung to him like a second skin, moving with him in perfect synchrony. A perfect fit.

As Elan surfaced, he marveled at the armor in the daylight. It shimmered with an inner luminescence, a silent tribute to Neptune's blessing. He knew he carried not just a piece of metal but a piece of history —a relic infused with tears shed by the god of the sea himself.

His task at Antium was complete; Elan now set his sights on Vulcan's lost forge. The next leg of his journey promised even greater dangers, for he would have to traverse lands fraught with volcanic vents spewing sulfurous fumes and ancient ruins that whispered secrets long forgotten.

Elan traveled northward, guided by Nykronus' cryptic messages and an old map depicting Italy as it once was—a land of fire and myth. The terrain grew more rugged with each passing mile, the earth beneath his feet cracked and scorched from past eruptions.

The cryptic messages that came from Nykronus were in the form of ancient texts and arcane symbols, delivered by mysterious means. Sometimes, they appeared as glowing runes carved into the walls of long-forgotten ruins, or as whispers carried on the wind that only Elan could hear. Other times, they arrived as tattered scrolls, their edges worn and their ink faded, requiring careful study and interpretation to unravel their true meaning. Each message was a piece of a larger puzzle, a clue that hinted at the location of Vulcan's forge or the challenges that lay ahead.

The landscape sharply contrasted the watery depths from which he had just emerged. Here, fire ruled—a primal force shaping and reshaping the world in its image. Steam rose from fissures in the ground like specters haunting this desolate place.

Vulcan's forge was said to be hidden among these volcanic vents, a place where celestial fire met earthly craft. Elan felt the heat radiating from the ground through his boots; sweat dripped from his forehead despite the coolness of Neptune's armor against his skin.

He followed a path lined with statues of Cyclopes—the one-eyed giants of lore—each one positioned as if guarding something precious and powerful beyond mortal reach. Their stone gazes seemed to follow him, silently challenging his resolve.

Finally, after what felt like an eternity of searching and deciphering clues left behind in old tales and etchings on stone tablets, Elan stood before an entrance carved into a mountainside—a mouth leading into darkness framed by pillars adorned with Vulcan's symbols: hammer and anvil.

Papal State Territory (Present-Day Monte Albano), 842 A.D

Drawing *Winterstar* once more, Elan descended into Vulcan's realm. The sword's icy glow pierced the shadows that clung to every crevice like cobwebs. The heat intensified as he ventured deeper into the mountain's belly; beads of sweat turned to rivulets that traced paths down his back beneath the armor. Every breath he took felt like inhaling fire; each step forward was defiance against nature's fury.

Elan encountered physical and mystical challenges in this hidden realm of fire and earth. Golems forged from molten rock lumbered towards him with fists that could shatter bones. But Elan danced between them—each movement deliberate and precise—using their momentum against them until they crumbled back into lifeless stone. *Winterstar* made a thunderous noise with each strike.

At times it seemed as though the very mountain sought to spit him out—eruptions shaking its foundations, spewing forth rivers of lava that sought to claim him as another relic entombed within this fiery crypt. His chest plate made him immune to the intense heat.

As Elan pressed on through the perilous depths, his thoughts turned to Kaira and the life she might have lived in the twenty years since her disappearance. In his mind's eye, he saw her finding moments of joy and peace amidst the challenges of medieval life. Perhaps she had found solace in the simple pleasures of tending a garden, her hands coaxing life from the soil just as she had once brought light to his world. Or maybe she had become a teacher, sharing her knowledge of the universe with eager young minds, her passion for learning undiminished by the passage of time. Yet, even as he imagined her thriving, Elan couldn't shake the fear that she had faced untold hardships and dangers, her safety and happiness threatened by forces beyond her control.

Hours turned to days—or perhaps it was minutes stretched into eternity—time held little meaning in this place untouched by the sun or moon.

Then came the moment when Elan entered a chamber so vast it might have housed all the stars if they fell from heaven. At its center stood an anvil larger than any he had seen before—its surface scarred from countless strikes yet unyielding as ever. Above it hung a massive hammer suspended in mid-air by chains forged from materials darker than night itself.

And there it was—leaning against the anvil—the shield forged by Vulcan's fire captured from the forge itself. Its surface was ablaze with images depicting heroes and gods locked in eternal combat—a masterpiece wrought in steel yet light as air when he lifted it from its resting place. Among the many images, one stood out to me: that of St. Michael locked in a fierce battle with Lucifer at the gates of hell.

The shield thrummed with power at his touch—a living force that resonated with *Winterstar's* hum. Together, they were a force to be reckoned with, a flawless combination of power and precision. One oozed a raw, low rumble like a bass guitar's thunderous chords, while the other roared with the intensity of an epic rockstar's solo. Their harmonies could cut through chaos like knives, leaving behind a symphony of order in their wake.

Yet as Elan prepared to take leave of Vulcan's domain with the shield in hand, he knew better than to think this journey would end without one final trial—a test not just of courage but also ingenuity and spirit...

Elan stood before the anvil, his hand resting on the shield's heated surface. The room thrummed with a resonance that seemed to beat in time with his own heart. He had come far, but he knew this was not the end. The forge of Vulcan was alive and aware, and it would not relinquish its treasure without a final test.

The air shimmered, and from the fiery glow emerged creatures born of flame and fury. Salamanders, the mythical spirits of fire, skittered across the walls and floor, their bodies a mosaic of molten rock and ember. They surrounded Elan, a ring of fire that threatened to consume him.

Elan tightened his grip on *Winterstar*. The salamanders lunged in a coordinated dance of destruction, their movements as unpredictable as wildfire. But Elan was a tempest of his own—a storm that had braved the crashing waves and now faced the inferno.

He pivoted and swung *Winterstar* with precision, its icy blade extinguishing each salamander it touched. The sword's chill countered the forge's heat, leaving trails of steam in its wake. With every defeated salamander, the shield seemed to pulse stronger in his grasp, as if acknowledging his worthiness.

But the salamanders were many, and Elan was one. They regrouped swiftly, adapting to his tactics with sinister surveillance. They drew upon the forge's heat, growing larger and more aggressive with each assault.

Elan realized brute force would not be enough; he needed to outthink these creatures of pure element. He scanned the chamber for anything that could aid him—his gaze settling on the chains that held Vulcan's massive hammer aloft.

A plan sparked within his mind like flint to tinder. With a series of feints and dodges, Elan maneuvered himself beneath the suspended hammer. The salamanders followed eagerly, their fiery forms illuminating Elan's silhouette against the forge's shadow.

The sound of the salamanders' approach filled the chamber, growing louder and more menacing with each passing second. Elan could hear the skittering of their claws against the rock, a discordant chorus that echoed from every direction. Low, guttural growls mingled with the hissing of their breath, a cacophony of hunger and malice that set his nerves on edge. The flickering light of the forge cast twisted shadows on the walls, making it impossible to gauge their numbers or anticipate their attack. Elan's heart pounded in his chest as he strained to track their movements, his senses on high alert as he prepared to face the unknown threat. The tension mounted with each step they took, the air growing thick with the promise of violence and the primal fear of the prey in the presence of the predator.

He called upon every reserve of strength and agility he possessed— leaping aside at the last moment as the salamanders converged where he had stood.

Winterstar cleaved through a chain as though it were no more than twine. The hammer plummeted down with an earth-shattering crash directly onto the unsuspecting salamanders below. The ground trembled under its weight; lava splashed high into the air like waves against cliffs.

The surviving salamanders recoiled from their fallen kin—now mere smoldering stones—and retreated back into the walls from which they had come.

Elan breathed heavily, sweat mingling with ash on his unshaven cheeks. The room quieted save for the crackling of cooling rock and his own labored breaths.

The shield felt different now in his hands—warmer but lighter—as if it had been waiting for him to prove himself before fully yielding its powers.

With admiration for Vulcan's craftsmanship, Elan slung the shield over his back behind *Winterstar*. It settled against him comfortably—a testament to its divine origin—and together they made their way back through the labyrinthine passages of the forge.

The return journey was not without its perils—the mountain rumbled with displeasure at being plundered of its treasure—but Elan moved with purpose, undeterred by falling debris or shifting ground beneath him.

As he ascended towards daylight, each step felt like shedding a layer from an ordeal that would be branded into his very soul—a trial by fire that left an indelible mark upon both man and myth.

As Elan emerged from the depths of Vulcan's forge, the sun kissed his face, and fresh air filled his lungs. He savored the warmth and the sweetness of the breeze, a welcome respite after the oppressive heat and darkness of the underground labyrinth. Yet, even as he relished the simple pleasures of the surface world, Elan couldn't ignore his journey's toll on his body. His joints ached with a dull, persistent pain, a reminder that he was no longer the young, invincible warrior he had once been. His breath came in short, ragged gasps, his lungs straining to adjust to the sudden change in air quality. For a moment, he allowed himself to feel the weight of his years, the accumulated scars and sorrows that marked his life like the rings of an ancient tree. But then, with a deep breath and a shake of his head, Elan pushed the weariness aside. His maturity had brought with it a clarity of purpose and a depth of understanding that his younger self had lacked.

Elan turned away from Monte Albano with two parts of Kaira's salvation secured—a symbol not just of protection but also resilience— the armor blessed by Neptune's tears and now this shield forged by

Vulcan's fire; two halves of a whole that would guide him on his quest for Kaira's return and put a stop the Order's enemies.

His trials within Vulcan's forge were over, but echoes remained—whispers that clung like shadows at dusk or memories surfacing from depths unknown; reminders that though battles may be won alone, it is rarely without cost or consequence... The war was raging.

Papal State Territory (Present-day Casenthinesi Forest) 842 A.D.

Ivar Ghostcloak slipped through the trees, his blond hair like a pale flame against the emerald backdrop. The forest hummed with a deceptive peace, sunlight dappling through the canopy in patches of warm gold. But he knew better than to trust the serene facade. Juno's breath had touched these woods, and its enchantment was as perilous as it was beautiful.

The rogue's blue eyes scanned the surroundings with vigilance sharpened by the loss of his brother. His journey had brought him here in search of scales—ethereal remnants that shimmered with Juno's essence. He trod softly, avoiding twigs and leaves that might betray his presence to unseen watchers.

Suddenly, the peace shattered as mystical beasts emerged from the thickets—a pack of lupine creatures with fur that rippled like liquid moonlight. Their eyes glowed with an unearthly light, fixating on Ivar with an intelligence far beyond any common wolf.

Ivar stood motionless, calculating his odds. These were no mere animals; they were guardians of the forest, their very presence a challenge to any who dared seek its belongings.

He drew a short blade from his belt—a weapon forged from Scandinavian iron and tempered by vengeance. "I seek passage," he spoke firmly, "for justice demands, I find what was lost."

The lead beast tilted its head as if considering his words before issuing a low growl that set the others on edge. With reflexes honed by years of thievery and survival, Ivar moved like a wraith among them—his blade a silver arc in the dappled light.

Each strike was measured, and each dodged an answer to the silent song of combat that filled the air. The beasts fought with a grace that matched their ethereal beauty, but Ivar fought with desire—a burning need that could not be satisfied by fang or claw.

In time, the creatures withdrew, recognizing Ivar's upper hand—a force driven by something greater than mere survival. They vanished as mysteriously as they had appeared, leaving Ivar alone once more with nothing but whispers of leaves to mark their passing.

He continued deeper into the heart of the enchanted woods until he came upon a glade bathed in a light that seemed untouched by time. There, nestled among moss and ancient roots, lay the scales—delicate and iridescent, breathing faintly with Juno's power. Each side pulled at each other's balance.

Ivar reached out with caution to collect the scale small enough to fit in his rucksack—a small victory in his quest; one step closer to avenging Leif and aiding those who had become his unlikely companions on this grander journey.

Papal State Territory, Lazio Region (Present-day Monte Terminillo) 842 A.D.

Isolde pressed on through biting winds that whipped across her path—a blizzard's fury unleashed upon the Terminillo Mountain's slopes. Snowflakes clung to her braids like pearls woven into black silk while her punchy green eyes remained fixed on her goal—an ancient gem said to be imbued with magic as old as time itself.

Each step was a battle against nature's wrath—the storm seeming almost sentient in its determination to cast her down from these duplicitous heights. But Isolde was no stranger to misadventure; she carried within her songs of heroes who had braved far worse for far less.

Beneath Isolde's upbeat demeanor lay a well of sorrow and heartbreak that few had ever glimpsed. She had lost her family to the machinations of the Malefic Assembly, their lives snuffed out in a single, cruel stroke that had left her adrift in a world that turned suddenly cold and hostile. In the aftermath of that tragedy, Isolde had thrown herself into her music, pouring her grief and rage into melodies that spoke of loss and longing, of the unquenchable thirst for justice that burned within her heart.

Her misadventures had begun then, a series of daring escapades and narrow escapes that had taken her from the glittering courts of kings to the shadowed alleys of forgotten slums. She had faced danger and betrayal at every turn, her quick wit and quicker blade the only things standing between her and oblivion. Yet, through it all, she had clung to the stories of heroes past, drawing strength and inspiration from their tales of courage and sacrifice. In time, those stories had become her own, a tapestry of song and myth that she wove around herself like a cloak of resilience and hope.

She wrapped her cloak tighter around herself, its fabric straining against gusts that sought to unravel both weave and wearer. Yet her voice rose above the howling wind—a melody that spoke of warmth and hearth, an incantation against cold and despair.

Hours passed amidst this frozen tempest until, at last, Isolde stumbled upon a cave hidden beneath an overhang of ice. Its mouth sleepily wide like an invitation—or perhaps a challenge—to those who dared seek shelter within its depths.

With careful steps, Isolde entered, her breath forming clouds in the air before her. The cave stretched deep into the mountain's heart—a silent sanctuary against nature's chaos outside.

There she found it—the gem radiating power so profound it seemed to pulse in time with her own heartbeat. Its surface caught what little light there was within the cave and scattered it like stars trapped within the stone—countless colors reflecting off walls amplified with reflection from frost.

Isolde reached out slowly—her fingers trembling not from cold but from awe—as she cradled the gem within her palm. It warmed at her touch—an ember awakening from slumber—and she knew she held not just a stone but a divine relic; a testament to magic that defied elements and endured beyond ages.

Eastern Alps, Kingdom of Italy, Carolingian Empire, 842 A.D.

Under an ocean of stars, Wulfstan trudged across rocky terrain that rolled like violent waves towards horizons unseen. The landscape stretched before him—an expanse vast enough to swallow empires whole—and yet he followed a map written not on parchment but in constellations above; celestial guides charting his course towards legend.

His armor gleamed dully beneath Luna's gaze—golden yet subdued amidst sand's silver glow. His red hair was a flag of defiance against night's embrace while his eyes remained ever watchful for signs along this sandy sea—a dragon's tooth fabled for wisdom long forgotten.

As he navigated by stars once studied by sages and seers alike, Wulfstan felt their silent stories seep into his soul—tales of battles fought beneath these same heavens; sagas etched into eternity for those willing to listen... or brave enough to seek their truths firsthand.

A violent storm erupted suddenly, the sky above the cathedral transforming into a roiling mass of clouds and fury. Thunder boomed, its deafening crashes shaking the very foundations of the ancient structure. Lightning tore through the air in jagged bolts, each flash casting stark, fleeting illumination over the scene below. The wind howled like a vengeful spirit, whipping through the streets and tearing at the heroes' clothing with icy fingers. The air crackled with tension and the tang of ozone, the palpable energy of the tempest bearing down upon them with almost physical force.

Yet within this chaos lay startling—for as rocks shifted, so too did secrets long buried, unveiling paths hidden from sight but known to heart or instinct alone...

When calm returned—stars once again unveiling themselves like jewels upon velvet night—he found what he sought half-buried beneath drifts newly settled: a skull larger than any beast he knew save those borne from dream or nightmare...chiseled with runes whose meanings whispered wisdom across ages—a language understood not through words but through warrior's spirit forged in trials both physical and metaphysical alike...

A single tooth remained on the long-forgotten dragon's head. It was a thing of awe and terror, its size and shape, unlike anything Wulfstan had ever seen. It was as long as a man's forearm, its curved, serrated edges gleaming with a wicked sharpness that spoke of the primal power of the creature it had once belonged to. The tooth's surface was a mottled ivory, its hue a testament to the countless ages it had endured since the dragon's fall. Wulfstan pried it from the beast's head. As he took it in his hands, he could feel the weight of its history, the echo of the great beast's fury and majesty that seemed to thrum through the ancient enamel like a pulse. It was a relic of a forgotten age, a reminder of the mythic beasts that had once roamed the earth, their presence now confined to the realm of legend and the whispered tales of fireside storytellers. In that moment, as he held the tooth aloft, Wulfstan knew that he grasped not just a weapon, but a symbol of the untamed forces that shaped the world, a primal essence that could be harnessed for good or ill in the battle against the encroaching darkness.

Through the whispering leaves and across the wind-swept peaks, a mystical connection hummed into life, bridging vast distances with the subtlety of an ancient spell cast by Nykronus. Though scattered across realms and histories, each member of Elan's assembled team felt a sudden warmth, a call to share triumphs won in solitude.

Standing at the foot of Monte Albano with the heat of Vulcan's forge still lingering on his skin, Elan lifted his eyes to the horizon. A shimmering in the air before him coalesced into a vision, revealing his battle buddies, each surrounded by their own hard-won victories.

In the heart of Casenthinesi Forest, Ivar Ghostcloak leaned against an ancient oak. His youthful face was marked by fatigue, but his eyes shone with fierce pride as he pulled forth the delicate scales from his rucksack. "Breath of Juno," he whispered, holding them up to the light. They glinted, reflecting myriad colors that seemed to dance like fireflies caught in twilight's embrace.

The vision shifted, and Isolde appeared amidst the ice-encrusted walls of her shelter on Monte Terminillo. Her breath came in puffs of white mist as she cradled the gem in her hands—a stone alive with an inner light that pushed back against the surrounding gloom. "Jupiter's Bolt," she announced with reverence. Her voice carried through the connection like a song sung to ward off darkness.

High in the Eastern Alps, Wulfstan stood resolute against a backdrop painted with stars. The dragon's tooth was in his grasp, its surface etched with wisdom older than empires. He held it aloft for all to see—his red hair whipped about by mountain gusts as if in salute to his feat. "Dust from Saturn's Ring," he declared. The runes upon the tooth glowed faintly as if acknowledging their new master.

Lastly, Elan stepped forward within their shared vision—a figure tempered by trials both past and present. The shield upon his back caught an errant ray of sunlight, casting patterns that danced upon his face. "Vulcan's Fire," he stated simply. His voice carried weight—a testament to battles fought and scars borne both within and without. The sigil on his chest plate glimmered under the moonlight, "and Neptune's Tears."

As each member beheld one another through this dreamlike meeting place—a convergence of wills across time and space—they shared not just artifacts but experiences; tales woven from courage and cunning alike.

They spoke not just to brag or commemorate but to affirm—a recognition that though they each bore burdens unique unto themselves, they were bound by a common cause, a tapestry of fates interwoven through shared purpose and kinship alike. They, indeed, were the Knights of St. Michael's Order. Laughter intermingled with serious nods as tales were shared - moments when comedy cut through the stress like a blade through butter amid turmoil or instances where quietness created room for contemplation beyond what words could convey.

And as they exchanged their tales—an unspoken understanding grew amongst them; that these relics were more than mere objects. They were symbols—each artifact representing not just divine favor but personal metamorphosis; tokens earned through trial and adjustment alike.

As each hero prepared for their impending union, their minds focused on unwritten futures. They remained unaware of eyes that watched from afar and saw not hope but opportunity in their gathering.

Papal State Territory, Rome, 842 A.D.

In Rome's underbelly, where whispers slithered like serpents through ancient corridors and ambitions brewed darker than any poison known to man or god alike, there lurked figures cloaked in malice. They gathered around a table etched with symbols that writhed beneath flickering candlelight—each mark an oath to powers unfathomable and fearsome.

A figure emerged from shadows' embrace—a woman whose eyes held neither warmth nor mercy but instead burned with ambition's unquenchable flame. She traced her fingers over the table's surface—a caress that seemed almost loving were it not for its underlying cruelty.

"They gather relics," she spoke, her voice devoid of any tremor despite speaking of forces that could rend souls from bodies or call down stars from heaven itself. "But they do not comprehend what they truly hold."

Her confidants—a motley collection of sorcerers and schemers—listened intently as she unveiled plans conceived in darkness's heart; machinations designed to twist fates and subvert destinies towards ends only she fully envisioned.

"Let them come together," she continued, "for it is in unity that they shall reveal their true power—and it is then we shall strike; tearing apart bonds forged in trust and turning dreams into nightmares."

Her words slithered across cobblestones like venom seeping into the earth—each syllable a harbinger of calamity yet to unfold; promises not merely spoken but etched into the very air breathed by those present—an oath is sworn upon night's cloak and sealed by malice deep-rooted as Rome's foundations themselves.

Above ground, where citizens walked oblivious to machinations unfolding beneath their feet—the sky seemed to shudder at intentions now set in motion, clouds swirling as if mirroring turmoil within human hearts below...

ACT THREE

"As far back as I can remember I have unconsciously referred to the experiences of a previous state of existence."

- Henry David Thoreau

CHAPTER
ELEVEN

Byzantine Empire, Sicily, 835 A.D.

The ancestral home of Nykronus held the relics and documents of countless secrets, each forged into the stone walls and hidden within the tapestries that embellished the chambers. On this night, in particular, flickering flames from a single fireplace fought against the darkness, casting long, trembling shadows that seemed to dance as if they were alive.

Nykronus stood beside a bed where his father, Felix, a revered figure within the Order of St. Michael, lay draped in linens that seemed far too large for his atrophied body. The air was filled with the scent of medicinal herbs and the feeling of impending loss. Nykronus's hands tugged at the sides of his tunic, a rollercoaster of emotions at war within him as he watched his father's chest rise and fall in shallow, wearisome breaths.

The old man's eyes fluttered open, their once vibrant hue dimmed by pain yet still lighted with determination. With a feeble gesture, he signaled Nykronus closer.

"Nykronus," his voice was no more than a rasping whisper, "the time has come for truths to be revealed."

Nykronus leaned in, his ear close to his father's lips. He could feel the heat of fever radiating from his skin.

"The Malefic Assembly," his father continued, "their shadows are spreading across our world. They plot to unleash darkness upon us all."

A chill crept up Nykronus's spine as he absorbed each word. The Malefic Assembly—a name spoken only in hushed tones among the highest ranks of the Order—was a gathering of sorcerers and malcontents who sought to overturn the natural order through forbidden magic.

His father grasped Nykronus's hand with surprising strength. "You must commit your life to the Order, my son. Only through St. Michael's guidance can their monstrous schemes be thwarted."

Nykronus nodded solemnly. "I am ready, Father," he said firmly. "I will uphold our sacred charge."

A look of profound relief softened the old man's features as he sank back against his pillows. His gaze drifted to a mezzanine where relics and symbols of their Order stood vigil—swords that had struck down evil, shields that had protected the innocent, trophies of conquests, and tributes to the brothers and sisters Magus Felix fought alongside.

With exhausting effort, he lifted his head slightly and locked eyes with Nykronus again. "There is one more thing," he breathed out, each word seeming to draw upon the last vestiges of his strength. "*Pugio Mysticus Amoris*... it is not merely a legend."

Nykronus listened intently as his father described an ancient weapon—a dagger forged with divine intent and bound by sacred vows. The *Dagger of Love*.

"It is said that within its blade lies the key to unlocking St. Valentine's power—a symbol of sacrifice and love that holds power beyond comprehension. It was a blade owned by a jailer's daughter. St. Valentine cured her blindness before he was executed."

His words trailed off into silence as he laid his head back down. The grip on Nykronus's hand slackened but did not release; it was as though, in this final moment, there remained an unspoken covenant between them—a passing of responsibility from one guardian to another.

With labored breaths growing ever fainter, Nykronus's father whispered one last declaration—a name shrouded in mystery that would become a beacon for Nykronus's path forward.

"Seek... seek it out... before it falls into shadow..." His voice was carried away into silence as his chest stilled and his soul departed from the earth to the heavens above.

Nykronus remained still for a long moment after his father's passing—alone now with his legacy and a newfound purpose burning within him like an unquenchable flame. The shadows cast by relics seemed to bow in reverence as if acknowledging the weight now placed upon Nykronus's shoulders.

Outside, beyond the stone walls of their home, stars shone brightly against the canvas of night—a silent testament to the eternal struggle between light and dark. And somewhere out there lay a relic steeped in love and sacrifice, waiting for its protector to emerge.

With dawn approaching and destiny calling, Nykronus knew there was no turning back from the path ahead.

The ancient chapel of the Order marinated in history, its walls evocative with the echoes of countless vows taken by those who had walked its holy grounds. Stained, intricate, colorful glass windows bathed the interior in an array of light that danced upon the stone floor and the solemn faces of the gathered knights. Each ray seemed to bear witness to the gloominess of the ceremony unfolding within.

Nykronus stood at the altar, a lonely figure amidst the artifacts of power that surrounded him. Swords with blades that had tasted battle, shields scarred yet resolute—each a testament to the Order's relentless fight against darkness. He felt their silent watch, a reminder of the path he was about to walk.

The chapel hummed with low chatter as members of the Order filled every pew, their presence a mix of aged young and old. All eyes were upon Nykronus, whose gaze remained fixed ahead, his expression masked with determination.

Quiet fell over the crowd as the Grand Magus stepped forward, his gait measured and deliberate. His robes whispered across the floor, the only sound in an otherwise silent room. He raised his hands, and the silence deepened as if even air itself dared not disturb.

"Nykronus," he began, his voice resonating within the stone confines. "You stand before us ready to take the oath that binds your soul to our cause. Are you prepared to uphold our values and mission?"

Nykronus looked into the eldest mage's eyes, his voice steady as he replied. "I am Grand Magus."

The Grand Magus continued, "Repeat after me: I solemnly vow to uphold the tenets of St. Michael's Order."

"I solemnly vow to uphold the tenets of St. Michael's Order," Nykronus echoed.

"To stand against darkness wherever it may rise."

"To stand against darkness wherever it may rise."

"To protect the innocent and wield my power with justice."

"To protect the innocent and wield my power with justice."

"And to seek out evil in all its forms and vanquish it from this world."

"And to seek out evil in all its forms and vanquish it from this world."

The words lingered in the air like a sacred incantation as Nykronus spoke them, binding him everlastingly to his chosen path.

Two knights approached as he finished his vow, each bearing a small chest. They set it upon the altar with reverence before stepping back into line with their brethren.

The Grand Magus opened the chest to reveal its contents: a mantle emblazoned with St. Michael's insignia—the sword and scales—and an amulet made of silver that sparkled even in the soft light.

"With this mantle," intoned the Grand Master as he draped it over Nykronus's shoulders, "you carry upon you our trust and commitment."

He then lifted the amulet from its velvet cradle. "And with this amulet," he said while placing it around Nykronus's neck, "you bear our legacy—our hopes for a future free from shadow. Your father's legacy."

Nykronus felt their weight settle upon him—a physical manifestation of his promise to his father, Felix.

With the sacred symbols of duty and honor, Nykronus turned to face his brothers and sisters of arms. Their looks were resolute. Some bore scars from battles past, while others held innocence untested by war. Yet all shared a common bond—their oath to uphold the light of St. Michael.

The ceremony drew nearer to its end as attendants extinguished candles one by one until only daylight remained, streaming through stained-glass windows that cast multicolored patterns upon stone statues of saints and martyrs.

In this sacred room, the Grand Magus approached Nykronus once more, this time privately at an alcove set aside for counsel.

"Nykronus," said the elder mage softly yet firmly. "Your journey begins under threatening omen. You must tread carefully; enemies, both seen and unseen, lay in wait for those who carry our charge."

Nykronus met his gaze squarely. "I understand," he replied simply.

"The Malefic Assembly is but one threat among many," continued the Grand Master, each word laden with significance. "Their reach is long, and their intentions are poisoned by malice."

Nykronus's jaw set in determination as he absorbed these warnings; they did little to quench the fire within him—a fire kindled by his father's last words and fueled by his own stiff heart.

"You must also seek out *Pugio Mysticus Amoris*," the Grand Master said gravely. Its power is compelling; in the wrong hands, dark forces can use it to do the unthinkable."

Nykronus inclined his head to acknowledge the Grand Master's words, a solemn pledge forming on his lips. "I shall locate it," Nykronus avowed.

The Grand Magus's hand came to rest upon the young warrior's shoulder, an action that conveyed not merely encouragement but also the passing of a sacred duty from elder protector to fledgling defender.

"Go now," he said finally. "Fulfill your destiny—and may St. Michael guide your soul true."

In the center of the Order's grand library, with its towering shelves burdened by centuries of knowledge, Nykronus's gaze drifted over the warren of tomes. The room smelled of old leather and parchment, suggesting hidden truths and antique enlightenment. High above, small windows allowed tiny beams of light to pierce the dimness, each ray a magnifying glass illuminating the dust particles that shimmied in their warmth.

The historian of the Order, an elderly woman named Theodora, stood across from Nykronus at a heavy oak table strewn with texts. Her fingers, gnarled by time yet precise in their movements, turned the pages of an illuminated manuscript until she came upon an image that caused Nykronus to lean in closer.

"Behold," Theodora's soft voice carried the weight of unspoken mysteries, "the *Pugio Mysticus Amoris*."

Nykronus examined the illustration—a dagger with a blade that seemed to shimmer even within the confines of ink and lambskin. The hilt was fancy, crafted with symbols of love and sacrifice interwoven into its design.

"The dagger's legend is intertwined with Saint Valentine himself," Theodora continued. "It is said that on the eve of his execution, Valentine touched this blade to the heart of his jailor's blind daughter and whispered a vow of protection over all she would love truly. Her love was pure and untainted. It is said the grace of God spared her from her blindness. She begged her father to help him escape execution, but there was nothing he could do."

Nykronus's attention was captured as Theodora detailed the profound power infused within the Dagger, its mysteries yet to be uncovered.

"The Dagger's allure has beckoned many," Theodora said, her eyes clouded by remembrance. "Knights and seekers have journeyed far, drawn by tales of its power. Alas, most have faltered; some were led astray by false hopes while others succumbed to darkness lurking within their own hearts."

A shiver traced Nykronus's spine at these words. He understood then that this quest would test him like no other—that finding the Dagger was not merely a matter of strength or wit but one that demanded purity of spirit.

"Your journey will be unabridged with danger," Theodora warned, her voice lowering as if to confine their conversation away from prying ears. "The Malefic Assembly seeks what you seek—they understand not love but only desire for dominion."

Nykronus nodded once, silently acknowledging the risks and virtues of his cause. With each word spoken by Theodora, he felt his purpose morph further into something unbreakable.

The historian watched him for a long moment before carefully closing the ancient manuscript. "Prepare well," she advised. "And may your courage reflect the purity of your quest."

The morning sun stretched its gleaming fingers across the fortress of the Order, washing the ancient stones in a light that promised new beginnings. Nykronus stood at the edge of the fence, his eyes tracing the horizon that lay boundless and uncharted before him. The air was crisp and melancholy with the scent of wet grass and the smokey embers of last night's fires.

Beside him, Wulfstan the Steadfast shifted in his Temporal Knight gear, the armor's golden hue reflecting the sun's early rays. The insignia upon his chest—a wolf caught mid-howl—seemed to come alive in this light. He was a figure from another time, his red hair and massive frame a testament to countless battles waged and won.

"Are you prepared?" Nykronus asked, his voice steady despite the storm of thoughts raging within.

Wulfstan turned, his face set in a grin that belied the gravity of their mission. "Ready? I was born for this. Anything to honor Magus Felix's dying wish."

Nykronus couldn't help but mirror Wulfstan's infectious smile. The young Temporal Knight exuded a fervor that matched the bright flames dancing in the nearby torches. Nykronus's father had always spoken highly of Wulfstan, and there was no one he would trust more to accompany him on this dangerous mission. As they grasped each other's forearms in a warrior's grip, a silent understanding passed between them, solidifying their commitment to the task.

Wulfstan's skills as a Temporal Knight would be invaluable on their journey. Mastery of time-related magic was a rare gift that could turn the tide of their quest. His understanding of temporal flows and his ability to navigate them were tools as potent as any blade or spell.

Together, they turned to regard their assembled companions—a motley crew drawn from far-flung corners of the world, each bearing unparalleled talents and bound by a shared purpose. The group stood ready, a fusion of tradition and innovation.

Wulfstan clapped Nykronus on the shoulder. "We face peril," he said, "but also glory beyond measure."

Nykronus nodded. "Aye," he agreed. "We walk into legend."

As they descended from the fence to join their waiting companions, Nykronus felt the weight of his father's legacy settle upon him like a mantle. Each step he took resonated with purpose.

The fortress's gates groaned before them, revealing a world bathed in the sun's embrace. They embarked on their quest, not to the sound of trumpets, but with resolute steps that carried them into an odyssey shrouded in peril and uncertainty.

Yet as they crossed the threshold into the wilds beyond, it was not fear that filled Nykronus's heart but rather a blossoming sense of confederation—with Wulfstan at his side and their fellowship at their back, they ventured forth to seize destiny by its throat.

When a veiled figure emerged from the tree line, the morning sun had barely begun to crest the distant mountains, casting long shadows across the dew-laden grass. Shrouded in a cloak that seemed to drink in the light, the figure watched the fortress of the Order of St. Michael from a distance. The Order within was oblivious to this silent observer whose presence was as sinister as it was concealed.

Nykronus and Wulfstan had already turned their backs on the rising sun, leading their small band towards their ambiguous fate. They were unaware of the malevolent gaze that followed them and the dark machinations that turned like cogs in the shadows.

The veiled figure's eyes glinted with malice, each movement calculated and precise. With fingers nimble as a thief's, they reached into the folds of their cloak and withdrew a small object, holding it up to catch the light—a coin emblazoned with a sigil that whispered of darkness and treachery.

In an instant, as if alerted by some unseen signal, the figure melted back into the forest's embrace, leaving no trace of their presence save for the coin they had left perched upon a stone—a silent herald of the Malefic Assembly's knowledge and intent.

As the sun broke entirely, casting away the remnants of shadows, Nykronus halted mid-stride. An inexplicable chill scurried down his spine, causing him to scan their surroundings with sharpened focus. He felt a prickling sensation at the back of his neck—an animalistic warning that something was awry.

Wulfstan noticed Nykronus's sudden pause and depicted his vigilance. Their eyes met briefly, and wordless communication flowed between them. Trust your instincts.

"Something wrong?" Wulfstan asked in hushed tones, his hand unconsciously resting upon his sword hilt.

Nykronus shook his head slowly but did not respond immediately. Instead, he strode forward and picked up the coin that seemed out of place against nature's color wheel. As he examined it, recognition dawned within him—a sinking realization of what it represented.

He clenched his fist around it tightly as if by crushing it, he could crush its threatening significance. Turning back to face his companions, who watched him with a mix of curiosity and concern, Nykronus felt resolve to harden within him like forged steel.

"We are not alone," he announced with quiet intensity. "The Malefic Assembly is aware of our quest."

His words hung heavy in the air. The faces around him paled slightly at their implications but then set into gestures of fierce spiritedness.

Wulfstan stepped forward. "Then let us not tarry," he said grimly. "We have much to do and little time for mind games."

Nykronus agreed and released his grip on the coin, letting it fall to the earth again.

"Let this serve not as a warning," Nykronus declared as he met each pair of eyes, "but as fuel for our fight. We walk a righteous path—one that we will defend against all threats."

With these words bolstering their spirits against an enemy unseen yet indisputably near, they set forth once more on their journey. Each step took them further from safety but closer to fulfilling Nykronus's father's last wish and preserving the noble cause they all championed.

TWELVE

In a secluded grove, the flare of a campfire cast much-needed warmth upon the faces of Elan's assembled team. The fire's warmth wrapped around them like a veil as each member found consolation in their own silent trance. Isolde's fingers brushed against the lustrous surface of Jupiter's Bolt, tucked the gem securely within a fold of her cloak before she settled against a tree.

With its storm-born origin, the gem seemed to emit a thunderous energy that tussled with the surrounding woods. Isolde's eyes lingered on it, her gaze as sharp as the green that flecked her irises. This gem was not merely another relic; it was the heart of their mission, the key to piercing veils unseen and binding what was sundered.

A frigid breeze whispered through the copse, its icy tendrils threading through the flames' heat and weaving an undercurrent of unease that permeated the air. The group's laughter had dimmed with the setting sun, leaving in its wake an undemocratic quietness.

Elan shifted uncomfortably on his makeshift seat, feeling the disquiet gnaw at his insides. He caught Isolde's eye; she returned his glance with a tight nod, her lips pressed into a thin line. There was an unspoken understanding that something was amiss—a thread pulling too taut amongst them.

Wulfstan leaned forward, his gaze scanning their perimeter with habitual alertness. "Restlessness stirs in our midst," he spoke, more to himself than to any of them. "A specter of doubt haunts our resolve."

Ivar Ghostcloak, perched on the opposite side of the fire from Isolde, let out a quiet huff—a sound that could have been amusement or scorn. His eyes remained hidden beneath his hood but were undoubtedly alert and watching.

Isolde closed her eyes for a moment and took a deep breath. They cut through the dim light with precision when she opened them again. She had always been attuned to the unspoken words carried by music and whispers alike. Now, she felt those silent chords of discord strumming through their group.

As the night deepened around them and watch shifts were taken up in silence, each member wrestled with their thoughts—their faith in one another, an ember that refused to die but struggled against an encroaching iniquity. Suspicion hung heavily in the atmosphere as if awaiting a single spark to burst into flame.

Moonlight filtered through the leaves, casting dappled shadows across the campsite. The team had settled into a tempo of rest, their breaths even in the stillness of the night. Isolde, her senses honed by countless nights under open skies, slept with a lightness that belied her surroundings.

Ivar Ghostcloak's silhouette merged with the darkness as he inched towards Isolde's resting place. He crept forward with deliberate precision, placing each foot delicately to prevent the slightest noise from rousing the sleeping bard. The scar on his cheek was a pale streak against his otherwise shadowed face, and his eyes reflected a glint of moonlight as they fixed on the gem's hiding spot.

Isolde's eyelids fluttered at the disturbance in the air—a subtle change only one as attuned as her could sense. As Ivar's fingers grazed the edge of her cloak, her eyes snapped open, piercing through the night directly into his.

For a suspended moment, their gazes locked—hers filled with shocked realization, his with a desperate determination. The stillness shattered like glass.

"*Vade retro, Satana!* What are you up to, Ivar?" Isolde's voice cut through the silence like a knife. She rolled away from Ivar's grasp, snatching up the gem and putting distance between them.

Ivar stood up quickly, backing away as if her accusation stung him physically. "Isolde," he began, but she cut him off.

"Your intent is clear as day," she said, her voice rising. "*Cinaedus*! You dare steal from those you claim to ally with?"

Ivar's face was a mask of mutiny now; whatever remorse he might have felt was buried beneath layers of resolve and anger. "I seek justice for my brother," he spat out. "The gem is but a means to an end."

Isolde stood firm, Jupiter's Bolt clutched in her hand. Its surface was aglow with a fierce light that seemed to pulse with her heartbeat's rage. Her stance left no room for doubt; she would not let Ivar's betrayal pass unchallenged.

Elan's instincts snapped into action, propelling him to his feet instantly. His hand wrapped around the hilt of *Winterstar* with a fierce grip, ready for battle. The firelight cast sharp shadows on his features, transforming them into a chiseled mask of determination and power. "Ivar," he growled, voice low and commanding. "Explain yourself."

The others quickly formed a semi-circle around Ivar, their faces twisted in confusion and anger. Wulfstan's jaw clenched tightly, his muscles straining beneath his skin in anticipation.

"I...I had no choice," Ivar stammered, his voice shaking under their intense stares. He glanced down at his tingling hand, still reeling from the near touch of Jupiter's Bolt. "They forced me."

"Who forced you!" Wulfstan shouted.

Isolde stepped forward, her expression softening just slightly. "Tell us the truth, Ivar," she urged gently. "The darkness cannot hide from those who are willing to see."

With a trembling breath, Ivar lifted his gaze to meet theirs once more. "It was the Malefic Assembly," he confessed, the scar on his cheek as a stark reminder of past battles. "They took my brother Leif and sent him on a mission to retrieve that cursed dagger. They promised me they could bring him back to life if I helped them."

A flash of bitterness crossed his face as he continued, "I do not serve the Order. They let my brother die under their watch. I serve only myself and my own desires. And now...I have endangered us all."

An uproar erupted among the group, each member struggling to process this betrayal mixed with empathy for Ivar's pain. Isolde's eyes held a glimmer of understanding amidst her disappointment.

"They seek the same relics we possess," Ivar went on, desperation creeping into his voice as he unburdened himself of the secret. "I thought...if I could just give them what they want..."

Wulfstan growled with rage. "You would trade our mission and our lives for your own gain?" His accusation hung heavy in the air.

Elan stepped between them, his hand raised for silence. His face remained stoic as he grappled with this new information, the weight of leadership weighing heavily on him.

"I only sought to bring back my brother," Ivar whispered, his eyes searching each team member before finally dropping to the ground in shame. "But now I see...I have put us all in danger."

A tense silence descended upon the group, each grappling with mixed emotions: betrayal, anger, understanding. Trust was frayed but not completely broken. Despite the strain on their trust caused by Ivar's betrayal, the group's bond remained unbroken. Their shared experiences, sacrifices, and commitment to a common cause had forged deep ties that couldn't be easily severed. They understood Ivar's misguided actions were driven by love for his brother and a desire for revenge. This empathy, along with the gravity of their mission and the need for unity against the forces of darkness, allowed them to maintain hope for reconciliation and keep their trust from unraveling completely. The success of their mission now hung on a delicate balance between human frailty and determination, and Elan knew that how they responded to this revelation would define not only their quest but also their loyalty as allies—and perhaps even as friends.

As the first blush of dawn stretched across the sky, a hesitant sun pierced the night's darkness, casting the party in a soft, melancholic light. The revelation of betrayal and the weight of their quest marked their faces with sorrow and disbelief. They stood, a tableau of shadows against the dawning day, finding no solace in the promise of the new light.

Ivar, embodying betrayal, distanced himself from the group, his youthful face marred by the depth of his treachery and fear. His hands trembled as he drew two slim daggers, their blades coated with a lethal toxin, symbolizing his desperation and final resolve. Ivar stood apart from the group, his shoulders hunched and his gaze downcast, unable to meet the eyes of those he had betrayed. The weight of his actions seemed to bear down on him, a physical manifestation of the guilt and shame that coursed through his veins. His once proud posture was now diminished, his confidence shattered by realizing the damage he had wrought. The distance between him and his former allies was not merely physical but emotional, a chasm carved by the knife of betrayal that he had wielded against them. At that moment, Ivar embodied the very essence of treachery, a living reminder of the fragility of trust and the consequences of misplaced loyalty.

The group's heated discussion on trust and justice was shattered as Ivar, in a moment of despair, lunged toward Nykronus with the poisoned blades, intent on a drastic final act of murder. His eyes, filled with a tumult of emotions, locked with theirs, signaling a farewell filled with remorse.

Isolde, with reflexes honed by countless battles, intercepted Ivar's charge. The confrontation was brief but fatal; her actions, driven by the instinct to protect, ended Ivar's life. He fell to the ground, a silent testament to the tragedy of their intertwined fates.

A collective gasp cut through the air as the group processed the abrupt turn of events. Wulfstan's shout of dismay echoed unanswered, and Isolde turned away, a single tear trailing down her face in mourning. Elan, paralyzed by the scene, displayed the agony of their collective loss—a stark reminder of the Malefic Assembly's looming shadow.

In the wake of this somber moment, Nykronus stepped forward. His face, grooved with ancient wisdom and unspoken sorrows, commanded the attention of the grieving assembly.

"The Assembly's roots extend beyond the reaches of history, entwined with the ancient cult of Mithras, and now guided by the malevolent Femina Perfida," Nykronus declared, his voice steady amidst the storm of their despair. "We face a formidable enemy."

He unveiled an ancient scroll, introducing the mythical Dagger of Love, rumored to be forged with St. Lazarus of Bethany's blood and said to wield the power of resurrection combined with St. Valentine's essence. The revelation of such a potent artifact, coupled with the mission to retrieve St. Valentine's heart from Terni, imbued their quest with a new sense of urgency and purpose.

With a solemn ritual, Nykronus transformed Wulfstan's dragon tooth into a magical compass, its emerald light pointing unwaveringly toward their destiny. The act served as a beacon of hope, knitting the fragments of their resolve into a unified determination.

As they watched the compass settle, a renewed commitment and clarity emerged among them. The path ahead was clear: to secure St. Valentine's relic before it could fall into the wrong hands.

Once a place of camaraderie and laughter, the grove now held a solemn vibe tainted by the echo of betrayal. Yet, as the sun rose higher, its rays seemed to cleanse the site of its sorrowful past.

Elan stood at the edge of the clearing, his eyes fixed on the horizon where light vanquished shadow. The night's events lingered in his mind, but a waned fire within him came with the new day. He turned to face his companions, each shouldering their own silent burdens.

"We leave this place not as we entered," Elan said, his voice cutting through the morning's stillness. "We carry heavy hearts, but our purpose has never been clearer."

Elan's gaze drifted to the horizon, his thoughts torn between his duty to the Order and his burning desire to find Kaira. The weight of his responsibilities pressed upon him was a constant reminder of his sacrifices and the battles yet to come. But even as he grappled with the enormity of his task, his mind kept circling back to Kaira, the love they had shared, and the future that had been stolen from them. He could still see her face in his mind's eye, her smile a beacon of hope in the darkness that threatened to engulf him. Elan knew that his role within the Order was crucial, that the fate of the world rested on their shoulders, but he also knew that he would never be truly whole until he found her, until he could hold her in his arms once more and promise her that everything would be alright.

Isolde looked Elan in his eyes, the sun intensifying the green pigment in her eyes, with agreement, her fingers distractedly tracing over her lute. Jupiter's Bolt was humming in unison with her pleasant strums.

Wulfstan gathered his golden armor and strapped it on with undaunted motions. He looked to each group member with an unspoken promise to guard them against any storm they might face.

As they prepared to depart from the grove, a soft breeze stirred the leaves around them, carrying the sweet scent of renewal. The team moved as one, their steps firm upon the earth as they left behind the site of Ivar's fall.

A solitary silhouette emerged from the austere backdrop, initially blending with the ascetic environment. Upon closer inspection, the figure appeared to be a nun, scarcely beyond her second decade. Her manifestation was sudden and unforeseen, startling in the tranquil landscape.

"I am Sister Livia," she said, her voice imbued with a gentle strength. "I've come to guide you through these lands and offer my aid in your quest."

Livia's attire epitomized monastic modesty: a tunic of undyed wool fell in simple lines down to her feet, overlaid by a scapular signifying her dedication to a life of service and prayer. A plain-colored mantle wrapped around her shoulders, warding off the chill of the stone walls, its fabric whispering of her vow of poverty and the practicalities demanded by her vocation.

Livia may have seemed an unassuming presence to those who judge by appearances alone, perhaps easily overlooked. Her features were homely, her stature neither commanding nor diminutive, yet there was an unmistakable aura of resolve. It was not the flamboyance of warriors or the ostentatious wisdom of scholars that marked her significance; instead, Livia carried within her an unwavering faith and a dedication to the divine that bestowed an inner strength as formidable as it was quiet.

Elan exchanged a glance with his companions before stepping forward. "We appreciate your offer, Sister Livia, but how did you know of our quest?"

Livia's eyes sparkled with a hint of mischief. "The divine works in mysterious ways, my friend. Let's just say that your journey has not gone unnoticed by those who serve the light."

Isolde, her curiosity piqued, asked, "What can you tell us about the challenges we face ahead?"

"The path before you is filled with danger," Livia replied, her tone growing severe. "But I have knowledge of these lands that may prove useful in navigating the paths ahead."

Wulfstan grumbled as he looked at Livia with annoyance and impatience. "Are you a warrior like us?" He asked.

Livia chuckled softly. "Not in the traditional sense, red beard. But I believe that faith can be a weapon as powerful as any blade, and I am ready to stand with you against the darkness."

As the group continued their journey, Livia fell into step beside Elan. "Your quest is a noble one," she said, her voice filled with conviction. "But I sense that you carry a great burden, a personal mission that weighs heavily upon your heart."

Elan was taken aback by Livia's insight.

Livia placed a comforting hand on Elan's shoulder. "Have faith, Elan. The divine tapestry is complex, woven with threads of fate and choice. One that may yet guide you to the answers you seek."

CHAPTER

THIRTEEN

Rietti, Duchy of Spoleto, Frankish Kingdom, 842 A.D.

The chaotic streets of Rietti burst with color and sound, an unexpected backdrop to the mighty purpose that drove Elan and his companions. Banners shook in the breeze, and musicians played as villagers and travelers gathered to celebrate the festival. Laughter mingled with the melodies of lutes and flutes, the scent of roasting meats and sweet pastries abundant in the air.

As Elan's eyes scanned the bustling surroundings, a pang of guilt hit him. How could he enjoy the lively atmosphere on such a crucial mission? Elan's thoughts drifted to Kaira, and he couldn't help but wonder how she would have reacted to the vibrant festivities surrounding him. He could almost picture her, her eyes sparkling with excitement as she dragged him into the throng of dancers, her laughter ringing out above the music. Kaira had always been the more adventurous of the two, and her zest for life and love of new experiences perfectly complemented Elan's more reserved nature. She would have reveled in the sights, sounds, and tastes of the festival, her curiosity and joy infectious to all around her.

His hand instinctively reached for the Mazza family heirloom in his pocket, a constant reminder of his duty and the weight of responsibility on his shoulders. Yet, a small part of him couldn't help but be swept up in the joyous energy around him. He had to stay focused, but it was becoming increasingly difficult with each passing moment.

Isolde, with her bard's divination, sensed opportunity amid the parties. Her seductive green eyes scanned the crowd for familiar faces and conversations that might hint at Kaira's whereabouts. She adjusted her braids, a black waterfall down her back, and straightened her posture.

"Let's split up," she suggested to the group, her voice cutting through the noise easily. "We'll cover more ground that way."

Wulfstan grunted in agreement. "Keep your eyes open," he cautioned. "We know not if our enemies have eyes here."

Sister Livia clasped her hands together, her plain habit making her almost invisible among the extravagant attire of festival-goers. "May providence guide us," she whispered.

Livia stood a short distance from the group, her hands clasped in front of her and her plain habit blending seamlessly into the background. Despite her unassuming appearance, there was a quiet strength about her. Her eyes, a deep and soulful brown, held a wisdom that seemed to stretch beyond her years, and when she spoke, her voice carried a gentle authority that commanded attention. It was clear that Sister Livia was no ordinary nun but rather a woman who had dedicated her life to a higher calling, one that had led her to this very moment to stand with Elan and his companions in their fight against the darkness.

With a shared look of ascertainment, they mingled with the crowd. Isolde approached a group of locals clustered around a storyteller, her ears perceptive to tales that might bear clues. She let her company blend into the flock, appearing as another festival-goer mesmerized by ancient legends and juicy gossip.

She drifted closer to a group deep in conversation about pilgrims passing through Rietti—pilgrims who spoke of strange manifestations and missing persons in their travels. Isolde's heart rate increased; this was just the lead she hoped to find.

As she listened intently, a woman with silver hair caught Isolde's attention from across the square. The woman's gaze persisted on Isolde before she turned away, slipping through the crowd with a glamour that belied haste. Isolde's instincts told her there was more to this woman than met the eye—perhaps even a connection to Kaira's fate.

Isolde darted through the crowd with astonishing agility, her mind ablaze with determination. The pulsing lights and pounding music fueled her as she chased after the mysterious woman.

Isolde moved through the crowd, her ears tuned to the catchy voice of an elderly storyteller perched on a rickety stage. His face was punchy with the wit of years, and his eyes held a spark that spoke of long-forgotten tales. As she approached, his story flapped like a banner in the wind, capturing the curiosity of all who passed.

"Twenty winters ago," he began, his voice rising above the din, "a woman of mystery graced our village. She came without warning, her presence as sudden as a storm over the Apennines."

Isolde edged closer, her instinct nuzzling that this was no ordinary tale.

"The villagers," he continued, "they spoke of her beauty, ethereal as if not of this world. But her eyes held the truth of her burden—eyes that had seen worlds beyond our reach."

The crowd gasped with interest, hanging on his every word. Isolde felt a tingle travel down her spine.

"She spoke in enigmas," the storyteller said with a heart-stopping pause, "clues jumbled with fate. 'When the time comes for the heart to seek its other half,' she said, 'look to where angels dream and demons weep.'"

Isolde's breath caught in her throat.

"The mysterious woman," he went on, "left as suddenly as she arrived, but her words lingered like morning mist upon the Tiber. Some say she was an oracle; others claim she was a witch."

Isolde stepped forward, unable to contain her curiosity. "Did she leave anything behind? Are there any... noticeable clues?" Her voice was steady despite her racing heart.

The storyteller peered at Isolde through squinting eyes as if measuring her worthiness of what he was about to disclose.

"Aye," he whispered, leaning in so only she could hear. "A pendant —a piece shaped like half a heart. She entrusted it to a young girl with fire in her spirit and sorrow in her eyes. She returned this girl to her father, a nobleman living just outside town."

Isolde's mind was whooshing with possibilities, and she had to know more.

"Who was this girl?" Isolde pressed.

The storyteller's lips curved into a knowing smile as he scanned the crowd again.

"Ah, my dear," he said with a glitter in his eye, "*that* is a story for another time."

The outskirts of Rietti unfolded into expansive territory, the lush greenery a crisp contrast to the busy festival they had left behind. Elan's gaze swept over the luscious hills as the team approached a nobleman's villa, its walls washed in a warm pigment by the setting sun. The marble facade promised tales hidden within its tranquil stones.

The nobleman, a figure of muscularity and gravitas, welcomed them into a sitting room rich with artworks that whispered of ancient magnificence and countless battles. His silver hair rested on his shoulders, and his eyes told stories of a man who missed little.

"You seek information of a woman of mystery," he began without preamble. "Twenty winters have not dulled the memory of her passage through these lands."

Elan leaned forward, every muscle tensed like a bowstring. Beside him, Wulfstan stood immovable as if carved from stone while Isolde's gaze flashed with eager interest.

"She came to us during times troubled by Byzantine strife," the nobleman recounted. "A healer to some, a seer to others. Her counsel calmed many a restless heart. I will never forget her for what she did for my family. I rewarded her for bringing my daughter back to us after we were separated during a storm—aided her in her travels."

"And where did she go?" Isolde inquired, her voice laced with urgency.

The nobleman waved towards an aged map unfurled across a cherrywood desk. His finger traced a path winding from Rietti to Benevento. "She sought solace in pilgrimage," he revealed. "I pointed her to this route; it leads to sacred places, shrines where one might speak to God or... other entities."

Elan studied the map, etching every turn and marker into his mind's eye. "Did she seek anything in particular on this pilgrimage?" he asked.

"A question she kept close to her heart," the nobleman mused. "But she mentioned 'the place where angels dream and demons weep.' I knew not what she meant then, nor do I now."

A spark ignited within Elan's chest—hope. The nobleman's words echoed a storyteller's, bridging past and present.

"Thanks," Elan said with genuine appreciativeness. "You helped more than you know."

As they rose to leave, the nobleman fixed them with warning. "Take heed on your journey," he cautioned. "The road is riddled with more than just physical dangers."

Elan felt a chill run down his spine at the nobleman's words, a sense of unease settling in the pit of his stomach. He had faced countless dangers in his time as a Marine, had stared death in the face and come out the other side, but the thought of the unknown perils ahead filled him with a new dread. He knew that the road to finding Kaira would be physically and mentally difficult, but hearing it spoken aloud made it all the more real. Elan took a deep breath, steeling himself for the journey, knowing he would stop at nothing to find the woman he loved and bring her home safely.

Underneath the leaves of an ancient oak tree, Elan and his party assembled in a compact circle. The grand villa of the nobleman stood proud in the background, its marble pillars towering over the gang assembled before it. The dim light of a single lantern, casting contour and underlining their earnest expressions, threw their faces into bright alleviation. The night aria was firm with tension and implications as they gathered in secrecy under the watchful gaze of the dignified structure behind them.

Elan derived the route to Benevento on the map with his finger, the others leaning in. The clues they had collected lay sprinkled before them like pieces of a heavenly puzzle, each waiting to find its rightful place.

"The mysterious woman, she is your Kaira, right?" Sister Olivia turned to Elan.

"It has to be. There's no doubt about it." Elan closed his eyes, filled with hope.

"Kaira spoke of angels dreaming and demons weeping," Isolde mused. "The nobleman repeated those very words. There must be a connection."

Wulfstan's face twisted in confusion, "Is it a puzzle or a veiled message of pain and loss?" he wondered aloud, torn between excitement and apprehension at the possible significance behind the riddle.

Elan folded his arms, considering their words. "The pilgrimage route—do you think it's literal or another puzzle?"

Isolde tilted her head, considering. "I believe it's both. Pilgrimage routes are drenched in spiritual intention, and if Kaira was seeking something sacred..."

Sister Livia interjected softly, "Pilgrimages often lead to enlightenment or discovery. It could be that she sought an answer or an artifact of great power."

"Perhaps she was searching for a way home," Nykronus added.

The team pondered this in silence for a moment. The concept that Kaira's evanescence was coupled with such a pilgrimage was both intimidating and hopeful.

"The route to Benevento passes through shrines and holy places," Elan said with renewed focus. "Could one of these be 'where angels dream and demons weep'?"

Wulfstan ran a hand through his red hair. "If we are to follow this path, we must prepare for what lies ahead. It will not be just our feet that are tested but our spirits as well."

Isolde nodded, "We'll need to understand the local lore and traditions," she added. "Knowledge may prove as valuable as any blade."

Isolde's green eyes flashed with a fierce determination that bordered on stubbornness. She had always been stubborn, her will as unyielding as the steel of her blade, and once she set her mind to something, there was no turning back. This tenacity had seen her through countless battles and hardships, which drove her to see this mission through to the end, no matter the cost.

Elan folded the map with care, slipping it into his pocket. Their course was set; they would follow the pilgrim's path to Benevento.

As they stood up to leave their temporary sanctuary beneath the oak tree, there was a sense of unity among them—a shared belief that they were on the cusp of unraveling the larger mystery that held Kaira's fate in its grasp.

The morning sun had only just begun to grace the cobblestone streets of Rietti with its golden touch when Elan and his companions convened in the town square. They established themselves, turning away from the memory of the previous night's festivities—the lingering sounds of laughter and melody now quiet by the punctilious sounds of their collected equipment. The team had awakened alongside dawn, each individual portraying a calm reflection of the prudence of their quest.

Elan expertly inspected the contents of his pack, ensuring the security of the map and other indispensable items. His actions were a ritual that Elan had performed countless times during his days in the Marines, a habit that had become as much a part of him as breathing. It was a task that brought him a sense of calm and order amidst the chaos of battle, a way to focus his mind and prepare himself for whatever lay ahead. As he meticulously checked each item, ensuring everything was in its proper place.

Next to him, Wulfstan examined his armor, its brilliant golden sheen catching the nascent light. The knight's impressive features were a satisfying beacon of doughtiness and unshakeable permanence.

Isolde approached a shopkeeper determined to procure last-minute necessities. Her braids danced with each calculated movement as she negotiated effortlessly. She rejoined her friends, and a new bag containing medicinals and jangling vials was in tow.

Livia approached her religious vestments pristinely presented, holding a satchel that cradled ancient scrolls and texts steeped in the region's lore. "The wisdom within these may guide us through the puzzles we confront," she conveyed, her tone brimming with orderly parole.

Nykronus stood slightly removed from the group, his gaze sweeping their environs with a guarded demeanor. The mage might have seemed sublime, but something was clearly on his mind.

Elan surveyed each team member consecutively. "We head out for Benevento," he proclaimed. "We got what we need to locate Kaira. We need to remain alert and always at the ready."

Wulfstan affirmed with a nod.

Isolde hoisted her lute upon her shoulder, determination quelling in her stare. "Our saga continues onward," she affirmed with enthusiasm, "and along with it, the lyrics we create."

Casting one lingering look back at Rietti, Elan guided the group forward.

Nykronus sighed, almost a low groan, the sound emanating from deep within him as his tired voice called out to Elan. "Benevento will have to wait."

"Excuse me?" Elan's face showed a mixture of disgust and resignation.

As Nykronus opened his mouth to speak, Elan knew what was coming deep down, but he couldn't bear to hear it out loud. Every second that passed felt like another step closer to losing Kaira. But facing the harsh truth made him hesitate, unsure if he was ready.

"Every moment we delay could mean losing Kaira," Elan stated.

Elan's conviction that each second was crucial in finding Kaira came from his experience as a Marine, where he learned to act decisively and trust his instincts. He felt Kaira was out there, and every moment delayed meant she remained lost and alone.

Nykronus stepped forward, his face etched with an intensity that matched Elan's own. "You must reconsider. Terni holds a key we cannot afford to ignore."

Elan frowned, confusion clouding his brow. "The nobleman's lead is to Benevento. That's where we'll find her. Why wait until now to say something?"

Nykronus insisted, "Terni is not a diversion. It's a necessary step towards unraveling the greater mysteries that determine Kaira's destiny." It had been two decades since the nobleman had last caught sight of this enigmatic woman. It could hold for a little while longer."

Wulfstan interjected, his voice a deep rumble of support for Elan. "The clues point us to Benevento, Nykronus. We must trust what we've uncovered."

Nykronus held Wulfstan's gaze steadily. "And what of St. Valentine's heart? Terni may reveal much about the forces we face and arm us better for what's ahead."

Isolde sensed the rising tension and unslung her lute from her back, plucking a soothing chord that rippled through the complex air like a pebble across still water.

"Both paths have merit," Sister Livia said softly, almost lost under the melody Isolde coaxed from her instrument. "Perhaps there is wisdom in considering both."

Elan looked between his companions, torn between urgency and strategy.

Nykronus continued, "I have walked these lands longer than you, Elan. We have come this far. Trust that I do not guide you astray."

Isolde's music swelled, weaving a tapestry of sound that seemed to knit the group together despite their differences.

"We are not just chasing Kaira," Nykronus added while Isolde's lute sang of ancient days and hidden ways. "The forces at play here are more intricate and far-reaching than we can fully grasp now. Our fates and the fate of the world itself are intertwined in ways that we are only beginning to understand."

Elan closed his eyes briefly, taking in the bard's tune and Nykronus's words. When he opened them again, they were clear with a reluctant decision.

"If Terni is so important," Elan conceded, "then we'll go there first."

Wulfstan grunted in acknowledgment but did not look convinced; his gaze lingered in Benevento's direction.

Livia's hand gently rested on Isolde's shoulder. She listened to her play, a peaceful smile spreading across her lips as she observed Isolde's clever tactics for diffusing tension. The soft, melodic notes of the instrument filled the room, creating a tranquil atmosphere. Livia was proud of Isolde's ability to soothe others through music, a skill that often went unnoticed but held great power.

Isolde's fingers danced across the strings, crafting an uplifting melody that seemed to speak of new beginnings and complex choices made right.

As they prepared to continue their journey, Elan took one last look at Rietti's fading silhouette against the dawn sky.

The team set off with Isolde's lute continuing its gentle serenade—a reminder that though their course was adjusted, they moved forward together as one toward Terni and the next chapter of their journey.

CHAPTER

FOURTEEN

Rome, April 825 A.D.

Kaira stood amidst a bustling market square, washing over her like a wave from an unfamiliar sea. Her eyes, comprehensive with wonder and apprehension, darted across the scene. Vendors shouted prices of goods she barely recognized, their Latin tongues wrapping around words that sounded harsh yet musical to her modern ears.

She stared at the ring that had been her anchor through time, constantly amidst the chaos. The cool metal of the ring pressed against Kaira's skin, reminding her of her mother's touch. Its smooth surface brought a sense of calm and familiarity, a tangible connection to her past life. The stone paths under her feet were worn smooth by centuries of footsteps that had tread before hers, and now she added her own, a temporal intruder in an era long past.

Kaira's heart pounded as she struggled to calm the rising panic. She had always been resilient in the face of change, but the world she fell into seemed like an entirely different realm. Kaira's life had been a tapestry of change and adversity, each thread a testament to her unwavering spirit. From the loss of her father at a young age to the financial struggles that had threatened to derail her dreams of studying architecture, she had faced every challenge with a quiet determination and a refusal to let circumstances define her.

As she took in the grandeur of the ancient city, she couldn't help but feel small and out of place. With every breath, she was torn between her curiosity to explore life here and her desire to escape this unfamiliar reality. The conflicting emotions threatened to suffocate her as she fought to find a way out of this nightmare.

The scents of olive oil and fresh bread mingled with the less pleasant odors of a city that knew nothing of modern sanitation. Kaira wrinkled her nose briefly before disciplining her features into an expression of neutral curiosity.

She walked past stalls displaying vibrant textiles and jewelry that glinted under the sun's unforgiving gaze. The voices around her rose and fell in an almost orchestrated rhythm—the lifeblood of Rome's heart.

"I need to get out of these clothes," she whispered, feeling the task's weight ahead. "I need to blend in if I'm going to survive. This isn't a dream, is it Kaira?"

Kaira glanced down at her outfit, suddenly acutely aware of how much she stood out among the sea of medieval attire. Her modern, form-fitting jeans and bright, patterned blouse were a jarring contrast to the simple, earth-toned tunics and dresses worn by the people around her. She might as well have been wearing a neon sign proclaiming her foreign status, and she knew that if she wanted to blend in and avoid unwanted attention, she would need to find clothing that would allow her to integrate into this new world seamlessly.

A fruit seller caught her eye—a woman whose hands moved deftly as she smiled and handed over apples. Kaira approached tentatively, watching the exchange between merchant and customer.

"Quid hoc est?" Kaira asked, pointing to an apple with hesitant Latin, a phrase she had rehearsed countless times during her first few days lost in her era.

The woman looked up at Kaira, eyes sharp but not unkind. "Mala," she replied, holding one for Kaira to take.

Grasping the apple firmly, Kaira smiled gratefully and moved on, feeling a spark of accomplishment for navigating even this small inter-action. With each step through Rome's thrumming streets, she fortified herself with thoughts of home and family—anchors just as vital as the bead at her neck. She was all alone.

Determined to discover a new existence in this historical tapestry, Kaira moved through the city with deliberate strides, knowing full well that adaptability was now her only ally.

San Francisco, California, December 2001 A.D.

Kaira went through the foggy San Francisco streets, the brisk winter air nipping at her cheeks. Her confident strides carried her towards Fisherman's Wharf, a popular tourist destination and iconic neighborhood in the city. Clutched under her arm were her carefully crafted architectural sketches, her passion project that she was eager to present to the university panel waiting for her. The rhythmic clicking of her heels against the sidewalk was like a familiar soundtrack, offering comfort and a sense of belonging as she traversed through the bustling city she had grown up in and come to love.

Her world tilted slightly on its axis at the entrance to the pier. A street performer had drawn a small crowd, his hands moving with the deft precision of a magician. Elan Durant stood still in a flannel and jeans, his presence like a magnet pulling Kaira's attention from her destination.

Their eyes met, and for a moment, the liveliness of tourists faded into soft background noise. Kaira felt something stir within her—a recognition of something she couldn't yet name. She approached slowly, caught in an invisible pull.

Elan's smile was warm and inviting as he concluded his act—a simple trick with cards that seemed to dance at his command. Applause rippled through the crowd, but his gaze never left Kaira's.

"Enjoy the show?" Elan asked as the crowd dispersed, leaving them in an intimate bubble of space on the crowded sidewalk.

Kaira nodded, her smile breaking free. "It was impressive," she admitted. "You've got quite the skill."

The cards seemed to spring into his nimble fingers, guided by movements perfected through countless rehearsals. "Elan, delighted to make your acquaintance," he said in a playful tone.

"Kaira," she said, extending her hand.

His grip was firm and sure—comforting in its strength. In that handshake lay unspoken promises of potential—shared laughter and whispered confidences.

They talked then as if they had met for the first time. Although they'd known each other for years, Elan grew up with her younger sister Reagan. Their conversation flowed effortlessly, topics weaving from art to history, touching lightly on their dreams and fears.

Elan suggested coffee at a nearby café, and Kaira agreed without hesitation. Their cheerfulness felt like slipping into a favorite pair of shoes—familiar and just right.

As they sat across from each other at a small table by the window, their connection deepened with every shared story and glance. The warmth in Elan's eyes when he looked at her made Kaira's heart flutter like never before.

The café around them hummed with life, but time seemed to slow in their little corner of the world. They procrastinated over their drinks long after they'd finished them, neither wanting this unexpected encounter to end.

As the sunset cast golden hues across the city, Kaira felt something bloom within her—a sense of belonging tethered not to place but to person. In Elan's company, San Francisco took on new colors that were vibrant and full of possibilities.

As they parted ways that evening, with plans to meet again soon, Kaira walked home with a pep in her step and an undying hope for what might unfold between them.

Under the warm glow of the restaurant's pendant lights, Kaira leaned forward, her eyes alight with the fervor of shared dreams. The small, intimate table between them drew their words into a close-knit complexity.

"I've always wanted to create something lasting," she confided, her fingers tracing the rim of her coffee cup. "To design buildings that would stand the test of time, like the ones I've studied from Ancient Greece."

Elan watched her, captivated. Her passion was vibrant and infectious. "And you will," he assured her. "You've got the talent and the drive."

Kaira smiled, warmth spreading through her chest. Elan's belief in her felt like a foundation being laid for her future.

As days turned to weeks, their bond deepened. They wandered through museums, where Kaira spoke of architecture with a knowledge that left Elan in awe. They strolled along the Embarcadero, where Elan shared stories of his time spent in the Philippines with his mother, each account a brushstroke in the portrait of his life.

Eventually, on an evening walk, Kaira reached for his hand, threading their fingers together. Elan's grip was steady and reassuring, an unspoken vow that resonated within her.

They found joy in simple moments—laughing over shared meals in dimly lit restaurants, watching the city lights flicker on as dusk embraced the city. Each encounter was a cord weaving them closer together until they were bound by something more potent than mere affection.

In quiet libraries, surrounded by the commotion of city life, they bared their souls to each other. Kaira spoke of her family—the strength she drew from Reagan and her inherited wisdom from their mother. Elan listened, his eyes reflecting a respect that bordered on devotedness.

In these exchanges, love took root, blossoming with every word and touch. They were two people learning the shape of each other's hearts—building a foundation.

One evening, as they sat overlooking the bay, Kaira whispered words she'd held close for too long. "I love you," she said, voice trembling.

Elan turned to her, his face open and honest, and replied with a truth that had grown quietly within him. "I love you Kaira Mazza."

In that confession lay an understanding—a realization of something profound and life-altering. Kiara and Elan were no longer unaccompanied souls navigating through life; they were partners sharing a journey woven from dreams and love.

As they sat together, watching the waves dance beneath the moonlight, Kaira knew she had found a companion and a person who would shape her life in ways she never could have imagined on her own.

~

Benevento, Lombard Principality, 842 A.D.

The ancient city of Benevento cradled secrets in its bosom, among them the birth of twins to a woman out of time. Kaira, her body weary but her spirit ablaze with fierce love, brought Myst and Maya under a sky masqueraded in stars that exclaimed of destiny.

The twins were born in a small chamber, its walls thick with the scent of herbs and the warmth of a crackling firebox. Kaira cradled her children, one in each arm, their tiny fingers curling around hers with an instinctive trust that made her heart erupt.

Raising children in this era was a complexity spun from threads of exultation and demand. With his eyes wide open, Myst was calm and thoughtful even from his earliest days. With the fiery sunset in her gaze, Maya was fierce and unmalleable in her cries for attention.

Raising children in a time so far removed from her own was a constant challenge for Kaira. She struggled to balance imparting the values and knowledge she had gained in the modern world and ensuring the twins could thrive in the reality of medieval life. Kaira often found herself biting her tongue, resisting the urge to speak out against the societal norms and expectations that she found stifling and oppressive. She knew she could not change the world around her, but she was determined to raise Myst and Maya to be strong, independent children, regardless of the limitations they placed upon her by the time they lived.

Kaira navigated motherhood with an animation born from the knowledge that she alone must be a rock for her offspring against the world's cruelties. She taught them with patience; her words laced stories of far-off lands and times yet to come—a heritage she alone could gift them.

As they grew, so too did Kaira's motivation to protect them. She patiently antiquated their lives, blending into the community while guarding the truth of their origins like a rare diamond in her chest.

Her love for Myst and Maya was timeless, its depths fathomless and filled with intention for their future. She pictured them prospering—strong, wise, and kind—lights unto themselves in this distant past that had claimed her. Kaira recognized Elan's essence, which was reflected within Myst and Maya.

As she watched them sleep quietly, Kaira whispered promises into the stillness—a mother's vows to guard their innocence and foster their growth. And in those hushed confessions lay all her hopes for what they might one day become.

In the hush of her modest Benevento home, Kaira lived a life wrapped in the fabric of secrecy. The sun dripped through the windows, lighting the room where her children played. Myst's quiet concentration mirrored his mother's scholarly nature as he assembled blocks into intricate structures. On the other hand, Maya was the spark of their home, her laughter ringing out as she chased after a ball of yarn with the limitless energy of youth.

Her days unfolded with routine and purpose. Mornings were spent tending to their needs and teaching them letters and numbers—a head start for the bright futures she envisioned. As the twins napped, Kaira poured over ancient texts and scrolls, her mind lighted with inquisitiveness. Her research delved into legends and myths that might hold clues to reconnecting with Elan, her heart's compass.

The room where she studied was lined with shelves filled with leather-bound tomes and parchment that rustled like autumn leaves at her graze. Here, Kaira found comfort in her scholarly pursuits; each page brought her a step closer to understanding the alluring forces that had brought her to this place in time.

In the soft candlelight of evening, she would document her findings in a journal bound by worn leather—the edges frayed from constant handling. Her handwriting flowed across the pages in neat lines, a testament to her implacable decision to sustain a bridge between past and present.

Kaira's life was a delicate balance between motherhood and her quest for knowledge. She kept their existence tucked away from nosy eyes, wary of the possibility of drawing unwanted attention to their peculiar little family. Her days were filled with teaching moments and quiet research, while nights held silent prayers for Elan's wellbeing.

As dusk painted the sky in shades of fading amber, Kaira often stood at the window watching the stars emerge like tiny beacons. She whispered wishes upon them for reunion and strength—each word a thread weaving hope into her quiet life of secrecy.

Kaira's fingertips traced the worn edges of the parchment, her eyes devouring the ancient text that sprawled before her. The candlelight flickered, but her focus never crumbled. She was deep within the confines of Benevento's library, a place where time seemed to bend and twist around the weight of history held within its walls.

She had encountered a tome—a compendium of legends and myths about worlds layered upon their own. The book was heavy, bound in leather that whispered of centuries passed. It was a fusion of knowledge, a motherlode that few eyes had seen and even fewer minds had comprehended.

Kaira's breath caught as she pieced together narratives that wove through time like a fine-tuned tapestry. One legend spoke of the Loom of Fate, an artifact said to weave the destinies of mortals and gods alike. Another recounted the tale of Aion's Mirror, a reflective surface that could reveal truths hidden to the naked eye.

Each story pulsated with potential—keys that might unlock the mystery of her shift in time. Kaira's mind raced with possibilities as she philosophized how these myths could collide with her own life's thread.

A particular legend resonated within her—a tale about the Celestial Crossroads, where paths between different eras intersected under specific celestial alignments. Her pulse quickened as she considered this might be her avenue back to Elan and her original time.

A flicker of doubt crept into her mind as Kaira considered the possibility of returning to her own time. What if Elan had moved on, his love for her fading with the passage of years? What if he no longer wanted her, the memory of their bond erased by time and distance? The thought was painful, but she knew she could not let it consume her. She had to hold onto hope, to believe that their love was strong enough to transcend the barriers of time itself.

With every turn of the page, Kaira felt a surge of exhilaration tempered by the gravity of her discoveries. Knowledge was power, but it bore a weight—a responsibility settled on her shoulders like a mantle.

Her hand paused over an illustration depicting St. Michael wielding his sword against a shadowy figure—representing good battling evil.

The burden of understanding settled upon Kaira like dusk upon the day. These myths and legends were not mere stories but tangled with the fabric of reality, threads that could guide or entrap those who dared to pull at them.

Kaira leaned back in her chair, absorbing what she held in her hands. Her eyes lifted to the darkness beyond the candle's reach, and she contemplated how this knowledge might shape their fates.

The candle flickered once more as if acknowledging the weight of discovery—and Kaira drew in a deep breath, ready to delve deeper into the secrets held within these forbidden pages.

In the stillness of her room, as twilight merged with the shadows, Kaira settled at her worn wooden desk. The twins slept soundly, their breaths a soft counterpoint to the scratching of her quill. She dipped the tip into the inkwell and pressed it to parchment, her heart guiding her hand.

"Dearest Elan," she began, each word a droplet of her soul spilling onto the page. "As I write this, our children are asleep—their presence a constant reminder of our love, an enduring testament to what we created together."

She wrote of Myst's keen mind and how he would lose himself in building structures that defied his tender age. "He has your focus," she penned with a smile. "That same intense concentration that I fell in love with."

Kaira's hand hesitated as she began to describe Maya. A breath escaped her—a mother's mix of pride and wonder—as she continued, "Maya is a force, Elan. She's fierce and brimming with life, challenging the world as if she could command the winds themselves."

Her quill was choreographed across the parchment as she described their life in Benevento. The simple joys and daily trials they faced in a time that was not their own—a narrative punctuated by her unwavering strength and determination.

Kaira found life in medieval Italy a constant battle. Each day brought fresh trials, from cooking without modern conveniences to navigating foreign social norms. She bit her tongue, unable to protest the injustices she saw, knowing her words would be ignored. Even basic hygiene and health required unaccustomed effort and creativity. Yet amidst the struggles, Kaira discovered simple joys in the close community and her children's love—moments of happiness that fueled her strength to greet each new day with a smile and hope.

"And you are here with us," Kaira wrote, "in everything I teach them, in every story I share that has your laughter laced through it. You are as present in this unconventional home as the very air we breathe."

She told him of her scholarly pursuits—of days spent scouring ancient texts for any sliver of hope or clue that might bridge the rift between them. Kaira's scholarly nature set her apart in the community. While others focused on household duties, she poured over ancient texts, her mind craving their wisdom. Whispers about her oddness grew, but Kaira refused to be deterred from her passion for learning, seeing it as a gift she would not let the era's expectations stifle. Her breakthroughs unfolded on the page before him—the Loom of Fate, Aion's Mirror, and most compellingly, the Celestial Crossroads.

"I believe there's a way back to you," Kaira confessed, her hand trembling with excitement and fear. "These legends whisper promises of crossing time, and I cling to them as I cling to the memory of you."

The candle beside her fizzled as she concluded her letter—a letter heavy with lonesomeness and coupling with a perennial hope.

"I hold onto the belief that these words will find you, that through some twist of fate or magic, you will know our story," Kaira wrote with finality. "Until that day comes, know that my love for you is as boundless as time itself."

She sealed the letter with wax and pressed her signet ring into it—a seal that carried the weight of their shared past and longing for reunion.

Kaira placed the letter in a small casket alongside other treasures—a lock of Myst's hair tied with a ribbon, Maya's first drawing rough against her fingertips. There, it would remain hidden but never forgotten—a tangible link between past and future borne from a love unyielded by time or distance.

Kaira's gaze lingered on the casket, her fingers caressing its cured wood before she withdrew the letter she had sealed moments ago. She moved to the window, peering at the evening sky, where stars began their nightly vigil. The air was crisp, carrying the scent of woodsmoke and the distant gab of the town.

She thought of Elan, his face etched in memory's deepest recesses—his unwavering strength and the tenderness that had drawn her to him. He had been her anchor, her confidant, her love. And though years and realms now separated them, she felt his presence in every part of her being.

Her heart ached with longing, but it was an ache piqued by the joy their children brought. Myst and Maya were living legacies of their love, embodying hope for a future she dared to envision. She saw in Myst's contemplative nature a reflection of Elan's cheerfulness and in Maya's zingy spirit an echo of their shared eagerness for life.

With a deep breath, Kaira turned away from the window. Her children were asleep, safe in the world she had crafted for them—a world filled with stories of where they came from and where they might go. In them lay the promise of tomorrow.

She wrapped the letter in a cloth and placed it back in the casket.

Kaira knew that entrusting her letter to another was a risk, but it was one she needed to take. Her friend, a monk who frequented the library and shared her thirst for knowledge, had proven himself trustworthy and kind.

She found him in his modest quarters within the abbey, surrounded by books and scrolls—a man as much at home among ancient texts as she was. His face lit up with quiet understanding as she explained her need for the letter to be delivered.

"Take this," Kaira said, pressing the bundle into his hands. "Should you ever find a way or hear a tale of someone who can traverse the veil between times..."

The monk nodded solemnly, recognizing the weight of what he held. "I will guard this with my life," he promised, tucking it into his robes.

Kaira smiled gratefully, speaking volumes of her trust in him and fate. As she left him standing among his precious manuscripts, she believed that somehow, her words would find Elan.

With that act done—a mother's wish cast into an uncertain future—Kaira returned home to her children. There, she would continue to build a life filled with love and learning, ever hopeful for a reunion with her heart's counterpart.

FIFTEEN

Desperation and isolation consumed Elan's thoughts as a relentless gale whipped through the carriage's opening, causing the timeworn scroll to flutter. The terrain raced past in a haze of emerald and rock, each kilometer propelling him farther from Kaira's ultimate whereabouts and closer to an undefined predicament.

Nykronus rode his horse beside him, his face set with the harshness of their mission. His voice cut through Elan's daydream with an intensity that matched the breezy air.

"Terni is crucial, Elan. It is where we'll find the the heart of St. Valentine." Nykronus reminded him, his gaze fixed on some distant point only he could see.

Elan's jaw tightened as he absorbed Nykronus's words. He understood the weight of their mission and the need to circumvent the Malefic Assembly's dark plans. Yet his heart ached for Benevento and for any clue that might lead him back to Kaira.

"I get it," Elan said, his hands tightening. "But every second we spend chasing these relics is another second Kaira drifts further away. Decades, years, months, weeks, days, it *doesn't* matter. Every second matters."

Nykronus regarded Elan with patience born from bearing his

burdens. "I know where your heart lies, but we must not let grief blind us to the situation at hand. The Assembly grows stronger even as we speak. In this immense world, their needs must take precedence. Will Kaira not want this?"

Elan's throat tightened at Nykronus's gentle warning. The balance between personal needs and duty had always been more clear.

"My heart's torn in two," Elan confessed, the words like gravel in his mouth. "Part of me died when I lost Kaira; you know that. But here I am chasing shadows when all I want—no, all I need—is closure."

The silence that followed was filled with an understanding too profound for words. Nykronus placed a hand on Elan's shoulder—a gesture that spoke volumes of their shared moment.

"We tread a path full of shadows," Nykronus finally said. "But remember, it is in darkness that light shines brightest."

Elan inhaled slowly, allowing Nykronus's wisdom to mend into his resolve like rain into parched soil. The conflict within him remained—a whirlwind of obligation and heartbreak—but Nykronus's presence was a light guiding him through the storm.

Nykronus watched the weakening light snuggle the ancient stones of an abbey, his outline embossed against the night sky. He stood with a swagger that seemed to anchor him to the complex framework of time. Nearby, Elan conveyed the visage of a man bracing against a storm only he could feel. He looked toward the horizon where Terni waited for them.

As nightfall disguised the world in colored hues, Nykronus turned to Elan, his eyes projected a well of unuttered knowledge.

"Leadership is not merely a role we assume; it's a mantle we wear," Nykronus began, his voice steady as bedrock. "It is our charge to rise above personal desires, to see beyond the veil of our individual needs."

Elan met Nykronus's gaze, finding a resilience that had withstood centuries in those ancient eyes. He felt the weight of his leadership—the lives that had depended on him, the choices that had shaped his path.

"The stakes have never been higher," Nykronus continued his voice grave. "If we fail, the darkness will engulf our world, twisting it into a nightmarish realm where suffering and despair reign supreme. The Malefic Assembly seeks to corrupt the very fabric of reality, to reshape it in its own twisted image. Only by standing together and finding strength in each other and ourselves can we hope to prevent this catastrophe and protect the countless lives that hang in the balance. Winning means preserving the light, the goodness, and the love that makes our world worth fighting for."

Elan's fists clenched at his sides. The echo of Kaira's laughter still haunted him, her absence a gorge in his soul. Yet, in Nykronus's words, he found a tether—a reminder that something larger was at play.

"We must stand as fortification against the darkness," Nykronus said, "The mission transcends us. Our sacrifices pave the way for a future we may never see but one we shape with every choice we make."

Elan nodded slowly.

Nykronus placed a firm hand on Elan's shoulder, grounding him in the present. "Remember this," he said softly yet with an iron resolve, "Leadership is not about bearing burdens alone; it is about knowing when to share them and when to trust in others as they trust in you."

As midnight approached, wrapping its quiet blanket around their slunk forms, Elan drew a deep breath. In Nykronus's enlightenment, he found comfort and sturdiness—enough to face tomorrow and all its unknowns.

Rain fell over the camp where Elan and his companions had gathered, the sound of a soothing pitter-patter on the canvas of their improvised shelter. The air is filled with the crisp, fresh scent of rain, mingling with the earthy aroma of wet grass and pine needles.

Inside, a rough-hewn table bore the weight of their gathered intel—various maps, manuscripts, and arcane texts. Around it, Elan's squad swapped glances that spoke volumes. They had each come from divergent paths, but their motivation now was one.

Wulfstan ran a gauntleted hand along the edge of Terni on the map.

"The heart lies concealed within the Terni, hidden by enchantments and age-old secrecy. Our path will be full of danger."

Isolde plucked a string on her lute, a low hum that vibrated through the secrecy. "And yet," she said, her voice a melody fabricated with belief, "our combined talents have brought us this far. I say we're more than capable of facing what lies ahead."

Elan surveyed his allies—St. Michael's knights are destined by universal cause rather than blood. His gaze settled on Nykronus, who sat with an aura of indestructible forbearance.

"It's not getting just about getting St. Valentine's heart," Elan stated firmly. "We're saving *his* legacy—protection over love and sacrifice. That's what gives this mission its gravity."

Nykronus nodded in agreement. "Indeed, Elan. And we must remember that love itself is an act of defiance against despair—a beacon in our darkest hours."

The group succumbed to silence, each party member understanding their role in the tapestry of their shared events.

"Then it's decided," Wulfstan declared with an authoritative boom that seemed to echo off the canvas surroundings. "We set out for Terni with clear intent: to secure the relic and protect what Saint Valentine stood for."

The others broke the silence—vocalists of tenacity that filled the space between them.

"Let's go over it once more," Isolde suggested. "The Abbey at Terni first to gather intelligence and then—"

"—and then into the belly of mystery," Livia interjected, her voice light but her eyes aflame with passion.

Elan studied each face around him, feeling pride as they were bound together. They were more than a team; they were keepers of hope in a world that threatened to extinguish it.

"We move as one," he affirmed. "Together, we'll stand against whatever shadows we face."

~

Storm clouds loomed ominously on the horizon as Elan and his companions gathered their supplies and exited the campsite. The ground squished underfoot, a mixture of mud and damp leaves, releasing a pungent aroma that clung to their horses' hooves. The world seemed to hold its breath in anticipation as they departed, the weight of their quest pressing down upon them like a heavy cloak. The fleeting beauty of the waking forest was overshadowed by the urgency of their mission, reminding them of the fragility of life in the face of danger.

Elan reluctantly mounted his horse, trying to push away the feeling of dread in his gut. The chestnut mare's gentle temperament only served as a stark contrast to his cynicism. Nykronus, with Livia riding at his back, was ready to lead the way, but Elan couldn't shake the unease that clung to him like a shadow.

It was a feeling he had experienced before in the Marine Corps. He remembered a mission in Afghanistan, where his instincts warned him of an impending ambush. Despite the spooky stillness and the lack of concrete evidence, Elan had trusted his gut and ordered his squad to take a different route. Later, they discovered that their original path had been heavily mined, and Elan's intuition had saved their lives. Now, Elan knew he had to trust his instincts again, for the stakes were even higher.

Isolde and Wulfstan pushed forward, their grace and unrelenting determination reminding him of their heavy burden. As they rode into the unknown, Elan couldn't help but wonder if they were truly prepared for this quest.

As they rode through the serendipitous countryside, vineyards and chromatic groves passing by in viridescent waves, Elan's thoughts were fixed on Terni—their next pitstop.

Wulfstan broke a silence among them, his voice a rumble akin to distant thunder. "We ride with more than just hope," he began, his gaze sweeping over each member of their fellowship. "We ride with a purpose carved by fate itself."

Isolde nodded, her green eyes reflecting the dawn light. "Aye, Wulfstan. We carry with us the echoes of those who fought for love's preservation—Saint Valentine's legacy."

Elan listened to his newfound brothers and sisters, their words perpetuating the tenet that had become his lifeline. He felt a kinship with these fighters, old and new, each driven by a cause greater than themselves.

"The path ahead is littered with challenges we can only guess at," Nykronus said, turning to Elan with an inexorable stare. "But in our hearts, we carry a flame that no darkness can extinguish."

Elan met Nykronus's gaze, finding solace in his timeless wisdom. "And it's that very flame that will guide us through Terni's mysteries," he added.

Their journey to Terni was not merely a traversal of land but an odyssey through layers of history and mysticism—a quest bound by sacrifice and secured by unity.

Terni, Duchy of Spoleto, Frankish Kingdom, 842 A.D.

Elan found himself staring at the ancient stone façade of the Terni Cathedral, the dusk gracing its weathered contours with the last remnants of sunlight. The atmosphere hung heavy with the scent of rain, foretelling an impending storm, but it also mingled with the earthy, mossy smell of the old stone, giving a sense of history and gloriousness.

The scene weighed heavily on the small group as they stood at the threshold of a moment they had all sensed would be a fulcrum in their travels. Elan's jaw was set, and his eyes narrowed in determination as he surveyed the ancient structure. Wulfstan's hand rested on his chest-plate, his knuckles white with tension. Livia and Isolde exchanged glances, their youthful faces pale in the moonlight but their stances resolute. Nykronus, his enigmatic face lined with concern, placed a comforting hand on Elan's shoulder, a silent gesture of support.

The door groaned open, its sound slicing through the muzzle that had set over them. Inside, cobwebs clung to the walls like ancient secrets, their presence a palpable force that seemed to reach out and touch the core of Elan's being.

They were not alone.

A figure emerged from the cloistered darkness, his sinister presence illuminated by the flickering candles in their sconces. The man's short, dirty frame was hunched and crooked, his matted hair clinging to his scalp in greasy patches. Most of his teeth were missing, and those that remained were jagged and yellowed. A chilling cackle escaped his lips, resembling the sound of gremlins chattering in the dark. He wore a tattered cloak adorned with holes and tears, hinting at the atrocities he had committed while wearing it.

Wulfstan's eyes widened in recognition, a look of disgust and anger contorting his features. "Warin," he growled, his hand instinctively reaching for his sword. "I should have known you'd be involved in this madness."

"So you've come for the heart," Warin's cold and venomous voice slithered through the air, "But do you understand what you're meddling with?"

Elan stepped forward, his body tensed for what was to come. "We're here to make sure it stays out of your hands and remains a symbol of protection," he shouted, his voice echoing off the stone walls.

Warin laughed, a sound devoid of humor. Warin's laughter echoed through the chamber, a sound so devoid of humor that it sent shivers down Elan's spine. The cold, mirthless noise seemed to suck the warmth from the air, leaving behind a sense of unease that settled in the pit of Elan's stomach. "Protection? Is that what you think this is about?" He took a step closer, his voice dropping to a dangerous whisper. "The Malefic Assembly does not seek protection, Elan. We seek power—the kind that will reshape this world. We will make it *better*."

Isolde moved beside Elan, her lute clutched in her hand like a shield. "You'll not have it," she challenged, her voice harmonious despite the quivering in her breast.

Warin's eyes shrunk as he regarded them all, taking in their mettlesome stances. "You may think your quest noble," he sneered, "but what do you know of loss? Of true sacrifice?"

Elan's heart clenched at Warin's words—each syllable a knife twisting deeper into his soul. Memories of Kaira swarmed before his eyes—her smile, laughter, and touch.

"More than you know," Elan shot back through gritted teeth.

Warin's stare fixated on Elan for a long minute before shifting to Nykronus. "And you," he addressed him with loathing cascading from every word. "A guardian of ancient relics? A puppet dancing on the strings of time?"

Nykronus remained unmoved by Warin's taunts, his presence a renitent force in the cathedral. "We stand against you as one," he stated plainly. "And we will not falter."

Warin took another step forward, and the candles seemed to burst with his growing rage. "Then come," he beckoned with a twisted smile. "Let us see if your resolve is as strong as your words."

The door slammed shut, trapping them outside in the desolate darkness. Sealed off from the hallowed sanctuary, they found Warin's menacing presence lingering like a sharp blade at their backs. Above them, the sky churned with ominous storm clouds that seemed to merge into one, casting a ghostly death mask over everything. The air crackled with electricity as they stood there, sending shivers down their spines. Elan couldn't help but be reminded of the war-torn landscapes he had experienced in his past life or perhaps in his future. The deafening booms echoed through the night, a haunting soundtrack to their terrifying encounter.

Elan leaned against the cold stone wall, his face etched with the exhaustion of a man who had glimpsed too much of humanity's abyss. The confrontation had laid bare the stakes of their quest, a reminder that they contended with forces that sought not just to claim but to corrupt.

They contended with forces that sought not just to claim but to corrupt, hoping to create a world where darkness reigned supreme. The Malefic Assembly's ultimate goal was to twist reality and reshape it in their image—a nightmarish landscape where suffering and despair were the norm, and hope was nothing more than a distant memory. They sought to extinguish the light of goodness and love, sever the bonds that held humanity together, and create a realm where their twisted desires could be fulfilled without restraint. It was a vision of Hell on Earth that Elan and his companions knew they had to prevent at all costs.

Livia knelt close, her voice low and steady. "Warin's words are toxin, constructed to weaken our spirit. But we've seen through his veneer."

Wulfstan grunted, his king-sized reprise emitting a long shadow on the archways. "Aye, Sister Livia. His talk of power is nothing but fear, disguising oneself as ambition. We know what we fight for."

Isolde's fingers danced absently over her lute strings, coaxing out a somber tune that seemed to encapsulate their mood. "Our path is one of sacrifice," she said. "But it is also one of hope—hope that what we do here will echo in a brighter tomorrow."

Nykronus's eyes held each of theirs in turn, his gaze as unwavering as it was ancient. "Warin seeks to unmake the world we cherish," he declared. "We mandate as its shield—a guard against the impending darkness."

Elan straightened up, feeling their collective resolve knit together like chainmail around his heart. "You're right. We stand as one. We may each carry our own scars," he acknowledged. "But it's those very scars that remind us why we can't—and won't—give up."

Their shared silence was an agreement made without words, a comprehension that rose above their fears and doubts.

Livia's hand brushed her mantle as she looked skyward, where thunder rumbled a distant warning. "Then let us be the storm that breaks upon Warin and his Assembly," she said.

The party turned back towards the cathedral door, its ancient wood now a barrier between them and their nemesis. They knew what lay ahead would test them in ways they could hardly imagine.

ACT FOUR

"I am confident in the belief that there truly is such a thing as living again, and that the living spring from the dead, and that the souls of the dead are in existence, and that the good souls have a better portion than the evil."

- Socrates

SIXTEEN

Elan pressed his ear against the cathedral's heavy wooden door, his forehead creased as he listened for movement within. Silence adorned the cathedral like a mask, yet it seemed to hum with latent energy. He traded glances with his companions, each nod betraying their mutual discomfort.

Isolde's fingers traced the intricate carvings on the door's surface, her eyes reflecting the torch-lit sparkle from the pillars along the corridor. "We need another way in," she whispered, her voice lost in the vastness of Terni Cathedral's sacred walls.

Wulfstan's armored hand found leverage on a brick relief, pushing against it with a force contradicting his age. The wall gave way with a hushed groan, revealing a tight passage neglected by years of abandonment and darkness. "This may lead us to where we need to be," he grunted.

They filed into the passage one by one, Elan taking point with Nykronus at his back. The corridor twisted and turned, leading them further into the entrails of the cathedral. The dust of ages muffled their footsteps, their passage a ghostly operation through time-worn halls.

Livia trailed behind, her fingers brushing against her rosary as she silently recited the prayers that had been her constant companions since childhood. Despite the gravity of their situation, Livia's faith remained unshakable. She found solace in the familiar words, drawing strength from believing that a higher power watched over them. Yet, beneath her serene exterior, Livia's mind raced with thoughts of the challenges they would face.

Each hero was lost in thought as they traversed the maze of passages. Elan's meditativeness persisted in the beauty of Kaira; every step he took was for her, and every breath was a promise to bring her back. Isolde considered the tales that would emerge from their adventure—the ballads of gallantry and sacrifice that would be sung for centuries.

Wulfstan's mind was on his glory days, each victory fueling energy into his body and soul—a feeling he carried like armor into this new conflict. Nykronus felt the weight of his father's countless attempts to retrieve the dagger upon him; this was but another chapter in an endless saga that he had witnessed unfold time and again.

They emerged from the passage into a chamber adorned with a giant mural depicting scenes of St. Michael's valorous deeds. Sanctity enveloped them as they prepared for what lay ahead—each donning their metaphorical shielding in anticipation.

And then, without warning, Warin jumped out from the shadow of an alcove—like a vulture emerging from its lair. His presence was like poison seeping into their bones, an embodiment of malice that turned even holy ground into a coliseum for hostilities.

Elan met Warin's gaze head-on, sharpening himself against the dread clawed at his resolve. They had arrived at this moment—the calm before the storm—and there was no turning back now.

Inside the cavernous Terni Cathedral, the day's last rays painted the cold granite floor with a tesserae of colors. They filtered through the dirty stained-glass windows, casting a dreamlike and gloomy glow that seemed to waver between the sacred and the profane. In this divine sanctuary, Elan and his party found themselves confronted by Warin, his form starkly contrasting the holy artistry around them.

The dagger Warin gripped pulsed with a sickly, green light that seemed to emanate from its twisted blade. The once pure metal was tarnished, its surface marred by dark veins that pulsated with malevolent energy. Once adorned with symbols of love and sacrifice, the hilt had been grotesquely transformed, now bearing the marks of the Malefic Assembly's vile intentions. As Warin held the dagger aloft, the air around him seemed to grow colder, as if the weapon's very presence was enough to suck the warmth and hope from the room. *The Pugio Mysticus Amoris*, a relic meant to embody the purest form of love, had been corrupted beyond recognition, its purpose now a mockery of everything St. Valentine had stood for.

"We… must retrieve that dagger," Nykronus murmured in a barely audible tone

For the first time since Elan met Nykronus, in both time periods, he saw a slight look of defeat in Nykronus's demeanor. His eyes were fixed on the dagger and frozen in place.

Warin's lips twisted into a sneer as he toyed with the dagger, his tongue trailing along its smooth edge and his voice echoing through the vast hall. "You're too late! I've pierced the heart of St. Valentine with *my* dagger. You're standing on the brink of futility," he taunted. "Do you even understand the power I possess? This blade was never intended for your kind - pitiful creatures pretending to be heroes. Your Order knows who crafted it and who it was meant for. We know its capabilities and potential. Did you really believe your beloved St. Valentine would succumb to your delusions? It was your kind who martyred him for what? Why don't you make this easy for yourself and hand over Vulcan's shield?"

Elan's grip on *Winterstar* tightened the scars on his knuckles, whitening with self-controlled rage. "You can't intimidate us, scumbag," he retorted. "We know what right looks like, and we won't let you destroy what we know is sacred."

Isolde stepped forward, her voice serene despite the danger. "You do not deserve that blade. However you obtained it must have been through treachery, and that will not serve you here."

Warin laughed—a hollow sound that seemed to feed off the shadows. "Oh, dear bard," he said, shaking his head with mock pity, "it was almost too easy to strip it from one who dared meddle in affairs beyond their grasp."

Wulfstan stepped up beside Elan, his presence like a rampart against Warin's hostility. "Your threats are as empty as your soul," he hissed.

Livia remained silent, her demeanor peaceful even in the face of Warin's gloating. Her eyes locked onto the *Pugio Mysticus Amoris*, recognizing the good it did for this world. She saw it as both weapon and key—essential to their mission yet corrupted with evil.

The tension thickened like thick fog rolling into a bright summer day. Each hero braced themselves for what was to come—a battle not just of steel and strength but of wills and destinies woven.

The center altarpiece of the cathedral, once a haven of solace and worship, now bore witness to an inevitable battle. The echoes of prayer had vanished, replaced by the racket of steel against steel as Warin's minions descended upon Elan and his allies.

Elan parried a whack, the clang of *Winterstar* ringing true, emitting a thunderous but low hum with each hit. He danced between foes with a warrior's precision, each movement measured and lethal. Years of off-duty martial arts training were being put to the test. Yet even as he fought, he couldn't help but feel the diabolical transformation of the *Pugio Mysticus Amoris* within Warin's grasp.

Isolde, her eyes alight with the fire of battle, wielded her instrument like a weapon of old. Notes soared through the air—sharp enough to cut through doubt, powerful enough to bolster her comrades' will—a spell buffing them with her strength. She ducked under a swinging blade, her counter swift and sure as she disoriented her attacker with a well-placed kick.

Wulfstan stood like a titan among mortals, his golden armor gleaming amid a raging tempest. With every strike and parry, his body absorbed and redirected the force with supernatural ease, each blow growing more ferocious as he tapped into ancient powers. His violent roar echoed through the chaos, inspiring his allies to fight on while striking fear into the hearts of their foes who were no match for this unstoppable force.

Warin's grip on the dagger tightened, sending tremors through the air that seemed to warp reality. The *Pugio Mysticus Amoris* radiated a malevolent crimson glow, its power palpable and overwhelming as if twisting the very fabric of their world against them. Despite their valor and prowess, they were at the mercy of this cursed weapon, feeling its immense power shift the balance in favor of their enemy.

Livia moved through the chaos with a nimbleness that contradicted her humble appearance. Her tunic swirled around her as she dodged and weaved, her hands finding weak spots to attack in armor and resolve. Her movements were not just those of a warrior but someone who understood that sometimes faith could be sharper than any blade.

Livia's movements were fluid and precise, each step a testament to her unwavering faith. As she dodged and weaved through the chaos of the battle, her lips moved in silent prayer, the words a constant rhythm that guided her actions. Her faith was not just a comfort but a weapon in its own right, a shield that protected her from the darkness that threatened to overwhelm them. When her hand struck out, it was with the surety of one who knew that a higher power guided her every move.

The villains lunged forward with savage determination, wielding the enchanted dagger that dripped with dark magic. Elan was quickly overwhelmed as multiple adversaries closed on him, their weapons striking with brutal force. The echoing clang of metal on metal filled the holy sanctuary, shaking the ancient stone walls that had stood for centuries and would hopefully remain standing until 2024, a testament to the ferocious battle.

With every passing moment, the heroes fought not just for Kaira or their quest but for something greater—the essence of love and sacrifice that St. Valentine himself had championed. Each assault they bought was proof of the Order's worthiness in the face of the darkest times.

Yet Warin watched from afar with a cruel snicker playing on his lips as he juggled the dagger between his grimy hands—the balance ever-so-slowly tipping in favor of malice and decay. Elan's heroes were outnumbered five to one.

The once grand cathedral was now a battleground, its towering stained glass windows shattered and stained in red. Flickering torches replaced the peaceful glow of candlelight, some extinguished by spilled wine, casting an eerie glow on the fading toward impending darkness—symbolic of light being extinguished by dark. Glimpses of armored figures darted through the pews, struggling to keep their swords and shields upright from fatigue in a dance of death and destruction.

Isolde, her voice a weapon against the encroaching darkness, wove her melodies into protective wards around her comrades. Isolde's melodies were more than just music; they were a tangible force that wove itself into the very fabric of the battle. As her voice rose and fell, the notes seemed to shimmer in the air, creating a barrier of sound that protected her comrades from the onslaught of their enemies. The magic of her song was ancient and powerful, a gift passed down through generations of bards who had used their talents to defend the innocent and fight against the forces of darkness. With each chord, Isolde poured her heart and soul into the music, her love for her friends and her determination to see them through this trial fueling the protective wards surrounding them. The shadows seemed to recoil from the light of her song, unable to penetrate the shimmering wall of melody between them and their prey. But even as her song swelled, a shadow detached itself from the chaos—a savage look on Warin, with the *Pugio Mysticus Amoris* in hand, aiming for her heart.

Time seemed to fracture at that moment, a mosaic of possible futures splintering into infinite directions. Wulfstan the Steadfast, now more courageous than ever before, thanks to his experience in countless battles, recognized the trail of ill intentions directed towards Isolde. He charged forward to protect her with a thunderous roar that echoed through the heavens.

The knight's body collided with Isolde's, sending them both sprawling to the ground as the attack connected with him instead. Pain erupted through Wulfstan's torso—a searing fire that threatened to consume him from within. He became dizzy from the unfathomable pain.

Isolde lay beneath him, her eyes wide with shock and fear as she gazed upon the knight who had shielded her from a mortal attack. Her hands trembled as they reached up to touch the battle-damaged armor that had borne the brunt of her fate.

Wulfstan grunted through clenched teeth and reached beneath his mantle with strength born of desperation and duty. His fingers closed around the dragon's tooth, its surface pulsing with celestial energy drawn from Saturn's Ring. The air crackled around them as he brought forth the relic, its power an untamed beast awaiting release.

His scream tore through the cathedral—a primal sound filled with pain and fury. The sound wave resonated with *Winterstar* in Elan's grasp, creating a harmonic convergence that unleashed a torrent of raw energy. A blinding light exploded from the union of dragon tooth and sword, washing over friend and foe alike. With a fierce cry that echoed through the air like a deafening aria from an opera, Isolde summoned a protective shield around Wulfstan and their party. The shield crackled with energy, pulsing with the strength of her determination to keep them safe. Her voice trembled with power as she shouted out, her green eyes blazing with unbridled magic and a matching glow.

The attackers faltered under the onslaught of power that cascaded from Wulfstan's bellow and Elan's *Winterstar*. One by one, they crumbled, their bodies unable to withstand the celestial force that tore through their ranks. Lightning-connected them like anchor links on an anchor chain so they could not escape an electrifying jolt. It was as if the very heavens had descended upon them in judgment with lightning to inflict the most painful punishment—a one-way ticket to Hell.

In the wake of destruction lay Isolde—her breath shallow as she clutched at her side where Wulfstan had protected her. Her eyes fluttered closed, and for a moment, all was still save for Livia's soft chanting as she knelt beside them both.

During the fiery chaos, a dark figure moved with silent precision, like a thief among shadows. With lightning-quick hands, the thief snatched the gem from the pouch at Isolde's waist, their movements so swift and subtle that the bard didn't even feel the loss of weight. The gem, crackling with Jupiter's raw power within its facets, had been protected by Isolde's life, a testament to its importance in their quest. Now, as the thief melted back into the chaos of the battle, Isolde remained unaware that the precious artifact had been stolen from right under her nose, focusing solely on the melodies that she wove around her comrades.

Wulfstan lay sprawled a few feet away, his golden armor darkened by the shadows of defeat. The courageous knight, who had been a bulwark against despair, now breathed shallowly, his life force waning with each ragged inhale.

"We can't stay here," Nykronus rasped, his voice edged with urgency. He was right; the battle had taken its toll on them all, and with Warin's remaining minions regrouping, they were sitting ducks in a field far too treacherous.

Elan nodded stiffly. His mind screamed to stand his ground and fight, but reason—cold and unforgiving—whispered of survival. "Let's go," he commanded, steeling his voice against the aftershock of emotion that threatened to fracture his resolve.

Livia looked up from Isolde's still form, her eyes pools of firm faith amidst pandemonium. "We can't leave her," she murmured, gently brushing a stray lock from Isolde's pale forehead.

Elan knelt beside them, placing a gentle hand on Isolde's shoulder. "She's alive," he affirmed softly, though his heart clenched at her vulnerability.

With a signal from Nykronus, they fashioned a makeshift stretcher from debris and cloak. Carefully lifting Isolde onto it, they retreated through the labyrinthine catacombs beneath the cathedral—a maze that promised obscurity from their pursuers.

The trek was silent save for the soft patter of their footsteps and Wulfstan's labored breathing as he was half-carried by Nykronus and Elan. The weight of their getaway was not just physical but weighed heavily on their egos—their quest ravished, their comrade fallen, and the entirety of Felix's dying wishes teetering on the brink of failure. The

Each step away from the battlefield felt like an echo of loss resonating through their bones. Elan's jaw set in a hard line as he focused on putting one foot in front of the other, leading his defeated band away from the jaws of death towards an ambiguous safe haven.

The darkness enveloped them like a blanket as they disappeared into the depths of history once more—a small band of weary souls carrying with them the heavy burden of retreat and loss.

Elan and his allies emerged from the catacombs' mouth onto the outskirts of Terni Cathedral. The night was quiet, a sharp contrast to the uproar of battle that still rang in their ears. They settled among the ruins of an old monastery garden, its walls providing scant shelter from prying eyes.

The atmosphere was drenched with despair. Wulfstan lay on a bed of dumpy raiments, his breathing shallow but steady—alive against all odds. Isolde's form was motionless beside him, her chest rising and falling with the faint rhythm of life.

Elan surveyed his friends, their faces painted with blood, fatigue, and sorrow. "We can't stay here," he sighed, more to himself than to the others. "We need to go back to Cassino; we'll find sanctuary with the Order—regroup...find backup…we barely made it out alive…"

Nykronus merely looked at Elan, his teary eyes reflecting the flicker of distant torches from the city. "We need to plan," he said quietly. "We must understand how Warin has twisted the dagger's power before we face him again. We have failed. The dagger now bears the blood of St. Valentine."

Livia gently dabbed a damp cloth on Isolde's forehead, her touch gentle despite the urgency of their predicament. "Do not give up. Our faith will see us through this," she offered with quiet conviction.

Elan crouched beside Wulfstan, clasping the knight's massive hand. "You saved her," he said. "If it weren't for you…she would have died. Now we need to save ourselves—live to fight another day."

Wulfstan's eyes cracked open, a glimmer of strength fighting through the pain. "For Lady Kaira, for Grand Magus Felix," he rasped, each word a struggle.

"For all of us," Elan corrected softly, squeezing Wulfstan's hand before addressing the rest.

He looked around at his tired band of comrades. "We cut our losses, rest, recuperate, but come morning, we roll out. We've been dealt a shitty hand but not a death knell. I don't know how or why, but St. Michael's relics saved our asses." His voice carried gratitude and strength that seemed to stitch the broken edges of their willpower.

Nykronus rose to his feet, his gaze locking with Elan's. "Cassino will offer us refuge and resources," he confirmed. "We regroup there, heal, and sharpen our strategy."

As they trudged through the beautiful Italian countryside, Elan couldn't help but feel a sense of surreality wash over him. The lush green hills and the warm sun on his face starkly contrasted the world he had left behind, a reminder of how far he had come from his home and friends in the future. Isolde's sleeping form, cradled in the arms of one of their companions, was a somber reminder of the confrontation they had just faced, the battle that had left them all battered and bruised. The shield, its surface gleaming with the imperceptible light of Vulcan's Fire, was strapped across Elan's back—a tactile remnant of hope amidst their tribulations.

The night had been long, filled with unsettled sleep and attentive eyes. But now, as the first rays of sun osculated the horizon, Elan felt a disturbance within him. *Risorgimento*-a resurgence of purpose. They had kept the shield safe from Warin's grasp; it was a small victory but one that steeled his resolve.

As they moved silently, each step away from Terni was measured and heavy with repose. Elan replayed the battle in his mind, analyzing each move and counterattack. The sting of defeat was still fresh, yet it was piqued by the reassurance that not all was lost. The shield on his back was a testament to their tenacity—a symbol that they could still turn the tide against the Malefic Assembly.

Wulfstan moved with difficulty, his wounds requiring attention that they could not afford to give just yet. But even through his pain, he projected an aura of invincible spirit—the essence of steadfastness that had earned him his title.

Livia signaled the group to stop as she knelt beside Isolde, her hands hovering over the bard's unconscious form. She closed her eyes, her lips moving in silent prayer as a soft golden light emanated from her palms. The light seemed to seep into Isolde's skin, seeking out the injuries that marred her flesh and knitting them together with a gentle, soothing warmth. Livia's brow furrowed in concentration as she poured her faith and healing magic into the bard, her touch a balm that slowly coaxed Isolde from the brink of darkness. It was a slow process, but Livia undertook it with unwavering devotion, her hands working tirelessly to subdue the bard's injuries and bring her back to the waking world.

Nykronus led them onward with a map unfurled in his hands. His features were embedded with concentration as he steered through the switchback terrain between them and Cassino. Occasionally, he would pause to consult the stars or read the wind.

Elan felt it in every fiber—this journey back to Cassino would mark more than just miles traveled; it would be where they mustered their strength and honed their will against Warin's wrong-doing. The shield upon his back would protect them and remind them that in their darkest hour, as they sought to retrieve the *Pugio Mysticus Amoris*, they still had something Warin needed. The Order of St. Michael would restore balance to a world crumbling on the edge of night.

Under a tapestry of stars, the road to Cassino unfurled before them, a literal and symbolic path. The serene night echoed the subdued tenacity settling in each of their hearts.

Cassino, Duchy of Benevento, 842 A.D.

Elan found himself in a quiet corner of a local tavern, his thoughts consumed by the day's revelations. The weight of the nobleman in Rietti's tale pressed heavily on his mind, urging him to take action.

With a deep breath, he sought out Nykronus. He found the archaic mage in a small library, poring over ancient texts and manuscripts.

"Nykronus," Elan began, his voice steady despite the tumult of emotions within him. "I need to go to Benevento. I did as you asked; I went to Terni. I can't ignore this lead."

Nykronus looked up from his studies, his eyes filled with under-standing and concern. "I know the heart's pull, Elan," he said softly. "But we must also consider the larger picture. The Malefic Assembly grows stronger by the day, and we cannot afford to divide our forces now that we know they have that dagger."

Elan nodded, his jaw set with determination. "I understand, but this is something I have to do. I need to find out what happened to her after she came to this..time. For Kaira... for myself. I promise I won't lose sight of our ultimate goal. I'll be back and I *will* help you fulfill your promise to your dad."

Nykronus sighed, a faint smile playing at the corners of his mouth. "Very well, Elan. Go to Benevento and follow the path Kaira's diary has laid out for you. But remember, you are not alone in this. Your allies, your friends... we are here for you, always. Take Sister Livia with you."

Elan clasped Nykronus's shoulder, a gesture of gratitude and understanding. "No, this is something I have to do on my own. You'll need everyone's help to make sure we're ready for our next showdown."

As Elan turned to leave, Nykronus called out once more. "Elan, while you pursue this lead, the rest of us will continue to gather our strength. The Malefic Assembly's influence spreads like a plague, and we must be ready to counter his every move. Be well. Find Kaira."

With a final nod, Elan strode from the library.

And so, as Elan set forth on his quest.

CHAPTER

SEVENTEEN

The chamber where Kaira pursued her scholarly endeavors was a hallowed repository of ancient knowledge. In this place, the insights of long-dead philosophers whispered their arcane truths from the pages of weathered tomes. The walls, lined with shelves sagging under the weight of time, seemed to lean in closer as the sage spoke, her voice whispering and toting the melancholy of yesteryear. Dusty artifacts and ancient scrolls adorned the room, their faded colors hinting at the stories they held. Relics of bygone eras adorned every surface, each piece a testament to the history they stupefied. In the heart of this tiny room, with an overabundance of knowledge, Kaira sat across from an advisor whose reputation as a learned sage had drawn her to seek her counsel.

"The Dagger of Love, Kaira, is not merely a relic," she said, brushing her fingers over a page yellowed by the march of countless days. "It is a key—one of many artifacts needed to weave a spell effective enough to awaken St. Valentine himself from his eternal slumber."

Kaira leaned forward, her fair skin reflecting the flicker of candlelight as she absorbed his words. Her hands, poised above an open tome, trembled slightly with the magnitude of what she was learning.

The *Pugio Mysticus Amoris* had always symbolized mystery and reverence within her family's lore. Now, its true purpose was unfolding before her like the petals of some rare mesopic flower.

The sage continued with each word being purposeful and intertwined with ominous undertones. "The dagger embodies sacrifice and protection, intrinsic to its power." She paused for a moment, locking eyes with Kaira. "Its theft in darker times was no mere misfortune—it was a calculated act by those who sought to twist its destiny."

A chill threaded through the room despite the warmth from the hearth. Kaira felt it crawl up her spine as she considered his warning. The consequences should such an object fall into malicious hands were dire and far-reaching.

"Malevolent desires must not overshadow the dagger's light," she warned. "Its destiny is intertwined with that of true love and sacrifice —should it be corrupted, the balance could be irrevocably tipped."

Her gaze held Kaira's for an eternal second before she looked away, allowing Kaira to process the importance of their discussion. The air around them grew heavy with unspoken implications—a portentous quietness filling the study like dust upon untouched relics.

Benevento, Lombard Principality, 839 A.D.

In an unfrequented glade, where light danced through the leaves and the air's aroma blessed with the serenity of untouched nature, Kaira sat cross-legged, her teenage children Myst and Maya at her sides. The three formed a triangle, the ground beneath them rich with the history of their secret meetings. Here, Kaira had taught her twins the art of meditation—her modern-day practice from the future morphed into the power of listening to the undertone of the earth.

Kaira's journey with meditation began long before she found herself in the past. It was a skill she had learned alongside her sister, Reagan, when they were just children. Their wise and gentle grandmother had recognized the power of mindfulness and sought to pass this knowledge on to her granddaughters. She would sit with them in the quiet of her garden, guiding them through the basics of breathing and visualization, planting the seeds of a practice that would grow and flourish throughout Kaira's life. As Kaira faced the challenges of high school and beyond, she found solace in the stillness of meditation, a way to center herself and find clarity in chaos. It was a gift she would carry with her through time and space, a constant companion in her journey to navigate the complexities of her new reality.

Kaira's voice carried the weight of wisdom beyond her years as she began to speak. She pulled out a shimmering gem from her leather tunic, its inner light shining brightly. According to legend, this gem was infused with the storm at Jupiter's peak when he cast a bolt into it. "A friend from a noble order entrusted me with this gem," Kaira said, her eyes locking onto Myst's as she emphasized the moment's significance. "She promised to come back for it one day. I need you to keep it safe for me."

Maya watched, her curiosity piqued as she noticed how the gem seemed to pulse in time with their mother's heartbeat. "Mother, I can see the storm manifesting within the gem. It's beautiful," she remarked.

Kaira's lips curved into a slight smile as she presented Maya with a shield, it's surface unadorned but gleaming like the fire of Vulcan from which it was forged. "This shield is now yours to protect and defend yourself with," she declared. "Legend has it that it possesses the unique ability to absorb and contain multiple spells' energies."

Myst cradled the gem in his hands as if it were the most brittle creature on earth while Maya ran her fingers over the cool metal of the shield, feeling an energy that seemed eager to erupt.

"These relics," Kaira continued, "were once owned by St. Michael himself. They can channel energies necessary for a spell of great importance." Her voice grew heavy. "In the wrong hands, these could be used for evil and plots beyond our worst nightmares."

She paused, looking between her son and daughter with pride and an indisputable sense of purpose. "I believe in your roles within a greater destiny," she confessed. "I was transported from the future for reasons and pulled hundreds of years away from your dad. We are part of a grand scheme that involves both of you more than any of us can understand."

Myst and Maya, their young faces fixed with awe and anxiety, regarded their mother's words with the solemnity of children far beyond their nine years. With a clarity that belied their age, they understood that the relics they now held were not merely playthings but burdens that carried the weight of expectation and responsibility. These artifacts would shape not only their own lives but the lives of countless others, a legacy that stretched far into an uncertain future. As they gazed upon the shield and gem, their tiny hands trembling slightly, Myst and Maya knew that they were being entrusted with a task that would define them in ways they could only begin to imagine.

Kaira reached out, placing a hand on each of their shoulders. "Guard them well," she implored. "Your stewardship will shape what's yet to come."

Benevento, Lombard Principality, 840 A.D.

Rain fell in thick sheets, obscuring the landscape and painting the town a blurry mix of muted colors. Each drop created ripples in puddles and dripped from rooftops, creating a serene scene. The ambiance was filled with the deep smell of damp earth and a hint of barbecue, likely from a gathering at a nearby home. Kaira walked beside her children, Myst and Maya, their footsteps mashing softly on the leaf-covered path.

A mysterious figure lurked in the nearby woods, his breath misting in the chill air as he watched them approach. His fingers caressed the hilt of his scimitar, anticipation coiling inside him like a viper poised to attack. The *Pugio Mysticus Amoris* was within reach and, with it, power beyond his understanding. He waited for the black of night to surround them.

With the *Pugio Mysticus Amoris* within reach, Warin could almost taste the power that would soon be his. He envisioned himself wielding the dagger, bending the very fabric of reality to his will. With this ancient relic, he could reshape the world in his twisted image, creating a dark paradise where his every desire would be fulfilled. He longed to unleash the dagger's full potential, to revel in the chaos and destruction it would bring, and to stand as the supreme ruler of a realm forever shrouded in shadow.

As they neared a cluster of large oak trees, Warin charged from his skulking location with a wild cry. Maya squealed out in alarm as Kaira spun around, her eyes wide with shock. Myst galloped forward, reaching for his hatchet.

"Run!" Kaira shouted at her children, her voice cutting through the sudden chaos like a shard of ice.

Warin's attack was swift and merciless, his blade catching the glint of twilight shining through a break in the storm clouds as he aimed for Kaira's heart. She dodged at the last second but not fast enough to avoid injury altogether. The dagger found its mark on her side, inducing a gasp of pain from her lips.

Maya scrambled to shield her brother with Vulcan's forged creation while Kaira grappled with Warin. Each movement she made was an agonizing dance between survival and sacrifice. Blood seeped through her tunic, staining it red as she fought back with every last ounce of strength she had left.

Warin laughed, a sound that mixed with the howl of an icy wind sweeping across the land. Kaira felt a visceral fear grip her heart. The sound was a chilling reminder of the darkness that threatened to engulf them, a twisted melody that seemed to seep into her bones. He thrust repeatedly, each time more furious than the last as he sought to wrestle away the Dagger of Love.

Kaira deflected a blow that would have been fatal for Myst, absorbing the brunt of it herself. She staggered back under its force, feeling life's warmth ebb away from her body. With a final act born of desperation and love, she threw herself at Warin to shield her children from his malice.

Her sacrifice bought precious seconds for Myst and Maya to escape into the darkening woods. The assassin's laughter turned to fury as he realized his prey was slipping away.

The world shrunk to pain and struggle as Kaira collapsed under Warin's brutal attack. Her vision blurred, and her breath came in ragged gasps as she felt him pry the dagger from her weakening grip.

As Warin fled into the night with his prize clutched tightly in his hands, Kaira lay motionless on the ground—her lifeblood seeping into the earth that had been witness to so much history and so much more to come.

Snuggled within the forest's hug, a concealed cubbyhole shielded from the rest of the world served as Kaira's shelter. Water dripped from the surrounding leaves, creating a hushed symphony that resonated with the sanctity of the moment. With Myst and Maya by her side, Kaira felt the wisps of her life beginning to fade away. Her breaths came in labored gasps, yet her eyes fought back with an intensity that contradicted her weakening state.

The twins knelt beside their mother, their expressions entrenched with concern and confusion. Maya sobbed as her brother attempted to console her as they now faced a reality they were unprepared for.

"Myst, Maya," Kaira began, her voice barely above a whisper as she clasped their hands within her frail ones. "I left instructions for you in my diary back home. Listen to me. I am so proud of you. I see so much of your dad in you, and I know in my heart you'll see him again."

Tears welled in Maya's eyes as she tightened her grip on her mother's hand.

Kaira offered them a smile that held both love and sorrow. "The relics you hold," she continued, looking toward the gem cradled in Myst's hands and the shield beside Maya, "are more than mere objects. They are embers of hope for a future you must help forge, and I am convinced they are what will bring you back to the rest of our family."

Myst's body tensed as he grappled with his mother's words. He knew not the weight of what was asked of him, but he felt its gravity nonetheless.

Kaira drew a painful breath before speaking again. "You both are destined for great things—things I will not get to see for myself." She paused, collecting the last ounces of her strength. "But know that I will *always* walk alongside you."

Maya leaned forward, pressing her forehead against their mother's. "I love you, Mom," she dedicated through quivering lips.

Kaira's gaze shifted between them one final time—a silent conveyance of all the wisdom and courage she sought to impart. "Protect each other," she implored with a hurry that pierced their hearts. "Let love guide your path."

With those final words, Kaira Mazza entrusted her legacy to her children. The weight of their responsibility settled upon them like an unseen mantle—a charge they would carry beyond this alcove and into the vastness of an uncertain future.

Myst and Maya sat in tense silence after burying their mother. The stillness of the night was suffocating, and each rustle of leaves reminded them of her absence. The storm had passed, but the lingering clouds mirrored the storm brewing inside them. They didn't know how to face this new reality without their mother.

They remained motionless for a long time, the gravity of their loss anchoring them to the earth. The gem and shield rested at their feet, emblems of an obligation that tugged at their souls more than any other burden.

Maya broke the silence first, her voice a fragile thread in the stillness. "We have to do this, Myst. For her—for all she believed in."

Myst paused, his solemn expression reset into determination. "I know," he assured her, though his voice trembled with emotion. "We'll keep these safe and use them as she intended. We're not just protecting relics; we're preserving hope."

Maya reached for her brother's hand, her grip firm and resolute. Together, they stood up, facing each other.

"We make this vow," Maya began, her eyes never leaving Myst's.

"To honor our mother's last wishes," Myst continued, picking up where his sister left off.

"And to safeguard these relics with our lives," Maya added.

"And finding our dad," Myst concluded.

The solemn promise hung between them like an indestructible chain, linking their fates irrevocably to the future. They understood that their journey would be full of danger and that each step forward would be in honor of everything their mother had prepared them for.

In that hallowed space under the watchful eyes of the stars, Myst and Maya Durant embraced their destiny.

Fragmented Territories, Italy, 841 A.D.

Maya, now a sixteen-year-old woman, stood at a hidden cave entrance, her fingertips grazing the cold, textured surface of the shield. Her dark hair, the same rich hue as her mother's, cascaded down her back in gentle waves, contrasting with the pale green of her eyes. The sound of the crashing waterfall filled her ears, droplets of mist kissing her cheeks and creating a natural curtain that separated her from the outside world. With the courage and composure of one far beyond her years, Maya took a deep breath and stepped into the unknown, ready to embrace her destiny.

Inside, shadows clung to every crevice, reluctant to part even for the determined flame of her torch. This was one of the secret locations their mother had spoken of—a sanctum where power and secrecy entwined like the roots of an ancient tree. Maya placed the shield upon an altar carved from stone, feeling a thrum of energy as if the earth acknowledged its return.

Meanwhile, Myst treaded toward the top of the highest mountain with Jupiter's Bolt securely in his satchel. He pushed through the thick snow that froze his clothing, each step a silent testament to his dedication. He arrived at a hidden cave where ice protected the entrance. With careful hands, he withdrew the gem and set it into a recess within the cave walls. A pulse of light surged from within it, sealing its place.

The twins had other relics to secrete away—the armor blessed with Neptune's Tears that Maya slipped beneath the roots of an olive tree rumored to have been planted by a demigod in a secluded garden in Antium; Maya's shield was returned to the very forge it was created in a mountain; scales touched by Juno's Breath that Myst hid within a nest of golden eagles atop an enchanted forest known only to those who flew; and finally, the dragon tooth filled with dust from Saturn's Ring that Myst concealed within an ancient ruin, in the Eastern Alps, whose origins were lost to time.

Each relic found its home in silence punctuated by heartbeats and whispers of cloth or leather against ancient stone and soil. Each placement was an act completed with precision—a ritual that held more significance than mere safeguarding.

Myst and Maya felt a growing sense of purpose with each relic placed, knowing that their actions were part of a grander tapestry. They understood that their role was to lay the foundation for a future quest, one that would be undertaken by someone they had yet to meet.

CHAPTER

EIGHTEEN

Cassino, Duchy of Benevento, 842 A.D.

Elan stepped through an ancient stone archway, his heart pounding with anticipation as he entered the city of Benevento. The brick-paved streets, worn smooth by centuries of footsteps, seemed to grumble secrets of the past. He inhaled deeply, the atmosphere heavy with the scent of history and the promise of answers.

As he made his way through the winding alleys, Elan couldn't help but feel a sense of familiarity wash over him. It was as if the city recognized his presence, welcoming him back like an old friend, even though he was nothing more than a stranger in a world he wished he knew. He approached a group of locals gathered around a fountain, their faces impressed with the wisdom of generations.

"Excuse me," Elan said, his voice steady despite the nerves fluttering in his chest. "I'm looking for information about a woman named Kaira Mazza. She lived here some time ago."

The locals exchanged glances, their eyes sparkling with recognition. An elderly man stepped forward, his weathered hand resting on Elan's shoulder. "Ah, Kaira," he said, his voice thick with emotion. "She was a beloved member of our community. Her home is not far from here."

With directions in hand, Elan set off, his strides purposeful. The streets seemed to guide him, leading him through a maze of ancient buildings until he stood before a modest stone house. The wooden door, adorned with intricate carvings, stood slightly ajar as if inviting him inside.

As Elan stepped into the house, he was struck by a sense of familiarity, as if the very essence of Kaira permeated every corner. Though he had never seen the interior before, it felt like a reflection of her spirit, each detail a testament to her presence.

Dust motes danced in the slanting sunlight that streamed through the windows, casting a warm glow over the room. Elan ran his fingertips along the rough surface of the stone walls, tracing the lines of history inscribed into their surface. He could almost feel Kaira's presence lingering in the air, a subtle reminder of their shared love.

Elan's gaze fell upon a small wooden box resting on a shelf as he explored the house. He reached for it with trembling hands, his breath catching in his throat as he lifted the lid. Inside, nestled among scraps of parchment and dried flowers, was a single rosary bead—the very same one that had brought him to this moment.

Elan's grip on the bead tightened, its weight and power giving him a sense of purpose. He understood this was only the first step in his quest to find Kaira, one element of the larger picture.

As Elan explored the depths of Kaira's home, his heart raced with each step, his mind consumed by the possibility of uncovering a clue that would lead him closer to her. His surroundings hung heavy with memories, and the silence was broken only by the creaking of ancient floorboards beneath his feet.

"Excuse me." A voice called from the entrance door.

Startled, Elan turned around, "Huh?" His hand subtly reached for *Winterstar*.

"I have something for you," the monk said, pulling a cloth-wrapped letter from his robe's pocket—the same letter Kaira had entrusted him years ago. "A letter."

"A letter for me? That's impossible." Elan reached for the letter and stared at it with awe.

"Kaira entrusted it to me to give to anyone asking about her in town." The monk solemnly looked into Elan's eyes.

"Kaira?" Elan was speechless and on the verge of tears. "Thank you."

"It was an honor to be entrusted with this. It must be important. I will leave you to it." The monk exited the house with reverence.

He found himself drawn to a dusty desk tucked away in the corner of the room, its surface untouched by time. With trembling hands, Elan brushed away the layers of dust, unwrapping the letter addressed to him in Kaira's unmistakable handwriting. His breath caught in his throat as he carefully unfolded the fine parchment, his eyes hungrily devouring every word.

The letter spoke of Kaira's life in this ancient world, of the joys and challenges of raising their children, Myst and Maya. Elan stood in stunned silence, his mind reeling as he tried to process the revelation that he had children. The idea that Kaira had raised their twins, Myst and Maya, in a time so different from theirs was awe-inspiring and overwhelming. He felt a surge of emotions - joy at the thought of being a father, sorrow for the years he had missed, and a profound sense of disbelief at the extraordinary circumstances that had brought them to this moment.

As Elan read on, his heart swelled with a bittersweet mixture of love and longing. Kaira's words hinted at the legends and myths she had begun to uncover, whispers of ancient gods, and powerful relics that seemed to hold the key to their fate. With each revelation, Elan's resolve grew more robust, his determination to find her burning brighter than ever.

He carefully folded the letter, tucking it close to his heart as a tangible reminder of their love. The discovery of Kaira's words had ignited a reoriented sense of purpose within him, a fierce desire to unravel the mysteries that separated them and bring their family back together.

Elan stood from the desk, his gaze sweeping over the room one last time. The dusty relics and faded memories surrounding him served as a testament to the life Kaira had built in his absence, a life he longed to be a part of once more.

As Elan's eyes traced Kaira's words, a wave of emotions crashed over him, threatening to sweep him away in its current. Joy swelled in his heart as he read about the life she had built with their children, Myst and Maya, in this ancient world. He could almost hear their laughter echoing through the stone walls and see Kaira's brilliant smile as she watched them play.

Elan struggled to comprehend the reality before him - he was a father to twins Myst and Maya, born and raised in a time far removed from his own. The shock of this revelation sent his mind spiraling, questions and emotions colliding in a dizzying whirlwind. How had this happened? What had Kaira endured, raising their children alone in a world so different from the one they knew? The weight of the years he had missed pressed upon him, a bittersweet mix of joy and sorrow that left him reeling.

Yet, despite those challenges, Kaira's love and strength shone through her words. She spoke of motherhood's simple joys, watching Myst and Maya grow and learn, and their family bond. Her message was a testament to her soul's resilience and the devotion and hope she held for their eventual reunion.

As Elan read and re-read her words, he felt a deep connection to Kaira, a bond that cut across time and space.

Now, as he stood in the quiet of Kaira's bedroom, the letter felt like a lifeline, a tangible connection to their love. Tears pricked at the corners of his eyes as he held the letter.

The letter was more than words on a piece of paper; it was a reminder that their bond could never be broken even in the darkest times. It anchored Elan's grief, transforming it from an abstract ache into something he could hold onto and read through the adversities ahead.

A wave of emotion crashed over him, and he found himself sinking to his knees beside the bed, his legs no longer able to support the weight of his grief. Hot and heavy tears began to stream down his face, tracing paths through the dust and grime accumulated during his journey.

He pressed the letter to his chest, his fingers trembling as he held it close as if he could somehow absorb the essence of Kaira's presence through the faded parchment. The words she had written, the love and longing that poured from every carefully crafted sentence, tore at his heart, ripping open wounds that had never truly healed.

Elan's shoulders shook as he wept, the pain of separation and loss overwhelming him. The room seemed to close around him, the stone walls amplifying the echoes of his sorrow.

But even as he wept, even as the pain threatened to consume him, Elan knew that his tears were not a sign of weakness but rather a testament to the strength of his love. They were the tears of a man who would stop at nothing to find his way back to his family, moving heaven and earth to hold them in his arms once more.

As Elan knelt beside Kaira's bed, his body shaking with the force of his grief, a soft sound from the doorway pulled him from the depths of his sorrow. He raised his head, tears streaming down his face, to find two figures standing at the threshold, their silhouettes bathed in the warm glow of the setting sun.

For a moment, Elan thought he was dreaming, his mind conjuring up an impossible vision to ease the ache in his heart. But as the figures stepped forward, their features coming into sharp focus, he realized this was no dream.

Myst and Maya, the children he had never had the chance to know, stood before him, their eyes wide with a mixture of uncertainty and hope. They were young adults, and their resemblance to Kaira was unmistakable. The twins had inherited Kaira's striking blue eyes and the subtle curve of her smile. When he tilted his head in thought, it was as if Elan was looking at a reflection of Kaira's reflective moments. Maya's bright and melodic laughter echoed Kaira's joyful spirit. The way she moved, with graceful confidence, was a mirror image of her mother's self-assured nature.

Elan rose to his feet, his legs unsteady beneath him as he took a tentative step forward. "Myst? Maya?" he whispered, his voice hoarse with emotion.

Myst and Maya, now 18, exchanged a glance, a silent communication passing between them before they turned their attention back to Elan. Maya, with her mother's dark curls and soulful eyes, was the first to speak. "Father?" she asked, her voice unnerved with a fragile hope.

That single word, spoken with such tender uncertainty, was all it took to break through the walls of Elan's grief. He stumbled forward, closing the distance between them in a few short strides, and gathered his children.

Tears of joy mingled with sorrow as Elan held them close, their bodies pressed against his chest, their heartbeats echoing his rhythm. He breathed in their scent, committing every detail of this moment to memory, a balm to soothe the ache of the years they had spent apart.

For a long moment, they held each other, basking in the warmth of their newfound connection. The pain of the past, the sorrow that had consumed Elan mere moments before, began to fade, replaced by a glimmer of hope that burned brightly in his chest.

With Myst and Maya in his arms, the pieces of his shattered heart began to mend, the jagged edges of his grief smoothing into something softer, something that could heal with time and love. Their presence was a reminder that even in the darkest of times, there was always a chance for a new beginning, an opportunity to forge the bonds of family that had been denied to them for so long.

As Elan, Myst, and Maya settled into the living room of Kaira's home, the weight of their shared history was oppressive. The siblings exchanged a glance, a silent understanding passing between them before Myst began to speak.

"Father," he started, his voice steady despite the emotion that swirled in his eyes, "there's so much we need to tell you."

Maya reached out, placing a comforting hand on her brother's arm, before gazing at Elan. "Mother left us with a mission, a purpose that has guided our every step since the day she was taken from us."

Elan leaned forward, his heart racing as he listened to his children's words. They spoke of Kaira's final wishes, of the secrets she had entrusted to them in the face of an unseen danger.

Myst's voice grew stronger as he recounted their journey and their trials in their quest to honor their mother's legacy. "She knew that the Dagger of Love held the key to our family's fate, that it was a relic of immense power that could not fall into the wrong hands."

At that moment, Elan felt a surge of hatred for Warin, the man who had murdered the love of his life. As he tried to grasp the complexity of the situation, his mind briefly wandered to thoughts of revenge. But this fleeting daydream was abruptly cut short when his daughter interrupted his thoughts.

Maya nodded, her eyes shining with determination. "We've spent years preparing ourselves, Father. Training our bodies and minds for the battle that lies ahead."

As Elan listened to their stories, he felt pride mingling with the ache of loss that had become his constant companion. His children, the living embodiment of his love for Kaira, had grown into fierce and determined warriors in his absence.

Their words painted a picture of their lives, the trials they had faced, and the unbreakable bond they shared with their mother, even in death. Each revelation was a thread that wove them closer together, binding them as a family united by a common purpose.

Myst leaned forward, his gaze intense as he locked eyes with Elan. "We know who murdered our mother, Father. And we will not rest until justice is served and the Dagger of Love is safely returned to our hands."

"Elan reached out, clasping his children's hands in his own. The warmth of their skin and the strength of their grip were tangible reminders of the love that had created them and sustained them through the darkest times. 'We're going to Cassino to get the Dagger back,' he said firmly. 'Somehow, someway, your mom was chosen to wield that dagger, and she died because of it. It doesn't belong to Warin or the Malefic Assembly. We're getting it back—for your mom.'"

Elan looked at his children, marveling at the strength and resilience he saw in their eyes. They had grown into remarkable individuals, shaped by the love and guidance of their mother, even in her absence. Since Kaira's passing, they felt a loss that had left an indelible mark on the family. In the wake of their grief, Myst and Maya had leaned on each other, their bond as siblings growing even more vital as they navigated the challenges of life without their mother. They had taken on responsibilities beyond their years, Myst stepping into a protective role, ensuring Maya's well-being. At the same time, Maya's nurturing nature provided emotional support and kept Kaira's memory alive in their home.

Myst and Maya, in turn, saw in their father a reflection of their resolve. The years had defined lines of grief and longing into his face, but beneath the weight of his sorrow, they recognized the same fierce determination that had driven their mother to entrust them with her final wishes.

As they sat together, their hands clasped in a symbol of their unbreakable bond, the family acknowledged the roles they each had to play in the journey that lay before them. With his skills honed by years of military service, Elan would be their protector and guide, a steady presence in the face of the dangers they would inevitably face. He had decades of wisdom and knowledge to pass down to his children, a side of him that Kaira never had the chance to witness.

With his keen intellect and strategic mind, Myst would be the architect of their plans, the one to unravel the secrets of the Dagger of Love and chart their course through the labyrinthine web of their enemies' machinations.

Maya, with her unwavering faith and ability to see the truth in others' hearts, would be their moral compass, ensuring that they never lost sight of the values that had defined their mother's life and legacy.

The first light of dawn spilled across the cobblestone path, casting a soft aureate hue over the threshold of Kaira's home. Elan stood in the doorway, his silhouette framed by the blossoming light, Myst and Maya flanking him on either side. The morning air was crisp, carrying the promise of a new day, a fresh start.

As they stepped over the threshold, their shadows stretched long behind them, tethered to the place that had once been a sanctuary of love and laughter. They turned their backs on the house, not in abandonment but with a reverence for what it represented—a legacy of love that Kaira had nurtured within its walls.

Myst adjusted the straps of his pack with purposeful movements, each buckle and tie a silent testament to his readiness. Beside him,

Maya stood resolute, her eyes reflecting the steel and softness that their mother had bequeathed her. In their stance, there was an unspoken vow to carry forward Kaira's unassailable anima.

Elan surveyed his children with pride, swelling his chest. They were no longer just fragments of a scattered past; they were whole, united by shared blood and purpose. His gaze shifted from them to the path ahead, where the journey to Cassino awaited—a path he now walked not alone but with his family at his side.

They moved as one entity down the path leading away from Kaira's home. The quiet of the morning was punctuated only by the sound of their boots against stone and earth. Each step was deliberate, a conscious movement toward destiny.

Elan felt a shift within him as they reached the outskirts of Benevento, where grass breathed secrets to the wind, and trees stood as silent sentinels to their passage. The grief that had once threatened to consume him had found its counterweight in hope. In Myst and Maya's presence, he found solace and strength.

The trio paused at a rise in the path that afforded them a view back toward Kaira's home. They stood shoulder to shoulder, watching as light painted the walls and windows with strokes of warmth.

"It's time," Elan murmured, his voice carrying both an end and a beginning.

Myst nodded solemnly while Maya placed a hand on Elan's arm—a gesture filled with comfort and resolve.

CHAPTER
NINETEEN

Cassino, Duchy of Benevento, 842 A.D.

As they approached the entrance of the Abbey of Monte-cassino, Elan's gaze fell upon a group of familiar figures emerging from the shadows. Nykronus, Wulfstan, Livia, and Isolde stood waiting, their faces grooved with anticipation and concern.

"Nykronus, my friend," Elan called out, firmly clasping the mage's hand. "I told you I'd be back."

Nykronus's smile broadened as his gaze shifted to Myst and Maya. The wise man's eyes twinkled with recognition. "Introductions are unnecessary, Elan Durant. Their likeness to you is unmistakable."

Myst stepped forward, his gaze filled with curiosity. "I am Myst; this is Maya. You're the one who's been guiding our father?"

"Indeed," Nykronus replied, his voice warm. "And I look forward to hearing about your adventures."

Wulfstan approached, his golden armor glinting in the sunlight. "Myst, Maya," he said, his voice gruff but kind. "I am Wulfstan, a Templar Knight. Your father is full of bravery."

Maya beamed, her eyes shining with pride. "Thank you, sir. We're ready to do our part in this fight."

Livia and Isolde stepped forward, their smiles gentle and welcoming. "Welcome home," Livia said, her monastic robes swaying in the breeze. "The Order has been eagerly awaiting your arrival, Elan."

Isolde nodded, her lute slung across her back, and her attention shifted to the twins. "I want you to tell us all about your mother. I cannot wait to sing tales of the one who lived in a world different from her own. We're honored to have you join us in this quest."

As they gathered in a secluded chamber within the Abbey's heart, Elan felt the weight of anticipation settle upon his shoulders. The room, illuminated by the soft glow of flickering candles, seemed to hold its breath as Myst and Maya stepped forward, their eyes glinting with a newfound purpose.

Myst's steady and clear voice cut through the silence. "We have discovered the resting place of St. Valentine." His words shifted the mood, a revelation that sent ripples of excitement through the assembled group.

Maya continued, her gaze sweeping across the faces of their companions. "His body lies within the hallowed walls of St. Paul's Basilica in Rome. It is there that we must journey if we are to unravel the secrets of our quest."

Elan leaned forward, his heart pounding in his chest. The knowledge that they now held a tangible destination, a sacred site that could hold the key to their mission, filled him with fire.

Nykronus nodded solemnly. "The basilica holds great significance in the tapestry of our journey. It is a place of power, where the threads of fate converge."

Wulfstan spoke with a voice that resonated with the weight of his experience. "The Order has long suspected that St. Valentine's remains held a crucial role in the unfolding of these events. Now, with this revelation, we can move forward with clarity and purpose."

The bard's eyes shining with quiet determination, Isolde added, "And find out what these dark forces are up to. The journey to Rome will not be without obstacles, but we must not falter. The stakes are too high, and the consequences are too dire to turn back now. If we fail, the

Malefic Assembly will gain control over ancient relics of immense power. They already have the dagger...and Jupiter's Bolt. With these artifacts in their grasp, they could unleash untold devastation upon the world, enslaving humanity and plunging us into an age of darkness and despair. Countless lives hang in the balance, and the very fabric of reality itself could be torn asunder. We cannot allow that to happen, no matter the cost."

As the group absorbed the gravity of Myst and Maya's revelation, Elan felt a heightened sense of urgency course through his veins. The path ahead was littered with danger, but with the knowledge of St. Valentine's resting place, they now had a clear direction, a beacon of hope to guide them through the darkness.

Elan's heart raced as he listened to the revelations unfold, each word an arrow piercing the veil of deception that had shrouded their journey. Myst and Maya, their faces seared with anger and disbelief, recounted the tales they had uncovered during their time in the past.

"Verendana, a devout follower of St. Valentine, was the one who sent Warin after our mother," Myst's voice trembled with emotion. "She was the one who orchestrated her death, all in the name of her twisted devotion."

Maya, her eyes glistening with unshed tears, added, "She had been hiding in plain sight all along, manipulating events from the shadows. *Femina Perfida*, the very embodiment of treachery, was none other than Verendana herself."

Nykronus placed his hand on Maya's shoulder. "Verendana's betrayal runs deep, a wound that has festered for centuries. Her actions have set in motion a chain of events that threaten to unravel the very fabric of our world."

Wulfstan bellowed with a voice that resonated with the weight of his experience. "The Order has long suspected Verendana's involvement, but the extent of her treachery was hidden from our sight. Now, with this revelation, we must confront the true nature of our enemy."

Elan felt a wave of anger and grief wash over him, the realization that Verendana had played a role in Kaira's death, adding a personal vendetta to their already daunting mission. The betrayal cut deep, a wound that would not quickly heal.

As the group absorbed the gravity of the revelation, a heavy silence settled over the chamber. Each party member grappled with their emotions, the weight of the truth-bearing upon them like a physical force.

Isolde broke the silence. "We cannot let Verendana's betrayal go unanswered. Our mission has taken on a new urgency, a personal stake that drives us forward."

With the knowledge of Verendana's true identity, they now had a solid target and a focus for their righteous anger. The quest for justice and the desire to stop the Malefic Assembly's plans burned brighter. They knew that time was of the essence and that every moment spent in contemplation was a moment their enemy could use to their advantage.

Elan rose to his feet, his eyes blazing with determination. "We can't let this revelation break us," he said, his voice steady and robust. "Verendana may have betrayed us, but we still have a mission to complete. We have to press on, now more than ever."

Nykronus nodded with sincerity. "Elan is right. We must use this knowledge to our advantage, to anticipate Verendana's next move and stay one step ahead."

The others conveyed their agreement, their faces set with a grim tenacity.

Elan stood at the center of the makeshift war room, his eyes scanning the faces of his companions as they gathered around the weathered wooden table. The fading candlelight cast shadows across the ancient walls of their Cassino hideout, a testament to the task's weight before them.

Nykronus leaned forward, his gaze intense. "*Femina Perfida*, or Verendana as we now know her, will not be easily thwarted. She has had centuries to plan and manipulate events to her advantage."

"We need to focus on the task at hand," Elan said, his voice cutting through the tension. "St. Paul's Basilica is our target, and we have to plan our approach carefully."

Wulfstan leaned forward, his brow furrowed. "What do we know about the basilica's layout? Any potential entry points or hidden passages?"

Isolde pulled out a set of ancient blueprints, spreading them across the table. "According to these plans, there are several hidden chambers beneath the main structure. If Verendana is hiding something, that's where we'll likely find it."

Livia nodded, her eyes scanning the documents. "We'll need to be cautious. Verendana is cunning, and she will have traps and defenses in place."

"Then we'll just have to be smarter," Maya said, her youthful face filled with determination.

As the group nodded in agreement, a sense of unity and purpose settled over the room.

Elan felt a surge of pride as he looked upon his companions, each a vital piece in the intricate puzzle of their mission. With their strategic planning complete, they were ready to embark on the final leg of their journey, to confront Femina Perfida and unravel the secrets that had haunted them for so long.

Nykronus placed a comforting hand on Elan's shoulder. "We have come far, my friend. The strength of our unity will be our greatest weapon against the challenges that lie ahead."

Livia nodded in agreement. "The Order has always believed in the power of unity. It is through our collective resolve that we will triumph over the darkness."

Wulfstan the Steadfast, his golden armor a beacon of courage, spoke with a voice that resonated with determination. "We have each faced our own trials and losses, but it is in coming together that we have found the strength to persevere."

Isolde, the bard's eyes shining with fierce loyalty, plucked a gentle melody from her lute. "Our stories, our pain, and our triumphs are woven together in a tapestry of resilience. It is this bond that will carry us through the battles to come."

Myst and Maya, their youthful faces scored with wisdom beyond their years, and they looked to Elan with unwavering trust. "We have found a family in this group," Myst said softly. "A family that will stop at nothing to protect each other and see this mission through to the end."

"Mom would have loved this," Maya added.

Elan held his children close, feeling emotions rushing through him. As they hugged, he couldn't ignore his happiness and love, but it was tinged with the memory of his mother's words echoing in his mind: "Things happen for a reason."

Elan's thoughts drifted to his mother's words, a bittersweet mix of frustration and longing washing over him. He had always struggled with her sayings, finding them more platitudes than comfort. Yet now, in the face of this challenging situation, he couldn't help but wonder if there was some truth to her wisdom. He smirked at the idea he was now saying it to his children.

Elan felt a swell of emotion rise within him as he looked upon the faces of his companions. Each one had become an integral part of his life, a piece of the puzzle that had brought him closer to the truth and the memory of Kaira.

CHAPTER

TWENTY

Papal State Territory, Rome, 842 A.D.

The journey to St. Paul's Basilica was one of tense anticipation and unquestionable commitment. Elan led the group through the outskirts of Rome, his senses heightened, alert for any signs of danger. Their surroundings felt heavy with the weight of their mission, the silence broken only by the soft whooshes of their footsteps and the occasional whisper of the wind.

Myst and Maya walked beside their father, their young faces etched with a resolve contradicting their years. They had grown so much since Kaira's death, their experiences shaping them into formidable allies in the fight against the Malefic Assembly. Elan's heart swelled with pride and fierce protectiveness as he watched them navigate the shadows, their movements precise and purposeful.

Elan had never imagined himself as a father, his life consumed by the demands of his military career and the weight of his personal struggles. But as he watched Myst and Maya, their presence a tangible reminder of his love with Kaira, he felt a sense of completeness that he had never known. The fierce protectiveness that surged through him was a revelation, a primal instinct that overshadowed everything else.

At that moment, he knew he would move heaven and earth to keep his children safe and to give them the future they deserved.

Nykronus followed close behind, surveying the surroundings for any signs of trouble. His presence was reassuring and constant, a reminder of the ancient knowledge and power that guided their steps.

Wulfstan moved with the grace and precision of a seasoned warrior, his hand resting on the hilt of his sword, ready to defend his companions at a moment's notice. With her lute slung across her back, Isolde moved with a quiet determination, her green eyes sharp and alert. She had seen the horrors of the Malefic Assembly firsthand, and her resolve to end their conspiracies was relentless. Livia walked beside her, her robes a whisper in the night, her faith a beacon of hope in the darkness.

Elan's thoughts turned to the remaining relics they vowed to protect as they approached the Basilica. *Pugio Mysticus Amoris*, the Dagger of Love, the key to thwarting the Malefic Assembly's plans, weighed heavily on his mind. He knew that the fate of countless lives rested on their success, and the responsibility settled on his shoulders like a physical burden.

But as he looked around at his companions, at the determination and courage etched on their faces, Elan felt a surge of hope. They had come so far and faced many challenges yet remained united in their purpose. Together, they would see this mission through to the end, no matter the cost.

A sense of discomfort settled over Elan. The shadows seemed to sparkle with an unnatural power, and the atmosphere shifted with anticipation. Suddenly, the clang of footsteps smashed the stillness, and a group of hooded figures emerged from the darkest alleys, their stances set with malevolent intent.

In the ancient corridors, a figure emerged, her striking presence commanding the space. Verendana bore her rich heritage in her features - dark, curly hair framing her face and deep brown eyes holding centuries of wisdom and secrets. A scar above her nose added a rugged aspect to her serene appearance.

The shadows emphasized her dark circles, hinting at sleepless nights spent pursuing goals or guarding secrets too heavy to share.

Verendana's curvaceous figure radiated strength and set her apart from her peers.

She stood at the forefront, sneering. "Your journey ends here," she declared. Beside her, Warin's crooked form twitched with excitement, his fingers curling around his weapon.

Elan's squad immediately fell into a defensive formation, their weapons at the ready. Myst and Maya flanked their father, their stances mirroring his own, while Nykronus and Wulfstan positioned themselves to protect the group's back. Isolde and Livia stood back-to-back, their eyes scanning the shadows for any signs of movement.

The scene crackled with tension as the two groups faced off, each waiting for the other to make the first move. Then, with a guttural cry, Verendana's followers surged forward, their weapons flashing in the moonshine.

The skirmish was fierce and chaotic, the sound of clashing metal and grunts of exertion filling the night air. Elan fought with relentless strength, *Winterstar* a blur of motion as he parried and thrust, protecting his children and companions with every ounce of his strength.

Myst and Maya fought with a skill beyond their years; their movements synchronized as they covered each other's backs. Nykronus's magic crackled through the air, his incantations sending bolts of energy sizzling toward their enemies. Wulfstan's sword sang as it sliced through the air, his movements precise and deadly.

Isolde and Livia fought with grace and agility that belied their gentle natures, their fists, and their weapons, finding their marks with unerring accuracy. Together, the group formed an unbreakable wall of resistance, their unity and toughness shining through in every moment of the battle.

Elan battled with a desperate ferocity, *Winterstar* felt light, channeling his strength with each swing from the hilt to the tip of the blade. The clash of steel against steel reverberated through his bones, each impact sending shockwaves up his arms. Sweat stung his eyes, and his lungs burned with exertion, but he pushed on, driven by the knowledge that he was the only thing standing between his companions and certain death. Vulcan's shield was not only a talisman of hope symbolizing the unbreakable bonds that united them, but also possessed the ability to autonomously block adjacent attacks as if endowed with a defensive peripheral vision. And so he fought, his body a weapon, his will an indestructible force, determined to protect those he loved or die trying.

Despite his skill and strength, Elan found himself surrounded, the enemy pressing in from all sides. He could hear the shouts of his allies, the continuing clash of metal on metal, but he was cut off from them, isolated in a sea of aggressors.

A blow from behind sent him stumbling, his vision blurring as pain exploded through his skull. He fought to stay on his feet, his sword arm trembling with exhaustion, but another strike sent him crashing to the ground, the shield clattering from his grasp.

Through the haze of pain, Elan saw a hooded figure standing over him, a triumphant sneer on their face. They reached down, snatching up the shield and *Winterstar*, and everything went black.

Myst and Maya stood just outside the skirmish site, their hearts racing with fear and adrenaline. They had seen their father fall and watched helplessly as the enemy dragged him away, the shield lost to the Malefic Assembly's clutches.

The remaining group members gathered around them, their faces grim with determination. Nykronus's eyes flashed with arcane power while Wulfstan's hand rested on the hilt of his sword, ready for battle. Isolde and Livia stood shoulder to shoulder, their expressions fierce and unyielding.

"We have to go after him," Myst said, his voice trembling with emotion. "We can't leave him in their hands."

Maya nodded, her eyes hard with resolve. "We'll get him back," she said, her tone leaving no room for doubt. "And we'll make them pay for what they've done."

The group exchanged glances, a silent understanding passing between them. They had come too far, fought too hard, to let the Malefic Assembly win now. With a nod, they set off into the night, their footsteps quick and purposeful as they followed the trail of their captured leader.

Myst and Maya took the lead, with much of Elan still visible to the entire group. They had already lost their mother to the Malefic Assembly's meddling; they would not lose their father. Whatever dangers stood between them, they would face them together, united in their resolve to rescue their father.

Elan's head throbbed as he slowly regained consciousness, his vision blurry and his thoughts scattered. He stumbled as he tried to recall the last thing he could remember, but it was all hazy. As his surroundings became focused, he found himself in a barely lit chamber, the walls embellished with dark artifacts and strange symbols that seemed to pulse with dark energy.

Elan struggled against his bonds, the coarse ropes biting into his skin with every movement. The cold, unyielding stone beneath him seeped into his bones, chilling him to his core. The rough surface scraped against his back, adding to the pain that wracked his body. He tried to focus on his breathing, to center himself amidst the pain and the fear, but the weight of his predicament bore down upon him like a physical force. The darkness pressed in on him from all sides, a tangible presence that seemed to mock his helplessness.

A figure emerged from the shadows, her presence commanding and unsettling. Verendana stepped into the flickering light, her eyes gleaming with triumph and something else—a deep, unsettling conviction.

"Ah, you're awake," she said, her voice smooth and cold. "Just in time to witness the culmination of my life's work."

Elan's eyes darted around the room, taking in the strange machine that dominated the center of the chamber. It was a contraption of gears and levers with a central platform designed to hold something of great importance.

"What do you want with me?" Elan demanded, his voice hoarse from dehydration and exhaustion.

Verendana smiled, a cruel twist of her lips. "You? You're merely a means to an end. It's the *Pugio Mysticus Amoris* that I'm interested in."

She held up the time-weathered blade, its surface gleaming in the dim light. "This dagger, imbued with the power of St. Lazarus himself, is the key to unlocking a ritual that has been centuries in the making. I mean, it is *my* dagger anyway. I was just taking it back."

Elan's heart raced as he realized the gravity of the situation. "What ritual? *Your* dagger?" he asked, dreading the answer.

Verendana's gaze grew unfocused as though peering into realms unseen beyond the room's walls. "A ceremony to channel the might of St. Valentine's essence contained within this holy artifact - his conserved cardiac muscle, long concealed by your Catholic institution. This power shall meld with the ichor of St. Lazarus, which is already flowing through this armament. I shall enact a rite to imbue myself with the ability to remold reality itself to my design. Indeed, St. Valentine bestowed this upon me on the eve of his demise. I am forever in his debt."

She turned back to Elan, her gaze intense and unwavering. "You see, I have a personal connection to St. Valentine. He was my father's prisoner, and he was murdered for what? Marrying people behind a lunatic's back? He did nothing wrong! He loved a Church that let him be murdered for nothing. He was betrayed, his teachings twisted and corrupted by those who sought to control the masses."

Verendana's voice took on a fervent, almost fanatical tone. "I will restore his legacy, and in doing so, I will claim the power that is rightfully mine. After all, he is *my* Valentine. For all the trouble you have caused me, Elan Durant will bear witness to the dawn of a new era."

Elan struggled against his bonds, his mind racing as he tried to escape this nightmare. But as Verendana turned back to the machine, her movements precise and purposeful, he knew that time was running out. He could only hope that his companions would find him before it was too late before Verendana's dark ambitions could be realized.

Verendana moved with a sense of purpose; her every action was precise and calculated as she assembled the machine, which would bring her dark ambitions to fruition. The contraption was a masterpiece of arcane engineering, a fusion of ancient magic and intricate mechanics. Its surface was a tapestry of interlocking gears and pulsing runes, each component honed to perfection by the skilled hands of long-dead craftsmen. The central platform was a raised dais of polished obsidian, its surface inlaid with swirling patterns of silver and gold. From this platform, a series of levers and pulleys extended outward, their purpose both esoteric and ominous. The dim light of the chamber played across the machine's surface, casting eerie shadows that seemed to dance and writhe with a life of their own. It was a thing of terrible beauty, a testament to the ingenuity and hubris of those who sought to harness the very forces of creation.

Verendana placed the Dagger of Love at the center of the machine, its blade pulsing with otherworldly energy. The shield, forged by Vulcan's fire, and the gem, struck from Jupiter's bolt, were carefully integrated into the machine's mechanisms, each component vital to the ritual's success.

Elan watched helplessly as Verendana worked, his mind racing with the implications of what she was attempting. This looked like an invention that couldn't even be built in his time. The power she sought was beyond anything he had ever encountered, and the thought of it falling into her hands filled him with dread.

He struggled against his bonds, the ropes biting into his skin as he fought to break free. But the knots held fast, and he could only watch as Verendana continued her preparations, her eyes gleaming with a fanatical light.

As she made the final adjustments to the machine, Verendana stepped back, a triumphant smile playing across her lips. "It's almost time," she said, her voice barely above a whisper. "Soon, St. Valentine will be mine, and the world will tremble at my feet."

Elan's heart raced with fear as he processed the severity of the situation. If Verendana succeeded in her ritual, the outcome would be devastating, and there was no telling what destruction she could unleash. Negative thoughts flashed through his mind: letting down his companions and the Order of St. Michael, failing Kaira and allowing her death to be in vain, not being able to bring her or their children back to Reagan or their family at home. Anger burned within Elan as he desperately searched for a way to halt Verendana's plans, break free from her grasp, and end her madness before it was too late. But as he looked around the chamber, taking in the ancient symbols and dark artifacts surrounding him, Elan knew he was running out of time.

"When that red-bearded companion of yours used the dragon's tooth, it infused this sword of yours with Saturn's elements. Fools!" Verendana's wicked, conceited smile stretched the wrinkles from her face.

The machine hummed with power as Verendana used *Winterstar* to supply its raw power, the Dagger of Love glowing with an eerie light at its center. And Verendana stood before it all, her eyes fixed on the horizon, ready to claim her twisted destiny.

The weeks of gathering intelligence on Verendana's whereabouts, piecing together fragments of rumors and ancient lore paid off. They had consulted with mortal and divine allies, following the threads of fate that seemed to converge on this remote location. Nykronus led the way, his arcane senses alert to any magical wards or traps their foe might have laid. Wulfstan's armor gleamed faintly in the moonlight, his every step deliberate and silent despite the weight of his gear.

Isolde's fingers brushed her lute strings, ready to weave a melody that could soothe or startle, depending on the need. Livia walked with them, her hands clasped tightly together, a silent prayer on her lips for the strength to face what lay ahead.

As they neared the lair, they could see its ancient stones bathed in an otherworldly glow, the energy from within pulsing like a tumorous heartbeat. The group exchanged glances, their resolve hardening. This was it—the moment they had prepared for.

Nykronus raised a hand, signaling them to halt. He whispered an incantation under his breath, and a ripple of energy spread out from him, seeking out any unseen dangers. Satisfied that their path was clear, he nodded to the others.

They moved forward as one.

As they breached the threshold of Verendana's lair, they were met with resistance—a group of acolytes devoted to her cause. But Wulfstan charged forward like a battering ram, his sword cleaving through the air as he dispatched foe after foe. Myst followed close behind him, his movements a blur as he fought with a precision that belied his youth.

Isolde strummed her lute fiercely, sending discordant vibrations that disoriented their enemies long enough for Maya's arrows to find their marks. Livia chanted loudly over the din of battle, her voice rising above the chaos as she invoked protection upon her allies.

They fought deeper into the lair until they reached the chamber where Elan was held captive. Verendana stood before her machine, oblivious to their approach as she focused on completing her ritual.

With no time to waste, Nykronus unleashed a torrent of magical energy toward Verendana, aiming not to harm but to distract. In that moment of confusion, Myst darted forward with all his speed and agility.

He reached out toward the humming machine at the ritual's center and—with a swift movement born of desperation—knocked *Pugio Mysticus Amoris* from its place among gears and coils. The dagger clattered away from its arcane setting just as Verendana turned with a snarl of rage upon realizing her plan had been thwarted—for now.

Verendana's eyes blazed with fury as she whirled to face Myst, her hand outstretched, dark energy crackling at her fingertips. "You foolish child," she hissed, her mouth dripping with saliva. "You dare interfere with my destiny?"

Myst stood his ground, the Dagger of Love clutched tightly in his hand. "Your destiny is built on lies and betrayal," he said, his voice steady despite the fear that gripped his heart. "We won't let you twist St. Valentine's legacy for your own gain."

Maya stepped up beside her brother, her bow drawn and aimed at Verendana. "It's over," she said, her eyes narrowed. "Release our father and surrender, or face the consequences."

Verendana laughed, a harsh, grating sound that echoed through the chamber. "Consequences? You have no idea what power I wield, the forces I have at my command."

The bolt of dark energy crackled and hissed as it surged toward Myst and Maya, the air around it vibrating with malevolent power. The sound was a discordant symphony of rage and hatred, a cacophony of shrieks and wails that seemed to pierce the soul. It was the sound of a thousand tortured voices crying out in unison, a chorus of the damned that chilled the blood and set the teeth on edge. As the bolt drew closer, the sound grew louder, building to a deafening crescendo that threatened to overwhelm the senses. It was a sound that spoke of annihilation and despair, a harbinger of the unimaginable agony that awaited those caught in its path.

They braced themselves for the impact, knowing there was no time to dodge or deflect. But the blow never came. Instead, a figure leaped before them, taking the full force of Verendana's attack. It was Elan, his bonds broken, his body shielding his children from harm.

He staggered under the onslaught, his teeth gritted in pain as the dark energy coursed through him. But he stood firm, his love for his family giving him the strength to endure.

"Dad!" Myst and Maya cried out in unison, their voices filled with anguish and fear.

Elan turned to them, his face pale but his eyes shining with determination. "I won't let her hurt you," he said, his voice strained but unwavering. "Your mother did an amazing job raising you two. This is the least I could do to hold up my end of the bargain. Nothing will ever compare, but I hope this makes up for some of the lost time. I'm proud of you both!"

Verendana's eyes widened in disbelief, her confidence faltering for the first time. "How?" she demanded, her voice shaking with rage. "How did you break free?"

Elan smiled a weak but triumphant grin. "Love granted me the strength I needed," he said. "The love I have for my family, for Kaira, for the world she fought to protect. The love I never truly understood my entire life until now. That's something you'll never understand, Verendana. And that's why you'll never win."

"Lux Aeterna Vinculum!" Nykronus roared with a voice that shook the very foundations of the room holding Juno's scales in his hand. The aura around him crackled with raw power as he channeled all of his rage and fury into the ancient incantation, unleashing a torrent of energy that threatened to tear reality apart.

As the blinding light from Nykronus's spell and Verendana's ritual engulfed the room, chaos erupted. Elan shielded his eyes, the intensity of the clashing energies nearly overwhelming him. Through the glare, he could see Nykronus standing firm, his hands outstretched as he poured every ounce of his power into the spell.

Verendana, her face contorted with rage and determination, gripped the Dagger of Love tightly as she thrust it into the heart of the machine. The ancient contraption hummed and pulsed, its gears turning faster and faster as it absorbed the dagger's power.

Across the chamber, Wulfstan, Isolde, and Livia faced off against Warin, their battle dance of steel and shadow. Wulfstan's sword clashed against Warin's blade, the sound of metal on metal ringing above the din of the magical maelstrom. Isolde's voice rose in a haunting melody, weaving a spell of confusion and disorientation around their foe.

Livia, her faith unwavering, called upon the power of the divine to bolster her allies and weaken their enemy. Warin, his eyes gleaming with malice, fought back with a ferocity born of desperation, his movements swift and deadly.

Myst and Maya, their hearts pounding with fear and determination, watched the battles unfold, ready to lend their aid. They knew that the fate of the relics, and perhaps the world itself, hung in the balance.

As the light from Nykronus's spell and Verendana's ritual reached a blinding crescendo, the light seemed to shimmer and warp. The lights pulsed rapidly, its brilliance undulating and disorienting. Amidst the pandemonium, an agonized cry tore from Verendana's throat. When the coruscating luminescence finally ceased its wild throbbing, the priestess had vanished without a trace. Tremors rippled through the earth underfoot as the chamber's walls quivered, buffeted by the mighty forces unleashed. The luminosity began to pulse again with escalating fervor, methodically eradicating the assailants in a relentless onslaught until the Malefic Assembly ceased to exist, vanquished by the inexorable power arrayed against them.

A haunting feeling settled over the chamber as the blinding light faded and the chaos subsided. The chamber was empty, with only the Order of St. Michael still standing.

Elan, his body battered and his life force fading, fell to the ground, his children rushing to his side. Myst and Maya knelt beside their father, tears streaming down their faces as they cradled him in their arms.

"Dad, stay with us," Myst pleaded, his voice cracking with emotion. "We need you."

Elan's eyes fluttered open, a weak smile playing across his lips. "You have each other," he whispered, his voice barely audible. "And you have your mother's strength within you. That's all you need."

Maya's hand found Elan's, her fingers intertwining with his. "We'll find a way to save you," she said, her voice fierce with determination. "We won't let you go."

Nykronus approached the fallen hero, his countenance a map of fatigue and grief, the depths of his feelings uncharacteristically visible in this unguarded moment. "Your father's sacrifice has bought us time," he said, his voice heavy with the weight of his words.

Having won their battles, Wulfstan and Isolde joined the group, their faces somber as they took in the scene before them. Isolde knelt beside Maya, her hand resting comfortingly on the young woman's back as she wept.

Myst and Maya knelt beside him, their faces streaked with tears as they clung to their father's hand, desperate to hold onto the precious moments they had left with him.

Elan's mind drifted, the pain in his body fading into the background as he focused on the two young faces before him. At that moment, he saw not just his children but a reflection of his love with Kaira—a love that had transcended time and space and brought these two remarkable beings into the world.

As he gazed upon Myst and Maya, Elan felt a wave of emotion wash over him. Elan had carried the weight of Kaira's disappearance for years, and the guilt and sense of failure were constant companions in his quest for answers. He had never let go of the past, never allowed himself to fully heal from the loss of the woman he loved. It was this unresolved pain that drove him forward and fueled his actions. Now, faced with the ultimate test, he had proven his love in the most profound way possible—by laying down his life for his children.

A sense of peace settled over Elan, a calm acceptance that he had finally found his purpose. He had always been worthy of love, even if he couldn't see it himself. In this final act of sacrifice, he shows the depth of his devotion to his family.

With a trembling hand, Elan reached up to caress Maya's cheek, his fingers brushing away her tears. "Don't cry, you two," he whispered, his voice weak but filled with tenderness. "I'm so proud of you both. You've grown into such strong, brave individuals. Your mother did an amazing job raising you."

Myst leaned in closer, his eyes glistening with unshed tears. "We couldn't have done it without you, Father," he said, his voice cracking with emotion. "You've always been our hero, even if you didn't know it."

Elan smiled. He had spent so long running from his past, from the love he thought he didn't deserve. But here, in the arms of his children, he finally understood the truth—that love had always been within him, waiting to be embraced.

Elan squeezed his children's hands one last time as his vision faded and his breath grew shallow. "I love you both so much," he mumbled, his words barely audible. "Never forget that."

As the dust settled and the echoes of battle faded, the group gathered in the ruins of the lair, their hearts heavy with the weight of their loss. Nykronus, his face etched with sorrow, surveyed the scene before him, taking in the devastation wrought by their confrontation with Verendana and her forces.

Livia, her eyes closed in solemn reverence, stepped forward, her hands clasped before her. "Let us pray," she said, her voice soft but filled with strength. "For Elan, a true hero who gave his life to protect those he loved. May he find peace in the embrace of his beloved Kaira, watching over his children from the heavens above."

The others bowed their heads, joining Livia in her prayer. Myst and Maya, their faces streaked with tears, clung to each other, drawing strength from their shared grief and the knowledge that their father's sacrifice had not been in vain.

As the prayer ended, Isolde stepped forward, her lute in hand. "I have a song," she said, her voice trembling with emotion. "A tribute to Elan, who embodied so many virtues."

With a deep breath, Isolde began to play, her fingers dancing across the strings as she wove a melody of love, courage, and sacrifice. Her voice rose, clear and powerful, as she sang of Elan's life and legacy.

"A hero, a lover, a warrior true,

A Marine, a fighter, with dreams anew.

A leader, a friend, a father so brave,

His love and his strength, forever he gave."

Wulfstan, his hand resting on the hilt of his sword, spoke up, his voice cantankerous but filled with boldness. "We will not let Elan's sacrifice be in vain," he said, eyes blazing with righteous fury. "We will protect the relics and stop whatever remains of the Malefic Assembly, no matter the cost."

ACT FIVE

"Since the soul is not found without body and yet is not body, it may be in one body or another, and pass from body to body."
  - Giordano Bruno

CHAPTER
TWENTY-ONE

Oceanside, California, June 3, 2024 A.D.

Elan Durant rode his motorcycle along the winding California coastal road, the summer breeze whipping through his hair. The sun hung low on the horizon, painting the sky in hues of orange and pink as he navigated the familiar twists and turns, his mind heavy with the weight of recent events. The smell of the ocean fueled his sense of freedom.

He pulled off the road at a secluded lookout point, the engine roar fading to a gentle purr as he brought the bike to a stop. Swinging his leg over the side, Elan dismounted, his boots crunching against the gravel as he made his way to the edge of the cliff.

The vast expanse of the Pacific Ocean stretched out before him, the waves crashing against the rocks below in a rhythmic symphony. Elan leaned against the weathered wooden railing, his eyes fixed on the distant horizon, as he allowed himself to breathe and process the whirlwind of emotions that had consumed him since his deployment.

Images flashed through his mind—the faces of his squad mates, his best friends Reagan and Austin, their eyes filled with love and admiration; the ruins of Afghanistan, the dust still settling in the aftermath of a battle; and Kaira, her presence lingering like a ghost, just out of reach.

Elan closed his eyes, the weight of his sacrifice bearing upon him. He had given his life to protect his country and those he loved, to ensure they remained safe and the world would not fall into darkness. But in doing so, he had left behind a void, a space that could never be filled—an unsatisfied heart—a life without love.

The solitude of the lookout point enveloped him, the gentle whisper of the wind and the distant cry of seagulls his only companions. In this moment, Elan allowed himself to feel the full depth of his loneliness, the ache in his chest that seemed to grow with each passing second.

He knew his journey was far from over. In the stillness of the evening, Elan surrendered to the emotions that had been building within him, letting the tears fall freely as he mourned all that he had lost and had yet to gain.

As the sun dipped lower on the horizon, its rays painted the sky in a breathtaking array of colors unlike anything Elan had ever witnessed. The vibrant oranges and pinks blended seamlessly with the deep purples and blues, creating a masterpiece that seemed to stretch into infinity—a true California sunset. Despite the beauty before him, Elan found himself lost in the depths of his mind, the weight of his past bearing upon him like an inescapable burden.

Memories of his childhood flooded Elan's consciousness, the echoes of his father's absence and the occasional moments of warmth now tainted by the realization of the man's true nature. Growing up, Elan had always focused on the good memories, suppressing the painful truth of his father's shortcomings. He had clung to the rare moments of affection, the fleeting glimpses of a loving father, while ignoring the signs of verbal and physical abuse, the womanizing, and the alcoholism that had torn his family apart. It was only now, with the clarity of hindsight, that Elan could see the whole picture, the depths of his father's betrayal and the final act of infidelity that had shattered his mother's heart and fractured their family beyond repair.

Early in life, Elan learned love and affection were luxuries he could not afford and the only way to survive was to build walls around his heart and never let anyone in. He constantly sought acceptance from those he encountered, whether colleagues, mentors, peers, or subordinates. He always put others before himself, never considering his needs to be the priority.

But then Kaira had come into his life, a beacon of light in the darkness that had consumed him. She had seen past his rough exterior, past the scars that marked his body and soul, and had loved him unconditionally. For the first time, Elan had allowed himself to hope and dream of a future where he could be happy and finally find peace.

But fate had had other plans. Kaira's disappearance had shattered his world, leaving him lost and adrift in a sea of despair. The pain of her loss had been unbearable, a constant ache that never seemed to fade, no matter how much time passed.

Elan clenched his fists, his knuckles turning white as he gripped the railing tightly. He could feel the tears welling up in his eyes, the dam he had built to hold back his emotions threatening to burst at any moment. He had spent so long running from his pain, burying it deep within himself and pretending it didn't exist. But here, in the solitude of the lookout point, with the weight of the world pressing down upon him, Elan could no longer deny the truth.

He had been shaped by his trauma, molded by the pain and suffering he had endured throughout his life. It had driven him to join the Marines, to put his life on the line for a cause greater than himself. But it had also left him broken, unable to trust or open himself up to others fully.

Memories of his recent missions flashed through his mind—the close calls, the near misses, the moments when he had hesitated or made the wrong call. He had always prided himself on being a strong leader, making tough decisions, and guiding his team to victory. But now, he realized that his unresolved issues had been clouding his judgment, making him second-guess himself and putting his team at risk.

Elan felt a sense of acceptance settle over him as the last rays of sunlight faded from the sky. He knew that he could no longer run from his past, that he had to confront the demons that haunted him if he ever hoped to find peace.

Perched on the edge of his twin-size air mattress, Elan surveyed the sparse and bare studio he had been living in since packing his belongings for his upcoming move.

Elan leaned forward, resting his elbows on his knees and clasping his hands together. He had been in therapy before and had spent countless hours talking about his childhood and the trauma he had endured. But he had never truly committed to the process, had never fully opened himself up to the possibility of healing.

As he sat in the quiet of his room, Elan knew he could no longer run from the truth. He needed help, someone to guide him through the darkness and help him find his way back to the light. It would not be easy; he knew that.

With a deep breath, Elan reached for his phone, his fingers trembling slightly as he scrolled through his contacts. He had the number of a therapist he had seen years ago, someone who had helped him through some of his darkest moments. He hesitated for a moment, his thumb hovering over the call button. But then, with a surge of courage, he pressed down, bringing the phone to his ear as he waited for the familiar voice on the other end.

"Hello, this is Dr. Samantha Furse's office. How may I assist you today?"

Elan took a deep breath, his voice steady as he spoke. "Hi, this is Elan Durant. I was a patient of Dr. Furse a few years ago, and I was wondering if I could schedule an appointment."

Elan sat in the waiting room of Dr. Samantha Furse's office, his leg bouncing nervously as he waited for his appointment. The room was designed to be welcoming, with soft lighting and comfortable chairs, but Elan couldn't shake the feeling of unease that had settled in his gut. *Tactical scenarios were more effortless than this,* he thought.

When the receptionist called his name, Elan stood up, taking a deep breath before following her to Dr. Furse's office down the hallway. The therapist greeted him with a warm smile, gesturing for him to sit on the plush couch across from her.

"It's good to see you again, Elan," Dr. Furse said, her voice gentle and reassuring. "I know it wasn't easy for you to take this step, but I'm glad you're here."

Elan smiled, his throat tight, as he tried to find the words to express the turmoil that had been building inside him. He had always struggled with vulnerability, having found it easier to bury his pain and pretend that everything was okay. But now, sitting across from Dr. Furse, he knew he could no longer run from the truth.

"I've been struggling," he admitted, his voice barely above a whisper. "Ever since I lost Kaira, I feel like I've been drowning. I know it's been twenty years, but it's something I have never been able to fully accept. And with my retirement from the Marines coming up, I don't know what I'm going to do. I'm not sure I know who I am anymore. I feel like I don't know who I ever really was."

Dr. Furse nodded with an expression of understanding and compassion. "Losing someone we love is never easy," she said. "And when we've built our identity around a particular role or career, to cope, it can be incredibly disorienting to let that go."

Elan felt a lump in his throat, his eyes stinging with unshed tears. He had never allowed himself to grieve Kaira's loss fully and had never permitted himself to feel the depth of his pain. But now, in the safety of Dr. Furse's office, he could no longer hold back the flood of emotions.

"I miss her so damn much," he whispered, his voice breaking. "And I'm scared. I'm scared of what comes next and who I'll be without the Marines."

Dr. Furse leaned forward, her eyes filled with empathy. "It's okay to be scared, Elan. It's okay to feel the feelings! But you have to let yourself *feel* those feelings. You don't have to face this alone. We can work through your grief together and help you find a new sense of purpose and identity."

Elan nodded, feeling hope for the first time in months.

As Elan settled into the familiar rhythm of his therapy sessions with Dr. Furse, he began unraveling the tangled web of emotions holding him back. Twice a week, he would enter her office with a sense of trepidation, knowing that he would be forced to confront the painful memories and unresolved traumas that had shaped his life.

At first, the process was slow and difficult. Elan struggled to put his feelings into words, to give voice to the pain and anger that had been simmering inside him for years. But with Dr. Furse's gentle guidance and unwavering support, he gradually began to open up and share the stories and experiences that had left him feeling broken and alone.

They talked about his childhood, about the abuse he had suffered at the hands of his father, and watching his mother endure and put up with his narcissism. Elan's voice shook as he recounted the countless nights he had spent huddled in his room, trying to block out the sound of his father's drunken rages and his mother's tearful pleas.

Dr. Furse listened intently, her eyes filled with compassion and understanding. She helped Elan see the patterns that had emerged in his life and how his early experiences had shaped his beliefs and behaviors. Together, they worked to challenge the negative self-talk that had become so ingrained in his mind, replacing it with a more balanced and compassionate perspective.

As the weeks turned into months, Elan began to feel a shift within himself. He no longer felt the need to bury his emotions or push them away, instead learning to sit with them and allow them to pass through him. He started to see himself in a new light, not as a broken or damaged person, but as someone who had survived incredible hardship and emerged more assertive on the other side.

He finally understood resiliency in a different capacity.

Elan became more involved in his community, volunteered at local charities, and mentored young veterans struggling with the transition back to civilian life. He took up hiking, finding solace in the peaceful solitude of nature and the physical challenge of pushing his body to its limits. Through these new experiences, Elan began to forge new friendships, connecting with people who shared his values and desire to impact the world positively. These tangible changes in his daily life reflected his internal transformation, a testament to the power of healing and self-discovery.

Through the process of therapy, Elan began to understand the impact that his emotional baggage had had on his life. He saw how his fear of vulnerability and his need for control had held him back in his relationships. He recognized how his unresolved grief over Kaira's loss had left him feeling stuck and unable to move forward.

With each session, Elan felt a sense of hope and possibility growing within him. For the first time in a long time, he felt a sense of purpose and direction, a belief that he could create a life filled with meaning and joy, even in the face of his pain.

As Elan continued his journey of self-discovery and healing with Dr. Furse, he began to learn valuable coping mechanisms to help him navigate the turbulent waters of his depression and anxiety. In each session, Dr. Furse introduced him to new strategies and techniques, guiding him through incorporating them into his daily life.

One of the first tools Elan learned was deep breathing exercises. Dr. Furse taught him how to focus on his breath, inhaling deeply through his nose and exhaling slowly through his mouth. She explained that this simple act could help calm his racing thoughts and soothe his frayed nerves, providing clarity and peace amid his emotional turmoil.

Elan diligently practiced the breathing exercises, taking time each day to sit in quiet contemplation and focus on his breath. At first, it felt strange and unfamiliar, but as the days turned into weeks, he began to notice a difference. He found that he was able to approach stressful situations with a greater sense of calm and clarity, his mind no longer consumed by the swirling vortex of his anxiety.

Dr. Furse also introduced Elan to mindfulness, teaching him to stay present and observe his thoughts and emotions without judgment. She encouraged him to take time each day to simply be, to notice the sensations in his body and the world around him without getting caught up in his mind's endless chatter.

Elan found that practicing mindfulness helped him to gain a new perspective on his struggles. He began to see his thoughts and emotions as passing clouds in the sky, temporary and fleeting rather than permanent and all-consuming. He learned to approach his challenges with curiosity and openness rather than fear and avoidance.

Elan's work with Dr. Furse allowed him to develop greater self-compassion. He learned to treat himself with kindness and understanding rather than the harsh self-criticism that had become so ingrained in his mind. He began to see his struggles not as personal failings but as a natural part of the human experience, which everyone grappled with in their way.

❧

As Elan settled into the worn leather couch in Austin's living room, he felt a sense of warmth and familiarity wash over him. The room was filled with the soft glow of lamplight, casting a warm and inviting atmosphere. Austin sat across from him, his blue eyes filled with concern and understanding.

"I'm really proud of you for taking this step, man," Austin said, his voice gentle and sincere. "I know it couldn't have been easy."

Elan nodded, his throat tight with emotion. "It's been a long road," he admitted, his voice barely above a whisper. "But I'm finally starting to feel like I'm making progress."

He took a deep breath, gathering his thoughts before continuing. "Dr. Furse has been amazing," he said, a small smile tugging at the corners of his mouth. "She's helped me see things in a different light, to understand the patterns holding me back for so long."

Elan's decision to confide in Austin was a significant step in his therapy, a sign of his growing willingness to open up and share his struggles with those closest to him. He had always seen Austin as a rock, a steadfast friend who had been by his side through the best and worst times. But it was only now, with the encouragement of Dr. Furse, that Elan felt ready to let his guard down and allow Austin to see the vulnerable parts of himself.

Austin leaned forward, his elbows resting on his knees. "That's incredible, man," he said, his voice filled with genuine pride and admiration. "I know how hard you've been working, and I'm just so glad to see you taking care of yourself. But between you and me, I couldn't even tell you needed therapy. You have a great poker face. I am so damn proud of you."

Elan had always struggled to open up to others, to let them see his vulnerable parts. But sitting here with Austin, he felt a sense of safety and acceptance that he had never experienced before.

"I couldn't have done it without you and Reagan, of course," Elan said, his voice trembling slightly. "Knowing that I have your support, that you two are here for me no matter what... it means everything."

Austin reached out, placing a comforting hand on Elan's shoulder. "I'll always be here for you, brother," he said, his voice filled with conviction. "No matter what."

At that moment, Elan knew that he had made the right decision to confide in his friend and that Austin would be there to support him every step of his journey of healing and self-discovery.

As Elan sat in the quiet of his boxed-up apartment, his mind wandered to the breakthroughs he had experienced in therapy. The walls he had built around his heart were finally beginning to crumble, and he was learning to embrace the vulnerability beneath.

A knock at the door startled him from his thoughts. He opened it to find Reagan standing there, a soft smile on her face.

"Hey," she said, her voice gentle. "I just wanted to check in on you and see how you're doing."

Elan stepped aside and invited her in. As they settled onto the couch, he took a deep breath and gathered his courage.

"I've been thinking a lot about what Dr. Furse said," he began, his voice hesitant. "About how vulnerability isn't a weakness, but a strength."

Reagan nodded, her eyes filled with understanding. "It takes a lot of courage to open up like that," she said, To let yourself be seen— *really* seen."

Elan felt a lump in his throat, his eyes stinging with unshed tears. "I've spent so long trying to be strong, trying to hold it all together," he said, his voice breaking. "But I'm starting to realize that true strength comes from facing your fears, from being honest about your struggles."

Reagan reached out, placing a comforting hand on his arm. "You're one of the strongest people I know, Elan," she said, her voice filled with conviction. "And I'm so proud of you for taking this journey, for being willing to do the work."

Elan felt a sense of warmth and gratitude wash over him. He knew he was not alone and had the support and love of those closest to him.

"Thank you," he said, his voice barely above a whisper. "For being here, for believing in me."

Reagan smiled, her eyes shining with tears. "Always," she said. "No matter what."

~

Camp Pendleton, California August 25, 2024 A.D.

The last notes of evening colors faded into the night sky, and Elan stood alone on the empty stage, the silence enveloping him like a comforting embrace. The rehearsal for his retirement ceremony had ended, and he found himself lost in thought, reflecting on the journey that had brought him to this moment.

As Elan prepared for retirement, his daily life began to reflect the internal changes he was experiencing through his therapy sessions with Dr. Furse. He found himself waking up earlier, taking the time to meditate, and setting intentions for the day ahead. He started cooking more, experimenting with healthy recipes, and finding joy in the simple act of nourishing his body and mind.

Elan's newfound sense of peace and clarity at work translated into a more focused and effective leadership style. He found himself more attuned to the needs of his fellow Marines, better able to support and guide them through the challenges of military life. His impending retirement became a source of excitement rather than anxiety, a chance to explore new opportunities and continue his personal growth in different ways.

In his free time, Elan began to explore new hobbies and interests. He took up writing, finding beauty in the world around him and capturing it on paper. He started attending local art shows and cultural events, immersing himself in the richness and diversity of his community.

These welcomed changes in Elan's daily life were a testament to the power of his internal healing journey.

As he stood on the stage, Elan realized that the changes he had experienced in therapy were not confined to the four walls of Dr. Furse's office. They had begun to spill over into every aspect of his life, influencing how he approached his relationships, work, and even his quest to find Kaira.

He no longer felt the need to shoulder the burden of his past alone, to push away those who cared about him in a misguided attempt to protect them. Instead, he had started to lean on his loved ones, allowing himself to be vulnerable and accepting their support.

Elan knew that his healing journey was far from over and that there would be hurdles and setbacks along the way. But as he stood on the stage, surrounded by the peaceful stillness of the evening, he felt proud of the work he accomplished and was looking forward to the rest of his life to figure things out.

CHAPTER
TWENTY-TWO

Benevento, Lombard Principality, 840 A.D.

Overcast heavens obscured the sunlight that would otherwise illuminate the peaceful countryside surrounding Benevento. A soft wind whispered through the foliage, bearing on its currents the delicate fragrance of blossoming flora and the faraway pealing of church bells. Amidst this placid backdrop, a gathering of people had converged, united by a common objective and a deep, shared grief.

They stood in a loose circle, their faces displaying sorrow and reverence. Among them were familiar faces—Myst and Maya, the children Elan and Kaira had cherished; Nykronus, the ally who had stood by their side through countless trials past, present, and future; Wulfstan, Isolde, and Livia, the loyal companions who had fought alongside them in their quest.

But Elan and Kaira's journey touched others in many ways. There was the old monk who had safeguarded Kaira's letter, the nobleman who gave Elan the clues necessary to reconnect with his children, and the countless others whose paths had crossed with theirs over the years.

As the sun dipped lower on the horizon, bathing the scene in a soft, ethereal light, the group began to move forward, their steps slow and measured. They carried simple wooden caskets, each adorned with a single flower—a rose for Kaira and a gladiolus for Elan.

Nykronus guided the mourners to a remote copse he had meticulously selected for its serenity and innate splendor. The venerable trees loomed majestic and dignified, their limbs entwining above to form a verdant awning that sifted a lone ray of sunshine emanating from a bleak, cloud-covered firmament into a tender, viridescent luminescence. Feral blossoms flourished in sporadic clusters, their fragile corollas swaying in the mild breeze.

Nykronus gestured for the group to halt. He knelt, his fingers tracing the outline of a diminutive, rectangular plot of earth that had been carefully dug out for the caskets.

"Here," he said, his voice low and reverent. "This is where they will rest together, forever."

The others nodded solemnly, their eyes fixed on the spot where Elan and Kaira's bodies would soon be laid to rest. Myst and Maya stepped forward, gently lowering the coffins into the earth. Tears streamed down their faces as they did so, mingling with the soil below.

"May you find peace in each other's arms," he murmured. "And may your love endure, even in death."

Myst and Maya began to throw dirt onto the caskets. Wulfstan and Isolde moved to join them, each taking a turn to sprinkle a handful of earth over the coffin. They whispered prayers and blessings, their words carried away on the breeze. Other mourners began to shovel dirt into the grave.

Livia stood apart from the others, her head bowed in silent prayer. In her hands, she held a small, leather-bound book—a journal in which she had begun to record the experiences and lessons she had learned during her time with the group.

As the last of the earth was smoothed over the grave, Nykronus stepped forward again. He placed a hand on the small mound, his eyes closed in concentration.

Nykronus stepped forward, his eyes fixed on the Dagger of Love before him. The blade glinted in the fading light, its ornate handle adorned with symbols of devotion and sacrifice. Around the dagger, an array of items had been carefully arranged - Jupiter's bolt and dust from Saturn's dragon tooth were on each side of the scales touched by Juno's breath. Elan was wearing Neptune's armor, and *Winterstar* was lying with Kaira.

Nykronus took a deep breath, his hands trembling slightly as he reached for the dagger. He knew that what he was about to attempt was a long shot, a desperate bid to defy the cruel hand of fate. But he also knew that he owed it to Elan and Kaira, to the love they had shared and the sacrifices they had made.

With a solemn nod to the gathered mourners, Nykronus began to chant, his voice low and steady. The words were ancient, a language long forgotten by all but a few. As he spoke, the air around him seemed to shimmer and crackle with energy, a palpable sense of power building with each syllable.

At the crescendo of the chant, Nykronus plunged the Dagger of Love into the earth between the two graves. He closed his eyes, focusing all his will and energy on the blade, channeling it to pierce the veil between life and death. As the dagger sank into the soil, Nykronus felt a jolt of energy surge through his body, as if the essence of life and death flowed through his veins. His muscles tensed, and a sheen of sweat formed on his brow as he poured every ounce of his will into the blade, willing it to pierce the veil and summon the spirits of Elan and Kaira from beyond.

For a long, tense moment, nothing happened. The gathered mourners held their breath, their eyes fixed on the dagger as it quivered on the ground. And then, slowly, almost imperceptibly at first, a soft glow emanated from the blade.

Nykronus's eyes snapped open, his heart racing with hope and anticipation. He watched as the glow intensified, spreading from the dagger in shimmering waves and touching the gathered mourners. It washed over the graves, bathing them in a warm, green light.

But as quickly as it appeared, the light began to fade. Nykronus's face fell, his shoulders slumping in defeat. He knew, with a crushing certainty, that the ritual had failed. He could not bring Elan and Kaira back despite his power and knowledge. His efforts proved that he needed more time to be a Grand Magus.

As the ritual's light faded, a somber silence descended upon the gathering. The weight of Nykronus's failure hung heavy in the atmosphere, an overwhelming grief permeating every heart. But even in their sorrow, there was a flicker of confidence, a determination to honor Elan and Kaira's memory in the only way they could.

Myst stepped forward, his eyes glistening with unshed tears. He looked at the assembled crowd, his gaze lingering on each face. "My parents," he began, trembling slightly, "were the bravest, most loving people I have ever known. They taught me what it means to fight for what you believe in, to never give up, even in the face of impossible odds."

He paused, taking a deep breath to steady himself. "But more than that, they taught me about the power of love. Their love was a force beyond reckoning, a bond that transcended time and space. It was that love that carried them through every trial, every hardship. And it was that love that ultimately led them to make the ultimate sacrifice."

Maya moved to stand beside her brother, her hand resting gently on his shoulder. "Mom and Dad's journey was not an easy one," she said, her voice clear and strong. "They faced countless challenges and fought against unimaginable odds. But through it all, they never lost sight of what mattered most - their love for each other, and their love for us. Despite missing a lifetime together, they loved us all the same."

She turned to face the gathered mourners, her eyes shining with a fierce determination. "We may not have been able to bring them back, but we can honor their memory by living our lives with the same courage and the same unwavering commitment to what is right. We can carry on their legacy and ensure that their sacrifice was not in vain."

Nykronus stood at the head of the grave, his face marked by gloom. He had known Elan for centuries and had fought alongside him in countless battles. But more than that, he had been a true friend, a constant source of strength and support.

Beside him, Myst and Maya stood hand in hand, their faces streaked with tears. They had lost a father and a mentor, a guiding light. The pain of that loss was almost too much to bear, but they drew strength from each other and from the knowledge that their father's legacy would live on through them.

The others stepped forward one by one to pay their respects. Wulfstan placed his armored hand on. "Rest well, my friend," he murmured, his voice thick with emotion. his chest plate. Your battle is over, but your memory will never fade."

Her eyes glistening with unshed tears, Isolde laid a single white rose atop the grave. "May your soul find peace," she whispered, her words carried away on the gentle breeze.

Livia kissed her rosary and reverently placed it on Elan's marker, whispering a prayer to herself. Despite her quiet voice, the group gathered around could still make out her words.

As the last of the mourners stepped back, Nykronus raised his hands, his voice clear and strong. "We lay to rest Elan Durant, a true hero, a loyal friend, and a loving father. May his spirit find its way to Kaira's side, where they can be together for all eternity."

The assembly stood silently, their heads bowed in reverence.

"Elan's journey may have come to an end," Nykronus said, his voice filled with a quiet determination, "but ours continues. We will honor his memory by fighting for what is right and standing together in the face of darkness. For as long as we hold true to those ideals, Elan's spirit will live on, guiding us and inspiring us until we, too, can rest beside him and Kaira in eternal peace."

The last echoes of Nykronus's words faded into the stillness and a profound silence descended upon the assembled mourners. It was a silence born not of emptiness but of a shared grief, a collective sorrow that bound them together in that moment, transcending the boundaries of time and space.

After the mourners began to disperse, Nykronus slipped away from the graveside, seeking a moment of solitude to process his thoughts and emotions. He found a quiet spot beneath a gnarled oak tree, its ancient branches stretching like a canopy above him. The *Pugio Mysticus Amoris* weighed heavily in his hand, a tangible reminder of his failure to resurrect Elan and Kaira.

Wulfstan, noticing Nykronus's absence, followed him to the

secluded spot. He approached the mage with a look of concern on his weathered face. "Nykronus," he said softly, placing a comforting hand on his friend's shoulder. "You must not blame yourself for what happened."

Nykronus sighed heavily, his eyes fixed on the dagger in his grasp. "I thought I had the power to bring them back, Wulfstan. I believed that my knowledge and the *Pugio Mysticus Amoris* would be enough to defy death itself. But I was wrong. I failed them, and now they are gone forever."

Wulfstan shook his head, his voice firm but gentle. "You did not fail, Nykronus. You brought us this far and guided us through countless trials and challenges. Without you, we would never have even had the chance to say goodbye, to honor their memory as we did today."

Nykronus looked up at his friend, his eyes glistening with unshed tears. "But what good is all my power and knowledge if I cannot save the ones I love? If I cannot bring hope in the face of such loss?"

"Hope is not found in the ability to change the past, Nykronus," Wulfstan replied, his gaze unwavering. "It is found in the strength to accept what we cannot change, to find meaning and purpose in the face of adversity. Elan and Kaira's legacy lives on through all of us, through the love and courage they inspired in everyone they touched. That is the true power of hope."

Nykronus nodded slowly, his grip on the *Pugio Mysticus Amoris* loosening as he considered Wulfstan's words. "You are right, my friend. I may not be a Grand Magus, but I am no longer just a magelight. I am a Magus, and my purpose is to guide and protect those who remain, to ensure that Elan and Kaira's sacrifice was not in vain."

CHAPTER

TWENTY-THREE

Rome, Italy, September 8, 2004 A.D.

Kaira stirred from her slumber, her mind still entangled in the vivid threads of her dream. As the first light of dawn seeped through the curtains, she struggled to discern the boundary between the dream world and reality. The images and emotions from her past life lingered, as tangible as the warm sheets wrapped around her body.

In her dream, Kaira found herself walking through the halls of an ancient Roman village. The buildings were adorned with intricate frescoes depicting scenes from mythology, and the air was rich with the alluring scent of incense and spices. She could feel the weight of her silk robes against her skin, and her feet were clad in delicate sandals. As she moved through the villa, she was filled with a sense of familiarity and belonging, as if she had walked these same halls a thousand times before. Yet, beneath the surface, there was also a sense of unease, a feeling that something was not quite right. It was as if she was a stranger in her own life, a visitor from another time and place.

She sat up slowly, rubbing her eyes with the back of her hand, and swung her legs over the side of the bed, her bare feet touching the cool hardwood floor. She glanced at the clock on her nightstand, the glowing numbers indicating it was still early. She had planned to meet with Professor Xicato today at the university before their trip to Castel Sant'Angelo. But the dream had left her feeling disoriented and unsettled, and she knew she needed time to process what she had experienced.

She reached for her phone, her fingers hovering over the screen momentarily before she began typing a message to the professor. "Not feeling well today," she wrote, her thumbs moving swiftly across the keyboard. "Need to rest. Will reschedule our meeting."

She hit send and set the phone back down, her mind drifting back to the dream. She couldn't shake the feeling that it was more than just a figment of her imagination, that it held some deeper meaning or purpose. She remembered the day she had first met Professor Xicato, how he had seemed to recognize something in her that she hadn't even known existed.

Kaira stood up and walked over to the window, pulling back the curtain to gaze at the awakening city. The streets of Rome were already beginning to come alive, with the distant sound of traffic and the occasional chirping of birds. She knew she should probably try to go back to sleep, to push the dream from her mind and focus on the day ahead. But something told her this was just the beginning, that the dream was a sign of something greater.

Kaira's dreams persisted, each night unveiling a new piece of the intricate puzzle of her past lives. The visions were so vivid and intense that she found it increasingly difficult to dismiss them as mere figments of her imagination.

One night, she found herself in a grand hall, the walls adorned with tapestries depicting epic battles and heroic feats. She was dressed in a flowing gown, her hair intricately braided and decorated with delicate flowers. She could hear the distant sound of music and laughter and felt a sense of joy and belonging that she had never experienced in her waking life.

Another night, she navigated an unpaved road, her clothing flapping in the wind as she rode on a magnificent steed. She could feel the weight of a knife in her hand, the rush of adrenaline coursing through her veins as she charged toward an enemy. The smell of sweat and blood filled her nostrils, and she knew with absolute certainty that this was not the first time she had faced such peril.

Kaira noticed a pattern in her dreams as the days turned into weeks. Each night, she would experience a different memory from a different lifetime. Still, the memories seemed to occur in chronological order, so she continued to write these dreams in her diary.

She tried to go about her daily life as usual, attending classes at the university and meeting with friends for coffee or dinner. But the dreams consumed her thoughts, and she found herself constantly distracted and lost in thought. She began to carry a small notebook with her everywhere she went, jotting down the details of each dream as soon as she woke up.

Kaira knew she needed to talk to someone about what was happening to her, but she wasn't sure who to turn to. Her friends and family would likely think she was losing her mind, and she wasn't ready to face that kind of skepticism or judgment. She considered reaching out to Professor Xicato, but something held her back. She couldn't quite put her finger on it, but she felt he knew more about her situation than he let on.

As the dreams unfolded, Kaira realized she could no longer deny the truth of what she was experiencing. These were not just dreams but memories of lives she had lived before. With each passing day, she felt a growing sense of urgency to uncover the full extent of her past and the role she was meant to play in the present.

Kaira entered the Vatican Library, the musty smell of antiquated books and the soothing sound of pages turning enveloping her. Thanks to a recommendation from Professor Xicato, she had been granted special permission to access the library's extensive collection. As she walked through the towering shelves, her fingers trailed along the spines of the books, each holding the promise of untold knowledge.

She found a quiet corner and settled in, a stack of books on reincarnation and past lives piled high on the table before her. As she delved into the texts, Kaira's eyes widened with each page. The stories and accounts she read mirrored her own experiences with uncanny accuracy. Tales of individuals who had lived multiple lives, each building upon the last, resonated deeply with her.

Kaira's research took her deeper into the annals of history, and she began to uncover haunting similarities between the events in her dreams and recorded historical occurrences. A battle she had witnessed in her sleep matched the description of a long-forgotten skirmish from centuries ago. The grand hall she had found herself in resembled a castle that had once stood on the outskirts of Rome.

As she cross-referenced dates and locations, Kaira couldn't help but feel a growing sense of unease. The coincidences were too numerous to ignore, and the evidence seemed to point towards a truth she had been grappling with for weeks: her dreams were not merely her imagination but memories of a life she had lived before.

Kaira leaned back in her chair, her mind reeling with the implications of her discoveries. If her dreams were memories of past lives, what did that mean for her present? Was she meant to fulfill some greater purpose, to right some ancient wrong, or to complete an unfinished task?

She knew that she needed to delve deeper to uncover the full extent of her past and the role she was meant to play in the present. But as she sat there, surrounded by the weight of centuries of knowledge, Kaira couldn't shake the feeling that she was on the cusp of something far more significant than she could have ever imagined.

Kaira sat in her dimly lit apartment, the intensity of her secret pressing down on her. The once cozy space now felt like a prison, the walls closing around her as she grappled with the reality of her past life. She longed to call Elan, the one person who has always been her rock, to share the burden of her experiences but fear held her back. She had tried to share her experiences with a few close friends, but their skepticism and raised eyebrows deepened her sense of isolation.

She recalled her conversation with her friends just a few days prior. Kaira had hesitantly broached the subject of her dreams, hoping to find a sympathetic ear. But their response had needed to be understood.

"Past lives? Kaira, are you feeling alright?" Lena had asked, concern cut across her face. "I know you've been under a lot of stress lately, but this sounds like something out of a fantasy book."

Kaira tried to explain and share the vivid details of her dreams and the uncanny similarities to historical events. But the more she spoke, the more Maria's skepticism grew. In the end, Kaira had retreated, feeling more alone than ever.

Now, as she sat in her apartment's silence, Kaira couldn't help but wonder if she was losing her grip on reality. She hugged her knees to her chest, trying to find comfort in the familiar gesture.

Overwhelmed by the weight of her experiences, Kaira found herself pulling away from even her closest confidants, including her sister Reagan.

As if the weight of her past lives wasn't enough, Kaira had recently discovered she was pregnant. The news had come as a shock, adding another layer of complexity to her already turbulent life. She had always dreamed of starting a family, but the timing couldn't have been worse.

Amidst the turmoil, Kaira's thoughts drifted to Elan, wondering how he would react to the news of her pregnancy and the strange dreams that haunted her.

Kaira's hand drifted to her still flat stomach, a mixture of fear and wonder washing over her. How could she bring a child into the world when she felt lost and confused? The responsibility of motherhood was frightening and Kaira couldn't help but feel overwhelmed by the prospect.

She knew she needed to find answers and unravel the mystery of her past life and the role she was meant to play in the present. But as she sat alone in the darkness, Kaira couldn't shake the feeling that the way forward would be lonely. She had to tell Elan.

Elan landed in Rome, his heart buzzing with anticipation and apprehension for Kaira's sake. It had been months since they had last seen each other, and their separation was made all the more difficult by the strange experiences Kaira had been navigating alone. As he crossed the threshold, his eyes caught sight of Kaira seated at a table towards the rear, her features bathed in the gentle radiance of warm-colored light bulbs.

He made his way over to her, his footsteps muffled by the plush carpet of a nearby cafe. As he approached, Kaira looked up, her eyes meeting his with a warmth that made his heartbeat. They embraced, holding each other tightly for a moment before taking their seats.

"Ciao bella," his embrace and gentle kiss on her forehead gave Kaira a sense of inner peace, even as her mind swirled in turmoil.

"Hey, handsome. How was your flight?" She had practiced her speech countless times, reciting the words to her reflection until they were etched in her memory, desperate to share it all with Elan.

"Long, but totally worth it. You're a sight for sore eyes," Elan smiled.

As they settled in, Elan couldn't help but notice the tension in Kaira's shoulders and the way her fingers fidgeted with the edge of her napkin. He reached across the table, taking her hand in his.

"Is everything okay?" he asked softly, his fingers brushing her soft hands.

Kaira took a deep breath, her eyes searching his face. "Elan, there's something I need to tell you," she began, her voice trembling slightly. "I'm pregnant."

Elan's eyes widened, a smile spreading across his face. "Kaira, that's amazing news," he said, squeezing her hand. "I'm so damn happy for us."

But as he looked closer, he noticed the shadows beneath her eyes and how her smile didn't quite reach them. "There's something else, isn't there?" he asked gently.

Kaira nodded, her gaze dropping to the table. "I've been having these weird dreams," she said, her voice barely above a whisper. "Dreams of past lives. Dreams of battles and castles and people I've never met."

She explained her research and the similarities between her dreams and historical events. Elan listened intently with each passing detail.

"I know it sounds crazy," Kaira said, her eyes searching his face for any sign of disbelief or judgment. "But it feels so real, Elan. I can't shake the feeling that there's something more to all of this."

Elan leaned back in his chair, his mind reeling with the implications of Kaira's words. He wanted to believe her and support her in any way he could. But a part of him couldn't help but wonder if the stress of her studies and pregnancy had taken a toll on her mental state.

"Kaira," he said softly, choosing his words carefully. "I'm here for you, no matter what. But have you considered that maybe these dreams are just a byproduct of stress? I know you've been under so much pressure lately with school, living overseas for the year, missing home, and finding out we're pregnant. It's a lot to take in."

Kaira shook her head, her eyes filled with a determination that Elan had never seen before. "I know how it sounds," she said, her voice growing stronger. "But I can't ignore what I've seen and felt. I need to find answers, Elan. I need to know the truth. I can't do this alone. I need you."

Castel Sant'Angelo, Italy, January 23, 2005 A.D.

Kaira led Elan through the maze-like corridors of Castel Sant'Angelo, feeling as if an unseen energy guided her. Her mentor, Professor Xicato, gave her a key to gain entry after hours without asking questions—reminiscent of events in her alternate life. Despite her gratitude, a small part of Kaira couldn't help but wonder about Professor Xicato, a nagging sense that he knew more than he was letting on.

She had dreamed of this place before, and now it was unfolding in front of her, just as she had envisioned. Elan followed closely behind, his hand clasped tightly in hers, a silent show of support and trust.

They arrived at the entrance to Hadrian's tomb, a place that had haunted Kaira's dreams for weeks. It was a secret door unadvertised to the public. As they descended into the ancient crypt, the atmosphere grew heavy with the weight of centuries past. The walls seemed to whisper secrets, and Kaira felt a shiver run down her spine.

As they walked deeper into the tomb, Kaira suddenly stopped, her eyes wide with recognition. She unlocked a door with the key

Professor Xicato entrusted to her. "I've been here before," she whispered, her voice echoing in the stillness. "In my dreams, I was standing in that room. Before I open this door, I swear to you I have never been here, Elan. When we walk through that door, we will see the true burial site of Emperor Hadrian, surrounded by statues of Roman gods—Mars, Venus, Fortuna, and Saturn. And Mithras is there too."

Elan continued to hold Kaira's hand. "So you're feeling deja vu?"

"It's more than that. I can't explain it. They're memories I can clearly remember," Kaira said, looking Elan intensely in the eye. She took a deep breath and pushed the ancient door open.

Elan looked around, taking in the ancient stone walls and the intricate carvings that adorned them. Then he couldn't stop staring at the statues Kaira told him about mere moments before. He had never been one to believe in the supernatural, but standing here with Kaira, he couldn't deny the strange sense that washed over him.

"I believe you," he said softly, his voice barely above a whisper.

Kaira turned to him, her eyes shining with tears. "You believe me," she said, her voice trembling with emotion. "You *really* believe me."

Elan pulled her into his arms, holding her tightly against his chest. "Of course, I believe you," he said, his voice fierce with conviction. "I may not understand everything, but I trust you, Kaira. This is incredible."

They stood there for a long moment, their hearts beating in unison as they took in the weight of their shared experience. Kaira felt a sense of peace wash over her for the first time since the dreams had begun. She wasn't alone in this, not anymore.

As Elan and Kaira stepped out of Castel Sant'Angelo, the skies above Rome opened up, unleashing a torrential downpour. The couple hurried through the narrow, cobblestone streets, seeking shelter from the sudden storm, and found refuge in a small, dimly lit bar.

Elan and Kaira huddled at a corner table, steaming cups of coffee cradled in their hands. Kaira's revelations hung heavy in the air between them, and Elan struggled to understand the implications of her dreams.

"Kaira," Elan said, his voice strained with emotion, "the idea of past lives, fate controlling our destiny... it's a lot to wrap my head around. I need time to process it myself, and I can't believe you held this all in. You're not alone anymore."

Kaira reached across the table, taking Elan's hand in hers. "I know it sounds crazy," she said softly, admiring his face. "But I can't ignore what I've seen and felt. It's like a part of me has always known that there's something more to our story."

Elan sighed, running his free hand through his rain-soaked hair. "But what does it mean for us, Kaira? For our future, for our child? What does it all mean?"

Kaira's grip tightened on his hand, and her eyes filled with fierce determination. "It means that our love is stronger than time itself," she said, her voice unwavering. "It means that no matter what happens or what obstacles we face, we'll figure it out together."

"I love you, Kaira," he said, his voice flooded with emotion. "No matter what happens, no matter what the truth of your dreams may be, that will never change."

Kaira smiled, tears glistening in her eyes. "I love you too, Elan," she whispered. "Thank you."

As they sat there, hand in hand, the storm raging outside the café's windows, Elan and Kaira knew their love would be tested in ways they had never imagined.

As the days passed, Elan and Kaira encountered a series of uncanny coincidences that seemed to confirm the details of Kaira's dreams. It began with a visit to the Vatican Library, where Kaira had spent count-less hours researching for her architecture thesis. As they wandered through the stacks, Kaira suddenly stopped, her eyes widening with recognition.

"This book," she whispered, pulling a worn leather-bound volume from the shelf. "I've seen it before, in my dreams."

Elan looked at the title, his face tightening in confusion. "The History of the Order of St. Michael," he read aloud. "I've never heard of it."

Kaira flipped through the pages, her fingers trembling slightly. "It was a secret society within the Catholic Church," she explained, her voice barely above a whisper. "In my dreams, they were involved in a battle against an ancient evil."

Elan's remaining wariness subsided as he watched Kaira pore over the book, her features alight with recognition and understanding. He couldn't deny the specificity of the details she had dreamed about, nor how they seemed to align with the information in the book.

Well into the night, Elan and Kaira returned to her apartment. Once inside, Kaira led Elan to the small kitchen table, where she had spread a collection of notes and sketches. "I've been trying to piece together the fragments of my dreams," she said, her voice steady despite the gravity of the situation. "I think I know what we need to do."

Elan pulled a chair beside her, staring at the pages before him. "Tell me," he said, his hand finding hers beneath the table.

Kaira took a deep breath, organizing her thoughts. "The Order of St. Michael," she began, tapping a finger on a sketch of an ancient symbol. "I think we need to find and learn from them."

Elan nodded. "Okay," he said, his mind already working through the logistics. "But we also need to think about our safety, the safety of our loved ones, and the safety of our unborn child. This might not be the right time to do this."

Kaira met his gaze, her eyes filled with a fierce determination. "I know," she said softly. "That's why I think we should move back to San Francisco, to be closer to our families. We can't do this alone, Elan. We need their support and protection. Plus, I miss Reagan."

Elan squeezed her hand, a small smile tugging at the corners of his mouth. "I absolutely agree," he said excitedly as he changed the subject. "I've been thinking... I want to enlist in the military. I'm thinking Navy. Marines? I want to be able to protect you, to protect our child. And the training and the skills I'll learn could be helpful in whatever these dreams are leading you toward. I want to do something to make our baby proud of me."

Even before starting a family had taken root in his mind, Elan had always felt a pull towards military service. His uncle, a retired Master Chief in the United States Navy, had been a guiding light, symbolizing the sacrifices and dedication required to serve one's country. Elan had grown up listening to his stories of life in the Philippines and the journey that had brought him to America, and he knew he wanted to follow in those footsteps. He saw the military as a way to make a difference, to give back to the country that had given his family so much, and to forge a path toward a better life for himself and his loved ones.

Kaira's eyes widened, a mixture of pride and fear flashing across her face. "Our baby is already proud of you, Elan. I'm proud of you. Are you sure?" she asked, her voice barely above a whisper.

Elan nodded, his jaw set with determination. "I'm sure," he said, his voice unwavering. "We're in this together, Kaira. Whatever comes our way, we'll face it side by side."

CHAPTER
TWENTY-FOUR

The Durant-Mazza household was always buzzing with the lively energy of a growing family. Kaira expertly balanced her successful career in architecture with the demands of raising twins. Luckily, she had the unwavering support of her sister Reagan. The Durants were also a constant presence, with Elan's mom, Rose, brother, Jhan, and sister, Kristinn, playing crucial roles in Myst and Maya's lives. Of course, their family dynamic was still a bittersweet aspect as Elan fulfilled his Marine Corps duties at different duty stations worldwide. But they had learned to adapt and make the best of it.

As Myst and Maya grew, Kaira couldn't help but notice peculiarities in their behavior. It started with small things, like the way Maya would hum ancient melodies Kaira had never shared before or how Myst would correct historical inaccuracies in the stories she read to them. Still, she knew them as she had already walked this path with her children.

One evening, as Reagan prepared dinner, Kaira overheard Maya and Myst discussing the intricacies of medieval weaponry. Their knowledge was far beyond their years, and the passion they argued sent a chill down Kaira's spine.

"Myst, Maya, where did you learn about these weapons?" Kaira asked, her voice laced with curiosity and concern.

The twins exchanged a glance, their eyes holding a wisdom that seemed to transcend their age. "We just know, Mommy," Maya replied. "It's like we've always known."

Kaira shared her observations with Reagan, who listened intently, her brows furrowed in thought. "It's strange," Reagan admitted, "but maybe they're just gifted children. They might be absorbing information from the books and documentaries we watch. Or just watching you."

However, as the years passed, the incidents became more frequent and complicated to explain. Myst would correct Kaira's architectural drawings, pointing out elements reminiscent of ancient Roman structures. Maya would learn and speak in foreign languages quickly, her accent flawless, and her vocabulary extensive.

Kaira couldn't shake the feeling that there was something more to her children's uncanny abilities. She poured over old family records and ancient texts, searching for answers to questions she couldn't quite formulate.

Kaira found herself seeking solace in the tranquil beauty of Golden Gate Park, her mind swirling with the weight of her observations. She walked along the winding paths, the gentle rustling of leaves and the distant laughter of children providing a soothing backdrop to her tumultuous thoughts.

She settled on a bench overlooking a small pond, watching the sunlight dance on the water's surface. In the moment's stillness, Kaira fully resolved the growing suspicions in her mind.

The puzzle pieces began to fall into place, each peculiar incident and uncanny ability displayed by Myst and Maya forming a picture that was both astonishing and undeniable. The ancient melodies, historical knowledge, and foreign languages revealed a truth that defied conventional understanding.

Kaira's heart raced as the realization dawned on her: Myst and

Maya retained memories from their past lives. The thought was both exhilarating and terrifying, challenging everything she had ever believed about the nature of existence. Although these experiences had been happening to her, Kaira still struggled to reconcile the idea of past lives with her understanding of reality. It was one thing to have vivid dreams and unexplained memories, but to accept that she had lived before was a concept that shook her to her core.

She remembered her vivid dreams, those that had haunted her since college—dreams of ancient cities, love and loss, battles fought, and sacrifices made. Why did they have memories, but Elan did not?

Kaira reeled at the implications of this discovery. What did it mean for her children's future? For their family's destiny? She knew this knowledge would change everything and set them on a path fraught with wonder and danger.

~

San Francisco, California, 2015 A.D.

Kaira sat down with Myst and Maya in the cozy living room of their San Francisco home. The walls were adorned with family photos, capturing moments throughout their lives. Pictures of Kaira's grandma Giazza, Reagan and her boyfriend Austin, Grandma Rose, Jhan, and Kristinn, and various snapshots of Elan in his Marine uniform were scattered with images of their childhood and prom night. Books were strewn about the room, reflecting the family's shared love of knowledge and learning. The space felt warm and inviting, a testament to the love and memories built within its walls.

The twins, now ten years old, looked at their mother with curiosity and apprehension. Kaira took a deep breath, gathering her thoughts before she spoke.

"Maya, Myst," she began, her voice gentle but firm, "I've noticed some things lately that I think we need to talk about."

The twins glanced at each other, a silent understanding passing between them. They nodded, waiting for their mother to continue.

Kaira leaned forward, her elbows resting on her knees. "You both seem to have knowledge and abilities that go beyond what most children your age possess. The ancient melodies, the historical facts, the foreign languages - it's like you've lived these experiences before."

Myst and Maya looked at each other again, a flicker of recognition in their eyes. Maya spoke first, her voice barely above a whisper. "We thought it was just our imagination, Mom. But the dreams, they feel so real."

Kaira's heart skipped a beat. "Dreams? What kind of dreams?"

Myst chimed in, his brow grooved in concentration. "We see places we've never been to, people we've never met. But we know them like we did go there and know them."

Kaira smiled, her suspicions confirmed. "Oh my babies, this must all be so confusing for you. You're experiencing memories from our past lives. It's hard to explain, but it's true."

The twins were silent for a moment, processing their mother's words. Then, Myst spoke up, his voice filled with a sudden realization. "Mom, don't you remember training with us at our house in Benevento?"

Kaira's eyes widened, and a flood of memories rushed back to her. The ancient Italian city, the sprawling villa, and the hours spent honing their skills in the courtyard returned to her in a dizzying rush.

"I... I do remember," she whispered, her voice trembling with emotion. "But how is this possible? How can we all have these memories?"

Maya reached out, taking her mother's hand in her own. "Maybe we're meant to remember, Mom. Maybe there's a reason why we've been given this gift."

Kaira squeezed her daughter's hand, a sense of purpose settling over her. "You're right, Maya. We need to understand why this is happening and what it means for our family."

The three of them sat silently, each lost in their thoughts. Their shared memories hung heavy in the air, a bond connecting them across lifetimes.

Myst broke the silence. "So who's telling father?"

Kaira, Myst, and Maya sat in the living room, the weight of their shared memories hanging in the air. Kaira looked at her children, a mix of wonder and determination in her eyes.

"So, we all agree that these memories are real, right?" she asked, a hint of a smile playing at the corners of her mouth. "We're not just collectively losing our minds?"

Myst grinned, his eyes sparkling with mischief. "Well, if we are, at least we're doing it as a family."

Maya rolled her eyes but couldn't suppress a giggle. "You're always the jokester, Myst. But yeah, I think we're all on the same page here. These memories—they're a part of us."

Kaira nodded, her expression turning serious. "And if they're a part of us, then there must be a reason. We need to understand what these memories mean and why we've been given this gift."

Myst leaned forward, his brow furrowed in thought. "Mom, do you remember how you used to tell us bedtime stories about the future? About the adventures we'd have and the people we'd meet?"

Kaira's eyes widened, the memories flooding back to her. "I do, Myst. I remember telling you about the world I came from and my life before."

Maya chimed in, her voice filled with excitement. "And now we're living in that future, Mom! We're actually here, with Dad and everyone else. It's like a dream come true."

Kaira felt a warmth spread through her chest, the love for her family overwhelming her. "It is, Maya. And I'm so grateful to have you both by my side, no matter our challenges."

Myst's face lit up with a sudden idea. "Hey, Mom? When can we go back to Benevento? You know, to visit the places we remember? I liked it there."

Kaira smiled, the thought of returning to the ancient Italian city filling her with nostalgia. "Soon, Myst. We'll make a trip out of it when your father can take some leave. But first, we need to focus on understanding these memories and what they mean for our future."

Kaira, Myst, and Maya ventured into the darkest alleyways of San Francisco's Chinatown, their footsteps echoing against the wet pavement. The city was infused with the briny scent of the bay, mingled with the rich aromas of diverse cuisines from hustling street vendors and nearby cafes. They sought Nykronus, a mystical figure they hoped could shed light on their shared memories and the looming threat over their family.

Turning a corner, they stood before a nondescript door, its weathered wood adorned with intricate carvings. Kaira glanced at her children, a silent understanding passing between them. She raised her hand and knocked, the sound reverberating through the narrow alley.

The door creaked open, revealing a tiny room packed with antique artifacts and dusty books, giving the impression of a hoarder's living space. A man sat in the center of the room, his face lined with experience and knowledge. His eyes, a piercing blue, seemed to see right through them.

"Nykronus, Professor Xicato sent us here," Kaira said, her voice barely above a whisper. "We've come seeking your guidance."

The old man smiled, his eyes crinkling at the corners. "Kaira, Myst, Maya," he said, his voice soft but commanding. "I've been expecting you."

The three stepped into the room, the door closing behind them with a soft click. They approached Nykronus, their hearts racing with anticipation and a touch of fear.

"We've been having these memories," Kaira began, her voice trembling slightly. "They are memories of past lives, of a time long ago. We don't understand their meaning or why we've been given this gift."

Nykronus nodded, his expression thoughtful. "The memories you speak of are not mere dreams or figments of your imagination," he said, his voice filled with a quiet intensity. "They are echoes of your past lives, a reminder of the roles you have played in the grand tapestry of history. Whispers from a tomorrow that will never be. Memories of a yesterday that may have been, but now fades away."

Myst and Maya exchanged glances, their eyes wide with wonder and trepidation. "But why us?" Myst asked, his voice barely above a whisper. "Why have we been chosen to remember?"

Nykronus leaned forward, his gaze locked on the twins. "You are not the first to be granted this gift, nor will you be the last," he said, his voice filled with a quiet authority. "The memories you hold are a key to unlocking the mysteries of the past and shaping the future. That's all I can tell you; your memories will be revealed all in time."

Kaira felt a chill run down her spine. "And the threat we sense?" she asked, her voice barely above a whisper. "What does it mean for our family?"

"The Malefic Assembly seeks to unravel the fabric of reality, to tear down the barriers between worlds and unleash chaos upon the universe," Nykronus continued his voice grave. "They believe that by doing so, they can harness the power of the ancient gods and reshape existence to their own twisted desires. If they succeed, the world as we know it will be consumed by darkness, and all that we hold dear will be lost forever. They will stop at nothing to achieve their goals and use every means at their disposal to eliminate anyone who stands in their way."

The gravity of Nykronus's words sank in.

"What can we do to help?" Kaira asked, her voice filled with understated commitment

He placed an ancient tome on the table before them, its pages rustling softly in the firelight. "This book contains some of the secrets of your past, the key to deciphering the memories you are unlocking on a daily basis. Information that will guide you in the battles to come."

Kaira reached out, her fingers trembling as she touched the weathered leather. "And what of the threat we face now?" she asked, her voice filled with a quiet determination. "How do we stop the Malefic Assembly?"

"The path ahead will be fraught with danger and uncertainty," he said, barely above a whisper. "But you are not alone in this fight. Allies from your past lives will stand with you, united in the face of the darkness."

Redwood National Forest, California, July 17, 2016

Nykronus led Kaira, Myst, and Maya to a secluded clearing deep within the heart of the Redwood forest. As they walked, Kaira's thoughts drifted to Elan, currently deployed with the military. She had kept him informed of their experiences and the training they were undertaking, but she couldn't help but feel his absence keenly. She longed for his strength and support, for the comfort of his presence by her side. But she knew he was serving a greater purpose, and she drew strength from just knowing he was out there, fighting for their family and the world they held dear.

"This is where your training begins," Nykronus said, his voice low and measured. "Here, you will learn to harness the power that lies within you, to wield it as a weapon against the darkness that threatens to consume us all."

Kaira nodded, her expression determined.

Nykronus guided them through ancient rituals to unlock their latent abilities. He taught them to meditate, to reach deep within themselves and tap into the wellspring of energy that flowed through their veins. As they focused their minds and channeled their thoughts, they began to feel a tingling sensation in their fingertips, a warmth that spread throughout their bodies.

"Visualize the energy as a tangible force," Nykronus instructed, his voice soft but commanding. "See it taking shape before you, a glowing orb of light that responds to your will."

Myst and Maya closed their eyes, their foreheads creasing in concentration. Slowly, tentatively at first, tiny light spheres began forming in their immediate vicinity. The orbs grew larger and brighter as they became more confident, pulsing with an inner radiance.

"Now, direct that energy towards the targets," Nykronus said, gesturing to a series of wooden dummies in the clearing.

The twins focused their minds, willing the orbs of light to move. With a sudden burst of speed, the spheres shot forward, slamming into the dummies with a force that sent splinters flying.

"Good," Nykronus nodded, a smile playing at the corners of his mouth. "With practice, you will learn to shape the energy into different forms - shields to protect yourself, blades to strike at your enemies, and more. The possibilities are limited only by your imagination and your will."

As the days turned into weeks, the family's skills grew exponentially. Myst and Maya could now conjure shields of shimmering light capable of deflecting even the most potent attacks. They could hurl bolts of energy with pinpoint accuracy, quickly striking targets from across the clearing.

One day, as they rested between training sessions, Kaira approached Nykronus with a question weighing heavily on her mind. "What about Elan?" she asked, her voice barely above a whisper. "Why do our children have powers and he doesn't? How can we ever expect him to join this fight?"

Nykronus smiled, his eyes crinkling at the corners. "Elan has all the training he needs," he said, his voice filled with quiet confidence. "His path is taking him to where we need him to be."

Kaira nodded, a sense of relief washing over her. She knew that Elan was a skilled warrior, but the thought of him facing the dangers ahead without the benefit of their shared memories had been a constant source of worry.

Reagan joined the group as their training progressed, eager to learn from Nykronus directly. She took on the role of a spectator and scribe, documenting their progress and the ancient lore they uncovered. Nykronus explained that the Order of St. Michael was a secretive organization with few members scattered globally. They kept their whereabouts closely guarded, knowing that the Malefic Assembly had followers everywhere, waiting for the opportunity to strike.

As they gathered around a weathered stone table, Nykronus began to share his knowledge of the ancient arts. He spoke of the power that lay dormant within each of them, a legacy of their family and their roles in the eternal struggle against the forces of darkness.

Kaira listened intently, her eyes closed in meditation as she absorbed every word. She knew the future would be dicey with endangerment, but she was ready to do whatever it took to protect her family and the world they called home.

Myst and Maya sat beside her, their eyes wide with wonder as they listened to Nykronus's tales of ancient battles and the heroes who had fought them. They knew they were a part of something greater than themselves, a legacy that stretched back through the ages.

Nykronus, once a mysterious figure from their past, had become an integral part of their lives. He was more than just a mentor, more than just a guide. He was family in every sense of the word.

Reagan, ever the scribe, took careful notes, documenting every detail of Nykronus's teachings. She knew the knowledge they gained here would be invaluable in the battles to come, a guide to help them navigate the treacherous waters ahead. Kaira looked toward her sister with admiration.

Kaira and Reagan had always been close, their bond as sisters unbreakable from birth. Growing up, they had been each other's confidants and fiercest protectors, standing together against any challenge that came their way.

That bond grew stronger as they worked side by side, documenting Nykronus's teachings and developing their strategy. They moved in perfect sync, their thoughts and actions aligned as if they were two halves of the same whole.

"Do you remember when we were kids?" Reagan voiced softly, her eyes distant with memory. We used to pretend we were warriors, fighting against the monsters under the bed."

Kaira smiled, reaching out to squeeze her sister's hand. "Of course I do. We were unstoppable together."

"We still are," Reagan said fiercely, her grip tightening. "No matter what happens or what we face, I will always be by your side. Always."

Kaira laughed, shaking her head in mock exasperation. "What would I do without you, Ray?"

"Crash and burn, probably," Reagan teased, but her eyes were soft with affection. "But you'll never have to find out. I'm not going anywhere, not now, not ever."

Kaira leaned against Reagan's shoulder, feeling warmth and security washing over her. "I know," she said softly. "We've got this, you and me. No matter what comes our way."

∽

After a long and intense training day, the sun cast a warm glow across the secluded clearing where Kaira, Myst, Maya, Nykronus, and Reagan gathered around a weathered stone table for dinner. The ancient sequoia trees towered above them, their leaves rustling softly in the gentle breeze. The fresh wood scent gave a crisp, revitalizing, and soothing aroma.

Kaira looked around at her family, her heart swelling with pride and affection. Myst and Maya sat beside her, their eyes bright with determination and a touch of mischief. Nykronus, their mentor and guide, stood at the head of the table, his expression thoughtful.

Ever the pragmatist, Reagan cleared her throat and pulled out a few hefty tomes bound in brand-new leather. "Look, fam," she said, her voice filled with excitement. "This is a work in progress. It has your journals and diaries with your memories. It also has the experiences and training Grand Magus Nykronus has been giving us. Take a first look at 'The Mystic Chronicles,' Volumes 1 through TBD."

Kaira reached out and took one of the tomes, her fingers tracing the intricate designs on the cover. She opened it, her eyes scanning the pages filled with their collective experiences—memories of their past lives, challenges, and lessons they had learned. It was all here, a testament to their journey and shared bond.

Myst and Maya leaned in, their eyes wide with joy as they flipped through the pages. They pointed out specific entries, laughing and reminiscing about their shared moments. Nykronus watched them, a faint smile playing at the corners of his mouth.

"This is incredible, Reagan," Kaira said, her voice filled with awe.

As they sat around the table, poring over the pages of The Mystic Chronicles, they had the knowledge, skills, and love to face anything that came their way. Nykronus was delighted to know that the Durant and Mazza family legacy would become a part of the Order of St. Michael's archive, ensuring future generations could learn from their experiences—thereby continuing the ongoing saga.

At the conclusion of dinner, Nykronus gathered the family's attention. With a grave expression, he took a deep breath before beginning. "My dear family," he said, his voice low and measured, "the time has come for you to know the true nature of our adversary, Dante Malvagio."

Kaira leaned forward, her eyes intense, while Myst and Maya listened.

"Dante is a cardinal, cloaked in the guise of piety and charm," Nykronus continued, his words painting a vivid picture. "Yet beneath this facade, he harbors dark ambitions and a sinister secret. He is cunning and manipulative, using his position within the Church to influence and control those around him."

Nykronus paused, his eyes scanning the faces of his charges. "Despite his charismatic exterior, Dante's true nature is betrayed by his appearance. His hair is unkempt, his clothing greasy, hinting at a deeper rot within. He has gathered a cult following, drawn to his hidden sinister intentions. Think of the Malefic Assembly under a different name and leader. If I had to give them a name, it would be the Cult of St. Valentine."

Reagan was perplexed. "St. Valentine? Dante Malvagio is St. Valentine? So, did the Malefic Assembly succeed in resurrecting St. Valentine? Is this why Kaira's family is experiencing these memories? Were they resurrected?"

Nykronus considered Reagan's thoughts before responding, "No, they were not resurrected. They are experiencing echoes. Remember, they never existed in the past. Not in this timeline. Yes, Dante is St. Valentine."

A shiver raced along Kaira's vertebrae as the gravity of Nykronus's revelation draped her shoulders like a leaden cloak. Myst and Maya, their eyes wide, clung to each other, their youthful innocence suddenly faced with the harsh realities of the world they were destined to protect.

"But we are not without hope," Nykronus said, quiet and determined. Your unity, love for one another, and the knowledge you have gained thus far are your primary weapons against Dante's machinations."

The meeting concluded with a somber acknowledgment of the

enormity of the task before them. Confronting Dante would require more training, careful planning, and further investigation into his activities and cult. Nykronus suggested that their next move should be to gather more intelligence and possibly seek allies, as Dante's influence within the Church made a confrontation risky at this stage.

As the family dispersed, each lost in their thoughts, they remained united in their purpose. They knew they were not yet ready to confront Dante directly, but they were committed to stopping his dark plans, no matter the cost.

CHAPTER
TWENTY-FIVE

Dante Malvagio's early life was masked in mystery, a carefully crafted facade that concealed the truth of his origins. Born in Rome in 1979, he was raised by Verendana, a woman who had escaped death centuries ago and had been watching over him since his birth. She succeeded in casting a ritual that changed the course of her life and truly gave her a second chance. Verendana's influence on Dante's life profoundly shaped his worldview and guided his every step.

As a child, Dante was enrolled in prestigious military prep schools, where he excelled in academics and physical training. His instructors marveled at his natural leadership abilities and uncanny ability to inspire loyalty in those around him. Dante's charisma was evident even at a young age, and Verendana nurtured this talent, knowing that it would serve him well in the future.

After graduating from prep school, Dante studied theology and philosophy at the University of Philadelphia, an Ivy League school. His professors were impressed by his keen intellect and ability to grasp complex concepts easily. Dante's time at university also allowed him to expand his network of contacts, forging relationships with influential individuals who would later prove invaluable to his cause.

Upon completing his undergraduate studies, Dante enrolled in seminary, where he honed his skills as a preacher and spiritual leader. His sermons were powerful and moving, captivating audiences with passion and intensity. Verendana watched from the shadows, pleased with her protégé's progress.

As Dante rose through the ranks of the Church, his reputation grew, and he began to attract a devoted following. His followers hung on his every word, drawn to his magnetic personality and promise of a better world. Verendana knew that Dante was destined for greatness, and she continued to guide him, always lurking just out of sight.

Dante's influence grew like a shadow, creeping across the globe with an insidious reach. He established a network of followers, a reestablished and modern Malefic Assembly, with hubs in major cities on every continent. From the crowded streets of New York to the ancient alleys of Cairo, Dante's presence was felt, his message whispered in the ears of the disillusioned and the desperate.

In the modern age, the Malefic Assembly has adapted to new methods of spreading its influence. It infiltrated boardrooms and political chambers, its influential and wealthy members pulling strings from behind the scenes. Through shady business deals and backroom negotiations, it slowly tightened its grip on the world's resources and decision-making processes.

At the heart of this web sat Vatican City, the headquarters of Dante's cult. It was here he held court, surrounded by his most devoted acolytes. They hung on his every word, their eyes gleaming with a fervor that bordered on madness. Dante's charisma was a tangible force, drawing in the lost and the broken and promising salvation in a world that had forgotten them.

Beneath the divine halls of the Vatican, Dante held clandestine meetings, his voice echoing off the ancient walls. He spoke of a new world order, a future where the Catholic Church would be cast aside and replaced by a new faith that embraced the darkness and forbidden. His followers listened, their hearts pounding with anticipation, their minds filled with visions of glory.

As Dante's cult grew, so too did his ambition. He began to reach out to influential figures, politicians, and business leaders, offering them a taste of the power he promised. Some resisted, but many fell under his sway, drawn in by his magnetic personality and the promise of untold riches.

Dante used these connections to further his agenda, leveraging their influence and resources to pave the way for his ultimate goal. He demanded unwavering loyalty and obedience in exchange for the power and wealth he promised. Those who proved helpful were rewarded; those who resisted or questioned his methods were swiftly and ruthlessly eliminated.

Dante's network spread like a virus, infecting even more places worldwide. In the slums of Mumbai, his followers preached to the poor and the desperate, offering them a way out of their misery. In the boardrooms of London, his acolytes whispered in the ears of the wealthy and the influential, promising them a share of the spoils.

Through it all, Dante watched, his eyes gleaming with a dark satisfaction. He knew that his time was coming, that soon, the world would be his to shape as he saw fit. The Malefic Assembly was rising, thanks to his elite sect, and nothing could stop it.

Dante knelt before the altar in his private chapel, his head bowed in silent contemplation. The flickering candlelight cast a supernatural glow across his face, highlighting the lines of anger and resentment on his skin. He had spent years climbing the ranks of the Church, believing that he was destined for greatness, only to be cast aside like a discarded pawn.

He remembered when everything changed when he realized that the Church was nothing more than a facade, a tool to be used in his grand plan. Verendana had guided him to infiltrate the ranks of the clergy and become a spy within the institution that claimed to serve God. As he rose through the ranks, he gathered information and secrets, building a network of loyal followers within the Church. But as he delved deeper into the inner workings of the Vatican, he discovered a web of lies and deceit that only fueled his ambitions.

The Church had betrayed him as it had betrayed countless others throughout history. It had used its power to manipulate and control, to crush dissent and silence those who dared to speak out against it. Dante had seen it all and vowed to tear down the institution that had robbed him of his innocence.

As he knelt before the altar, Dante's mind raced with thoughts of revenge. His new world order would eclipse the Church and its false promises. He would gather an army of the faithful, those who had been cast aside and forgotten, and together, they would overthrow the old guard and usher in a new era of darkness.

Dante's eyes gleamed with a fanatic light as he rose to his feet, his fists clenched at his sides. He would stop at nothing to achieve his goals, no matter the cost. The Church had underestimated him, and now it would pay the price for its arrogance.

With a final glance at the altar, Dante turned and strode out of the chapel, his footsteps echoing in the silence.

Dante strode into a dimly lit lodge, inspecting the faces of his most trusted acolytes. They were a diverse group, hailing from all walks of life, but united in their devotion to the cause. Some were wealthy businessmen, others were street rats, but all had been drawn to Dante's magnetic personality and promise of power.

"My friends," Dante began, his voice low and commanding. "The time has come for us to strike at the heart of our enemy. The Church has grown complacent and secure in its power and influence. But *we* know the truth. *We* know it is a corrupt institution, rotten to its core."

The assembled cultists rustled their assent, their pupils gleaming with a fanatic light. They had all seen the truth for themselves and had all been betrayed by the Church somehow. And now, under Dante's leadership, they would have their revenge.

We must be cautious," Dante continued, his gaze sweeping over the room. "The Church is powerful and will not hesitate to crush us if our true intentions are discovered. We must operate in secrecy, striking from the shadows as the final pieces are moved into place."

He pointed to a map on the table before him, its surface marked with cryptic symbols and annotations. "Our agents have been infiltrating the highest levels of the Church hierarchy. They will continue to gather intelligence, sow discord, and undermine the institution from within."

The cultists leaned forward, eager to participate in the grand plan. Dante smiled, a cold, calculating expression that sent shivers down the spines of those who saw it.

"But that is only the beginning," he said, his voice barely above a whisper. "We must also gather sacred relics that hold the key to our ultimate victory. With them in our possession, we will have the power to reshape the world in our image."

The chamber erupted in a chorus of cheers and shouts, the cultists caught up in the fervor of Dante's words.

Dante's vision for the world was one of absolute control, where he alone held the reins of power. He dreamed of a future where the masses bowed to his will, the strong ruled over the weak, and he was worshipped as a god among men. With the relics in his possession, he would have the power to reshape reality and bend the very fabric of existence to his desires. And anyone who dared to stand in his way would be crushed beneath the heel of his boot.

Sanctuary, a secret location in Redwood National Forest, June 2, 2024 A.D.

Kaira, Nykronus, Reagan, Myst, and Maya gathered in the family's stronghold, a sense of purpose and determination filling the air. The threat posed by Dante Malvagio loomed more immense than ever. In recent weeks, there had been a surge in supernatural activity world-wide - strange sightings, unexplained phenomena, and a palpable darkness on the horizon. Members of the Order reported whispers of a coming storm, a convergence of dark forces that threatened to engulf everything in its path. It was clear that Dante was on the move, and time was running out to stop him.

As they settled into their seats, Kaira couldn't help but smile as she saw Elan's face appear on the video chat screen.

"Chief Warrant Officer Durant," Kaira said, her voice playful yet filled with affection. "It's good to see you, even if it's just through a screen."

Elan grinned at the sight of his family, his face showing fatigue from the previous night's military operation. "Always a pleasure, Kai. I wouldn't miss this meeting for the world.'"

Nykronus cleared his throat, drawing everyone's attention. "Now that we're all here let's get down to business. Dante's influence grows stronger by the day, and we must act swiftly to counter his plans."

The group nodded in agreement, their attention sharpened by intense concentration. Nykronus began outlining their strategy, emphasizing the importance of training, recruiting allies, and consolidating their resources.

As the meeting progressed, Kaira's thoughts kept drifting to Elan. She was thankful for his unconditional love and support since the day she told him about her echoes. She knew he deserved to be here, to be a part of this fight. She had filled him in as much as she could during their brief conversations, but there was so much more to tell. She resolved to find a way to bring him into the fold and share the incredible truth of their family's destiny with him. He was a part of this, just as much as any of them, and she knew that together, they would be an unstoppable force against the darkness.

Reagan turned to Elan, a mischievous glint in her eye. "Hey, Elan, when you get a chance, can you give Austin a big hug for me? I miss that big lug."

Elan chuckled, nodding his head. "Of course, Reagan. I'll make sure to give him an extra squeeze, just for you."

Kaira watched the exchange with a warm smile, her heart swelling with pride as she saw her family maintaining a light-hearted spirit despite the circumstances. She caught Elan's eye, and the two shared a moment of silent understanding, their love for each other evident in their gaze.

Meanwhile, Myst and Maya were deep in conversation, their heads bent together as they discussed their plans for the upcoming battle. They were already proving themselves invaluable, and their youthful insights and talents added a fresh dimension to the group's efforts.

As the meeting concluded, Nykronus looked around the room, his eyes filled with pride and decisiveness. "We have a long road ahead of us," he said, his voice firm yet encouraging. "But I do not doubt that together, we will prevail. We have faced dark forces before and emerged stronger for it. The Order of St. Michael has been preparing for this moment for centuries - gathering knowledge, training warriors, and guarding the relics that hold the key to defeating Dante. We know what he plans to do with the power he seeks. And we will use every resource at our disposal, every ounce of our strength and courage, to stop him before it's too late."

The group clapped in agreement, Nykronus's words lifting their spirits.

Elan's face filled the screen, his expression full of determination and anticipation. Despite the distance between them, his presence was strong, a testament to their bond as a family.

"I have some good news," Elan began, his voice steady and clear. "My SkillBridge program and terminal leave have been approved. I'll be able to come home nine months earlier than planned before I retire."

The family erupted in cheers and applause, their faces beaming with joy at the prospect of having Elan back home sooner than expected. Kaira felt tears of happiness welling in her eyes, the weight of their long separation finally lifting from her shoulders.

Elan smiled, his eyes shining with pride and love for his family. "I want you all to know that I am fully committed to our plan," he continued, his voice growing more serious. "Even though I'm not there with you in person, I will do everything I can to support our cause from here."

Nykronus's demeanor was one of gratitude and respect. "Your support means the world to us, Elan," he said, his voice filled with emotion. "We know that you will be a valuable asset to our efforts, no matter where you are."

"We can't wait to have you home, Dad," Myst said, his voice filled with excitement. "But we know that you're with us in spirit every step of the way."

Elan's smile widened, his heart swelling with pride at his son's words. "I couldn't be more proud of all of you," he said intensely. "Together, we'll stop everything that gets in our way."

"And then what?" Myst asked, with excitement. "What happens after we win?"

Nykronus smiled, placing a reassuring hand on the boy's shoulder.

"Then, we rebuild. We take the lessons we've learned and the bonds we've forged and create a better world - one where the light always triumphs over the darkness."

Kaira added, her eyes shining with hope. "And we do it together, as a family. No matter what the future holds, we'll face it side by side, with love and courage in our hearts."

"Always," Reagan agreed, her voice fierce with determination. "We're in this together, now and forever. And nothing, not Dante, not the Malefic Assembly, not anything in this world or beyond, can ever tear us apart."

Nykronus and Reagan set out to gather allies for their quest, reaching out to those who had shown signs of remembering their past lives to strengthen the Order of St. Michael. They organized meetings in various locations, aiming to persuade these potential allies to join their fight against Dante Malvagio.

The first to arrive was Stanley Wyatt, a rugged man with a distinct red mustache and a cowboy hat. As he entered the room, his eyes widened in recognition of Nykronus. "I know you!" he exclaimed, his voice filled with awe. "You're the one from my dreams who guided me in my past life as Wulfstan the Steadfast. And I know your father, Felix. That life was real, wasn't it?"

Nykronus smiled, nodding in confirmation. "Indeed, Stanley. Indeed it was. It's good to see you again, my old friend."

Next to join was Zoe, a beach blonde woman with piercing green eyes. She, too, recognized Nykronus immediately. "In my past life, I was Isolde, the bard," she explained, her voice filled with emotion. "I've been having these memories come to me in waves since I was a kid. Since then, I've been singing songs based on my dreams. I *knew* I wasn't crazy."

Olivia, a librarian with a pixie cut, arrived shortly after. "I was *Sister Livia* in my past life," she said, her eyes meeting Nykronus's. "I've been dreaming of our adventures together for as long as I can remember. Where's Elan and the children?"

Nykronus gathered the group together, his expression grave. "I cast a spell in an alternate past," he began, "and it unleashed a wave that triggered a temporal echo. This echo has influenced your experiences, drawing us together once again. As for Elan Durant, the echo has not reached him yet.'"

Reagan couldn't contain her excitement. "This is incredible!" she shouted, her eyes shining madly. "As the Order's unofficial historian, I'll need copies of any dream journals or diaries you've kept. This information could be invaluable to our cause. And it's badass! We call them The Mystic Chronicles. It's a little name I cooked up myself."

Kaira entered the room, accompanied by Professor Xicato. His old eyes surveyed the gathered allies. As his gaze fell upon Nykronus, a smile spread across his face. "Nykronus, my old friend," he said, his voice filled with warmth and familiarity. "It's been far too long.'

Nykronus returned the smile, stepping forward to embrace the professor. "Indeed it has, Xicato. I'm glad you could join us."

Kaira watched the exchange with curiosity. As Professor Xicato turned to face the group, his eyes widened as they met Kaira's. "Kaira," he breathed, his voice filled with emotion, "I'll cut to the chase. I've been waiting to tell you since the moment I met you. In another life, I was the nobleman who helped you when you first arrived."

Kaira's eyes widened as she finally connected the dots. She remembered the nobleman's kindness and generosity, how he had taken her in and helped her navigate the unfamiliar world she found herself in. "Professor Xicato," she said, her voice filled with gratitude. "I can't believe you're really him! I mean he's really you. You know what I mean. Thank you for helping me all those years ago."

Nykronus cleared his throat, drawing the attention of the gathered allies. "Professor Xicato has been a trusted friend and a member of the Order for many years," he explained. "Together, we launched the plan to set everything in motion in the alternate past to ensure that this future would succeed. That plan is still in motion."

The group nodded, their faces surging with intensity. As the introductions ended, the allies pledged their support to the cause, ready to stand alongside the family in their fight against Dante Malvagio and the Malefic Assembly.

Kaira, Nykronus, Reagan, Myst, and Maya gathered around the central table in the command center, their faces illuminated by the soft glow of the holographic displays. The room buzzed with drive and decisiveness as they prepared for the final confrontation with Dante Malvagio and his malevolent forces.

Elan's face appeared on the main screen, his presence a reminder of the unbreakable bond that united the family, even across vast distances. "I've been monitoring Dante's movements from here," he said, his voice steady and resolute. "It looks like he's gathering his forces near the ruins of an old temple in the catacombs of Rome."

Nykronus nodded, his eyes scanning the map before him. "That makes sense. The temple holds a powerful nexus of magical energy. If Dante harnessed that power, it could give him a significant advantage. He could use it to bolster his abilities, making him nearly invincible in battle. Or worse, he could use it to tear open the veil between worlds, unleashing horrors beyond imagination. We cannot let that happen."

Kaira leaned forward in concentration. "Then we need to strike first before he can complete his ritual." She looked around the room, meeting the eyes of each family member. "We've all been preparing for this moment, training and honing our skills. Now is the time to put those abilities to the test."

Reagan stepped forward, her expression one of fierce determination. "I've been working on a plan to infiltrate Dante's inner circle," she said, pulling up a series of schematics on the display. "If we can get someone on the inside, we'll have a better chance of disrupting his plans."

Myst and Maya exchanged glances, their young faces filled with excitement and apprehension. "We've been practicing our combat skills," Myst said, his voice steady despite his age. We're ready to fight alongside you."

"After all, we have two lifetimes worth of training now," Maya added.

Kaira felt a surge of pride and love for her children; their bravery and dedication were a testament to their family's strength. "I know you're ready, and I know how special you are," she said, her voice soft but firm. "But remember, your safety is our top priority. If things get too dangerous, I want you to promise me that you'll retreat to the safe house."

Myst and Maya, now young adults, nodded solemnly, their eyes shining with a wisdom beyond their years. They understood the gravity of the situation, the weight of the responsibility that rested on their shoulders. But they also knew that they were ready, that their parents had prepared them for this moment all their lives. They knew their parents would do everything in their power to protect them, just as they would do everything they could to support the cause.

As the meeting continued, the family refined their strategies and assigned roles to each group member.

"I got my orders and tickets today. I'm flying out to Naples in the morning, and I'll get to Rome as quickly as possible," Elan announced triumphantly.

Throughout it all, Elan's presence remained a constant source of strength and encouragement, his love and devotion to his family a beacon of hope in the face of the coming darkness. As the final preparations were made and the group prepared to depart, they knew they were ready to face whatever challenges lay ahead, united in their resolve to protect the world from Dante's malevolent ambitions.

Somewhere over the Pacific Ocean, September 7, 2024 A.D.

Elan jolted awake, his heart pounding as the remnants of his dream clung to his consciousness. He blinked, taking in the empty plane around him, the hum of the engines a constant reminder of his journey from South Korea to Naples. The dream had been so vivid, so real, he struggled to separate it from reality for a moment.

In the dream, he had found himself in Rome, at Castel Sant'Angelo, alongside his best friend Reagan. They had discovered a sword, a weapon of great power and significance. But the dream had also carried with it a surge of emotions and thoughts, a glimpse into an alternate life where he had grown up alone and lost, without the love and support of his family.

Elan shuddered, the nightmare still fresh in his mind. He was grateful for his life and the family he had built with Kaira. Their love had been a beacon of hope in even the darkest times, a reminder of all that was good and worth fighting for. But he also knew that he could not take their happiness for granted, that there were forces at work that sought to take it all away. He would have to be vigilant to protect his loved ones with every ounce of strength he possessed. He reached for the airplane napkins, his hands shaking slightly as he began to write down the details of his dream. He titled it "The Mystic Chronicles: Elan Durant POV," the words flowing from his pen as he poured his thoughts and feelings onto the page.

When he finished, Elan took pictures of the napkins and sent them to the group chat with the caption "FINALLY!" He knew that his family would understand his dream's significance and its role in their shared destiny. He felt like a supporting cast member his entire adult life—he had a feeling that was about to change.

As the plane continued its journey, Elan leaned back in his seat, a smile spreading across his face. He whispered, *Stellata d'Inferno*. I'm coming for you, baby. My *Winterstar*." The words held a promise, a declaration of his commitment to the cause and to the woman he loved.

The Abbey of Montecassino, Cassino, Italy, September 11, 2024 A.D.

Kaira, Elan, Nykronus, Reagan, Myst, and Maya stood side by side, their faces determined as they surveyed the gathered allies before them. The command center buzzed with energy, a palpable sense of purpose and unity filling the air.

Professor Xicato, Stanley Wyatt, Zoe, and Olivia formed a semi-circle around the family, their expressions defined with the same fierce determination that radiated from Elan and Kaira. Their eyes blazed with an unwavering resolve, their jaws set in lines of grim purpose. They stood tall and proud, their postures exuding an aura of strength and unity that was contagious in the air around them. It was clear that they were more than just allies; they were a force to be reckoned with, a team forged in the crucible of battle and tempered by the bonds of friendship and loyalty. Each had answered the call to arms, their past lives and shared destinies intertwining to bring them to this pivotal moment.

Elan proudly scanned the gathered members of the Order of St. Michael. As he caught the faces of the knight, bard, and nun, he felt a rush of exhilaration, anxious to catch up on the memories he was about to experience.

Zoe spoke first. "I remember the night we first met, Elan," she said with a grin. "You were so serious, so focused on the mission ahead. But even then, I could see the heart of a true hero beating within you."

Stanley, his mustache twitching with amusement, chimed in. "I'll never forget when we faced those shadow demons in the catacombs beneath Rome. I thought we were done for, but Elan—you never wavered. You led us through the darkness and back into the light."

Olivia's pixie-cut hair bobbed as she nodded, adding, "Elan, you have always been our rock and guiding star. But it's not just your strength that sets you apart. It's your compassion and unwavering devotion to those you love. That's what makes you a true leader."

Kaira held Elan's hand, as he tried to understand the swirl of emotions he was feeling. He felt he knew these people and could hardly wait to know them again.

Nykronus stepped forward, his voice ringing out with clarity and conviction. "My friends, my allies, we stand here today united in our cause, ready to face the darkness that threatens our world. Each of you has been chosen; your unique skills and experiences are crucial to our success."

Kaira nodded, her eyes shining with pride as she looked upon the assembled group. "Together, we are stronger than any force Dante Malvagio can muster. We have trained and prepared, and now we are ready to take the fight to him."

Elan placed a hand on his wife's shoulder, his presence a steadfast anchor amidst the gathering storm. "We've faced challenges and obstacles at every turn," he said, his voice ringing with conviction. "From the moment we first met, our love has been tested by forces beyond our control. We've endured separation and heartbreak and fought battles, both physical and emotional. But through it all, we've remained united. Our love has been our greatest strength, it is now our most powerful weapon against the darkness that seeks to consume us. And it is that love, that unbreakable bond, that will see us through the trials ahead. Together, we are stronger than any force that dares stand against us."

Reagan, Myst, and Maya stood tall, their young faces filled with a fierce determination that belied their age. They had grown up knowing the weight of their destiny and the importance of their roles in the battles to come. Now, they stood ready to take their place alongside their parents and allies to fight for the future they believed in.

As the group looked at one another, they signed. They were no longer individuals but a cohesive unit, bound by the unbreakable ties of family, friendship, and destiny.

With a final nod, Nykronus turned to face the holographic displays, maps, and schematics of their battle plans glowing before them. "Let us begin."

CHAPTER
TWENTY-SIX

Rome, Italy, October 13, 2024 A.D.

Professor Xicato's mansion in Rome buzzed as the gathered allies convened in a secure meeting room. Elan and Kaira, commanding and resolute, stood at the head of the table, flanked by their children, Myst and Maya, and the Grand Magus Nykronus. The room was filled with familiar faces, each bearing the weight of their shared destiny.

Reagan, her blouse crisp and her demeanor focused, sat beside Stanley, the MMA fighter's muscles tensed with anticipation. Zoe leaned forward with her beach-blonde hair pulled back in a sleek ponytail, her piercing green eyes fixed on the holographic display before them. Olivia, the librarian from Egypt, her pixie-cut black hair framing her face, studied the ancient texts before her, her brow furrowed in concentration.

Professor Xicato, his aged face lined with wisdom and determination, stood beside Olivia, his presence a comforting anchor amidst the gathering storm. He spoke, steady and clear, "My friends, we have come together today to face the greatest challenge of our lives. The Malefic Assembly grows stronger by the day, and we must act now to stop them. Their influence can be seen in the growing unrest and discord throughout the world. Increased reports of strange occurrences and unexplained phenomena have reached our ears, signs that the Assembly is meddling with forces beyond their control. Just last week, reports of a small village in the countryside being consumed by an unnatural darkness reached us. When our agents investigated, they found the village abandoned, with no trace of its inhabitants. This is just one example of the Assembly's growing power and the chaos they sow."

Elan's mind drifted to the recent recollections that had filled his slumber over the past months. His gaze roamed the chamber, absorbing the resolute expressions of his companions. "Each of us has confronted personal trials and hardships, yet at this moment, we remain as one. United, we possess the power, the wisdom, and the determination to resist the shadows that imperil our realm."

Kaira placed a hand on the ancient map before her, her fingers tracing the lines of the hidden temples and sacred sites. "We know what we must do. We must gather the relics, the artifacts of power that can help us in our fight. But we must also be prepared for the challenges that lie ahead, the enemies that will stop at nothing to see us fail."

As the group leaned in, their attention focused on the plan before them; a sense of unity and determination settled over the room. They were no longer individuals but a cohesive unit bound by the unbreakable ties of destiny and purpose. With Elan and Kaira at the helm, they knew that they could face whatever lay ahead and emerge victorious in the battle for the fate of their world.

Nykronus tapped his hand on the table, drawing the group's attention. His eyes, deep pools of wisdom and experience, fixed upon Elan as he spoke, his voice resonating with the weight of his words. "Elan, there is a matter of great importance that we must discuss—a strategic detour if you will."

Elan leaned forward, his brow furrowed with curiosity. "What do you propose, Nykronus?"

The Grand Magus gestured to the ancient map before them, his finger tracing a path to a familiar location. "Castel Sant'Angelo. *Winter-*

star. It is crucial that you retrieve this weapon before we face the Malefic Assembly. I trust you remember how to get it?"

Kaira's eyes widened, recognition dawning on her face. "*Winterstar*... I remember reading about it in the ancient texts. St. Michael's Stellata d'Inferno. She's yours?"

Nykronus nodded, his gaze never leaving Elan's face. "Indeed, she's what allowed us to get to this point in the first place. And it is a weapon that will be essential in the battles to come. A weapon that has been fought in battles past and battles that exist only in some minds. With *Winterstar* at your side, once again, Elan, you will have the power to stand against even the most formidable of foes."

Elan's mind raced with the implications of Nykronus's words. He knew the dangers ahead, the enemies that would stop at nothing to see them fail. But with *Winterstar* in his grasp, he could face those dangers with renewed strength and resolve.

"I understand," Elan said, his voice steady and determined. "I'll retrieve *Winterstar* from Castel Sant'Angelo. But I can't do it alone."

Nykronus smiled, a glimmer of pride in his eyes. "You will not be alone, Elan. Your allies will be with you every step of the way. Together, you will face the challenges that lie ahead and emerge victorious."

The atmosphere in the chamber transformed as Myst and Maya approached. Their youthful visages bore striking resemblances to their parents, Kaira and Elan, displaying a blend of eagerness and resolve. Elan observed his offspring sharing a meaningful look before Myst grasped beneath the table and lifted an ornate, vintage chest onto the tabletop. The container was elaborately engraved, its rich timber shimmering under the gentle illumination of the conference area.

A chatter of curiosity rippled through the gathered allies as they leaned forward, their eyes fixed on the mysterious container. Maya's fingers traced the intricate patterns impressed into the wood before she looked up, her gaze sweeping across the room.

"So, about those temples and that plan to retrieve all these relics?" Maya's voice was steady, but her eyes showed a hint of mischief. "Um, we already did that."

Elan's eyes widened, and he exchanged a surprised glance with

Kaira. The room fell silent for a split second before erupting into a cacophony of questions and exclamations. Reagan leaned forward, her eyes narrowed. "What do you mean, you already did that?"

Myst grinned, his fingers working the latch on the box. "We've been busy. While you all were gathering allies and making plans, Maya and I were out there, tracking down the relics. I mean we already knew where they were anyway—for the most part."

As the assembled group marveled at the ancient relics before them, the air in the room seemed to crackle with energy. It was as if the artifacts were alive, pulsing with a power emanating from their cores. The hairs on the back of Elan's neck stood on end as he felt the thrum of magic coursing through the room, a tangible force that seemed to wrap around each of them, filling them with a sense of awe and trepidation. Even those without magical abilities could feel the weight of the power contained within the relics, a pressure that seemed to push against their very souls.

Maya reached into the box, her fingers closing around a small, intricate gem. She held it up, the light catching the delicate filigree. "This one is for you, Zoe. "

Zoe's eyes widened as she reached out, her fingers closing around the amulet. "Jupiter's Bolt! You, kids, are twice as badass as you were in 842."

Myst and Maya continued to distribute the ancient relics, each imbued with a power that seemed to resonate with its intended recipient. Stanley with his fiery red hair and mustache contrasting his modern attire, stepped forward as Maya held out a small, intricately carved box.

"For you, Stanley," she said, her voice filled with reverence. "The dragon's tooth, filled with dust from Saturn's Ring, collected from the cradle of creation."

Stanley's eyes widened as he took the box, his fingers tracing the delicate carvings. "It's like riding a bicycle."

Olivia, watched as Myst approached Professor Xicato with a shimmering armor set in his hands. "Professor, this armor was blessed with Neptune's Tears, collected from the deepest oceans. It will protect you in the battles to come."

Professor Xicato bowed his head, solemnly accepting the armor. "I am honored, Myst. I will proudly wear it, just as your father did over a millennia ago."

Kaira's eyes shone as Maya handed her a shield, its surface engraved with intricate designs. "Mom, do you remember when you gave us this shield? Now, it will keep *you* safe."

Kaira pulled her daughter into a tight embrace, her voice thick with emotion. She remembered the day she asked her children to protect the shield and the gem. "Thank you, Maya. I love you so much."

Olivia stepped forward, her eyes fixed on the scales that Myst held. "Olivia, these scales were touched by the Breath of Juno. They will help you cast judgment on our enemies."

Olivia took the scales, her fingers trembling slightly as she felt the weight of their power hearing the stories of their previous owner, Ivar Ghostcloak. "I will use them wisely, Myst. Thank you."

Reagan's eyes widened as Maya approached her, a single feather in her outstretched hand. "Auntie Ray, this feather is from St. Michael's wings. It will give you the ability to fly and cast divine intervention for a short time. The sun can recharge the feather, but that takes a lot of time."

Reagan took the feather, her eyes shining with awe. "I love you, kiddos. Thank you, Maya."

Myst approached Zoe with an electric lute as a final surprise. "Zoe, this is a replica of your old lute, with some modern adjustments. It symbolizes how the past has truly met with the future in the present."

Zoe's fingers closed around the lute, her eyes filled with wonder. "It's... it's perfect. Thank you, Myst."

As the gathered allies marveled at the ancient relics before them, Zoe's fingers caressed the electric lute, a spark of inspiration igniting in her eyes. She stood, her beach-blonde hair cascading over her shoulders, and strummed the first chords of a haunting melody.

Her voice, rich and soulful, filled the room as she began to sing, the words pouring from her heart like a sacred oath:

"In the shadows of the past,
The Order of St. Michael stands steadfast.
With swords of light and hearts so true,

We're here to fight, to see this through."

The allies watched, transfixed, as Zoe's music washed over them, the power of her words resonating deep within their souls. Her fingers danced across the strings, the electric lute humming with an otherworldly energy.

"We honor those who came before,
Their sacrifice, forevermore.
With angels watching from above,
We'll protect the future with strength and love."

Elan's chest swelled with pride as he listened to Zoe's song, the lyrics a testament to the unbreakable bonds that united them all. Kaira, her hand clasped tightly in his, smiled through the tears that glistened in her eyes, the weight of their shared destiny heavy upon their shoulders.

"The Malefic Assembly, they'll fall,
Before the might of St. Michael's call.
We'll take their names, we'll make them pay,
For the darkness they've unleashed today."

As the final notes of Zoe's song faded into silence, the room erupted into applause, the allies rising to their feet and cheering. Myst and Maya, their faces alight with fire, rushed forward to embrace their parents, their love and pride for their family, and their cause evident in every gesture.

Zoe lowered the electric lute, her eyes shining with the intensity of her convictions. "We've got this," she said, her voice steady and sure. "With the legacy of the Order of St. Michael flowing around and through us, and the angels watching over us, we'll face whatever comes our way. And we'll win."

Nykronus stepped forward. He pulled the *Pugio Mysticus Amoris* from beneath his robe, his fingers closing around the hilt. A shudder ran through his body as he felt the weight of its power.

"My friends," he said, his voice steady and clear, "there is one final task that I must undertake. One final battle that I must face alone."

Elan raised his eyebrow, his eyes searching Nykronus's face. "What do you mean, Nykronus? We're in this together, all of us."

Nykronus shook his head, a sad smile playing at the corners of his lips. "Not this time, Elan. This is a battle that only I can fight. A battle that has been centuries in the making."

He held up the Dagger of Love, its blade glinting in the room's soft light. "This dagger, imbued with the power of Saint Valentine himself, is the key to ending the threat of Verendana and Dante once and for all. I need to do this for my father. For Felix."

Kaira's eyes widened, understanding dawning on her face. "Nykronus, you don't have to do this alone. We can help you. We can fight alongside you."

He pivoted to address the assembled allies, his tone resonating with the depth of his beliefs. "You speak the truth, Kaira. *Together*, we shall confront Verendana and Dante. I will wield the Dagger of Love to vanquish them while concurrently annihilating it, ensuring an unending cycle of reverberations does not recur. Immortality is not the natural order. To cease their campaign of dread and restore tranquility to our realm once again, and guarantee we alone may defy mortality - you are correct. I shan't proceed unaccompanied. I require you, each and everyone, to remain at my side. To imbue me with your mettle and valor, whatever the price."

The aura in the meeting room became electrified as the allies gathered around the table again, their newly acquired relics humming with power. Elan stood at the head of the table, his eyes scanning the faces of his comrades, each one fueled with determination and resolve.

"Alright, let's get down to business," he said, his voice steady and commanding. "Myst and Maya, I'm so proud of you. We've got the relics thanks to you, but that's only half the battle. I still need *Winterstar*. We need to figure out how to take down Dante and his cult before they can do any more damage."

Nykronus nodded, his eyes glinting with wisdom. "Dante's power lies in his political influence and the loyalty of his followers. We need to undermine both if we hope to stop him."

Reagan leaned forward, her brow furrowed in thought. "We could expose his true nature to the public, show them the monster he really is."

Olivia shook her head. "It's not that simple. Dante's followers are fanatics. They won't be swayed by mere words."

Myst and Maya exchanged a glance, their eyes sparkling with mischief. "We might have an idea," Maya said, a grin spreading across her face.

Elan raised an eyebrow. "What do you have in mind?"

Myst leaned forward, his voice low and conspiratorial. "We've been practicing with our abilities, and we think we can use them to disrupt the cult's operations from the inside. Maya and I have been honing our skills in connecting with various relics and magical energy. Trust us."

Kaira's eyes widened, a mixture of pride and concern on her face. "Are you sure it's safe? We don't want you putting yourselves in danger."

Maya reached out, squeezing her mother's hand. "We'll be careful, Mom. We have to do this. It's the only way."

Professor Xicato stroked his beard, his eyes narrowed in thought. "It could work. If we can disrupt the cult's operations and expose Dante's true nature simultaneously, we might be able to turn the tide in our favor."

Elan bobbed his head, thoughts swirling with potential plans. "Okay, we'll go for it. Myst, pour your heart into it and hold nothing back. Maya, channeling your core power through the spell is crucial. As a team, you'll boost the potency of our relics. Meanwhile, the others will leverage your skills to the fullest."

Vatican City, Italy

In the heart of the Vatican, the towering spires of St. Peter's Basilica stood as a beacon of faith and tradition, symbolizing the Catholic Church's enduring presence in the world.

Dante Malvagio and his fanatical followers stormed the Vatican that night, their dark magic overwhelming the basilica's defenses. The Swiss Guard, armed with their traditional halberds and firearms, were no match for Dante's twisted power. He sent them flying through the air with a wave, their bodies crumpling like rag dolls against the unyielding stone. Verendana and the acolytes moved through the chaos like wraiths, their faces twisted with malevolent glee as they desecrated the sacred artifacts and relics that lined the basilica's halls. Dante strode through the massive doors of the Church, his black robes billowing behind him like the wings of a fallen angel. His eyes gleamed with a dark light, a hunger for power and domination that knew no bounds.

As they made their way down the central nave, their footsteps echoing off the marble floors, Dante's gaze fixed upon the high altar, where the Baldacchino stood as a testament to God's glory. With a sneer of contempt, he raised his hand, and a blast of dark energy erupted from his fingertips, slamming into the altar and sending shards of stone and metal flying in all directions.

Screams of terror filled the air as the faithful scrambled for cover, their eyes wide with horror at the sacrilege unfolding before them. Dante's followers surged forward, their weapons drawn, as they began to lay waste to the sacred space, smashing statues and tearing down tapestries with savage glee.

Elan and his allies watched the scene unfold through a magical scrying mirror from a hidden chamber beneath the Vatican. The scrying mirror, an ancient artifact passed down through the generations of the Order of St. Michael, had been a closely guarded secret known only to a select few. Nykronus had revealed its existence to Elan and his allies only recently, knowing that the time had come to use every tool in the fight against Dante and his forces. Now, they witness the horrors unfolding within the heart of the Vatican and gather the intelligence they need to mount a counterattack.

Their faces pale with shock and anger as they continued to spy with the mirror. Kaira gripped Elan's hand tightly, her eyes brimming with tears as she witnessed innocent people fall and the desecration of a place she held dear.

"We have to stop him," Elan growled, his voice trembling with barely contained rage. "Dante has gone too far. This isn't just an attack on the Church; it's an attack on everything we hold sacred. If he succeeds in harnessing the power of the Vatican, he'll be one step closer to his ultimate goal: total world domination. With the Church under his control, he'll have access to immense wealth, political influence, and the minds and souls of billions of followers. He'll twist the teachings of the faith to suit his dark purposes, spreading a message of hate and intolerance that will poison the hearts of men. We can't let that happen. We *will* stop him, here and now, before it's too late."

Nykronus nodded grimly, his time-worn eyes filled with a deep sadness. "This is a declaration of war," he said, his voice heavy with the weight of centuries. "Dante has made his intentions clear. He will stop at nothing to achieve his goals, even if it means destroying the very foundations of our faith."

The room buzzed with frenetic energy, and the once quiet space was now a hive of urgent mobilization. Elan paced the room, his eyes burning with a fierce determination as he addressed the gathered allies.

"Dante's made his move," he said, his voice cutting through the tense air like a blade. "He thinks he can strike at the heart of our faith and break us. But he's wrong. He's only succeeded in uniting us, in giving us a common purpose."

Kaira stood at his side, her hand resting on the hilt of her sword. "We've been preparing for this moment," she said, her voice controlled and hardy. "We have the relics, we have the knowledge, and we have each other. Dante may have his cult, but we have something far more powerful: the bonds of family and friendship."

Nykronus nodded, his ancient eyes shining with a renewed sense of purpose. "Kaira is right. Dante's actions have only served to sharpen our focus, to remind us of what's truly at stake. This is no longer just a battle for the world's fate; it's a battle for the very soul of humanity."

"Alright, everyone," Elan said, his voice ringing with newfound clarity and purpose. "Let's get to work. We have a madman to stop and a world to save. And we're going to do it together, as a family."

Their temporary foothold buzzed with a palpable strain as the alliance gathered around the central table, their eyes fixed on the maps and strategic documents before them. Elan stood at the head of the table, his gaze intense as he surveyed the faces of his closest allies: Nykronus, Kaira, Reagan, and Professor Xicato.

"Alright, everyone," Elan began, his voice steady and commanding yet tinged with a sense of urgency. "This is it. Our final chance to stop Dante and his twisted plans. We've got to make this count. If we fail, the consequences will be catastrophic. Dante will unleash a darkness upon the world like nothing we've ever seen. Innocent people will suffer, entire nations will fall, and all that we hold dear will be consumed by the shadows. We are the only thing standing between Dante and the world. We have to fight with everything we have, every ounce of strength, courage, and love that we possess. Because if we fail and allow him to succeed, there will be no going back. The world as we know it will be lost, and darkness will win."

"We won't fail Dad." Myst looked at her Elan with love and admiration, reminding him of who they were.

Nykronus nodded. "Dante's actions at the Vatican have shown us the depths of his depravity. We cannot allow him to continue unchecked."

Kaira leaned forward, her finger tracing a path on the map. "Our best chance is to confront him directly, at the heart of his power. If we can disrupt his ritual and destroy Nykronus's Dagger of Love, we'll end this once and for all."

Reagan frowned, her brow furrowed in thought. "But how do we get close enough? Dante's sure to have his most loyal followers guarding him."

Elan nodded, his eyes flicking to the twins. "We'll get close. Don't worry, Ray. Myst, Maya, you'll need to be careful. Stick to the plan and don't take any unnecessary risks."

The twins acknowledged. "We understand, Dad," Maya said, her voice steady. "We won't let you down."

Elan returned to the map, his finger tracing a path to the ancient catacombs beneath Rome. "No cowboy shit, Myst. Protect your sister. Nykronus and I will lead the main assault, using *Winterstar* and the Dagger of Love to confront Dante directly. Mazza women, you'll watch our six, ready to step in if things go south, and you'll lead the rest of the Order."

~

As the sun began to set over the ancient city of Rome, Elan, and Kaira, found themselves standing on a balcony overlooking the Tiber River. In the distance, the imposing silhouette of Castel Sant'Angelo loomed.

Elan leaned against the railing, his eyes fixed on the horizon. "It's hard to believe we've come this far," he said, his voice soft and reflective. "All the sacrifices we've made, the battles we've fought... it all leads to this moment."

Kaira moved to stand beside him, her hand finding his and intertwining their fingers. "We've been through so much together," she said, her voice filled with a quiet strength. "But I wouldn't change a thing. Every choice we've made, every path we've taken... it's brought us here, to this moment."

Elan turned to face her, his eyes searching hers. "We've also been through so much apart. I know the risks we're taking, Kaira. I know what we stand to lose. But I also know that we have no choice. We have to see this through, no matter the cost."

Kaira nodded, her gaze unwavering. "I'm with you, Elan. Always. We've faced impossible odds before and always come out stronger for it. Our love, our bond... our patience. It strengthens us to keep fighting, even when all seems lost."

Elan pulled her close, his arms wrapping around her tightly. "I love you, Kaira," he whispered, his voice thick with emotion. "No matter what happens, I will always be grateful for the life we've shared and the family we've built."

Kaira held him tightly, her face buried in his chest. "I love you too, Elan. More than words can say. And I know that, together, we can face anything. We will stop Dante, save the world, and do it side by side, as we always have."

Elan held Kaira close, his heart swelling with love and determination. "When this is all over," he whispered, his voice heavy with emotion, "when we've stopped Dante and saved the world, I want nothing more than to build a life with you. A life of peace and happiness, where we can watch our kids soar, and grow old together."

Kaira looked up at him, her eyes shining with tears and hope. "I want that too, Elan. More than anything. I want to watch our grandchildren grow up, find love, and start their own families. I want to travel the world with you to explore all the wonders we've never had the chance to see. But most of all, I want to wake up every morning in your arms, knowing that we've made a difference and left the world a better place than we found it."

Elan smiled, his heart aching with his love for her. "We will, Kaira. We'll have all of that and more. We'll find a quiet place by the sea where we can heal, rest, and be together. We'll tell our grandchildren stories of our adventures, of the battles we fought and the sacrifices we made. And we'll know that it was all worth it, every struggle and every scar, because it brought us to that moment, to that perfect peace we've always dreamed of."

As the last rays of the setting sun painted the sky in shades of orange and red, Elan and Kaira stood together on the balcony, their hearts filled with quiet resolution.

As the evening deepened and the moon was scarcely discernible in the heavens, the coalition assembled in a remote quad, their visages carved with resolve. As Stanley and Zoe provided ranged coverage from a nearby building, Elan was positioned at the vanguard of his ground unit, his gaze surveying the countenances of his allies. Everyone was heavily armed, their armaments glinting in the dim lunar glow.

Nykronus stood at Elan's side, his ancient eyes glinting with fierce resolve. He proudly held Pugio Mysticus Amoris in his hands, its blade thrumming with power. Kaira and Reagan flanked them, their swords sheathed at their sides and their armor glinting in the dusk.

Professor Xicato and Olivia stood nearby, their robes billowing in the gentle breeze. They carried ancient tomes and sacred relics, their knowledge and faith a weapon in its own right. Myst and Maya stood tall and proud, their abilities honed and ready to be unleashed.

Elan raised his hand, and the group fell silent. "This is it," he said, his voice enduring and influential. "We've come this far, and now it's time to end this. Dante thinks he can reshape the world in his own twisted image, but we're going to show him just how wrong he is."

The others knew the stakes, knew the risks they were taking. But they also knew that they had no choice. The world's fate hung in the balance, and they were the only ones who could tip the scales in favor of the light.

As one, the alliance turned and began to march towards Castel Sant'Angelo, their footsteps echoing off the cobblestone streets. They moved in formation, their weapons at the ready, their eyes scanning the shadows for any sign of trouble. They moved toward the divine place that started it all.

CHAPTER
TWENTY-SEVEN

Elan's footsteps echoed through the sacred chamber as he entered the Room of St. Michael, a reverence washing over him. The space was filled with artifacts and symbols honoring the archangel, each seeming to radiate with otherworldly energy. As he walked, Elan reached into his pocket, his fingers closing around the rosary bead that had once belonged to Kaira and Reagan's grandmother.

With a deep breath, he reached for an ancient rosary hanging on the wall, its beads gleaming in the soft light. Carefully, he inserted the missing bead into its rightful place, a soft click resounding through the room. As the bead settled into position, a shimmering blue light emanated from the rosary, growing brighter with each passing second.

The ethereal image of St. Michael towered over Elan, standing at least twice his height. The archangel's presence filled the room, his majestic wings spanning the entire width of the chamber. His gaze, fixed upon the shimmering pool, seemed to hold the weight of eternity itself. An ancient tome rested on a pedestal in the middle of the pool, its pages seeming to beckon Elan forward.

With the utmost confidence, Elan approached the pool, his heart pounding. The last time he did this, he had Reagan by his side. As Elan stood alone in the room, he couldn't help but think back to the last time he had been here, with Reagan by his side.

As he drew closer, he could feel the power pulsing from the tome, a palpable force that seemed to thrum through his very bones. With trembling hands, he reached out and lifted the book from its resting place, the weight of it both physical and metaphorical.

As he opened the tome, the pages crackled with age and power. Elan's eyes scanned the ancient text, his mind racing as he deciphered the spell written within. With a deep breath, he began to recite the words, his voice growing stronger with each syllable.

As the final word left his lips, a blinding light filled the room, and Elan felt a surge of energy coursing through his veins. Elan turned to face St. Michael, his eyes widening as he saw the archangel holding out the legendary sword, *Winterstar*. The archangel's expression was solemn pride, his eyes filled with a wisdom that seemed to stretch across the ages. There was a sense of sentience in his gaze, a deep understanding of the moment's gravity and the importance of the task. With hands that trembled with awe and trepidation, Elan grasped the blade's hilt, feeling the weight of destiny settling upon his shoulders.

As his fingers closed around the ancient weapon, a wave of deja vu washed over him, the knowledge of holding this sword before, in another life, another time. He could feel the blade's power thrumming through his arm, a tangible reminder of the weight of his destiny. It felt like home.

For a moment, Elan stood there, the sword in his hand, the tome at his feet. He knew that he could use the blade to travel back in time, to right the wrongs of the past. His mind raced with the possibility of rewriting history and preventing the rise of Dante and the Malefic Assembly before they could even begin. But as he looked towards the door, he knew his friends were waiting for him and needed him here and now. The image of Myst and Maya flashed before his eyes, reminding him of the future he fought for. And then there was the memory of Kaira, her love and strength, the anchor that kept him tethered to the present. Elan knew that he could not abandon them, not even for the chance to change the past.

With a deep breath, Elan picked up the tome and placed it in his suit pocket. Elan turned away from the pool, the sword held firmly in his grasp. He strode towards the door, ready for battle, knowing that he carried the legacy of St. Michael and the love and support of those who fought alongside him.

As Elan rendezvoused with his allies outside the castle's walls, the early morning hours garbed the group in secrecy as they marched from the bridge toward the entrance of Castel Sant'Angelo.

As they neared the entrance, the allies gathered in a tight circle, their hands instinctively checking their weapons. Elan's fingers brushed against the hilt of *Winterstar*, the sword's power thrumming beneath his touch. Kaira stood beside him, staring at the looming structure ahead, a quiver of arrows strapped to her back.

Nykronus whispered, drawing the group's attention. "Remember," he began, his voice low but firm, "unity is our greatest strength. We must stand together, no matter what challenges we face within these walls." His eyes met each of theirs, a silent understanding passing between them.

Elan's heart pounded in his chest as they crossed into the courtyard, the weight of their mission settling heavily upon his shoulders. Doubts began to creep into his mind, whispering insidiously of the evil ahead. *What if they were not strong enough to face Dante and his followers? What if their relics could not counter the Malefic Assembly's dark magic?* Elan thought of Myst and Maya, so young and yet so brave, and feared for their safety in the coming battle. He worried for Kaira, the love of his life, and the thought of losing her forever chilled him to his very core. But even as these fears threatened to overwhelm him, Elan drew strength from the presence of his allies, from the knowledge that they stood together, united in their cause. He knew they would face whatever came, no matter the cost, for the fate of the world itself hung in the balance.

As they moved deeper into the complex, the allies remained vigilant, their senses heightened for any signs of Dante or his followers.

Elan couldn't help but feel the weight of history pressing upon them as they waited. Castel Sant'Angelo had stood for centuries, witnessing countless battles and struggles. Now, it would serve as the stage for their defining moment, a symbolic battlefield where the world's fate hung in the balance.

Suddenly, marching feet echoed through the courtyard, and Dante's forces appeared on the horizon. They were a formidable sight, their armor gleaming in the rising morning light, their weapons held at the ready.

Dante stood at their head, his posture rigid with barely contained energy. His eyes blazed with a fanatic fervor, a madness that seemed to consume him from within. Every muscle in his body was coiled, ready to strike at a moment's notice. His hands, clenched into fists at his sides, trembled with the force of his conviction, the veins in his neck standing out in stark relief against his pale skin. There was a hunger in his expression, a desperate need to see his dark vision realized, no matter the cost. As Elan and his allies faced him across the courtyard, they could feel the weight of his malevolent gaze upon them, a palpable force that sought to crush their resolve and bend them to his will.

Elan's grip tightened on the hilt of *Winterstar*, the legendary sword seeming to hum with anticipation. Beside him, Kaira nocked an arrow, her gaze fixed on Dante's approaching forces.

Myst and Maya radiated an aura of power and impetus. They stood tall, their eyes locked on the enemy, ready to fulfill their roles in the coming battle.

As the two sides collided, the ancient battleground of Castel Sant'Angelo erupted into a fierce display of combat. Elan charged forward, *Winterstar* gleaming in his hand as he met the first wave of Dante's forces. The legendary sword seemed to sing as it sliced through the air, each strike a testament to Elan's skill and the weapon's power.

From afar, Zoe and Stanley let loose a volley of arrows, each finding its mark with deadly precision. Zoe's movements were fluid and graceful, a dance of death that left a trail of fallen enemies in her wake. Stanley grunted and shouted as each of his arrows connected with their targets. As they ran out of arrows, they raced down from their vantage points to join the fight on the ground.

Myst and Maya unleashed their mystical abilities, their faces embossed with concentration as they channeled the power of their relics.

Myst closed his eyes, reaching out with his mind to an ancient gem that hung around his neck. He could feel its energy thrumming through his veins, a crackling force that set his nerves alight. With a deep breath, he focused his will, shaping the power into a tangible form. A shimmering shield sprang into existence before him, a barrier of pure energy that pulsed with an otherworldly light. Bolts of lightning danced across its surface, ready to strike down any who dared to approach.

Meanwhile, Maya's hands moved in intricate patterns, weaving the air into a tapestry of illusion. Shimmering mirages sprang to life around her, each a masterpiece of deception. Phantom warriors, their forms crafted from mist and shadow, charged towards the enemy ranks, their spectral weapons raised high. Disorienting visions swirled before the eyes of the Malefic Assembly, causing them to stumble and lash out at empty air. Maya's illusions were a weapon in their own right, sowing confusion and chaos among the enemy ranks, buying precious moments for her allies to strike.

Nykronus, his dagger aglow with arcane energy, stood at the center of the fray, his ancient voice rising above the chaos as he called upon divine power. Stanley, Professor Xicato, and Olivia fought alongside him, their weapons flashing in the morning light as they pushed back against the tide of Dante's followers.

Reagan's police training was evident in every move; she fought aggressively, and her loyalty to her family drove her forward. She moved through the skirmish like a force of nature, her strikes precise and devastating.

Elan locked himself in a fierce duel with one of Dante's most skilled followers as the battle raged. The man was tall and lean, with silver hair gleaming in the fight's chaos. His eyes, a piercing blue, held a fanatic intensity as he lunged at Elan with a wicked-looking sword. The blade was infixed with dark runes that seemed to pulse with unholy energy, and the man's movements were lightning-fast and precise, honed by years of training and devotion to his dark master.

Dante's forces, though numerous, began to falter under the relentless onslaught of the Knights of St. Michael. The relics' power and their wielders' skill proved too much for the cult, and slowly but surely, they began to lose ground.

Yet even as the tide of battle seemed to turn in their favor, Elan and his family knew that the test was yet to come. Somewhere within the walls of Castel Sant'Angelo, Verendana and Dante themselves waited, their dark power a looming threat they would have to face before the day was done.

Elan locked himself in a fierce duel with one of Dante's most skilled followers as the battle raged. Their swords clashed, sparks flying with each impact. Elan's face was impressed with the challenge, his eyes reflecting the weight of his past and the hope for a future with Kaira and their children. Each strike was fueled by the desire to protect his loved ones and the world from Dante's malevolent ambitions. Every dodge was a grasp to hold onto the love he never experienced in an alternate life.

Nearby, Kaira engaged in a deadly dance with a group of cultists, her magic-infused brass knuckles finding their marks with unfailing accuracy and blocking their attacks with Vulcan's shield. The cultists, clad in dark robes and wielding curved daggers, swarmed around her like a pack of rabid wolves. They chanted in an ancient language, their voices rising in a discordant chorus as they sought to overwhelm her with sheer numbers. But Kaira was undaunted. She spun and dodged, her bow a blur as she fired arrow after arrow into their midst. The cultists fell, one by one, their blood staining the ground beneath them, but still, they came, driven by a fanatical devotion to their twisted cause.

As the battle raged on, Nykronus's eyes scanned the chaotic courtyard of Castel Sant'Angelo; he saw Dante marching into the war holding a relic in one hand, unsheathing his sword in the other, and taking manners into his own hands. The Grand Magus knew the time had come to implement their planned strategic move. With a swift motion, he signaled to the family, his gaze conveying the moment's urgency.

Dante's voice rang out across the courtyard, "Lieutenants, on me!" Menace and hatred emanated from every corner of his body as he screamed the command.

Elan, locked in combat, caught Nykronus's signal from the corner of his eye. With a final, decisive strike, he disengaged from his opponent and approached the courtyard's center, where Nykronus stood. Each step was an effort, his muscles screaming in protest as he forced himself to keep moving. Once gleaming and proud, his armor was now dented and stained with the blood of his enemies and his own. He could feel the exhaustion tugging at his limbs, the hours of fighting taking their toll on his battered body. But still, he pushed on, his jaw set. He would not falter now or when so much was at stake.

Olivia, her pixie-cut black hair drenched with sweat, noticed Elan's movement and quickly dispatched the cultist she had been fighting. She stepped beside him, her eyes fixed on Nykronus's position.

Reagan, showcasing her efficient movements, fought her way through many enemies. Her determination to reach Nykronus was unwavering. Myst and Maya followed closely behind, their mysterious powers on standby.

Distancing herself from her fistfight, Kaira barreled through assailants using her shield like a bulldozer, striking down any foe who dared to stand in her path. Her gaze locked with Elan's, a silent understanding passing between them as they converged on Nykronus's location.

As the family gathered around the ancient mage, they formed a protective circle, their backs to each other and their weapons facing outward. Dante, visible in the melee, his eyes blazing with malice, seemed to sense the shift in the battle's momentum.

Nykronus, rising above the din of combat, began to chant the spell's words. The air around them crackled with mystical energy, and the family could feel the power building within their circle.

Myst and Maya, their hands linked, added their voices to the incantation, their youthful tones blending with Nykronus's ancient timbre.

The relics they carried began to glow, their light pulsing in rhythm with the spell's cadence.

As the incantation reached its crescendo, the family's focus turned inward, their minds and hearts united in a single, powerful purpose. The courtyard seemed to fade away, and for a moment, they were alone in a world of swirling magic and unbreakable bonds.

As Nykronus's chanting reached a fever pitch, the luminous, arcane symbol beneath the family and their allies grew brighter, pulsing with otherworldly energy. The air around them crackled with power, and the ground seemed to tremble beneath their feet.

In his mind, Elan saw a future where their children could grow free from the shadow of the Malefic Assembly and explore their unique abilities without fear of persecution or harm. He saw Kaira by his side, her love a constant source of strength and comfort, and their family, united and unbreakable. He saw a world where the balance was restored, where the light of hope and goodness shone bright against the darkness. And he knew, with a fierce certainty, that he would do whatever it took to make that future a reality.

Myst and Maya, deep in concentration, channeled their mystical abilities into the spell, their relics glowing with an intense, ethereal light.

Reagan, her forehead wrinkled, lent her strength to the incantation, her loyalty to her family unwavering in the face of the chaos surrounding them. Olivia, Stanley, and Zoe stood shoulder to shoulder, channeling the power from their Roman god-infused relics directly into Nykronus's spell. Their combined resolve was a beacon of hope amidst the darkness.

Professor Xicato, his eyes wide with awe, watched as the spell took shape, culminating his years of research and dedication to the cause. He knew this moment would be a turning point in the battle against Dante's malevolent forces.

As the incantation climaxed, a brilliant beam of light erupted from the arcane symbol, piercing the sky and illuminating the battlefield with a blinding radiance. The beam shot towards Dante's power source, a dark and twisted artifact that pulsed with an unholy energy.

Dante, his eyes widening in disbelief, watched as the spell's power struck the artifact, causing it to shudder and crack under the onslaught. The spectacular display of the spell's power left Dante's followers momentarily stunned, their weapons lowering as they shielded their eyes from the blinding light. Some staggered back, their faces burned with fear. The family and their allies, seizing the opportunity, regrouped and caught their breath, their weapons still at the ready. They knew the reprieve would be short-lived, but they were grateful for the chance to gather their strength and prepare for the next wave of the battle.

The artifact, its surface now marred with glowing fissures, began to emit a high-pitched whine, its power fluctuating wildly. Dante, his face contorted with rage, let out a roar of fury as he realized the extent of the damage inflicted upon his power source. Dante's dark influence manifested as a pulsing, malevolent energy that seemed to leech the very light from the air around him. It was a tangible, cold, and oppressive force that sought to sap the will of those who stood against him. The shadows seemed to deepen and twist in his presence, and the foundation beneath their feet felt tainted by his malice. But as the spell's energy engulfed this dark aura, it began to fray and dissipate like mist before the rising sun. The shadows receded, and the air grew lighter as if a great weight had been lifted from the battlefield.

As the spell's energy dissipated, the family and their allies stood firm, their eyes fixed on the weakened artifact and the now-vulnerable Dante. They knew that the true test of their strength and unity was yet to come, but with the power of Nykronus's spell and the love that bound them together, they were ready to face whatever challenges lay ahead.

As the spell's remnants of energy pulsed through the courtyard, the family and their allies stood united, their hearts and minds intertwined in a tapestry of trust and love.

Professor Xicato, his eyes shining with pride and admiration, placed a gentle hand on Kaira's shoulder. "You have always been my favorite student," he whispered, his voice barely audible above the crackling energy surrounding them. "Your bravery and dedication inspire me."

Her face illuminated by the spell's ethereal glow, Kaira turned to her mentor, a smile of gratitude tugging at the corners of her lips.

Dante, his face contorted with rage and fear, watched helplessly as the spell's energy engulfed his dark influence, neutralizing its hold on the battlefield. His followers, their resolve wavering in the face of such overwhelming power, began to falter, their attacks becoming increasingly desperate and uncoordinated.

The family and their allies, their spirits buoyed by the spell's success, pressed forward, their weapons flashing in the mystical light as they drove back the enemy forces. They moved as one, their trust in each other guiding their every step, their love for one another fueling their determination to emerge victorious.

As the spell's final shockwave ripped through the courtyard, Dante's forces crumpled under its immense power. Some were flung back like ragdolls, their bodies broken and lifeless before they even hit the ground. Others collapsed where they stood, their eyes rolling back in their heads as the dark magic that fueled them was stripped away. The courtyard was littered with the fallen, and an eerie silence descended upon the battlefield, broken only by the crackling of residual energy and the labored breathing of the victors.

"No!" Dante roared, his voice raw and fury. "This cannot be happening! I am the chosen one, destined to rule this world!"

Elan, his eyes blazing with determination, stepped forward, *Winterstar* held high. "Your reign of terror ends here, Dante," he declared, his voice carrying across the battlefield. "The power of our love and unity will always triumph over your hatred and darkness."

Dante, his body wracked with spasms as the spell tore at his very essence, glared at Elan with a look of pure malice. "You fool," he spat, his words dripping with venom. "You think your pathetic love can defeat me? What do you know about love!"

Kaira, her hand clasped tightly with Elan's, met Dante's gaze unflinchingly. "You underestimate the strength of our bond," she said, her voice steady and resolute. "Our love is a force that cannot be broken, not by you or anyone else."

Myst and Maya, their relics glowing with an intense, otherworldly light, stepped forward; despite their teenage youth, their faces were populated with wisdom beyond their years. "It's over, Dante," Myst said, calm and assured. "You've lost. We're locking you away where you can't hurt anyone ever again."

Maya added, "We're throwing away the key, too."

Dante, his eyes wild with desperation, lunged forward, his hands outstretched in a final, futile attempt to grasp victory. But the family and their allies stood firm, their weapons at the ready, their love and trust in each other an impenetrable shield against the dark lord's malice.

Zoe reached for her electric lute but pulled her phone out instead. "Hey Siri, play The Power of Love by Huey Lewis and the News."

The rest of the party cheered.

As the chaos of the battle subsided, stillness settled over the courtyard of Castel Sant'Angelo. The family and their allies, their chests heaving with exertion and their faces smudged with grime, stood amidst the aftermath of their hard-fought victory.

Elan, his hand still clasped tightly with Kaira's, surveyed the scene before him. The once-pristine grounds were now littered with the bodies of Dante's fallen followers, their dark robes starkly contrasted against the ancient stone. Heavy with the tang of sweat and the coppery scent of blood, the smell seemed to press down upon them.

Nykronus moved among the survivors, offering words of comfort and healing where he could. He knew that the battle had taken a toll on them all, both physically and emotionally, and that the road to recovery would be long and arduous.

Reagan knelt beside a fallen bystander, her head bowed in silent prayer. She had seen death before, but never on such a scale, and the weight of it threatened to overwhelm her. Yet, as she looked up and met the eyes of her family, she found strength in their shared bond, which had been forged in the crucible of adversity.

As the family and their allies gathered together, they shared a moment of quiet reflection, each lost in their thoughts and memories. They had won, but the cost had been high, and they knew that the scars of this battle would linger long after the physical wounds had healed.

Yet, as they looked around at the faces of those who had fought beside them, they saw not just allies but a family bound by love, trust, and a shared purpose. They had faced the darkness together, and together, they would rebuild, stronger and more united than ever.

Nykronus, his robes tattered and his dagger hilt broken, surveyed the scene with a heavy heart. He had seen countless battles in his long life, but none had taken such a toll on those he held dear. The mage's eyes met Elan's, and a silent understanding passed between them—the cost of their victory had been high, and the scars it left would run deep.

The physical wounds of the battle were evident on every member of the group—gashes, bruises, and burns marred their skin, and many limped or leaned on each other for support. But it was the emotional wounds that cut the deepest. The weight of the lives lost, the horrors witnessed, and the sacrifices made hung heavy in the air, a palpable presence that threatened to suffocate them.

And yet, amidst the sorrow and the pain, there was a flicker of hope. They had achieved what many had deemed impossible—they had stood against the forces of darkness and emerged victorious. The world would never know the full extent of their sacrifice, but they would carry the memory of those who had given everything to protect it.

As they stood among the ruins of Castel Sant'Angelo, the family and their allies gathered close, their arms wrapped around each other in a silent embrace. They had survived the storm, but the quiet that followed was a stark reminder of the evil still lurking beyond. Together, they watched the sunlight drape the broken stones in shadows, a moment of peace amidst the uncertainty.

CHAPTER
TWENTY-EIGHT

Camp Pendleton, California, February 14, 2025 A.D.

The sun shone brightly over Camp Pendleton, California, seemingly shining brighter on the Order of St. Michael members. A gentle breeze carried the scent of the nearby ocean, mingling with the occasion's solemnity. Chief Warrant Officer 4 Elan Durant stood tall and proud, his uniform crisp and his medals gleaming in the sunlight and was surrounded by the people who had been by his side through the most challenging and extraordinary times of both of his lives.

Zoe smiled at him, her electric lute slung over her shoulder, as Olivia, with her short black hair styled in a pixie cut, nodded in appreciation from across the audience, her gesture a silent prayer of thanks. Stanley Wyatt, the MMA fighter known for his epic mustache and freshly trimmed beard, grinned broadly, signing autographs for fans at the retirement ceremony. Nykronus, the Grand Magus of the Order of St. Michael, stood quietly, his enigmatic eyes filled with pride.

Professor Xicato watched with a knowing smile, while Elan's beloved wife, Kaira, held his hand tightly, her eyes shining with love. Austin, Elan's best friend and fellow Marine, stood at attention, his uniform reflecting Elan's dedication. Myst and Maya, twins with a unique birth story spanning centuries, looked on with awe and affection. Reagan Mazza, resplendent in her police captain's uniform, stood tall, her glasses catching the sunlight.

Dr. Furse, who had tended to their wounds both physically and emotionally, watched with quiet satisfaction, aware of her crucial role in their lives. Grandma Mazza, the keeper of family relics and secrets, smiled knowingly, her eyes reflecting the wisdom of generations. Rose, Elan's mother beamed with pride, deeply appreciative of her son's sacrifices. Jhan and Kristinn, demonstrating their unbreakable family bond, stood united.

As the ceremony continued, Kaira looked adoringly at Elan, her expression one of pure devotion. Their eyes met, filled with mutual love and gratitude. Together, they turned to the assembled friends and family, silently expressing their appreciation for the unwavering support that had sustained them through the challenges and triumphs of their lives.

As the accolades and speeches concluded, there was a palpable sense of both ending and new beginnings. Elan looked around at the faces of those who had been by his side through it all, and he knew that whatever the future held, they would face it together.

Oceanside, California

Elan stood at a scenic lookout point overlooking the vast expanse of the Pacific Ocean. The retirement ceremony had been a whirlwind of emotions, and he had slipped away from the procession to the reception, taking a moment to himself. The salty breeze whipped through his graying hair as he let his mind wander back over the years of his service—both to his family and the Order of St. Michael.

From the day he enlisted in his first life, Elan knew his life would be one of sacrifice. He faced battles, both on the physical plane and in the realms beyond, each leaving its mark on his soul. The scars he bore, visible and invisible, were proof of everything he endured.

Yet, as he stood there, watching the waves crash against the rocky shore, Elan felt a sense of peace. He had fought the good fight and had given his all to protect those he loved and the world he cherished. As

Elan stood there, the weight of his responsibilities, once so heavy, seemed to lift from his shoulders.

This was only the first chapter, and the rest of his life was waiting to be written. His mind began to wander, contemplating the possibilities that lay ahead. He would finally have the time to pursue the hobbies and interests pushed aside during his years of service. He could see himself tinkering with old motorcycles, getting his hands dirty as he restored them to their former glory. Or he could write, putting pen to paper to capture the stories and emotions that had shaped his life. The future was a blank canvas, and Elan was excited about filling it with new adventures and experiences.

The sound of footsteps behind him drew Elan from his reverie. He turned to see Kaira approaching, her eyes filled with understanding and love. She slipped her hand into his, her touch a silent reminder of the life they had built together.

"Thinking about the past?" she asked softly, her voice barely audible over the crashing waves.

Elan affirmed, a small smile tugging at the corners of his mouth. "And the future," he replied, squeezing her hand. "We've been through so much, Kaira. But standing here with you, I know it was all worth it."

Kaira leaned her head against his shoulder, her presence comforting his soul. "And now, we have a whole new chapter ahead of us," she cried. "A life beyond the battles, beyond the sacrifices. A life where we can just be Elan and Kaira, husband and wife, parents and grandparents."

Elan turned to face her, his eyes shining with love and gratitude. "I couldn't have done any of it without you," he whispered, pulling her into a tight embrace. "You've been my rock, my guiding light through it all. I haven't told you this, but you saved my life."

It was a moment of perfect peace, a promise of the life they had earned together.

San Diego, California
His tribe surrounded Elan as the sun set below the horizon, casting

a warm glow over the Hard Rock Hotel's grounds. The retirement party had moved to a cozy gathering spot, where laughter and conversation flowed as freely as the drinks.

Reagan's eyes twinkled with amusement as she entertained the group with stories of their childhood exploits. "Remember when we tried to build a treehouse in your backyard?" she asked, nudging Elan with her elbow. "You insisted on using that rusty old hammer and ended up with a nail through your thumb!"

Elan chuckled, shaking his head at the memory. "I learned a valuable lesson that day," he said, his voice tinged with nostalgia. "Sometimes, it's okay to ask for help."

The conversation shifted as friends and family shared their stories of Elan's bravery on and off the battlefield. Austin, stout with emotion, spoke of the countless times Elan had saved his life, literally and figuratively. Her hand resting gently on Elan's knee, Kaira shared how his unwavering love and support had been her anchor through the storms of their lives.

As the night wore on, Elan opened up in a way he never had before. He spoke of his struggles with depression and anxiety, of the weight of the memories that haunted him. "I've been seeing a therapist," he admitted, his voice barely above a whisper. "It's been hard facing those demons. But I'm learning that it's okay to be vulnerable, to ask for help when I need it."

The group fell silent, their faces impressed with understanding and compassion. Her eyes shining with tears, Kaira pulled Elan into a tight embrace. "I'm so proud of you," she whispered, her voice trembling. "You're the strongest person I know, and I'm so grateful to be by your side."

As the night wore on, Elan found himself in a more intimate circle, surrounded by those who had been his closest companions through the most extraordinary times of his life. Nykronus, Zoe, Olivia, and Stanley Wyatt sat with him, their faces illuminated by the soft glow of the flickering candles on the table.

As Elan looked around at his closest companions, a flicker of worry crossed his mind. They had been through so much together, forging bonds that could never be broken. But now, as they each prepared to embark on their paths, he couldn't help but wonder if their tight-knit group would begin to drift apart. The thought of losing touch with these remarkable individuals, who had become his family, sent a pang of sadness through his heart. He knew their shared experiences would always keep them connected, but the idea of not having them all together was bittersweet.

The conversation had taken a more reflective turn, each pondering the following chapters in their lives. Elan, his voice steady, began to share his thoughts.

"I've been thinking a lot about the future," he said, his eyes scanning the faces of his friends. "About what I want to do with this new chapter in my life."

Nykronus nodded in understanding. "And what have you concluded, my friend?"

Elan took a deep breath, his gaze settling on the dancing flame of a nearby candle. "Well, Grand Magus, my old friend, we don't know where Verendana is, for starters. That's for future us to worry about. For now, I want to focus on what truly matters," he said, his voice barely above a whisper. "On my well-being, on adventure, and love."

Zoe shifted her posture with curiosity. "Oh? What does that look like for you, Elan?"

A small smile tugged at the corners of Elan's mouth. "It means taking care of myself, both physically and mentally," he replied, his voice growing stronger with each word. "It means continuing my therapy and learning to be kind to myself."

Olivia nodded in approval. "And adventure?" she asked, her eyes sparkling with excitement.

Elan's smile widened. "Adventure means embracing new experiences," he said, his voice filled with enthusiasm. "Traveling with Kaira, exploring the world, and creating new memories together."

Stanley grunted and chuckled softly. "And love?" he asked, his voice tinged with mischief.

Elan's eyes softened, his gaze drifting to where Kaira sat, deep in conversation with Reagan and Austin. "Love means cherishing every moment with my family; that includes our family, too, you know," he said, with calm emotion. "It means being present and showing them how much they mean to me every damn day."

As the conversation flowed, Elan felt a sense of excitement building within him. The future, once so uncertain, now seemed filled with endless possibilities. With his friends by his side and his family as his anchor, he knew he could face whatever lay ahead.

As the evening began to wind down, Elan found himself alone in a corner of the gathering space, his thoughts drifting between the memories of the past and the possibilities of the future. The soft glow of the overhead lights cast a warm ambiance, and the gentle sounds of conversation filled the air.

Nykronus approached Elan with a small, wrapped package in his hands. "Elan, my friend," he said, "I have something for you."

Elan looked up, curiosity chiseled on his features. "What is it, Nykronus?"

The mysterious figure smiled, holding out the package. "A gift to mark this moment in your journey."

With careful hands, Elan unwrapped the package, revealing a small, intricately carved wooden box. The box was a work of art, with delicate patterns and symbols permanently fixed on its surface. Elan's fingers traced the carvings, his eyes widening as he recognized the symbols of his past life intertwined with those of his present. The intricate patterns seemed to dance before his eyes, each triggering a flood of memories he had thought long forgotten. There, cut into the wood, was the sigil of a wolf, which had adorned Wulfstan the Steadfast's armor. Beside it, the delicate lines of a lute, a reminder of Isolde, the bard whose songs had the power to sway hearts and minds. And there, at the center of it all, was the unmistakable image of *Winterstar*, the legendary sword that had been his constant companion through countless battles and trials. As Elan's fingers moved over each symbol, he felt a deep sense of connection to his past self, a reminder that their struggles and triumphs were forever woven into the fabric of his being.

"Open it," Nykronus encouraged.

Elan lifted the lid, and inside, nestled on a bed of soft velvet, was a small, golden compass. Instead of pointing north, the needle pointed to a single word chiseled in elegant script: "Hope."

"This compass," Nykronus explained, his voice filled with warmth, "is a reminder of the path you're on. It points not only toward a direction but also to a state of being—a state of hope, healing, and self-discovery."

Elan lifted the compass from the box, feeling its weight in his palm. The metal was cool but radiated a gentle warmth as if infused with the love and support of those around him.

"Thank you, Nykronus," Elan whispered, his voice thick with emotion—tears fighting to stay contained. "This means more to me than you can know."

Nykronus placed a hand on Elan's shoulder, his touch comforting. "You are not alone on this journey, my friend. You have the love and support of all those around you. Let this compass be a reminder of that and the bright future ahead."

As the last guests bid farewells, Elan was surrounded by the people who mattered most—Kaira and their children. The soft glow of the fading evening light cast a warm, intimate atmosphere as if the world had narrowed down to just this tiny, precious circle.

Kaira took Elan's hand with her eyes filled with love and understanding. "You've come so far, my love," she whispered, her voice a gentle caress. I'm so proud of you."

Elan looked into her eyes. "I couldn't have done it without you," he replied, his voice thick with emotion. "Without all of you."

He turned his gaze to Myst and Maya, their faces marked with admiration and concern. "I know I haven't always been the father you deserve," he said, trembling slightly. "But I promise you, from this day forward, I'm going to be the best version of myself—not just for me but for all of you."

Myst and Maya exchanged a glance, their eyes glistening with unshed tears. They moved closer to their parents, their arms wrapping around them in a tight embrace.

"We love you, Dad," Myst whispered, his voice muffled against Elan's chest. "No matter what."

Maya nodded, her face pressed against Kaira's shoulder. "We're here for you, always."

Elan felt emotion wash over him, a mix of gratitude, love, and fierce grit. At this moment, surrounded by the unconditional support of his family, he knew that he could do anything.

"I'm making a commitment," he said, his voice steady and filled with conviction. "A commitment to myself to continue this journey of healing and self-love. Not just for me but for all of us. Because you deserve the best version of me, and I'm going to work every day to be that person."

Later that day, the Durant family gathered in the living room of their cozy home, the warm glow of the afternoon sun filtering through the windows. Elan sat on the plush sofa, Kaira nestled beside him, their hands intertwined. Myst and Maya, their faces still flushed from the ocean breeze, settled into the armchairs across from their parents.

"So," Elan began, "I've been thinking a lot about the future, about what we should do as a family."

Kaira nodded, her eyes shining with excitement. "I think it's time we start making some plans," she said, her voice filled with enthusiasm. "Plans that focus on our growth as individuals and as a family."

Myst leaned forward, his elbows resting on his knees. "What did you have in mind, Dad?"

Elan smiled, his gaze drifting to each family member. "Well, I think we should plan some trips together. We can explore new places and create new memories."

Maya's face lit up, her eyes sparkling with excitement. "That sounds amazing!" she exclaimed, bouncing slightly in her seat. "Where should we go first?"

Kaira chuckled, her hand squeezing Elan's gently. "I could use a vacation or two. We should all list places we want to visit, and then we can decide together."

Elan nodded, his heart swelling with love and gratitude for his family. "Exactly! Also, I think we should also focus on supporting each other's dreams and hobbies," he added, his voice filled with sincerity. "Whether it's taking a cooking class together, learning a new language, or spending more quality time with each other."

His mind began to wander, again thinking of the hobbies that had always piqued his interest but had been pushed aside in the chaos of his former life. On top of working on motorcycles and writing, he began to daydream. He had always been fascinated by woodworking, the idea of taking a raw piece of lumber and transforming it into something beautiful and functional. He could take a class, learn the basics, and share his newfound skills with his family. They could work together on projects, creating pieces that would become cherished heirlooms passed down through generations. Or he could ask Zoe to teach him so he could finally learn to play the guitar, something he had always admired but never had the time to pursue. He could imagine himself strumming away on the porch, his family gathered around him, their voices joined in song as the sun dipped below the horizon. The possibilities were endless, and Elan felt excited about exploring them together as a family.

Maya looked at Myst and immediately said, "We're in."

San Francisco, California, Spring 2025 A.D.

Elan sat in his new study, surrounded by the warm glow of the late afternoon sun filtering through the large windows of the home his architect wife designed. The room was filled with reminders of his journey—the compass gifted to him by Nykronus, a framed photo of his family, *Winterstar*, his military shadow box, dozens of books titled

"The Mystic Chronicles," and a stack of journals containing his thoughts and reflections.

He leaned back in his chair, his eyes drifting over the space he had created for himself. It was a sanctuary where he could explore his thoughts and emotions without fear or judgment. The walls, painted a soothing shade of blue, seemed to embrace him, offering a sense of calm and tranquility.

Elan's gaze settled on the compass, its golden surface glinting in the sunlight. He reached out, his fingers tracing the intricate engravings. The word "Hope" stared back at him, a constant reminder of his chosen path.

Elan felt a wave of emotion wash over him as he sat there. The journey he had undertaken, both physically and emotionally, had been one of the most challenging experiences of his life. He had faced his deepest fears and darkest demons and emerged a stronger, more resilient person on the other side.

Elan felt a deep sense of hope and gratitude. He was grateful for the opportunity to grow, learn, and love more fully, for his family's unwavering support, his friends' wisdom and guidance, and the chance to create a life filled with meaning and purpose.

As the sun began to set, casting a warm, golden glow over the room, Elan closed his eyes, taking a deep breath. He knew that whatever the future held, he would face it with courage, determination, and an open heart. And in that moment, surrounded by the reminders of his journey, he felt a sense of peace wash over him, a feeling of contentment and hope that would guide him through the days ahead.

CHAPTER
TWENTY-NINE

ome, Italy, October 13, 2025 A.D.

A year had passed since the climactic battle at Castel Sant'Angelo. Amidst the ruins of an ancient amphitheater, a somber gathering had been arranged. The sun cast a muted glow over the assembled crowd, a mix of local leaders, community members, and the family who had fought bravely to protect them all.

Elan stood at the center of the gathering, his family by his side. Kaira's hand rested gently on his arm, a silent show of support and love. Myst and Maya, now a year older and wiser, stood tall and proud, their eyes shining with the knowledge of their extraordinary destiny.

As the crowd settled, a local leader stepped forward, his voice filled with grief and gratitude. "We are here today to remember those who were lost in the battle against the forces of evil," he began, his gaze sweeping over the assembled crowd. "And to honor the family who stood against them, who sacrificed so much to protect us all."

The crowd bowed their heads in reverence, the weight of their losses hanging heavy in the air. Elan felt a lump form in his throat, overwhelmed by the outpouring of emotion.

The leader continued, his voice trembling with each word. "Elan,

Kaira, Myst, and Maya, you have shown us the true depth of your courage and selflessness. You have fought not just for yourselves but all of us, for the balance that keeps our world in harmony."

He turned to face the family directly. "On behalf of our community, we offer you our deepest gratitude and unwavering support," he said, gesturing to a group of children who stepped forward, each bearing a small, intricately crafted candle.

As the children placed the candles at the family's feet, Elan felt a sense of humility over him. He knew their battle had been fought not for glory or recognition but for the greater good, for preserving all that was right and just in the world.

Kaira squeezed his hand, her eyes glistening with tears. Myst and Maya stood a little closer, their demeanor filled with solemnity and determination as they accepted the quiet tribute.

As the ceremony finished, Elan and his family were ushered into a private meeting room, joined by their closest allies and confidants. The room was dimly lit, with ancient tapestries adorning the walls, their intricate patterns dancing in the flickering candlelight.

At the head of the table sat Nykronus, his weathered face scored with lines of wisdom and experience. Elan and Kaira sat beside him while Myst and Maya settled in across from them, their young faces alight with curiosity and anticipation.

The room fell silent as Nykronus cleared his throat, his voice deep and resonant. "My most trusted companions," he began, his gaze sweeping over the assembled group, "we have gathered here today to acknowledge the vital role each of you has played in the protection of our world."

He turned to Elan and Kaira, a smile tugging at the corners of his mouth. "Elan, Kaira, your bravery and devotion have been an inspiration to us all. You have faced unimaginable challenges and emerged stronger, united in your love and your commitment to the greater good."

Nykronus's gaze shifted to Myst and Maya, his eyes twinkling affectionately. "And you, young ones," he said, his voice softening, "have shown courage beyond your years."

He paused, his expression growing more serious. "But our work is far from over," he continued in a somber tone. "The forces of darkness will always seek to upset the balance, to plunge our world into chaos and despair. It is our duty, as protectors, to stand against them. Somewhere out there, Verendana is making her next moves."

Nykronus rose from his seat, his presence commanding the room's attention. "And so, I humbly offer my services as advisor and mentor to this extraordinary family," he said, his voice ringing with conviction. "My knowledge and experience are yours to draw upon, to guide you in the challenges that lie ahead."

Elan and Kaira gazed into each other eyes with gratitude and respect. They knew that Nykronus's wisdom would be invaluable in the coming years, a beacon of light in the darkness that threatened to engulf them.

San Francisco, California

Elan sat in their San Francisco home's dimly lit living room, his gaze fixed on the flickering flames of the fireplace. Kaira, Myst, and Maya were nestled beside him, a blanket draped over their laps. The room was quiet, save for the occasional crackle of the fire and the whisper of their breaths.

Elan's mind wandered to the past year's events, the battles fought, and the sacrifices made. He thought of the allies they had lost, the brave souls who had given their lives in the fight against Dante and his forces. Their faces flashed before his eyes, each a painful reminder of the cost of their victory.

Kaira's hand found his, her fingers intertwining with his own. She, too, was lost in thought, her eyes glistening with unshed tears. "We've lost so much," she whispered, her voice barely audible over the crackling of the fire.

Elan nodded, his throat tight with emotion. "But we've also gained so much," he said, his gaze drifting to Myst and Maya. "Our children, our future. They are the reason we fought so hard and will continue to fight."

Myst and Maya looked up at their parents. They had seen and

experienced things that no child should have, but they had emerged more vigorous and resilient.

"We won't let their sacrifices be in vain," Myst said, his voice firm and convictional. "We'll honor their memory by continuing the fight, by protecting this world."

Maya nodded, her hand reaching out to grasp her brother's. "We are the guardians now," she said, her eyes shining with determination. "It is our duty to carry on their legacy, to ensure that the balance is maintained."

Elan felt a surge of pride and love for his children, for the strength and courage they displayed in the face of such adversity.

As the fire began to die, the family huddled closer together, drawing strength and comfort from each other's presence. They knew the memories of those they had lost would forever be embedded in their hearts, a constant reminder of the price of their victory. But they also knew those memories would fuel their determination to continue the Order of St. Michae's ongoing fight against evil and protect the world they had fought so hard to save.

Elan and Kaira exchanged a meaningful glance as they surveyed the living room, its walls adorned with ancient tapestries and shelves lined with mystical relics collected throughout their extraordinary journey. Myst and Maya, now in their early twenties, sat cross-legged on the floor, their eyes alight with curiosity and wisdom beyond their years.

Kaira's voice was soft but filled with conviction as she addressed her family. "We've been through so much together and learned more than we ever could have imagined about the forces that shape our world."

Elan nodded, his hand resting gently on an ancient tome. "It's our responsibility to ensure that this knowledge is preserved, that the sacrifices made by our allies and ancestors are never forgotten."

Myst and Maya leaned forward, their gazes intent. "We want to help," Myst said, his voice steady. "We need to make sure that future generations are prepared and that they understand the balance that must be maintained."

Maya's eyes shone with determination. "We can't let the darkness catch them unaware like it did us. We have to give them the tools to fight back, to protect the world we've fought so hard to save."

Kaira smiled at her children, and pride and love were impressed on every line of her face. "You two are the future," she said softly. "The legacy of our family, of all those who have come before us."

Elan rose to his feet, his eyes sweeping over the room. "Then let's begin," he said, his voice ringing purposefully. "Let's gather our records, our artifacts, and our memories. Let's create a testament to the battles we've fought, the lessons we've learned, and the love that has sustained us through it all."

The family nodded in agreement, each member taking on a specific task. Kaira and Reagan began sorting through the countless journals and diaries they had kept over the years, carefully selecting the most important entries and arranging them chronologically. Myst and Maya cataloged the various artifacts and relics they had collected, each a tangible reminder of their challenges and victories.

Elan and Nykronus pored over ancient texts and manuscripts, seeking out the wisdom of those who had come before them, the guardians who had stood against the forces of darkness throughout the ages. They carefully transcribed the most relevant passages, adding their insights and experiences to create a comprehensive guide for future generations.

As the hours passed, the room began to fill with the fruits of their labor. Stacks of journals and manuscripts, carefully organized and annotated, began to take shape. Displays of artifacts and relics lined the walls, each labeled with its history and significance. And at the center of it all, a master document began to take form, another chapter in The Mystic Chronicles—a testament to the incredible journey they had undertaken and the lessons they had learned along the way.

And so, with hearts full of love and determination, the family began to weave their story, to create a tapestry of memory and knowl-edge that would endure long after they were gone, a beacon of hope for the generations yet to come.

~

San Lorenzo de El Escorial, Madrid, Spain

Olivia's office was a haven of tranquility and purpose. The ancient stone walls seemed to whisper secrets of the past, while the sunshine streaming through the stained-glass windows cast a color wheel across the room. The family had gathered here, united to preserve their extraordinary story for future generations.

Myst and Maya sat hunched over a large wooden table, their pens scratching against the parchment as they diligently recorded their experiences and lessons. Kaira and Elan, seated beside them, pored over ancient tomes and artifacts, carefully documenting the mystical knowledge they had acquired throughout their journey.

In the corner of the room, Austin and Reagan worked together to organize the vast collection of records and relics. The occasional laugh or exclamation of discovery punctuated their hushed conversations. The room was filled with camaraderie and purpose, a testament to the unbreakable bonds forged through their shared trials and triumphs.

As the hours passed, the stack of written pages grew, each one a piece of the intricate tapestry that was their story. Olivia moved among them, offering guidance and support, her experiences as a keeper of ancient knowledge invaluable to their efforts.

Elan paused in his writing, his gaze drifting to the faces of his family, each one forged with determination and love. He knew that their work here was more than just a record of their lives; it was a gift to the future, a beacon of hope and resilience in the face of the darkness that always lurked beyond the horizon.

Kaira looked up from the ancient text she was studying, her eyes meeting Elan's. At that moment, a silent understanding passed between them, and they recognized the importance of their task and the love that had sustained them through it all.

Southern Alps, South Island, New Zealand

Stanley's secret training ground was nestled in the heart of New Zealand's mountains, a hidden oasis of knowledge and power. The scenery sizzled with energy as Myst and Maya honed their skills under the watchful eyes of their mentors.

As Myst and Maya moved through intricate combat forms, their bodies flowed like water, each strike precise and powerful. Their eyes glowed with an otherworldly light, a testament to the unique abilities that coursed through their veins. The air around them seemed to crackle with energy, random sparks of electricity dancing along their fingertips as they channeled their inner power.

With each movement, the twins could feel the ancient knowledge of their past lives continuing to surge, complementing the wisdom they gained in this modern world. They could sense the presence of their ancestors, their whispered encouragement and wisdom echoing in their minds.

Myst and Maya closed their eyes as they completed their final form, feeling the power within them settle and recede. They knew this was just the beginning and that their abilities would continue to grow and evolve with more training. But for now, they reveled in the knowledge they were ready and had the strength and skills to stand alongside their family and defend the world against the forces of darkness.

Stanley nodded approvingly, with his dragon tooth now fashioned as a necklace around his neck,

Zoe sat beside him, strumming a haunting melody on her electric lute, the notes seeming to weave themselves into the fabric of the world around them.

Stanley halted the day's exercises as the sun began to dip below the horizon, casting a warm glow over the training ground. Myst and Maya gathered around him, their faces flushed with exertion but their eyes bright with the thrill of discovery.

"You two have come so far," Stanley said, his voice filled with pride. "Your parents would be proud of the guardians you are becoming."

Myst and Maya exchanged glances, their hearts swelling with love and determination. They knew that their family's legacy rested on their shoulders and that they were the future of the fight against the darkness.

As the group returned to the main compound, Zoe's music floating on the evening breeze, Stanley's mind drifted to his past, to the centuries he had spent as Wulfstan, a guardian of the ancient ways. He knew the road ahead would be long and treacherous, but he also knew the future was in good hands with Myst and Maya at the helm.

The Durant-Mazza family embarked on a journey of love and connection, visiting places with special meaning. In the Philippines, they walked along the pristine beaches, the warm sun on their faces and the soft sand beneath their feet. Rose shared stories of her childhood, her laughter mingling with the gentle crash of the waves.

In Italy, they explored the ancient ruins of Rome, marveling at the history surrounding them, this time as tourists, and visited the places where Myst and Maya grew up. Elan and Kaira walked hand in hand through the streets, their love for each other more potent than ever. Reagan and Austin joined them, their bond deepening with each passing day.

Egypt welcomed them with its timeless beauty, the pyramids standing tall against the endless sky. Kristinn and her significant other rode camels through the desert, the wind whipping through their hair as they laughed and held on tight.

Mexico's vibrant colors and lively music filled their hearts with joy. They danced in the streets, the rhythm of the mariachi bands guiding their steps. Jhan and his wife shared laughter with the Durant-Mazzas as their nieces and nephews ran and played, their innocence and happiness a balm to the family's souls.

In Alaska, they marveled at the majesty of the glaciers, the icy blue hues taking their breath away. They huddled around campfires, sharing stories and roasting marshmallows, the warmth of their love keeping the cold at bay.

Maine's rugged coastline and charming lighthouses provided a backdrop for quiet moments of reflection. They sat on the rocky shores, watching the waves crash against the cliffs, each lost in their thoughts but united in their love for one another.

The turquoise waters and white sandy beaches of the Bahamas offered a paradise of relaxation and rejuvenation. They swam in the clear waters, the sun warming their skin and the saltwater cleansing their souls.

In Paris, they climbed the steps of the Eiffel Tower, the city of love stretching out before them. They wandered through the Louvre, admiring the masterpieces and creating memories that would last a lifetime.

Tokyo's bright lights and bustling streets filled them with excitement and wonder. They sampled the local cuisine, and their taste buds danced to each new flavor. They explored the ancient temples, finding peace and tranquility amidst the chaos of the city.

Australia's vast landscapes and unique wildlife captured their hearts. They watched the sun set over Uluru, the ancient rock formation glowing red in the fading light. They swam with dolphins and walked through the lush rainforests, each moment a treasure to be cherished.

The list went on.

～

San Francisco, California

The Durant-Mazza family stood together on the Twin Peaks scenic overlook, their eyes fixed on the distant horizon, each lost in their own thoughts but united in their love and determination.

Elan's arm wrapped around Kaira's waist, and his touch was a silent reminder of their unbreakable bond. Myst and Maya stood on either side of their parents. Reagan and Austin stood nearby, their hands intertwined, symbolizing the love and support they offered the family.

Rose and Grandma Mazza watched their grandchildren with pride, their hearts swelling with the knowledge that the future was in good hands. Kristinn, Jhan, and their families completed the circle, their presence a testament to the strength and resilience of the Durant-Mazza clan.

As the last rays of the sun disappeared behind the horizon, Elan took a deep breath, his voice steady and filled with conviction. "It's like mom always says," he said, his gaze sweeping over his family. "Things happen for a reason."

Rose tightly hugged her son, Elan. "See? I told you, you never listen."

Kaira laughed, her eyes glistening with unshed tears. "He doesn't, does he, Mom? Our sacrifices. Everything that happened to this point. It's been worth it," she said softly. "We fought to create a safer world for Myst and Maya, for all the generations to come, and we succeeded."

Myst's voice rang with pride as he declared, "Whatever happens next, we're ready." His eyes lighted with pride, reflecting the strength and resilience sculpted through their incredible journey.

Maya met her brother's gaze, a silent understanding passing between them. They faced unimaginable challenges and emerged victorious, their bond unbreakable. With a confident smile, she echoed his sentiment, "Bring it on."

EPILOGUE

In the dense, lively jungle of the Philippines, a lone silhouette emerged, shrouded in the mystery of the deepening shadows. This was no ordinary individual but Nykronus, a custodian of timeless knowledge and enigmas. The jungle, teeming with the symphony of fauna and the whisper of foliage, seemed to halt in veneration of his existence. The jungle exuded a rich blend of earthy moss, sweet floral fragrances, and the tangy scent of tropical fruits.

In his presence stood an obscure-looking glass, a mystical threshold bordered by creepers and primordial rock unaltered by time. It glimmered with an ethereal radiance, a portal to unexplored domains awaiting its voyager to traverse.

Nykronus grasped a leather-bound volume in his hands, its surface adorned with the name "Elan Durant." This volume, brimming with the annals of valor, selflessness, and the might of steadfast optimism, was a tribute to the heritage of those who had fought gallantly to restore harmony to the world.

With grave reverence, Nykronus traced his fingers over the surface, sensing the gravity of the narratives contained within. He gazed again into the jungle as if bidding adieu to a long-time companion and tenderly placed the volume at the foot of the looking glass.

Inhaling deeply, Nykronus advanced, his silhouette enfolded in the dark mirror's embrace. As he traversed the threshold, the atmosphere surrounding the portal pulsated with energy, the fabric of reality yielding to the will of the ancient magic at work.

No sooner had Nykronus vanished into the looking glass than the heavens above the jungle roared to life. A colossal tempest, born of no typical weather, swirled with an intensity that seemed to lament the guardian's departure. Lightning forked across the sky, illuminating the dark recesses of the jungle in flashes of stark, white light.

Then, as if targeting the core of the magic that dared pierce the veil between realms, a solitary bolt of lightning struck the looking glass. The force of the impact shattered the portal into a thousand minuscule fragments, dispersing them across the jungle floor where they lay, shimmering faintly in the storm's aftermath. The sound was like a thousand mirrors breaking simultaneously, a cacophony of high-pitched tinkling that echoed through the trees and sent birds scattering from their perches.

The portal fragments lay scattered across the jungle floor, each one no larger than a fingernail. They sparkled and glinted in the fading light of the storm, catching the eye like stars fallen to Earth. As the wind began to die down, the gentle tinkling of the shards could still be heard, a faint and otherworldly sound that seemed to whisper the secrets and mysteries lost with the portal's destruction.

The jungle gradually resumed its chorus, the sounds of life weaving through the trees, indifferent to the enigmas that had unfolded in its midst. Under a stone archway, a leather-bound volume with "Maya Durant" on the surface remained by the ruins of the portal, a sentinel of stories waiting to be discovered by those who dare to venture deep into the heart of the unknown.

And so, Nykronus's odyssey continued beyond the realms of known maps into the stories yet to be told. The tempest faded, leaving a silence that spoke of endings and beginnings, of the eternal cycle of adventures that beckon from beyond the veil of the ordinary world.

Acknowledgments

Thank God for putting me on this Earth, allowing me to interact with the fantastic people in my life, and giving me the capacity to use my brain, heart, and soul in a meaningful manner.

To my mom, Rosana, thank you for molding me into the man I am today. That foundation you set "decades" ago made life more accessible than what most people have. Thanks for teaching me family values and, most importantly, how to be a good person. Thanks for binge-watching *Star Trek, Twilight Zone, and Supernatural* with me, getting me into a world of science fiction and fantasy, and making me the nerd I am today. You're right, Mom. Things happen for a reason. I love you.

Also, thank you to my stepdad, Dante, for caring for the most important woman in my life and showing me that love finds a way, even if it takes a lifetime.

To my siblings Felix, Christinne, Jhoanne, Daniel and Kelsie. Thank you for staying close and keeping me in your thoughts and prayers. While it has been a crazy few years, seeing you and your families grow has been an essential inspiration in this book, life, and beyond. Life is short, so love the one you've got.

To my friends, THANK YOU FOR LETTING ME BE MYSELF.

To my readers, thank you for reading my first book. I learned much through this process and can't wait to do it again. Thank you for the pushes and nudges to all the people I've met. Thank you for the support! You're all beautiful human beings.

I can't tell you enough how much I value human beings. So be good humans!

Also, since I have your attention I want to remind you to be the best version of yourself that you can be. Someone I care about told me she wanted to be the best version of herself for me, and I now know why. And now, I want to be the best version of myself for me so that I can be the best version of myself for you. (It makes sense in my head.)

To the women I loved in my life, thank you for the experiences; many of them played a factor in this Mystic Chronicles series. I believe. Love is the answer.

To the world's finest Chief's mess in the world's greatest Navy. Thank you for keeping me anchored, proud, motivated, and professional. What we do makes me so pleased to serve, and it's been the best chapter of my career. There are too many Chiefs to name specifically, but Amy. THANK YOU. Navy Chief, Always proud!

To the shipmates (Sailors, Marines, Airmen, and Soldiers), thank you for your sacrifice. It's been an honor to serve with you, and I'll continue to do that for as long as I live and breathe.

To my best friend Mel and best friend-in-law Ken, thank you for keeping me out of the darkness.

To my therapists (Caitlin, Melanie, and Sheryl). Thank you for keeping me sane!

To my beta readers, specifically Bree from Fiverr, thank you for your thorough and brutally honest feedback and for helping me to say what I mean!

To my babies, Debo, Sparky, Sandy, Rocky, Apollo, Storm, Crash, and Burn (and new nephew Bolt): I don't deserve you. People don't deserve animals.

Bard and Ari, thank you for inspiring me to turn a story I've been thinking about since 1997. Thank you for sharing your trauma with me so I could get through the grief. Your lives have been an inspiration, but your ability to share and get me back into poetry and reading has helped me put pen to paper.

Finally, to Ethan. Thank you for allowing me to be a dad. I'm so proud of the man you became and wish you were here to read this story. This whole time, I imagined bouncing ideas off of you while writing every chapter, just like I would do in the good old days with some of the crazy jack-of-all-trade ideas and hobbies I had in the past. I LOVE YOU CRAIG.

Oh yeah, Felix, thanks for being the best Ninong to Ethan. Love.

ABOUT THE AUTHOR

ERHROLE NAVARRO IS A FIRST-GENERATION FILIPINO AMERICAN AUTHOR, BORN AND RAISED IN SAN JOSE, CALIFORNIA. AS AN ACTIVE-DUTY MASTER CHIEF IN THE U.S. NAVY, ERHROLE HAS DEDICATED HIS LIFE TO SERVING HIS COUNTRY AND COMMUNITY. DESPITE FACING NUMEROUS CHALLENGES AND TRAUMATIC LIFE EVENTS, INCLUDING THE LOSS OF HIS SON ETHAN, ERHROLE HAS FOUND SOLACE AND PURPOSE IN HIS WRITING.

ERHROLE'S PASSION FOR STORYTELLING BEGAN IN THE 7TH GRADE WHEN HE PENNED HIS FIRST NOVELLA. YEARS LATER, HE TRANSFORMED THAT EARLY WORK INTO HIS DEBUT NOVEL, "ECHI ETERNI," WHICH EXPLORES THEMES THAT HAVE PROFOUNDLY IMPACTED HIS LIFE. THROUGH HIS WRITING, ERHROLE AIMS TO CONNECT WITH READERS DEEPLY AND EMOTIONALLY, OFFERING THEM THE SAME COMPASSION, UNDERSTANDING, AND WISDOM HE HAS GAINED THROUGH HIS EXPERIENCES.

DRAWING INSPIRATION FROM HIS FAVORITE BOOK, "TUESDAYS WITH MORRIE," ERHROLE SEEKS TO CREATE MEANINGFUL STORIES THAT OFFER HOPE, ENCOURAGEMENT, AND A SENSE OF BELONGING TO THOSE WHO MAY BE STRUGGLING. HE BELIEVES IN THE POWER OF LOVE, DEVOTION, AND THE HUMAN SPIRIT TO OVERCOME EVEN THE DARKEST TIMES.

WHEN HE'S NOT WRITING OR DEPLOYED IN THE NAVY, ERHROLE CAN BE FOUND SPINNING TUNES AS A BEDROOM DJ, IMMERSING HIMSELF IN THE WORLD OF COMIC BOOKS, OR RIDING HIS MOTORCYCLE ALONG THE BEAUTIFUL CALIFORNIA COAST. HE APPROACHES LIFE WITH THE PHILOSOPHY THAT IT'S TOO SHORT TO LAST LONG, EMBRACING EVERY MOMENT AND OPPORTUNITY TO IMPACT THE WORLD AROUND HIM POSITIVELY.

THROUGH HIS WRITING, MILITARY SERVICE, AND UNWAVERING COMMITMENT TO HIS COMMUNITY, ERHROLE NAVARRO EMBODIES THE SPIRIT OF RESILIENCE, COMPASSION, AND THE ENDURING POWER OF THE HUMAN HEART.

The Mystic Chronicles Between Realms

BY ER HR OLE NAVAR O